PRAISE FOR
Where the Heart Meets the Sea

"Drake conjures a deep sense of belonging to tell an emotional and heartwarming story of the search for family and the need to connect with the past in order to build a future." —Jayne Ann Krentz, *New York Times* bestselling author

"*Where the Heart Meets the Sea* is a rich, emotional story that sweeps readers to the beauty of Norway, is full of family drama and romance, and has a heroine readers will cheer for." —Jennifer Probst, *New York Times* bestselling author

"A richly atmospheric and emotionally layered novel, *Where the Heart Meets the Sea* sweeps you away to Norway's wild coast, where love and mystery intertwine. With graceful prose and haunting depth, it's a story about courage, renewal, and the secrets that can set us free." —Julianne MacLean, bestselling author of *These Tangled Vines*

"Kimbra Drake's *When the Heart Meets the Sea* is a delightful novel filled with everything I love: secrets, a found home, a plucky heroine, a gorgeous backdrop of sea and sky, and some romantic twists and turns that I didn't see coming. I'm ready to move to Norway after reading this beautiful book of second chances." —Maddie Dawson, bestselling author of *Matchmaking for Beginners*

"*Where the Heart Meets the Sea* is a beautifully atmospheric story that captures the captivating charm of Norway's coastal landscapes. The island of Lyngør feels like a living, breathing character, and the author's ability to transport the reader there is truly immersive. With themes of identity, family, and healing, the novel offers a heartfelt exploration of how the past can shape—and sometimes surprise—our future. A lovely and reflective read set against a stunning and unforgettable backdrop." —Jennifer Moorman, *USA TODAY* bestselling author of *The Vanishing of Josephine Reynolds*

"When Ella's grandmother dies and leaves her a house on a private island near a small town in Norway, she embarks on a journey of discovery that takes her not only to the land of her ancestors, but also deep into a mystery surrounding her mother's death. Kimbra Drake has woven a beautifully atmospheric story of family secrets, romance, and self-discovery that will delight armchair travelers everywhere." —Kerry Anne King, bestselling author of *Improbably Yours*

"Kimbra Drake's *Where the Heart Meets the Sea* is a deeply moving exploration of identity, legacy, and the ways love can both wound and heal across generations. For readers who love novels like *Our Italian Summer* by Jennifer Probst or *The Light Between Oceans* by M.L. Stedman, *Where the Heart Meets the Sea* offers that same blend of emotional honesty, mystery, and breathtaking setting. It's a book about rewriting the stories we tell ourselves about our parents, our choices, and the meaning of home. Ultimately, Drake delivers a story that lingers long after the last page." —Los Angeles Book Review

"When Ella Nilsen inherits her grandmother's seaside cottage on a windswept Norwegian island, she goes there from Colorado seeking closure. Instead, she uncovers the secrets her family left behind. With the help of Leif Arnesen—a quiet, intriguing boatbuilder bound to her past—Ella is drawn into a love story that unravels old mysteries and offers the chance to heal generations. *Where the Heart Meets the Sea* is a haunting, evocative tale of secrets, loss, and the journey home." —Patricia Sands, bestselling author of the Love in Provence series

"Set against the breathtaking backdrop of coastal Norway, Drake brings the setting to life with crisp, atmospheric detail, guiding readers through a story filled with subtle twists, tender surprises, and an undercurrent of mystery. A heartfelt love story about finding belonging, healing old wounds, and opening oneself to the possibility of new love." —Suzanne Simonetti, *USA Today* bestselling author of *The Sound of Wings*

"*Flott jobb* ('great job' in Norwegian)! Ella Nilsen, an American who inherits her grandmother's cottage on a remote Norwegian island, searches for answers in a page-turning story set in the land of the fjords. *Where the Heart Meets the Sea* is the memorable journey to Norway I have always wanted to take. —Marilyn Simon Rothstein, author of *Who Loves You Best*

"An evocative romance novel set on a picturesque island in Norway. . . . Lyngør not only serves as a beautiful setting but frames Ella's compelling emotional journey. . . . Readers will enjoy the novel's absorbing setting, authentic characters, and heartfelt scenes." —BlueInk Review

"Kimbra Drake's deft eye for detail creates a captivating main character of the Norwegian archipelagoes, and the chemistry between and mysteries uncovered by Colorado-born textile artist and designer Ella and stubbornly loyal boatbuilder Leif linger with the reader long after the final page. *Where the Heart Meets the Sea* is a love affair of place, a compelling love story, and a love letter to family lost and found." —Kelly Sokol, author of *Breach* and *The Unprotected*

"A little romance, a little mystery, a little island community in Norway—all are enticing elements in *Where the Heart Meets the Sea*, Kimbra Drake's delightful novel." —Jane Doucet, author of *Lost & Found in Lunenburg*

"Flavored with Norse mythology, this entertaining story is full of mystery and romance, danger and adventure, with characters so real you feel like you know them. An excellent read."—Kathleen M. Rodgers, author *The Llano County Mermaid Club*

"Kimbra Drake's dynamic, heartfelt coming-of-age debut mixes family drama with romance in a setting that sparkles with nostalgia. It's the kind of story that gently draws in the reader, each page a soft reminder of a time close enough to remember but distant enough to long for." —KJ Micciche, author of *The Book Proposal*

"Effortlessly evokes the romance of Norway." —Helen Fisher, author of *Space Hopper* and *Joe Nuthin's Guide to Life*

"In the heady romance novel *Where the Heart Meets the Sea*, an unlikely relationship develops in a moody Norwegian village." —*Foreword* Clarion Reviews

"Kimbra Drake's *Where the Heart Meets the Sea* is a deeply moving and gorgeously written novel that blends romance, mystery, and self-discovery in a setting as evocative as its characters are unforgettable. Drake's prose is lush and immersive, painting the Norwegian landscape with vivid sensory detail—salt air, heather-covered hills, and the ever-present sea become characters in their own right." —Steven Joseph, author of *A Grownup Guide to Effective Crankiness* and *Cranky Superpowers*

Where the Heart Meets the Sea

Where the Heart Meets the Sea

A NOVEL

KIMBRA DRAKE

Bleecker Street ✒ Books

Published by Bleecker Street Books

Edited and designed by Girl Friday Productions
www.girlfridayproductions.com

Cover design: Lauren Smith
Project management: Sara Addicott
Editorial production: Alyssa Brillinger
Image credits: cover © Adobe Stock/Friedberg

ISBN (paperback): 979-8-9993544-0-2
ISBN (hardcover): 979-8-9993544-3-3
ISBN (ebook): 979-8-9993544-1-9

Library of Congress Control Number: 2025920835

First edition

For Edel, Pål, and Dennis

NORWAY

Risør

Tvedestrand

Sandøya

Arendal

Kragerø

Jonfruland

1. Holmen
2. Odden
3. Lighthouse
4. Lyngør Grocery
5. Lyngørsida
6. Ringpynten
7. Speken
8. Gåsholmen

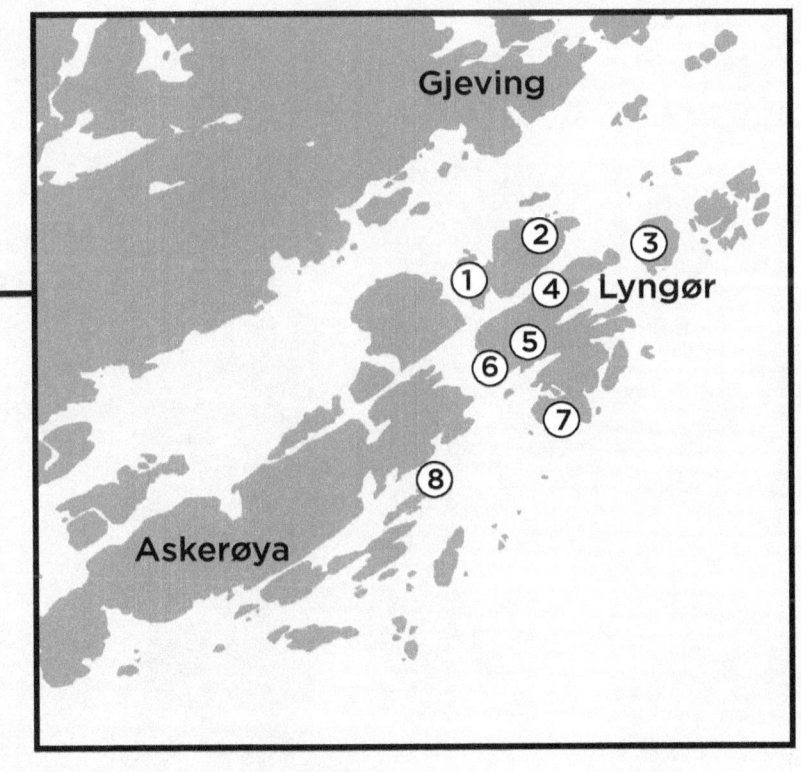

Gjeving

Lyngør

Askerøya

CHAPTER 1

Ella Nilsen first saw her grandma's cottage just before dusk, when the setting sun in Lyngør, Norway, washed its old stone walls in a luminous salmon color. The cottage, named Ring Point, or *Ringpynten* in Norwegian, looked like something out of a storybook; mossy granite blocks framed the mullioned windows, and fairy roses and ivy climbed the walls.

Her reserved Norwegian grandma, Hilda Nilsen, who had raised her since she was a baby and taught her the Norwegian word for grandmother, *mormor*, had never mentioned Ring Point to her. In fact, Ella hadn't learned about it until after Hilda's death six months earlier, when her grandma's lawyer informed her that Ring Point now belonged to Ella.

In this moment, as Ella stood on the ridge, gazing down over the cottage's slate roof, everything she'd been led to believe about her history collided with what was in front of her. It was almost too much for her to take in.

Tears stung her eyes, and she swiped at them. *Oh Mormor, you had to have known the news of the cottage would undo me. Why did you hide it from me all these years?*

Ella usually welcomed surprises, but this was something

else entirely. She knew that she was five months old when Mormor brought her from Norway to Boulder, Colorado, but her closemouthed grandma never spoke of their life in Oslo. Ella, of course, had no memories of Norway, and their lives had begun, as far as she knew, when they settled in Boulder, where Hilda taught Norwegian at a public school. Although Ella had begged Hilda to tell her stories about their shared history, her grandma only offered glimpses and generalities. She told Ella how much she missed seeing Norwegian *bunader* the traditional folk costumes, or that she craved *lutefisk*, cod fermented in lye. Hilda liked to joke that trolls still stalked the land.

Hilda didn't like speaking about her own daughter, Sara, who had died giving birth to Ella. Ella craved details about her mom. More times than she could count over the years, she had begged her grandma for information. Hilda had shared a few details, but they were vague, and she always shut the conversation down quickly, warning, "Let it go. Holding on to the past is too painful. It's impossible to heal."

Ella spotted a well-tended garden on the property with rows of berry bushes, flowering herbs bursting from wine barrel planters, and a sandbox-size plot with green shoots and fresh dirt. From what the lawyer had said, no one had lived in the house for almost thirty years, not since 1963, the year Ella was born. But someone had put a lot of love into that garden.

Ring Point looked exactly like the unsigned oil painting Hilda's lawyer had sent Ella, except that the canvas hadn't done the place justice. Each time Ella looked at the painting, she'd felt a little tug, which had grown into an overwhelming pull.

The painting had come with a note written in Hilda's loopy scrawl.

> Ella,
>   Scatter my ashes in Lyngør. But sell Ringpynten. It's worth a lot of money.

The lawyer can help you with that.
Hilda

Why hadn't Mormor sold the cottage years ago when she struggled to make ends meet, living hand to mouth on a teacher's salary? She'd complained about having to raise Ella in a cramped two-bedroom apartment in downtown Boulder, where car stereos blared, skateboards clacked, and drunk college students bellowed over each other at Bears Taphouse below. Or why hadn't she sold Ring Point when she retired and was barely surviving on social security?

Ella found it bizarre.

The cool breeze blew in off the sound and whipped Ella's hair around her face so that a wisp caught in her mouth. It tasted like sea salt. Here in Lyngør, it was impossible to avoid the water. Good thing she'd bought a life vest for the trip. She'd worn it on the eight-hour ferry ride from Oslo and kept it on as she disembarked and took the fifteen-minute walk along the waterside footpath to her cottage. Only upon her arrival there did she wriggle out of the life preserver, stuffing it into the over-size backpack at her feet. She'd never risk being near the deep blue without it.

She'd inherited her anxiety about the water from her grandma. That, along with her coppery curls and almond eyes. Strange that Hilda had wanted to own a waterside cottage for so many years, if she was afraid of the water.

So this was it. Ringpynten. Her family legacy. A home she'd just discovered but hoped to soon be rid of. She needed to sell the property, pronto. The $22,000 she'd inherited from Hilda initially seemed like a fortune but was nothing more than a few drops in the bucket. She was starting to think that she shouldn't have bought the little retail store back in Boulder so impulsively—what did she know about running a business?

But the shop was the perfect venue to sell the clothes she'd designed. It was a lavender one-story storefront on a lively street just a couple of blocks from Pearl Street Mall in the heart of downtown Boulder, and she'd named the boutique Little Bird. Hilda had always called her dreams unrealistic and "artsy-fartsy." Perhaps using her inheritance to buy the shop was a way of thumbing her nose at the bossy old woman. Whatever it was, Ella had dug herself into a deep financial hole.

She hoped selling the cottage wouldn't take long. Not only was she up to her ears in bills, but she had no idea how she'd spend her time in Lyngør until the place sold.

Back home was another story; her life there was crazy busy. She was simultaneously tending bar at a chophouse and preparing for the soft launch of Little Bird in two months. Before leaving for Norway, she'd rushed around town hunting for the perfect paint, fixtures, and fabrics for the boutique. She was also checking in on the renovation crew because she needed everything to be just right—there was no time for do-overs. Truth was, she had no choice but to work around the clock to make ends meet and to make sure her new business succeeded. Her bestie, Petal, and her coworkers at the chophouse all agreed that she needed a vacation, or a Xanax prescription—or both. It occurred to her that maybe staying extra busy was her way of coping with her fear and grief.

Hilda's death gnawed at her. Even though they weren't close, her grandma had always been her anchor. They argued constantly over what Hilda called Ella's "impractical and impossible" life choices and her far-fetched notions of someday making a living off her art. Hilda's gift of Ring Point had now paved the way for Ella to pursue her dreams. But first she had to sell it. And that meant staying on a tiny island in the middle of the Norwegian archipelago, surrounded by water, until she found a buyer.

Ella scanned her surroundings. Nautical, white wooden

houses lined the shores of the small, leafy islands and disappeared around their tips. There were no cars, streets, sidewalks, or stores, just lots and lots of water. She felt as if she'd arrived in Neverland.

She hoisted her pack, grabbed her guitar, and carefully cradled the box that contained the urn with Hilda's ashes. Descending the craggy hill that edged Ringpynten, she stepped around rock and root, her boots skidding on the polished granite. She stubbed her big toe, gritted her teeth as the pain shot up her foot, and then resettled the cardboard box.

"OK, you're finally home, Mormor. Are you happy now? Don't worry. You won't be in there for long." Ella swallowed the grief searing her throat. They hadn't parted on the best of terms. She'd always thought there would be time to work that out.

She'd had her last conversation with Mormor six months earlier, in Boulder. Her grandma had called on New Year's Day with advice on how to make good in 1992, and Ella hadn't wanted to hear any of it.

Quit that slutty bar job. Stop dressing like a hippie cowgirl. Forget that artsy-fartsy nonsense. Twenty-nine is old enough to grow up and find a husband.

Neither one had uttered the words *I love you*, and now it was too late for both of them.

Ella took one measured step down the hill, then another, and another, until she reached level ground. Past the garden, two wooden boats lay belly-up on the lawn. She shuddered. The last thing she wanted to do was board another boat. She tried to comfort herself with the thought that perhaps she could find out more about her mom while she worked on selling the cottage.

Turning the key in the door, she stepped into the foyer and, still cradling Mormor's ashes, let the rest of her belongings tumble into a pile on the frayed carpet. She flipped the light switch and a yellow glow from a wall sconce lit the narrow, pine-paneled room. The interior of the cottage looked much better than she'd imagined. Where were all the dust and spiderwebs? The scent of damp wool and stale woodsmoke filled the air, like mittens hung by a hearth.

It was strange how a place so foreign could feel instantly familiar, comfortable, like the soft Levi's she'd bought at a vintage clothing store. She traced her hand over a walnut bench in the entryway. Maybe her mother, Sara, along with all the other earlier generations of Nilsens, had sat there to put on their shoes. A shiver raced up her spine. This home held her history, which had always felt so far away, so unknown, yet was something she'd always wanted to understand. She felt an even stronger need to know it now.

To the right of the foyer was a small kitchen with worn wood cabinetry. An empty beer bottle and a recent Lyngør Grocery flyer, dated June 1992, sat on the oak countertop. Weird. The lawyer hadn't said anything about a caretaker, but clearly someone had been there.

"Hello? Anybody here?" she called out.

One thing the lawyer had told her was that the place didn't have a phone. There'd be no calling for help. The cottage was so remote, any squatter could have moved in and who would even notice? Her muscles tensed. She didn't like the idea of being all alone in an isolated cottage in an unfamiliar place. Thinking that maybe she hadn't thought this through, she wondered about the crime rate in Lyngør. She cocked an ear to listen for approaching footsteps or the click of a door latch—although who was she trying to kid? Even if the squeak of a floorboard did give her a teensy heads-up, it wouldn't be enough to save her in this isolated cottage, if someone meant to harm her.

There definitely was creaking coming from somewhere in the cottage. Worry ripped through her as she considered that perhaps the person who drank that beer was creeping around somewhere. No, Ella told herself, old houses creaked and groaned, especially in the evening when the temperature dropped. Was that cigarette ash in the kitchen sink? She heard a scratching sound and checked the cabinet beneath the sink, peering inside for reassurance or cleaning supplies, but found only mouse droppings. One more thing to take care of, unless someone on the island wanted to send over their cat.

She eyed the beer bottle again, still reasoning with herself. She turned on the tap, but it startled her by belching a blast of rust-colored water. That over, the most it could do was spit out a trickle of the same dirty water, which smelled of rotten eggs. The can of soda in her backpack would have to do until tomorrow, when she could head back to the dockside store that she'd seen when getting off the ferry.

Tonight would be used to make lists: items to buy, repairs to make, questions to ask. Near the very top of the list would be finding the best real estate agent in the area. She also wondered if anyone might remember her mother; maybe someone here had spent time with Sara before she died. Perhaps she could find someone who could tell her more about the Nilsens of Ringpynten. There was so much she wanted to know.

In the sitting room, Ella drew back the faded curtains. Choppy waters bordered the cottage on two sides, making her anxious. She wanted to be back in the safety of her city apartment, watching MTV's *House of Style*, and sketching her fashion designs . . . if only she could be home doing any of that instead of staying here in the Land of Too Much Water.

She moved to the far wall to examine the grandfather clock. Its pendulum was still, but like much of the rest of the house, it had a nautical flair. Just above the dial was a painting of a rocky seascape with a lighthouse. It was signed *Sailor Nilsen* in navy cursive. Perhaps she'd inherited her artistic talents from her ancestors; she sure didn't share their love of the water.

Near the brick fireplace, her eye was caught by the rooster-red floor-to-ceiling china cabinet, which was painted with strikingly colorful, fantastical-looking flowers, birds, and scrolls. She ran her fingers over them. Hilda had owned a breadboard with a similar decorative pattern, which she'd called rosemaling—a traditional Norwegian folk art. It was one of the few things Hilda had brought to Colorado, though she'd refused to tell Ella why it was special to her.

Ella thought she'd add the cabinet design to her sketchbook. Perhaps this trip would inspire designs for her future clothing line. But she couldn't even think about that until she got her financial situation settled. If the cottage didn't sell quickly, she wouldn't be able to pay the mortgage on her shop, or the rent on her apartment. Also, her 1970 VW Kombi Bus needed a new engine. It was permanently parked in front of her store until she could afford that. She darkly thought that at least the bus was big enough for her to move into, if it came to that, and ruefully recalled how Hilda had truly hated that sunflower-yellow "hippie-dippie" van.

Ella eased open the cabinet door and found three shelves crammed with delicate pink-peony china, a canister of peanuts, and a bag full of bear-shaped chocolates. The expiration dates on the snacks hadn't passed, so she pried open the lid on the peanuts, scooped a handful, and shoveled them into her mouth. She'd been so racked with travel jitters that she'd eaten only crackers since leaving Boulder twenty hours earlier. Temporarily setting aside her fear about whoever had been in the house, she decided that she could just about hug the person who'd left the food.

Someone had also left an unopened half gallon of twenty-five-year-old scotch in a round bottle with a silver hammer logo. She thought she'd replace the snacks and booze later, but then reminded herself that the cottage and everything in it belonged to her.

She cracked open the scotch and took a sip. It was smoky and tasted like dried cherries—close to perfection, a nine out of ten. She preferred her drinks neat, as opposed to the sugary cocktails that she was always mixing at the chophouse back home.

She took another sip, then ventured farther with the bottle and chocolate, looking for the bedrooms. At the upper-story landing she found three, each of them small with plain furniture and paintings of boats at sea. She suddenly thought of her grandfather, whom she hadn't known. He had died early, from cancer. Surely he must have spent the summers here too. She wondered where Hilda and Sara had slept.

What felt like a flutter of wings brushed Ella's throat. If her mom hadn't died in childbirth, would she have sung Ella to sleep as a baby? Perhaps a sweet cradlesong, like the one Hilda played on the piano when Ella was little—"Den Fyrste Songen." "The First Song." The melody was soothing and lilting, and the lyrics made Ella think of a mother standing over a cradle, her heartfelt lullaby calming her crying daughter.

Ella walked back down to retrieve her luggage, dragged it upstairs, and settled into the room closest to the staircase. She raised the blind and, in the last of the day's light, saw waves breaking against the granite dock below. She squeezed the aquamarine pendant dangling from a long strand of beads around her neck. She'd recently read in a book that seafarers wore aquamarine as a protective talisman. She gladly bought into this belief, especially since she'd decided to say goodbye to Mormor by scattering her ashes on her property perched above the sea.

How did people get around this craggy island? Ella wondered how she'd transport all the supplies she needed from the store. She certainly couldn't haul them back to Ringpynten in one trip, not without a mule. The hilly path to Lyngør Grocery took fifteen minutes on foot.

Her eyes fell on the two boats overturned on the lawn, still bathed in light. Now they made even more sense, but there was no way she could get around in one on her own.

Turning away from the sea view, she nearly choked when she noticed the painting mounted above the dresser: It was of a woman, seemingly in her early twenties, cradling an infant in her arms. Both the woman and the baby had almond eyes, red hair, and wide mouths—features that mirrored Ella's own. She pushed up on her tiptoes, leaned in, and lifted the painting from the wall. Her heart slammed in her chest as she took in the brushstrokes and the brilliant use of light. The style and technique were quite similar to the painting of Ringpynten that her grandma's lawyer had sent her. But this one was signed *Hilda Nilsen* and inscribed:

Lunch with Sara and Ella at Frogner Park
Oslo, Norway
May 1963

Ella reread the date in confusion. How could that be? It was two months after Sara had passed away giving birth. Maybe it was painted posthumously, as a tribute. Had Mormor tried to make herself forget, to comfort herself with this illusion? That didn't seem likely to Ella, based on what her grandma had told Ella about not holding on to the past. Ella hated to question her grandma like this, but she'd been truly shocked to learn about the secrets that had come to light since Mormor's death. If she'd hidden the cottage, was it unreasonable to think there could be more secrets still hidden away? Was Hilda hiding something about Sara? If Sara was still alive in May, as the painting suggested, then what really happened to her? And why would Hilda have kept it a secret all these years?

Also, Mormor never said she was an artist.

CHAPTER 2

Whittling knife in hand, Leif Arnesen chipped the start of a wolf's snout out of an oak block. The shavings fell to his feet. He was sitting in a chair in front of the kitchen fireplace built by his great-great-grandfather, and out of habit he kicked the shavings into the fire.

The moments before dawn were Leif's favorite time of day. This was when he carved wolves, ravens, serpents, flora, and fauna, all from images culled from the dozens of books he'd collected on Viking art. He'd whittled every morning over the last twenty-six years, since he was a boy of eight, and his guardian, Erik Olsen, first placed a knife in his hand. Erik was now his boss over at Lyngør Boatyard and Marina, and they were close, but Leif really wanted to design and carve wooden boats rather than work as Erik's number one boatbuilder and mechanic. He hoped that someday Erik would finally see him as an artist and let him take on design jobs.

The clock chimed eight. Leif had twenty minutes to meet Oskar, the fishmonger, on the water near Ringpynten to pick up his twelve kilos of fresh cod. He'd never hear the end of it if he didn't bring his fish cakes to the annual summer party, as he'd been doing faithfully for the last ten years. His friends kidded him that *tradition* was his middle name, but that was a nicer way of noting that Leif hated change.

He pocketed his boat keys. His socks, Chucks, and sweater—all blue—lay in a heap on the reindeer pelt beneath his feet. Leif's father, Bjorn, had died in a boating accident when Leif was five, leaving him an orphan. Even though the color was pleasing to Njord, the god who protected seafarers, Bjorn hadn't had a stitch of blue on him when he'd taken the boat out, and Leif had vowed to never make the same mistake. He'd worn blue ever since.

The Lyngør folk politely continued to call it an accident, but the awful truth was that Bjorn was drunk and lost control of his boat, killing himself and two men, out-of-towners, who were visiting from up north. Bjorn's best friend, Erik Olsen, had barely survived. After the accident, Erik raised Leif. It was just the two of them because Leif's mother had died from meningitis when he was only two years old.

He had no memory of her, but his father's death still haunted him. He often thought of the bedtime stories Bjorn had told about the importance of respecting the deep blue sea and protecting all the travelers on it. To this day, a sea of grief still sloshed inside him, and he wondered how his dad could've been so irresponsible. A small part of him had never forgiven Bjorn.

Setting aside his carving, Leif decided he needed more coffee. He still felt groggy; the day before, he'd had to fetch a couple of fiberglass skiffs and a red dinghy from a manufacturer in Oslo and haul them to the Lyngør Boatyard, where they'd be put up for sale. It had meant a late night. He refilled his blue thermos, which had been a recent gift from Erik in honor of Leif's thirty-fourth birthday.

He grabbed his wallet from the kitchen table. Next to it lay a business card from a prestigious shipyard known for its talented boatbuilders. The owner had offered him a boat-builder position yesterday. He'd applauded Leif's strong work ethic and attention to detail, even called him a brilliant crafts-man. Leif tossed the business card into the kindling basket. The recognition felt great, but he wouldn't accept the job, not in a million years. Sometimes Erik could be difficult to work for, but Leif had no interest in changing bosses or moving to a different place.

He liked his life exactly how it was. On Saturdays he played poker with his childhood friends at the local clubhouse. Once a week he bought *skolebrød*, a cream pastry, at Lyngør Bakery, a tradition established by Bjorn. The bakery owner shared Leif and Bjorn's love of Norse mythology, and Leif always looked forward to chatting with him.

Leif yanked the blue sweater over his shaggy blond hair. It stretched tight across his broad shoulders and strong biceps. The baker always insisted that Leif looked like a Norse god, but Leif didn't see himself as good-looking. He didn't waste time looking in the mirror.

Pulling the door shut behind him, Leif jogged down the two long flights of stairs to his dock. He'd built the two wooden boats that were tied there. The smaller of the two was an open twenty-foot double-ender with wolves and leaves carved into her railing. Leif had christened her *Skadi*, the Norse goddess who married Njord, the god of the sea. Leif's larger boat was a thirty-two-foot cabin cruiser with tendrils and serpents carved into the trim around her windshield and on her railing. He'd christened her *Rán*, the goddess of storms and the drowned.

As Leif stepped onto *Rán*, the boat dipped under his weight. He went to the helm and fired up the engine. Steering past the grocery, the sailmaker's workshop, and a couple dozen white clapboard cottages, and around the tip of Lyngørsida, he headed for the waters just offshore from Ringpynten. Ten

minutes later, he dropped anchor in the narrow channel near
the old Nilsen cottage. Small, rocky islands dotted water as
blue as Leif's clothes.

Oskar was late, as usual. Leif prided himself on his punc-
tuality. Thinking to kill the time by doing a little fishing, he
grabbed his pole from the deck just as a flash of color drew
his gaze to Ringpynten. Two throw rugs were draped over the
low rock wall, and the front door stood ajar. He wondered who
was there. Everyone knew that Mia, who oversaw the cottage
rentals, had canceled all visitors after hearing from the lawyer
in charge of Mrs. Nilsen's estate.

He ruled out his oldest friend, Inger, knowing she'd be
at work at the post office. A passionate gardener, Inger was
thrilled when Mia agreed to let her work the small plot of land
at Ringpynten. She planted peas, rhubarb for her wine, and
gooseberries for her jam, with the understanding that she must
respect the privacy of any renters. Both Mia and Inger were as
close to him as siblings. But while Inger was his oldest friend,
Mia, who also owned Lyngør Grocery, was his best friend.

He scanned the property and saw a laundry tub out on the
slate terrace. Perhaps Mia had hired a handyman to clean and
make repairs. Several tiles definitely needed replacing on the
cottage roof.

Fifteen minutes passed before Oskar approached in his
trawler, throwing a sharp wake that sent Leif's skiff rocking.
Bald, wind-burnt Oskar was the king of fishermen, and he
talked up a storm. He pulled up alongside Leif, threw over the
fenders, and dropped anchor.

"Trying to check out the new Nilsen tenant, are you? No
families this time around. Just the lone American woman.
Arrived yesterday."

Oskar grabbed five large fish from the catch bin on his deck
and began passing them over the railing to Leif. Leif dumped
the cod, one by one, into his marine cooler.

An American woman? Why hadn't he heard? He'd been in Oslo, that was why.

"She's a real knockout," Oskar persisted. "An answer to a lone boy's prayers."

"Right." Leif wasn't looking for a girlfriend. He was content with his life just as it was. And if he were looking, he had no intention of chatting up an American. They were an odd lot. Loud talkers. They put ice in their water and clothes on their dogs. And all that nonsense about inches and ounces instead of the metric system, like the rest of the civilized world.

Oskar slid a pouch of tobacco from the inside pocket of his grubby slicker.

"Yesterday my wife's knitting club was on the ferry. The girl there was on board." He pinched out a spot of tobacco and rolled it in paper. "The ladies figured she's one of those eccentric artist types, like you read about in the *sladder* rags. You know, gossip magazines." He chuckled open-mouthed, revealing crooked brown teeth. "The gossip made my wife so excited she came on to me last night."

Leif cracked open a snail with his fillet knife and slipped the jellied meat onto his fishing hook. He didn't want to think about Oskar and his wife fooling around.

Smoke streamed from the fishmonger's nostrils. "Why would a young American woman pay to rent a cottage in Lyngør? Any guesses?"

"Oskar, can you give me some space? You're frightening the fish, and I want to catch dinner before I head to work." It was Monday, which meant a fish supper. Nothing was better than fresh grilled fillets, but if he didn't land anything now, he'd have to buy days-old mackerel in Mia's grocery.

"Suppose I better be off." Oskar flicked his cigarette butt into the water.

"Come on, don't litter!" Leif snatched his minnow net

from the bucket on the deck and scooped up the butt before it floated away.

"Good luck with your cod cakes. Look forward to tasting them at the party," the fishmonger called back as he motored away.

• • •

A half hour passed and Leif still hadn't caught a single fish, but he decided to give it another twenty minutes. Then he needed to get to work. Mia had bought a new red dinghy, and he promised to deliver it to her today.

As *Rán* drifted offshore from Ringpynten, he balanced his pole against the gunwale and grabbed another snail. Faint music came from the cottage. A woman strumming a guitar and singing was sitting on the stone wall that skirted the dock. Russet ringlets tumbled over her shoulders and chest. She didn't look like the usual summer visitor; she wore a bright-yellow dress with a bold pattern and a big, floppy cowboy hat. It was exactly like the hats he'd seen on people in travel advertisements for America—ads that promised rodeos and steakhouses and balloon rides.

With that type of excitement, why would American tourists ever choose to come to Lyngør? It was known, if it was known at all, for being an idyllic village on the sea. The natural surroundings were incredible, but not much happened there. Life revolved around the water, and the everyday routine was about as bland as boiled parsnips. But that was just fine with Leif, who adored habits and custom. Sticking to his schedule gave him some sense of control over what had always felt, to him, like a chaotic and unpredictable world.

From what he could see from his boat, the woman at Ringpynten looked like a trendy city person. Mia, who was obsessed with movies set in big cities, would have loads to say about this.

The breeze picked up. The tourist took off her hat. Wisps of hair flew about her face, like the coppery threads on a red sailcloth. Oskar was right; she was attractive, and Leif liked what he saw. He recast his line with a steady flick of the wrist, willing his eyes to stay on the water, not on the woman, whom he could now only think of as Sunna, the Norse goddess of the sun.

CHAPTER 3

The first morning at Ringpynten, Ella shook out the throw rugs on the lawn, spinning dust out into the crisp, salty breeze. She really needed the cottage to shine to attract serious buyers and land a quick sale—and that critical infusion of cash. As she draped the carpet over the stone wall, the waves slapped against the dock.

She remembered this sound, the steady beating of waves, from the night before, and how it had frightened her until she'd pulled the covers over her head to silence it. Back home in Boulder, she'd used a different method to block out the sounds outside her window: She fell asleep with headphones clamped to her ears to mute the techno music that thumped from the dance bar on the lower level of her apartment building. Located between a microbrewery and a sports outfitter, the bar was always packed on weekends, though she'd never been there herself.

Ella was never alone but often lonely. She supposed that cities could be like that—lots of people in close proximity who didn't always connect with each other. But she thought it might be something specific to her too. She had felt for a

long time that she had trouble bonding with people in her adopted city. At the chophouse, she'd found her coworkers difficult to get to know. Although she was there six nights a week,
the staff was constantly turning over because it mostly con-
sisted of college students and ski bums, who tended to come
and go. She had nothing in common with the customers at
the bar either. Most of them loved to hear themselves talk, so
Ella listened when they cried over their beers about their latest breakups, and she laughed at their corny one-liners. They
could be so tiresome, though! She'd heard more than her share
of chatter about some new technology her customers were
calling the World Wide Web. The boring ones were prefera-
ble, though, to the ones who were disrespectful, referring to
her as "babe" or "hottie," and snapping their fingers to get her
attention or to signal for another round. Ella sighed. Their tips
covered her latte addiction, the lease on her moped, and fabric
for her fashion line. Not to mention the really big stuff, like her
rent, which was past due.

Jeez, she owed so much money right now! She'd hired
Petal to help with the soft launch of Little Bird and to oversee
the renovations while she was in Norway. Having no money
for payroll yet, she'd promised to pay Petal in cash as soon as
she sold the cottage, so she really had to unload the property
ASAP.

Petal, for her part, needed the money because she was
planning to move back to India. She was going to star in her
eldest brother's debut Bollywood film. Ella's heart squeezed at
the thought of her best friend moving to another country. But
she reminded herself that they didn't really spend much time
together anyway, since Petal was often caught up in the lives
of her seven siblings. Ella, an only child, couldn't even imagine
that; it sounded like a lot of work to her. As money was never
far from her mind these days, she sent up another prayer for
a quick sale so that she could pay Petal, as well as her bills.

She laughed as she remembered what Petal said right before Ella left Boulder: "Don't come home until you've landed a hot Viking dude!"

Ha. She had no time for romance.

Little Bird was where she was placing her expectations for happiness—not in some guy. As she surveyed the cheery pink fairy roses surrounding the cottage, she let her mind wander toward her future plans.

She thought about all the customers she'd have once she had the store up and running. Though she'd always suffered from impostor syndrome and doubts about her talent as a designer, she'd planned on the store grounding her in the local art scene. Besides selling her own fashion designs, she wanted to support other local artists by carrying their handcrafted goods: beeswax candles, gemstone rings, watercolors of the Rocky Mountains. She couldn't wait to invite them to cozy gatherings in her store—opening receptions, special events, maybe even birthdays and holidays. Ella was looking forward to creating for herself the sense of belonging that had always eluded her. She imagined that, with time, these customers and local artisans might become the caring and supportive family that she had always wanted.

Ella brought herself back to the present and mentally checked her ever-growing to-do list. She noticed the loose shutter hanging from a window on the upper story. It needed a new coat of paint. Come to think of it, so did the white clapboard on the house. She added *Find a handyman* and *Buy headphones (cheap)* to her list. Her bank account was almost empty, but she couldn't think about that right now.

Her watch read 9:00 a.m. According to the Lyngør Grocery flyer she'd found on the kitchen counter, the store opened in an hour. While she was in town, she thought she might as well ask around about her mom. Seeing the painting and its inscription had really gotten under her skin. She wondered once again about the date on the painting. How could Ella's mom have been alive when Hilda painted it? That would mean she hadn't died in childbirth, and it would be truly insane of her grandma to make up a story about her own daughter's death. Wouldn't it? Ella could hardly imagine it. And yet when Ella was a young girl, she'd begged Hilda to return to Norway so she could see where she was born. Hilda had refused, saying there was nothing left in Norway to call home anyway. She urged Ella to think of Boulder as home now, and not to be ungrateful or ask for too much. The trip would cost a fortune, she'd said, and she was having trouble making ends meet as it was.

Hilda had said all that while owning and renting out a cottage all these years and putting aside a sizable nest egg. Why had she lied about her finances? Why wouldn't she return to Lyngør? And just as puzzling, Hilda had painted that stunning double portrait of mother and daughter, set at Frogner Park in Oslo, but Ella had never even seen her color in a coloring book. So many of the things her grandma said and did were now questionable. In light of all this, Ella was ready to believe that she might have lied about Sara's death after all. But why?

Grief and anger over Hilda's secrets prickled at the edge of Ella's thoughts.

Ella did what she had always done when life got difficult: She turned to her art. Her Olympus OM-4T lay next to her guitar on the stone wall. She grabbed it and pointed the lens at the cottage, thinking that she'd like to hang pictures of both Ringpynten and Lyngør in her store to inspire future clothing lines. Maybe she could even save money on the property listing if she submitted her own photographs. As she framed shots of the cottage, she found it hard to believe that this mysterious and beautiful little house belonged to her now. It looked like something out of a fairy tale. Even if she hadn't had a family connection to the place, she couldn't deny it was utterly enchanting.

Back in the cottage sitting room, Ella ran a damp rag over the dusty bookcase. It was stuffed with tattered paperbacks and also, oddly enough, a framed, whimsical photograph of two pairs of shoes: men's loafers and women's ankle straps with bows. The shoes lay side by side on a colorful blanket that was spread out on the ground. The blanket was embroidered with bluebells and oystercatchers with spindly pink legs. She wondered who had stitched the needlework—was it Sara's or Hilda's creation? Maybe that was where Ella's love of textiles and design came from. She picked up the photograph, but before she could get a closer look, the dried-out wood frame fell apart in her hand. The picture poked out between the glass and the cardboard backing.

Ella pried away the cardboard and eased out the photograph. On the back of it was a detailed, red-ink sketch of a woman's face. Hearts surrounded her hair. Below the sketch was written, For Sara: Gåsholmen med min kjæreste. Juli 1962. "Gåsholmen with my sweetheart. July 1962."

That was a year before Ella was born.

Her breath hitched in awe. This had to be a sketch of her mother. Ella had never even seen an image of her until the night before, because Hilda hadn't saved anything associated with Sara. Knowing almost nothing about her mother had made it harder for Ella to deal with her absence, so she'd tried not to think about her at all. That was certainly what Hilda had encouraged.

As Ella studied the artist's rendering of Sara's long, wavy locks, she pushed her own curls from her shoulders. She didn't realize tears were running down her cheeks until they pooled on her lips. She remembered a time when she was five and bubble gum had gotten stuck in her hair, so Hilda marched her to the beautician. Ella had sobbed, knowing what was coming. She wiggled as her grandma plopped her into the booster seat at the salon.

Hilda bent down until her face was level with Ella's. "Be still." Hilda's pickled-fish breath caught in Ella's nose. "You look like a troll, with that messy mane of yours. Same as your mother's."

Hilda turned toward the beautician. "Cut it to her ears."

Ella's hair was just like her mother's and Hilda was going to take it away. She tried to shield herself but Hilda wouldn't allow it. Ella was able to grab one wisp of hair before it fell to the floor. She hid it under her salon bib, then cupped it in her pocket and brought it home, where she placed it in her empty Minnie Mouse PEZ dispenser for safekeeping. Although she knew it was her own hair, Hilda's offhand comparison had brought her about as close to her mother as she'd ever gotten. She pretended the hair was Sara's.

She turned over the photograph taken at Gåsholmen again. She looked more closely at the shoes. They lay side by side on the blanket, which was spread out near a big, slanted boulder. Maybe the men's loafers belonged to Sara's boyfriend. It was possible, considering the word *sweetheart* written there. Or maybe the loafers belonged to her father. Her father's identity remained a mystery to Ella, although Hilda had identified him as a Brit who was just passing through, crewing on a yacht.

"A good-for-nothing, a wandering traveler!" was how she put it once.

Was Gåsholmen within walking distance? She put this question on her list of things to ask when she got to the store. She needed plenty of food and supplies too. There'd better be a water taxi service to help her haul everything to Ringpynten, she vowed, because the boats in her yard would never see her backside unless she was walking away.

She put her ever-growing lists into her satchel. As she shut the door behind her and stepped outside, a glittering light drew her gaze to an empty whiskey bottle and a metal lighter on the stone wall. Were those there when she'd arrived yesterday?

The hair rose on her arms as her thoughts returned to someone lurking around the cottage. She didn't want to think about that, so she focused on the heather carpeting the ground. She'd like to find a fabric in that exact hue—a soft, soothing pinkish purple—and make a dress to match the flowers.

As Ella headed toward Mia's store, she marveled at Ring Point's garden. Spearmint and dill flowered in glazed ceramic pots near a plum tree. Next to them were several roses with tangerine-colored pods—probably for making jelly, as Hilda loved to do each summer. Leafy rhubarb, carrots, and staked peas thrived in the well-tended vegetable garden, which was the size of a large sandbox. A porcupine waddled around the lingonberry bushes, which were draped in ripe red fruit. Those berries reminded Ella of Christmas Eve dinner with Hilda: lingonberry gløgg—no one could make spiced mulled wine like Mormor—and *nissegrøt,* the hot rice pudding Ella would always think of as Santa's porridge. Ella loved how her grandma always hid one almond in the *risgrøt,* and whichever one of them found it in their serving won the *sjokolade julegris,* a small chocolate pig.

A fresh wave of emotions washed over Ella. Anger at the secrets her grandmother kept from her. Grief that she'd never celebrate the holidays with her again.

Trying to shake it off, Ella eyed the ugly chicken wire around the garden. She'd rip it out and add it to the junk pile. She didn't know who the gardener was, but the plot was now hers to manage until she handed the keys over to whoever bought the cottage.

As Ella walked past the plum tree, she wondered if her mother was buried somewhere on the isles of Lyngør, or maybe even here at Ringpynten. If she could find out, perhaps she could put Hilda next to her. But Ella didn't have any living family members to ask. All Ella knew was that her ancestors came from Oslo, that she was born there, and that her family summered in Lyngør.

Ascending the steep hill that edged her cottage lifted her mood. She'd been a hiker all her life, exploring Kohler Mesa Trail near Boulder as a small child with Hilda each Saturday morning rain or shine, or even snow. She'd cherished those mornings with her mormor because being out in nature like that was one of the few ways they really connected with each other. Mormor had taught Ella the importance of *friluftsliv*, "an outdoor life," a way of living that was deeply rooted in Scandinavian culture. Once again, Ella's heart squeezed at the memory of her grandma. She missed Hilda's cheeky grin when she won Monopoly or Go Fish. She missed Hilda's occasional yet squishy, comforting hugs.

• • •

As Ella walked along the uneven footpath toward the shop, she passed shuttered waterside cottages with glazed tile roofs, white crocheted curtains, and carved trim around the windows and doors. Tidy, quiet, and uniform. Maybe not her style but appealing—and nothing like her apartment building in Boulder, where decades of old chewing gum were ground into a colorful mosaic on the sidewalk out front and the hallway smelled of frying oil and chicken wings. Her windows looked out on Pearl Street Mall, the Boulder Bookstore, breweries, and college students kicking around hacky sacks near the record store. Ella loved the lively pulse of her adopted hometown, taking in shows at the Boulder Theater, buying homemade honey and peanut butter at the busy weekend market. But as she took in her surroundings here, she wondered what it would've been like to grow up in Lyngør.

As Ella rounded the corner of the two-story clapboard grocery store, she spotted a cuckoo perched on the store's picket fence, making *coo-coo* sounds. Maybe it was the same bird who'd awakened her at six this morning, squawking just outside her window. Perhaps her mother was woken by cuckoo birds when she spent her summers here back in the early sixties.

Ella's pulse spiked as she heard water slosh against the grocery store dock. She shoved her hand into her satchel to touch her life vest, comforted in knowing that she could put it on anytime she got too close to the water's edge. A sugary cake scent drifted from the store and distracted her. Bells tinkled as Ella entered the shop. She took in the fish charts and a poster of Edvard Munch's *Inger on the Beach* that hung on the cream walls. Potted violets and nautical instruments decorated the windowsills. The shop looked nothing like the sterile grocery stores back home, with their fluorescent lights and acres of linoleum.

A big cat with a bottlebrush tail made a beeline for Ella, rubbing his cheeks against the worn leather of her knee-high boots. She ran her coral nails over its thick fur, drawing a rumbly purr. Ella had never owned a pet because Hilda hadn't wanted her to get attached to something that could run away or die. Someday when Ella settled down and had more time, she'd adopt a shelter dog, or cat, or both.

"That cat usually doesn't take to strangers," the cashier said.

"Well, he has good taste. I'm an animal lover." She squatted and scratched the cat's ears. "What's your name, beautiful?" Her Norwegian was a bit rusty, but the cashier got the gist of it.

"His name is Bactus," the cashier replied.

The cashier was around Ella's age, late twenties. She had short, spiked platinum hair, an elegant neck, and a pronounced collarbone—Holly Golightly gone punk.

"Cool," the woman nodded at Ella's boots.

Ella had embroidered sparrows on the leather. The boots were unique, and she was proud of them. Hilda had hated them. She hadn't approved of much of anything about Ella, not her hand-sewn clothes, or her photography or music, not even her love of birds. Who didn't like birds?

"You're American, yes? I've met very few Americans. You've come pretty far," the cashier said and extended her hand. "Mia." Mia switched to English with ease, as if she'd had a lot of practice.

"Ella, from Colorado." She shook Mia's hand and smiled. "Yes, it felt like it took forever to get here, but I made it. You speak excellent English. Have you ever lived in the States?"

"Thanks. And no, I've never been to America," she laughed, "but all Norwegians are required to study English in school, starting in first grade. Norway is small, so we need to learn other languages, especially if we want to travel or work in business. I've always wanted to visit California and see Hollywood Boulevard where they shot *American Gigolo*, except that I'd have to board a plane." Mia studied Ella's satchel, which had several woven patches stitched onto the suede.

"What's that?" she asked, gesturing to a patch with a red mountain.

"Yeah, that's Red Rocks. It's a natural amphitheater. And this patch is from Bonnie Raitt's concert from her 1989 *Nick of Time* tour. An amazing night—the music, camping at Indian Paintbrush, the s'mores." The thought made her stomach gurgle. Since she arrived the day before, she'd only eaten the chocolate and peanuts she'd found in the cottage. "I'm absolutely starving. Do you sell cereal?"

"I don't sell cereal. It's hard to keep stocked—too popular." She slid a hard candy from her pocket. "You remind me of Julia Roberts."

Ella touched her mouth and hair and smiled her sincere megawatt smile. "Thank you. I'll take that as a compliment," Ella laughed. She was disappointed about the cereal. She had eaten cornflakes every day since she was a child.

"You're a bit early for summer folk," Mia said, then scribbled something on her clipboard. "*Fellesferie* isn't for three weeks."

"What's *fell-es-fair-ria*?" She pronounced it carefully.

"Fellesferie is when practically everybody in the country takes a three-week vacation, and the tourists arrive—mostly Norwegians, but a good number of Swedes—and it gets a little chaotic."

"Oh. But I'm not a tourist." Ella shrugged.

"Really. Where are you staying?"

"Ringpynten."

"Oh?" Mia scrunched up her nose. "I got a letter from the lawyer in charge of the owner's estate. Mrs. Nilsen died, and I was told to cancel the renters. Sorry, I thought I contacted everyone." Mia glanced around for the ledger. "What's your name?"

"Ella Nilsen. Hilda Nilsen was my grandma. She left me Ringpynten."

"You're Mrs. Nilsen's granddaughter?" Mia's voice rose an octave. She extended her hand again, and Ella shook it. "Mia Linn. I own this shop." Ella must've looked surprised, because Mia laughed and added, "I know, I look young for my age, but really, I'm twenty-nine. This store has been in my family for generations. My parents passed it down to me before they retired up north. I'm also in charge of Ringpynten's rentals and overseeing the maintenance. The lawyer didn't mention you were coming. The letter only said the property would be put up for sale. How long are you staying?"

"Um, I'm not sure yet. My plane ticket is open-ended, but I can't stay longer than two weeks. I have to get back to work."

"What's your job?" Mia laughed. "I'm nosy. And I love everything American! Do you know that song 'Fast Car' by Tracy Chapman? Do you like it?" She fiddled with her rainbow suspenders. "Tracy's the best, isn't she? I hope to see her in concert someday."

"Oh yeah, I play her album all the time when I work on my fashion line," Ella said with a smile. "I'm launching my own clothing store soon. I need to hire staff ASAP."

"That's so cool." Mia grinned before reaching beneath the register to retrieve a jar labeled *Inger's Stikkelsbær Syltetøy.* A hand-painted vine with red berries decorated the logo.

"Gooseberry jam. It's delicious! My friend Inger makes it from her gooseberry bushes. Here, try it. I'll introduce you to Inger. Please let her know if you like it. It's a Welcome-to-Lyngør present."

"Thanks. That's so sweet of you. I'd love to try it."

"Great!" Mia smiled. "I bet you have quite a bit on your grocery list."

"Yes I do. But first I need a real estate agent. Is there a good one in Lyngør?"

"Nope. The only businesses on the islands are this store, the post office, and the hotel. You'll have to go to the mainland, to Tvedestrand. That's where you'll find restaurants and bars and things that you can't find here at my shop." She wrapped up the gooseberry jam. "My cousin is an agent in downtown Tvedestrand. I can call her and give her the heads-up that Ringpynten is for sale and you're on a tight deadline. But I should tell you: The market is slow, so selling a pricey summer home could take forever."

"I hope that's not the case. But that's kind of you. Could you do that? I would really appreciate it." Ella had everything on the line and no one to lean on if it all blew up in her face. If the house didn't sell quickly, she could say goodbye to Little Bird and her dreams for her future.

Mia noticed the concern in Ella's eyes. "Don't worry," she said. "Ringpynten is amazing. Someone will eventually snap it up."

"I hope so . . . I mean, the cottage doesn't even have a street address, and so I don't know what to tell a real estate agent. Or even who to call to find out what it might sell for." She let out a sigh. "That's why I came here myself. And Hilda wanted her ashes scattered in Norway. Plus, I'm hoping to learn more about my family in Lyngør."

"Many of the cottages on the smaller islands, like Ringpynten, don't have addresses. But you know, Norway is one of the most expensive countries in the world." Mia gestured at the window and to the islands and water beyond. "It's stunningly gorgeous here. Old monied Norwegians and the nouveau riche here are willing to pay a fortune for vacation homes in Lyngør. Bottom line, your cottage is worth gobs of money."

"A fortune?" Ella stammered in surprise. "Are you sure?"

"You look confused." Mia laughed at Ella, who could only nod in agreement. "Let me try to explain better—as I said, I'm obsessed with the States," Mia said with excitement. "I saw a movie set in the Hamptons—New York, you know. That famous beach area and these isles in Lyngør are both playgrounds for rich vacationers and trust-fund kids. I suppose owning property in either place is a status symbol—you know, wealth, importance—and those things crank up the summer-home prices." She took a sip of soda. "I think the inheritance tax rate is fifteen percent, but I'm not sure. I'll check with my cousin in Tvedestrand and let you know."

"That's so kind of you. Thanks!" If this was true, Ella might have enough to get out of debt, buy Little Bird outright, and hire staff to help sew her line and to work the register.

"How is the cottage? Everything in order?" Mia asked. Bactus leaped onto the counter and let out a loud rumble while Mia scratched his ears.

"I think it has mice. You can send over Bactus anytime." Ella laughed. "And I'm only sort of joking. Do you happen to know who's been there recently? Someone left a beer bottle on the kitchen counter, and then this morning I noticed an empty whiskey bottle and cigarette lighter on the stone wall. I'm a little worried that someone's been hanging around."

"It's probably the handyman. I hired him to replace a cracked window. I'm so sorry if it alarmed you." Mia gave Ella an apologetic look. "He's a great worker, who works under the table. Cheap. Just a bit messy." She snorted. "But you know, there's no crime in Lyngør. I don't even lock my door."

"Good to know." Ella smiled with relief. "Do you think it'd be possible for me to hire this handyman to fix the sink and the tiles on the roof, plus do a bunch of other repairs?"

"No problem, I'll talk to him," Mia said. "Now what's on your list? What can I help you grab?"

Thirty minutes later, a pay-phone card, food, and supplies covered the checkout counter. Mia had talked Ella into buying everything from a strange, caramel-brown, cubed-shaped goat cheese to a Donald Duck comic book. It turned out Mia liked to sketch her own comics for stress relief.

Pulling two bottles from beneath the cash register, she said, "Inger makes rhubarb wine too. I have to keep it under the counter, though, because only government-owned liquor stores are allowed to sell wine." Mia grabbed a real estate pamphlet, held it up to make sure Ella noticed it, and slid it onto the stack of groceries. "Contact information for my cousin in case you'd like that. Anything else?" she asked as she gestured toward the aisles.

"Would you mind calling me a water taxi? There's no way I can carry all of this in one trip."

Mia smiled. "The taxi service isn't running right now. The owners are on holiday in Spain for another two weeks."

"Not running? How do people haul their stuff around if they don't have a boat?"

"You really don't know much about Lyngør," Mia said with a curious tilt of her head.

"Fill me in—please!" Ella felt a little silly for not researching Lyngør before arriving.

Mia began ringing up the pile of groceries before her.

"Translated, *Lyngør* means 'Isles of Heather.' It consists of four islands. Fewer than a hundred people live here year-round. Everyone owns at least one boat, so the water taxi is mostly for the tourists—we get hundreds of them."

Ella nodded with interest. Pity there wasn't a taxi service right now, not just to ferry her groceries home, but also to get her to Gåsholmen to see if she could find out anything about her mother. Even though Mia was too young to have known Sara personally, Ella felt like she was on a roll, so she took a chance. She dug inside her purse, pulled out the picture from the broken frame, and turned it toward Mia.

"The sketch is of my mother, Sara Nilsen. It seems she was at Gåsholmen with a man in July of 1962. She died when I was a baby." *How strange to think that maybe Mormor lied about my mother's death.*

"I'm so sorry to hear this," Mia said.

"Thank you, I appreciate that. I'd like to find out anything I can about my family. Especially my mother. My grandma told me nothing."

"Nothing at all?" Mia said.

"Nope. And she never will, since she died six months ago. I found her face down in her sardines and toast." Ella hadn't meant to sound glib, but with all her mixed emotions, that's how it came out. It didn't seem to faze Mia, who covered her mouth with her hand, suppressing laughter.

"I'm sorry for your loss," she managed to say.

Ella shrugged. "I'm fine. It *is* funny, in a dark sort of way." Truth was, Ella had walked around in a daze for some time after Hilda died. She was stricken to lose her only remaining family, and compounding the loss was the realization that any memories of her mother had also died with Mormor.

Hilda had once said, "You're just like her, and it breaks my heart, sadly enough." But Ella would never know what that meant, because Hilda refused to say anything more.

Mia, turning over the photo, tapped her finger against the inscription date on the sketch of Ella's mom. "I wasn't born yet. I'm afraid I can't help you."

"Do you have contact information for any of the tourists—the regulars? They might have stories about my family."

"No, not really. We don't tend to stay in touch like that."

"So Hilda never mentioned she had a daughter?"

Mia shook her head. "Hilda and I only talked about matters relating to Ringpynten, like repairs and renter issues."

"OK, but you must know someone who was around when my mother stayed here before I was born," Ella persisted.

"Well . . ." Mia chewed on her thumb. "My friend Erik would have been in his mid-twenties at that time, though I doubt he knows anything."

"Could you introduce us?"

"Yeah, all right. But don't get your hopes up—it's been a long time since your family vacationed in Lyngør." Mia handed back the photograph. "Good news is, Gåsholmen is only a five-minute boat ride from Ringpynten. You own two boats. Hilda had them serviced every summer, but I'll ask my friend Leif to hurry up and look at them now. He works with Erik at Lyngør's boatyard and marina. I bet he can lend you a dinghy to use for now."

Ella shook her head. She'd probably fall overboard and drown. She picked up the lists and sighed. "What about number five on my list? Where can I get bed linens and towels?"

"I washed Ringpynten's linens at the end of last Fellesferie. They're in my apartment upstairs." Mia pointed at the rafter ceiling.

"Great. Next, I need a pay phone. I'm surprised the cottage doesn't have a phone or even a television." It was 1992, but it might as well have been the 1850s. Ella needed to check in with Petal to see how the renovations were going.

"There's a pay phone here on the island, but it's out of order.

You'll have to go to the gas station on the mainland, Gjeving. That's a fifteen-minute boat ride. But you can use my phone whenever you like."

"Thank you," Ella said. "You're a lifesaver. But I still need to figure out how to lug all my supplies back. Do you have a cart or something I can borrow?"

"Nah, just take what you need right now." Mia motioned toward the counter. "I'll have Leif bring the rest—it might not be until tomorrow, but I'll send you home with a jug of water. Leif will do a great job on the boats."

• • •

As Ella retraced her steps on the uneven concrete path back to Ringpynten, she knocked on the doors of several shuttered cottages with Norwegian flags rippling out front. She felt hopeful that she'd meet some locals who might give her clues about her mom and maybe even Mormor. She wondered if she and her mom were as similar as Mormor had insisted they were. Not a single person seemed to be at home.

Disappointment clobbered her. The houses were probably second homes or reserved for tourist rentals, and as Mia had pointed out, Ella had arrived too soon in the season. Fellesferie wasn't for three weeks yet. Unfortunately, she couldn't afford to stay that long.

CHAPTER 4

Happy with the one good fish he'd caught for dinner, Leif fetched Mia's new fiberglass dinghy at the marina. He towed the boat beyond small, leafy islands; the hotel; and dozens of white-painted waterfront cottages. Plastic boats were soulless compared to traditional wooden boats, he thought as he tied the blasted dinghy to the dock at Lyngør Grocery. But these new ones were all the rage.

Mia's cat followed Leif into the store. No one was manning the till. "Morning, Mia!" he called out.

"Back here!" she hollered from the back room.

Refrigerated shelving lined the rear walls, where he found Mia restocking tubes of shrimp cheese and caviar. He smiled as she approached, her hair sticking out in all directions. "Styled your hair with an eggbeater again?"

"Says the weirdo who only wears blue."

"I dropped off your dinghy at the dock."

"Oh jeez. I can't afford it now. When you were in Oslo, my fridge died and I had to order a new one." She unpacked fish pudding from the box at her feet. "And don't be annoyed—you should have no problem finding another buyer. It's pretty and red."

"I don't blame you, and I'm not annoyed." He meant it. He just wasn't keen on being a salesman, chasing customers and brownnosing them. "I have to head to work. Erik's gone for the day. He's visiting Ragnar."

"OK, but just so you know, Ringpynten has a new owner. Mrs. Nilsen's granddaughter, Ella Nilsen, inherited it."

So Sunna had a name. Ella Nilsen. Leif shrugged one shoulder at Mia. Mrs. Nilsen hadn't set foot in Lyngør in as far back as he could remember. He had no recollection of her.

"I told Inger that the cottage is being put on the market and that she can't garden or harvest berries at Ringpynten unless she gets permission from the new owner," Mia said. She was sitting on a stool, shelving smoked cod roe. "Inger's heartbroken and depressed about it. You know how much she loves that property and gardening there. It's her sanctuary."

"Yes, I know," Leif said, shaking his head. "It's no secret that she's frustrated, maybe even a little bitter, that she can't afford to buy the property herself. Why doesn't she ask Ella if she could continue to plant there, or at least collect her berries and rhubarb for cooking?" He bent over to pet Bactus, who lay near his feet on the wood floor.

"Great idea. I'll suggest it to her. I'm sure it will all work out—Ella seems nice," Mia said. "Could you please hurry up and service Ringpynten's boats so she can get around?"

"That job's on the books for the third week of June." He'd have to work overtime to squeeze it in before then, throwing his routine out of whack. He began to reconsider even as he said it. He didn't care for the way his gut had warmed when he spotted her earlier this morning, with her cowboy hat and guitar. "I guess I could move the job up." He didn't mention that he'd already seen her. He didn't want to deal with Mia's teasing, or risk her telling anyone else.

"It needs to be done quickly. She needs to sell the place immediately and get back to the States." Mia squinted at the cooler. "Ella seems different from anyone I've ever met. And you know how I love different people. I might finally have a chance to get to know a real American! Please help her." She stood and faced Leif. "I don't think Ella knows how to do things around here."

From his experience, most women knew how to get things done well enough. Leif reached for a jar of *sursild*, herring marinated in mustard sauce. He twisted off the lid. "Put this on my tab."

"No problem," Mia said, turning back to shelve some tubed caviar, "but please go to Ringpynten today. Lend her the dinghy to use until you're done. You won't regret it. If anything, you'll find her charming."

Leif skewered a piece of herring. Ella, with her soulful singing, was definitely capable of charming him.

Mia jigged one leg, as she frequently did when something weighed on her mind.

"Spill it," Leif said.

"Ella bought a bunch of supplies from me. Could you take them to her? A favor to me."

"Fine." Leif sighed heavily. "Anything else?"

"She really wants to see Gåsholmen. It has something to do with her ancestors. Maybe you could offer to take her there?"

"You're asking me to chat up an American? You have to be joking." He wondered what he and Ella would even talk about. Rodeos, NASCAR, and cowboy music?

"Are you worried Charlotte's going to be jealous? She sure has gotten her claws into you." Mia retrieved two sour cream containers from the cooler and pressed them against her chest. Pushing out her backside, she swayed from side to side, blowing air kisses.

"Ha ha, you're a regular comedian. You know Charlotte

and I just fool around sometimes. Neither one of us is interested in taking it further."

Mia shook her head. "I just don't understand that. But whatever works for you."

"Right. I'll see you at the party on Friday." Leif tossed his empty herring jar into the rubbish bin at Mia's feet.

"Wait—could you also fix the sink in Ella's kitchen?"

He crossed his arms. Mia was really pushing it.

"Come on, just do it. You'll like her. She's colorful! A much-needed change around here."

Change was the last thing he wanted. And his routine with Charlotte was just about perfect. They'd been friends since their early teens, and he knew what to expect from her. On the weekends, they went skeet shooting, played squash, and watched cooking shows. Why would he want to do anything differently?

He reached for another jar of pickled herring and huffed. "Fine, I'll drop by on the way to work."

CHAPTER 5

Ella carried Hilda's urn carefully to the windowsill in the sitting room, where it caught the light and threw rainbows on the walls. The urn was sparkly bright, with swirls of electric pink and lemon. An acquaintance of Ella's had crafted it with care. Some years earlier, Ella had dragged her grandma to the glass-blowers' exhibition show. Hilda had practically drooled over the handblown Chihuly-inspired vases and bowls but insisted that she could never pay such a steep price for a nonessential.

She'd joked, "Ella, you can put me in one of those containers when I die."

When she was small, Ella tried to please Hilda. She made her bed every day and ate the peas from the TV dinners that Hilda served most nights, even if they reminded Ella of boogers. But no matter how hard Ella tried, it seemed she couldn't win her grandma's love. Now, after discovering the portrait of her mother and herself that had been painted with such care, she imagined that Mormor might've loved her after all.

The sore spot in her chest ached again. She wondered what life would have been like if her mother had lived. Would the three of them have been a happy family, spending their summers at Ringpynten, baking pastries and swimming in the sea together? Did Hilda ever play in the water? Maybe Mormor had cautioned Sara against swimming, just like she had Ella.

Her grandma's history was a box of riddles, and it niggled at Ella again, as it had always done.

Why hadn't Mormor told her even a single detail about this place?

She stared out the window in search of something inspiring to improve her mood. The islands across the narrow channel were lined with white, wooden Lyngør-style cottages that were part of her heritage. The red, white, and blue of the Norwegian flag flapped from a pole drilled into one of the docks. A pair of blond teenagers cannonballed into the water.

Ella broke out in goosebumps. She hadn't been in the water since she was eight, during her one and only attempt at learning to swim. She'd marched down to the local community center, proud of her customary stylish and colorful ensemble—flowered galoshes and pink arm floaties. When she arrived at the pool, the other kids called her a scaredy-cat for wearing floaties, so she stomped straight to the diving board and hurled herself into the blue water. To her surprise, it filled her mouth and she gagged, panicking as the weight of her galoshes pulled her down. Much to her embarrassment, the other kids pointed and laughed as the lifeguard dragged her out of the pool, scolding her. "What were you thinking?"

Ella had limped home in one boot. Mormor was furious, ranting about the dangers of water and how it swallowed people, even people with floaties on. Ella hadn't been a fan of water since, never learning to swim and never wanting to.

To let in the fresh air, Ella propped open the front door with the shoe tray that lived nearby. She supposed she should explore the cellar, which she suspected would be a creepy, spider-infested hole in the ground. She'd rather skip it, but

Mia had mentioned that it contained odds and ends, leftovers from decades earlier, and she'd offered to send over someone to haul away the garbage.

Ella's pulse quickened at the possibility of finding something important there. She unlatched the cellar door and flicked on the light. What if she got lucky and found something that belonged to her mother? As she rested her hand on the railing, her fingers snared a sticky web that made her skin crawl. She brushed her hand on her sleeve and let out a long, deep breath.

At the bottom of the steps, she surveyed the concrete room with its rough plaster walls. There was a taped-up garden hose and a wooden shelf holding canning jars full of applesauce. Two small engines were tucked into a mildewy corner; they probably belonged to the boats on the lawn. She'd sell those along with the boats. Mia's friend could trash everything else.

A moth tapped its wings against the dim ceiling bulb, then flitted away, settling on a tarp-covered mound near the underbelly of the staircase.

Ella folded back the tarp until it crumpled to the floor, leaving a cloud of dust that she waved from her face. She blinked in surprise at an old treadle sewing machine on an oak cabinet with cast-iron legs. No way could that beauty have belonged to Hilda.

Ella remembered how, at age twelve, she'd bought a yard-sale sewing machine and a stack of leftover fabrics with her own money. She'd earned it from mowing lawns and pet-sitting the neighbor's Saint Bernard.

Hilda had remarked, "You're just like her," but as always, she refused to say anything more, though she looked distant for the rest of the day. Hilda's comment had enraged Ella.

"You're an evil witch!" she yelled at her. "How can you keep this from me about my own mother! Does this mean my mom sewed?"

There was no answer, but that didn't stop Ella, who fired off question after question.

"What was her favorite food? What music did she like? Did she have a boyfriend?"

Something about the last question sent Hilda into a rage that almost equaled Ella's.

"Boys!" she sputtered, with spittle flying. "If it weren't for Sara getting pregnant, she would've lived. If it weren't for you, Ella, your mom would've lived!"

She paled and put her head in her hands and then, as if snapping back to reality, hugged Ella and sobbed. "Please be careful!"

Ella was shocked. It seemed she was to blame for Sara's death, and this was too awful for Ella to talk about, so she dropped the subject. Over the years, she stopped trying to extract any more information about Sara from Hilda.

In the cellar she studied the gold inlay near the spool pin on the sewing machine and two small identical birds that framed a name, Sara Nilsen. It belonged to her mother. For a moment Ella froze and stared in disbelief. Why would Hilda save this? From what she told Ella, Hilda had only saved a few of her own favorite belongings: her *bunad* and a rosemaled breadboard that matched the china hutch at Ringpynten.

"Everything else was pointless," Hilda had said with conviction. It was clear her grandma wanted to forget her past when she moved to Boulder.

In the drawer Ella found a hand-size sketchbook. The leather was embroidered with Sara's initials and a rosy starling with black and rouge feathers. Ella drew her fingers over the feathers and swallowed the lump in her throat. The needlework looked exactly like her own.

She paused in awe for a moment before opening it. On the first page, she found a sketch of a dress with a meadowy wildflower print, accompanied by her mother's signature. Such a gift! She quickly flipped through the book and saw that it was filled with sketches. She'd savor every page, but first she'd grab the scotch and find a sunny spot on the lawn. She inched the sketchbook into her pocket.

The sewing machine was too heavy to lug upstairs. She'd have to remove it from the cabinet to carry it. Maybe Mia could lend her some tools. Climbing out of the cellar and into the foyer, Ella jumped in surprise. A man filled the door frame.

"Who are you?" she demanded.

"Sorry, the door was open. I'm Leif Arnesen. Mia sent me," he said with a deep voice and a barely detectable Norwegian accent. In fact, he sounded like he'd lived in England for some years.

"Ella Nilsen. You're the boat guy," she said, smoothing her hair self-consciously. It was probably full of cobwebs.

Leif was tall and attractive, with shaggy blond hair, cheek-bones you could cut yourself on, and a light dusting of stubble on his strong jaw. He wasn't her type though. Mostly she dated the bad boys—dark, complicated, loner types who lived and starved for their art and drank way too much.

Her longest relationship had lasted a whopping four months. Petal had teased her about it: "You either never give a guy a chance and you ditch him, or you're so desperate for him to love you back that he gets scared and runs away."

And then there was her last fling, a psychology grad student who had actually said, "You know, it's clear that all your relationship issues come from trying and failing to win your grandma's love." This was after she'd dumped him.

But none of that mattered. Right now she had no time for distractions and too much on the line. She was leaving Lyngør anyway, just as soon as the cottage sold.

Leif reached out to shake her hand. She hesitated, then gave her fingers a quick wipe on her hip before accepting. She barely had a moment to register how tan and solid his hand was before he pulled it away.

His gaze settled on her sparrow boots. Did he just smirk? She flushed, conscious of the chocolate smudges and dust on her wrinkled dress. But why should she care? And who was he to smirk—what kind of guy wore an Oxford shirt to fix boats? He looked fit, though, carrying his broad shoulders like a jock, and so wholesome she bet he drank milk three times a day.

"Where should I put your supplies?" He pointed his thumb at the canvas bags piled on the floor behind him.

"I'll do it, thanks," she said in Norwegian before switching back to English, "I hope to learn more Norwegian while I'm here. I'm surprised at how well you all speak English. You have a slight British accent—did you ever live there?"

"No. I've only lived in Lyngør. But my English teacher, who taught me for eleven years, moved here from London. That would be where I got the British accent," he said with a laugh. "The skiff engines are in the cellar. Mind if I fetch them?"

"Yes please. Would you mind carrying up a piece of furniture while you're at it? It's a sewing machine and it's heavy."

"No worries." He unbuttoned his shirt cuffs and rolled up his sleeves in a way that suggested he could handle anything.

• • •

In the kitchen, Ella unpacked the supplies from Mia's shop and stole glances at Leif as he replaced the fuse on the water pump beneath the sink. His jeans hugged his body in all the right places, without being tight. He had what looked to be strong legs and a cute butt, probably from squatting when he worked on boats, or maybe cross-country skiing. Didn't all Norwegians ski?

"Mia told me to get to work right away," he said.

"Well," she said. "Thank you, Mia."

He worked in silence. She wiped down the stove and admired the view of him on his knees.

"Sink is fixed," Leif announced and then pointed at the kitchen counter. "Is that yours?"

She followed his gaze to the sunflower seed packet that had somehow made it through airport customs. Next to the seeds lay a drawing of a magpie in the cottage garden.

"Yes, I just drew it," she said. "And I packed the seeds for the trip and forgot to eat them, but now I think I'll plant them in the garden."

His brow twitched. "Are you staying?"

"No, but isn't it better to leave a place nicer than when you found it? At least, I think so."

He swept a hand over his mouth in answer, but she saw the twinkle in his eyes as he turned toward the middle of the kitchen and the sewing machine. "Where should I put this?" he asked.

"In the sitting room, please."

He lifted the machine as if it weighed nothing, his shirt sleeves snug against thick forearms.

Ella stopped with him near the folksy cabinet. It hadn't occurred to her that the only available free space was beneath the window that faced out to the choppy waters.

"Hmm. No, not there. I'd love to look out the window and see heather and evergreens. Could you do me a favor and switch that with the sewing machine?" Smiling at him, she pointed at the painted trunk that sat beneath the window overlooking the treed bluff.

He smiled back through gritted teeth. Grunting as he braced the machine against his body, he moved it to her liking. "Not keen on the water view?"

"Thanks. Not a big fan of the water."

"What the devil are you doing here, then?" he asked in a friendly way.

"I was born in Norway. My mother died when I was a baby, and shortly after that, my mormor and I moved to America.

She raised me." She considered telling him about the portrait she'd found in the bedroom yesterday, but the pain of that discovery was still raw, and she might not be able to keep her tears in check. That picture of the two of them was a homage to what might have been if Sara had lived. It suddenly occurred to Ella that maybe Hilda wanted her to come to Ringpynten to learn the truth about her mom on her own.

"I came here because I need to sell the cottage. It's too difficult to do from the States. Also, my mormor wanted me to spread her ashes in Lyngør."

"I see," Leif said, and politely turned back to his work.

Ella didn't want to miss her chance to ask some questions, though.

"Do you happen to know anything about my family, especially my mom, Sara Nilsen?" She clutched the sewing machine cord as she knelt on the floor to search for an electrical outlet. The sketchbook in her pocket dug into her thigh, so she slid it out and set it on the sewing cabinet.

"Nah, as far as I know, your family hasn't visited for almost thirty years. I'm sorry about your mormor though." That was almost exactly what Mia had said.

"Thanks. Mormor had a heart condition, so it wasn't a huge surprise." Ella plugged in the cord. As she straightened, she looked up at Leif. He held the sketchbook, his calloused fingers thumbing through the fragile pages. She was shocked. How dare he. She wanted to be the first person to look at them. She snatched the book from Leif. At the brief touch of their fingers, the air contracted and for a moment they stared at each other.

"I've got work to do," he said, the shine leaving his eyes. He turned on his heel and walked out the front door.

She pushed the sketchbook back into her pocket and fell into step behind Leif. Well, OK, maybe she'd been a little rude, but that book was one of the only links she had to her mother.

In the yard, Ella sat down on the low stone wall near

the dock. The brisk breeze coming in off the water matched the tension flowing between her and Leif. He frowned as he nudged his foot against the larger of the two boats that lay on her lawn.

Ella picked at the moss speckling the wall. She'd done nothing wrong, she told herself. Leif was full of himself. How could he not be, as good-looking as he was? If anything, *he* owed *her* an apology for looking at her things without permission. She itched to pore over the pages alone. He'd better hurry up, get her boats in the water, and leave.

"How long will this take?" she asked.

"Ten days."

"What! That long?" She'd hoped she could sell the boats immediately and then pay the rent on her apartment.

"Sanding and varnishing are time-consuming. The boats need to be submerged in water for a good five days." He poked at another plank. "On land, over the winter, the wood dries out and cracks. After a proper soaking, the planks expand, and the cracks seal up."

"Won't they sink?"

"Does a stick sink?" He snatched a stubby branch from the lawn and sent it sailing over the wall and sea grasses and into the aqua waters, where it drifted in the current beyond the cabin cruiser parked at her dock. A red dinghy hung off the back of the cruiser. She noticed that the big wooden boat had ornate carvings on the railing and around the windshield, both intricate and fabulous. She thought she saw wolves snarling between braided vines. Her fingers longed for her pencil and sketchbook to replicate the designs. As always, she saw inspiration everywhere. She needed a closer look than from thirty feet away. She grabbed her life preserver before she could change her mind or be chained in place by her fear of the water.

"What are you doing?" Leif raised an eyebrow at her.

"I need to see something. Just a moment!" she called over her shoulder, clipping on her vest as she descended the steps to the dock. Waves hissed. She could taste the salt thick in the air, and her stomach rolled as if she were seasick. Touching her aquamarine beads, she told herself to be brave. She recalled her art teacher quoting Van Gogh: "What would life be if we had no courage to attempt anything?"

Ella knew the world wouldn't stop spinning if she turned back now, but she was too proud to show her fear. On the dock, she closed her ears to the clapping waves and focused on the carved wolves, vines, and Viking runes on the boat railing. She brushed her fingers over two ravens, wings adjoined, and imagined those birds on her next line of dresses. With the artist's permission, of course.

• • •

Back on the lawn, she placed her preserver on the stone wall near Leif. "The carvings on your boat are stunning. I especially love ravens. I have a thing for birds." She smiled at him. "Do ravens have a special meaning in Norway?"

"Yup, the Norse god Odin owned two ravens who could understand humans, so he sent them out to fly around the world and return in the evening to tell him everything they saw. Ravens really are extremely intelligent. Vikings kept them aboard, and when they were out at sea they set the birds free to scout. If the birds didn't come back, that meant land was near."

"I love that. Do you happen to know the name of the artist who worked on your boat?"

"You're looking at him. Except I'm not an artist. I'm just a boatbuilder and handyman at the boatyard." He leaned over the larger of the two skiffs and stabbed at a rotten plank with the blade of his pocketknife.

"You're an artist, same as me." The realization tickled her

belly and danced through her. "You're an incredibly talented one. I'm impressed!"

"Thank you." He stood a bit straighter.

As Leif carried on with inspecting the engines, Ella caught him stealing glances at her. His eyes were Nordic blue. Had she combed her hair this morning? She couldn't remember. She had so much on her mind that she wouldn't be surprised if she hadn't: selling the house, navigating this unfamiliar place, finding a place to sprinkle Mormor's ashes, and soft-launching Little Bird just two months from now. Not to mention her questions about the oil painting of her and Sara, the drawing of her mom, and now the sketchbook. The sun beat down on them. Leif shrugged off his Oxford shirt and tossed it on the low wall, revealing a Bob Dylan concert T-shirt.

She decided to draw him in a little bit. "Do you know where Gåsholmen is?" she asked.

"Yes, but I don't go there. It's pretty touristy." As he spoke, he continued fiddling with one of the engines. Ella detected something like distaste in his tone, so she pressed him and he told her about the tension between locals and tourists. The tourists had money to spend, while the locals depended on that money. Leif considered the tourists snobs—relying on the locals for manual labor and expertise, while coming and going as they pleased.

"I inherited Ringpynten. Does that make me a snob?"

He shrugged at her. "I don't know. Does it?"

No one had ever called her a snob before. She thought it funny that he might see her like that.

"You can find me on the patio when you're done," she said, and as she brushed past Leif, he muttered under his breath.

She stopped to look at him. "I beg your pardon?"

He opened his mouth and closed it, and a flush crept up his neck. Had this wide-shouldered, Viking-like man just blushed at her?

A few heartbeats later he said, "Sunna. You're different."

"So I've been told." She winked at him. "But what's a Sunna?"

He grabbed the gunwale on the larger skiff and lifted it a couple of inches off the grass but said no more.

Evidently she was dismissed. She walked to the patio and didn't look back.

CHAPTER 6

Leif eased the skiff back to the ground. What had gotten into him? Sunna, the Norse sun goddess, for Loki's sake! The words had simply flown out of his mouth. His conversational skills fell apart in her company.

He'd noticed her professional-looking camera inside the cottage—and the sketchbook, of course. She was an artist type, and she'd called him an artist too. That idea melted him. He thought about taking her to Gåsholmen, though he feared he couldn't trust his mouth to work properly around her. He felt an unfamiliar yearning as he wondered what it would be like to be with someone like Ella. But she was just visiting, which was problematic enough. Why couldn't he find someone like her here?

Guitar music drifted from the patio, and she began to sing Eric Clapton's "Tears in Heaven," the same tune she'd played this morning as he fished offshore. His stomach went hollow. She was doing a beautiful job with the song—her voice was soulful, vulnerable—but each time he heard that song on the radio, he thought about his mother and father, and wondered if they'd know him if they saw him again. Perhaps Ella wondered the same thing about her own mother, and maybe even her father too.

After filling out the estimate for the boat repairs, Leif approached Ella where she sat strumming her guitar on the granite patio that edged the water. She wore large, sparkly rings on her fingers, and her lips were the color of raspberries. He held out the paper to her.

"Give me a moment—I'm working on a song. I need to write down the lyric or I'll forget it." She scribbled something in the notebook splayed open at her feet.

Mia was right; Ella *was* charming. If he was smart, he'd give the repair job to someone else and avoid any further involvement with her. She took the paper from him, scanned it, then folded her arms.

"You must be kidding."

"It's a fair price—more than fair. I've taken fifty percent off the price of the paint, since I've got some paint left over from an earlier job."

"No. This seems outrageous to me." Handing back the estimate, she said, "I think I'll get another quote."

"You won't find a better one." He didn't need this headache. Turning to leave, he tripped over the guitar case, and his face flushed.

She looked back down at her guitar and began to strum and sing: "I gave him some lip and sent him on a trip. Little Boy Blue—"

He erupted with sarcastic laughter, even though his stomach had gone hollow all over again. He pointed at the dock and said, "You can borrow the red dinghy until I complete the job. Don't let your boats fall apart. They have a terrific resale value."

"Do you happen to know how much they're worth?"

"The bigger of your two, the *skjekte*, is worth around thirty thousand kroner, and the pram runs around sixteen thousand."

Ella did mental math. "Wow. That's around eight grand in

US dollars . . . Well, OK then, please service them for me. I'd like to sell them quickly." With that kind of cash, she could pay Petal and even buy a new industrial sewing machine.

"Someone from the boatyard will get to it ASAP. The dinghy is seaworthy; you can row to Gåsholmen in fifteen minutes." He motioned at the island straight across the channel. "See the cottage, on the tip of that island? If you take the boat around that bend, Gåsholmen will be off to your left."

"Thank you, but I'll have to pass." Ella didn't like the look of the sea-foam edging the rocks. "Do you think you could recommend other places for me to visit while I'm here? I'd like to find out anything I can about my family."

"Not really," he said bluntly. "But you can always take the dinghy to explore the islands if you wanted to. Or you might want to hire a local schoolboy to ferry you around after he finishes his homework?"

Ella started strumming again, and he distinctly heard the opening chords of "Don't Come Around Here No More" by Tom Petty.

"Right. Go on, give the dinghy a try. Unless you're afraid you'll chip those lovely nails of yours."

Her cheeks reddened. She was flustered. Good. He secured the dinghy mooring lines to Ella's dock, and then he left.

CHAPTER 7

Ella fumed as Leif steered his boat into the channel. She wasn't a tourist! And did he really think she cared about her nails? She was perfectly capable of taking the dinghy out on her own, if she wanted to. She almost spluttered as she thought about teaching herself to play guitar like Patti Smith, making her own distinctive clothes, and performing on Pearl Street Mall. People even threw money into her guitar case. If she could do all that as a teenager, she could certainly master a dinghy now!

She channeled her anger by grabbing a broom and vigorously sweeping the patio as she aimed skeptical looks at the ocean. Taking a dinghy out in the channel went against everything she'd been taught and come to fear about the water. Mormor had always said that water swallowed people.

She looked at the dock again, then over the side, directly into the water. Her stomach felt woozy. Good thing she'd learned breathing techniques and other ways to control her fear. Plus, she assured herself, people swam and paddled on the sea every day. Besides, she came from a long line of seafaring Vikings, didn't she?

She wondered if Sara had rowed from Ringpynten to

Gåsholmen on the day the picture was taken. Perhaps Sara's sketchbook could give her some ideas about her mom's life. She took the book from her pocket and tears of joy welled in her eyes as she flipped through the pages, entranced with the playful designs: seabirds on flowy skirts, and a tea dress with a slipper orchid pattern. Ella couldn't believe the coincidence; she had photographed that same flower while hiking in the subalpine forest in the Rocky Mountains, falling in love with its delicate shape and reddish-brown petals. Not many would believe that this tropical flower could thrive in both Colorado and Norway, but it did. She brushed her hands over her tear-streaked face.

It seemed that nature inspired Sara, just as it did Ella. Seeing Sara's sketches brought Ella closer to her mother than she'd ever been, yet it also made her miss her even more. She felt herself growing angrier with Hilda.

She had to muster the courage to get in that dinghy. If she did, she could explore Lyngør, visit Gåsholmen, and go to the Lyngør Hotel bar. Maybe, by chance, she would meet an employee or guest who had spent time with her family. What else did she have to do while she worked on selling the cottage? And when would she get another opportunity to get answers to her questions about her family?

She looked at the red dinghy again. *Go sit in it,* she told herself. She thought it might be time to take a first step toward facing her fear. Plus Leif had gotten under her skin. She would love to prove him wrong.

Ella cinched the straps on her life vest before sitting down on the edge of the dock. The granite felt cold, and the damp seeped through her skirt. She breathed in the briny air and grasped the long strand of beads looped around her neck. Aquamarine was associated spiritually with courage, trusting, and letting go, and she leaned into that. She touched the dinghy with one of her bare feet. Leif's words taunted her. She pressed her foot harder against the dinghy. She told herself that she should at least sit in it, as a tribute to her ancestors. But she made no move to board the boat and instead reached for a snail shell that lay next to her. Tossing the shell into the water, she watched it sink, her stomach sinking with it. To distract herself, she trained her camera lens on a goose and four goslings as they paddled slowly through the cold waves.

She studied the algae-coated waterline on the bank as the sea slapped against it. It reminded her of the layer of green slime that had lined the granite fountain in the neighborhood where she grew up. As a teenager Ella had tossed pennies there, wishing for answers to her questions about her mom. How old was she when she got pregnant with Ella, and did she love Ella's father? Did she want Ella? Did music play a part in her life? Was she kind?

Gåsholmen. If only that island could talk! Ella knew she couldn't leave Lyngør without finding out if Sara really died while giving birth to her.

Caressing her necklace one final time, and with careful, measured movements, she lowered herself into the boat and settled on the bench. The natural tipping with the waves made her pulse go wild, so she focused on the teal water and the minnows darting through the seaweed. She stared at the oars. This felt like enough for today, but maybe tomorrow she would try them out.

CHAPTER 8

Early the next morning, Leif walked across the stone quay and into Lyngør Boatyard and Marina and entered one of its three white clapboard buildings. Each adjoining building featured blue trim and barn doors. At lunch, he'd drop by Ringpynten to deliver the paint and tools for the service job on Ella's two boats. Perhaps he should've offered to take her to Gåsholmen, but everything about her had tipped him a fraction off-balance. Ever since meeting her, he'd thought about her more than he cared to admit.

Inside the main building, Leif moved past the salt-smeared windows, oil-stained tarps, and tool bins. As he traced his hand along his current project, a wooden lapstrake boat, his shoulders relaxed a notch. This place had been his second home ever since Erik had taken him in after his father's death. Erik was barely able to take care of himself, but he'd raised Leif out of loyalty to his best friend, Bjorn.

When Leif was a child, he'd felt unmoored living with closed-off, unpredictable Erik, each of them overwhelmed by grief. Leif stuck closely to a daily routine. It was something he could count on. Something he could trust. After school and over his summer vacation, he shadowed Erik at the boatyard, learning to repair engines, weld metal, and mold oak planks into perfect curves. They had dinner at 4:00 p.m. sharp in Erik's office: fish cakes pan-fried on a two-plate burner while jazz played on the radio. Leif had his first taste of whiskey at age twelve.

Leif patted his pocket, relieved he'd remembered the paperwork for the boats he retrieved in Oslo yesterday. He was excited to tell Erik about what the marina owner had said about his carving skills and how he'd promised to put his designs on sailboat railings if Leif accepted the senior boatbuilder position. If Erik knew about the owner's enthusiasm, he might finally come to have faith in Leif too.

In the marina office, he found Erik with his feet propped up on his desk. An unlit cigar was clenched between his teeth as he soldered the wires on a transistor radio. He was barrel-chested and only fifty-four but his stooped posture made him seem a decade older. Erik fell apart every June on the anniversary of the boat accident that killed Leif's father and the two visitors Leif knew nothing about. Physically, Erik had recovered from his injuries, but mentally he remained broken, as the only survivor. Every year around this time, before the tourists arrived and the boatyard got too busy, he visited his best friend, Ragnar, at his cabin, to get away and recharge.

Leif thought Erik looked worse this June than any previously, and twice as burned out as he had before he'd gone away.

"How was your trip to Ragnar's cabin?" he asked.

"Ragnar was in fine form. Drunk by noon. Nonstop stories about our shenanigans in Lyngør, all those years ago. He always exaggerates about the old days. The stories get more ridiculous every year." Erik pulled his cap to his brow. "Thanks for fetching the boats. You look like crap. You all right?"

"Fine, yeah. I rolled in late. It was a great trip though. You know, the owner loves my carvings and wants to pay me to put my designs on his boats. He said he already has clients lined up, that some of them had seen my work on boats at the Risør boat festival and want the same designs on their railings."

Erik seemed unimpressed. Whenever Leif had suggested that Erik offer carving services at his boatyard, Erik chuckled as if it were a little joke. Mia always said that Erik intentionally undermined Leif's confidence to ensure that Leif stayed at the boatyard. Although Leif didn't enjoy feeling that he wasn't being taken seriously, the routine of working with Erik was comfortable, and there was security in that.

Erik shuffled papers on his desk. "Carving is a great hobby. But you are one of the best boat*builders* in the whole country, and that's why I need you here." He lit his cigar. "How about taking the morning off? Sleep, make some food, whatever. Just make sure to come back this afternoon—work orders are piling up."

"I'm good, just need some more coffee." Leif preferred to work, since it would take his mind off Sunna.

The workbench was cluttered with a cracked rudder, a carburetor, and a piece of old bread smeared with liver pâté. Leif reached for the coffee pot and found a clean-enough mug.

"Mia changed her mind on the dinghy, so I loaned it to Mrs. Nilsen's granddaughter, Ella," Leif said.

"Hilda Nilsen's granddaughter?"

"Hilda died. Her granddaughter is here to sell the cottage." Leif tossed Ringpynten's paperwork onto Erik's desk.

"Makes no sense," Erik muttered. He'd gone gray as a flounder belly.

"What?" Leif said.

"Forget it." Erik withdrew a fifth of whiskey from the desk drawer, took two large gulps, and wiped his mouth with the back of his hand. Erik seldom drank except in June, but when he did, he could fall in and out of lucidity. Occasionally he'd sob about the passengers on Bjorn's boat, muttering how the sea had taken them all. Frequently he let slip the same words, "It should've been me."

"Either she buys the dinghy," he said, "or you bring it back here immediately."

Leif frowned. "There's no harm in letting Ella borrow it. She's only here for a short time."

"No, she can't borrow the dinghy." Erik coughed through his clenched teeth. "She either buys it or returns it. I'm not a bloody rental agency."

"Did you ever meet Ella's mum, Sara Nilsen? She's hoping to find out more about her while she's visiting." Seeing the deep lines cut into Erik's face, he added, "What?"

Erik glowered at the whiskey gripped in his hand. "You know I don't associate with that lot, so why ask?" He stormed past Leif and left. Erik often complained about vacationers with their flashy boats and fat wallets wanting quick repairs and discounts every summer, but Leif wondered why he seemed especially angry today. What did he have against Hilda Nilsen and her granddaughter?

CHAPTER 9

In the cottage bedroom, Ella leafed through her mom's sketch-book for the dozenth time. Sara's wildflower patterns could have been drawn by Ella's own hand. Then she gazed at the portrait Mormor painted, wondering if that day at Frogner Park had really happened, or if it was imagined and painted after Sara died. Ella's heart wrung in pain each time she looked at the painting. It took her down the road of what might've been.

She wondered if she'd ever sat on her mom's lap, or on Mormor's, in this room. Finding remnants of her mother had put a fire in her belly to find out how she lived—and how she died. And Ella was starting to see her Mormor in a new light. She had never let anyone close, not even Ella. She wondered now if Mormor had never healed after her daughter's death . . . maybe her heart had stayed raw, pained, and bitter. Ella felt sad for Mormor, to have lived with that loss all those years.

Ella turned over the photograph and read the inscription again: Gåsholmen with my sweetheart. Who wrote this? Did Sara love him, or was he a summer fling? Gåsholmen obvi-ously meant something special to her mom, and Ella felt that if she went there, she would feel closer to her. It was time to row the dinghy.

• • •

Now Ella's bottom ached from sitting on the dinghy bench for what seemed like forever, and still she hesitated to untie the line. Wavelets struck the hull and rocked the boat from side to side. She fought the urge to climb back on the dock. As she cinched the straps on her life vest, Mormor's warnings about the dangers of water gnawed at her. She had forbidden Ella to Rollerblade on the trail that snaked along Boulder Creek because Ella might skid off the path, fall into the water, and drown.

Ella looked at the waves as if searching for answers. Just beyond Ringpynten, a wooden sailboat went by. Two couples lounged on board, everyone wearing smiles and sailing jackets but no life vests. They looked relaxed. They belonged to Lyngør.

But she belonged here on these islands too, she told herself.

And yet she couldn't relax on the water, could she? She tried to gather the courage to pick up the oars. Her heart scampered at the thought of untying the boat and crossing the open sea to Gåsholmen. She wasn't ready for that adventure yet, she thought with a shudder. Today she'd try out the oars and travel along the safety of the shore in the direction of the ferry slip where she'd landed a few days earlier. She told herself that the dinghy would be as easy to handle as the rowing machine at the Boulder YMCA. She tugged the line free and, before she could change her mind, grabbed the oars awkwardly. She plopped the blades clumsily into the water and pulled them back in such a way that they barely skimmed the surface. She loosened her grip and adjusted her fingers, carving the blades into the water over and over again, concentrating on each stroke before she finally figured out how to guide the dinghy into the peaceful channel.

As she powered the dinghy steadily forward, her adrenaline cartwheeled and sweat beaded on her brow, yet she couldn't help but smile. She was doing absolutely fine. In fact, rowing seemed to come naturally to her, as if she'd been in boats all her life. Maybe she had salt water running through her veins like her Viking ancestors.

Fifteen minutes later, she reached the tip of Lyngørsida, the island that held Ringpynten and the grocery. Glorious purple heather, which she'd always found so calming, shrouded the point. She remembered Mia saying that the name of this island referred to all that heather. Perhaps she could scatter Mormor's ashes in a field of flowers. Or maybe it was better to take her to a local church; Mormor had always attended Sunday services in Boulder.

A trawler plowed through the channel, and her dinghy tipped from side to side on the waves. She clutched the oars. Luckily Lyngørsida lay just off to her right. Under control again, her pulse slowed as she marveled at the maritime homes with cheerful wildflower gardens and fruit trees, and the way the sunlight bathed the stone docks in a warm golden light.

"Ella!" Mia was on the dock in front of the grocery store, and she motioned to Ella to come to shore. Rowing to the store meant traveling farther from Ringpynten. But she'd come this far, so she couldn't let her fear win, especially not in front of local folk.

. . .

At the Lyngør Grocery dock, Ella settled the oars into the dinghy and clutched one of the bumper tires anchored to the pier. Mia was chatting with a woman who had a cigarillo tucked between her strawberry-stained lips while fueling her boat at the gas pump. Mia turned to Ella. "This is my friend Inger."

"Nice to meet you." Ella smiled up at Inger from the dinghy.

"Great to meet you too," Inger said, giving Ella the once-over with the most striking wolf eyes. They reminded Ella of White Fang, the dog in her favorite children's book. She grinned at Ella. "Do you think I could practice my English with you? I want to impress Axel, my boyfriend. He's taking me to London for our two-year anniversary at the end of the summer." Then she flapped her hands at Mia. "Go on—hurry up and grab the list and tell Erik to get out here."

"He'll whistle when he's ready to pay," Mia said. "We have two hours before the Vinmonopolet closes." She turned to Ella. "That's the government store in town that sells liquor, and we need to get some for our annual summer party. Would you like me to grab you anything? You can pay me back later."

"No thanks. It's kind of you to offer, though. Some renters forgot their scotch at my cottage, and I'm drinking that. It's one of the best whiskeys I've ever tasted."

As Ella spoke, the sea air rustled the petals on the hydrangeas near the store's picket fence. Those same bushes grew on Ringpynten's property, and the thought reminded her of something from one of her to-do lists. "Mia, I need to hire someone to mow the grass and take down the mesh and wire fencing around the garden beds before the property hits the market. I want to make it as attractive as possible to potential buyers."

Mia opened her mouth to answer, and Ella couldn't help but notice that she quickly closed it when Inger shot her a stern look. Mia raked at her spiky hair as pink splotches erupted on Inger's neck. Inger scratched at them, and Ella was reminded that Mormor broke out in hives whenever she was upset.

"What?" Ella asked with concern.

Inger tapped her cigarillo ash and Ella noticed the inky stains on Inger's fingers. They were the color of the homemade wine Mia had sold Ella two days earlier.

Inger spoke up. "I'm the one who's been gardening at

Ringpynten. My property is shady and there's no dirt or grass, just rocks everywhere." She hesitated, then took several quick puffs on her cigarillo. She blew a smoke ring and continued, "Mia gave me permission to work the land at your cottage if I didn't pester the renters. Do you think it might be OK if I keep gardening there this summer?"

"Well, let me think about it." Ella smiled politely at Inger, but she seriously doubted she'd give her the green light to keep growing things at Ringpynten. The mesh and wire around the beds were an eyesore. She didn't want to disappoint Inger, but she knew what she was there for, and it wasn't to make friends, she told herself.

"OK. I understand," Inger said flatly, but something else flickered in her wolfish eyes.

For a brief and uncomfortable moment no one spoke. Ella tried to guide the conversation toward a less-controversial topic.

"Inger, would you happen to know anything about my relatives at Ringpynten? Or do you happen to know someone who might've spent time with my mom, Sara?"

"No. She wasn't local, so no," Inger scoffed.

As a rule, Ella gave people a second chance, so she ignored her. She turned to Mia and asked, "Did you happen to talk to your cousin about my cottage?"

Mia nodded. "She confirmed what I told you, that the market is extremely slow right now, and expensive summer homes aren't exactly selling quickly. She's vacationing in Oslo, but she knows people there who are super keen on buying a cottage in Lyngør. She promised to call me back after she spoke with them. Meanwhile, I could send over a photographer to take pictures of Ringpynten for advertisement."

"Thank you for checking with your cousin; I appreciate it. But no need to send over a photographer—I've already taken some pictures of the property."

"Fantastic! If you give me the film, I can get it developed

for you. There's a place in Tvedestrand, near the real estate office where my cousin works."

Inger cut in. "How much commission are you getting for this, Mia?"

"Very funny, Inger."

"Inger, I love your rhubarb wine," Ella said. "I'd like to buy a couple more bottles." She knew she was sucking up, a habit she'd learned in childhood. Mormor hadn't been overly generous with her compliments, so Ella looked for approval from other people.

"I don't usually sell to vacationers. I kind of like to keep it local, you know."

"There's still bottles in the shop," Mia said. Inger made a face at her.

"That's great! Reserve a bottle for me, will you? I've tried some of your gooseberry jam too—delicious! And it inspired me to sketch out a purse with a seed pattern. When I get back home, I'm going to buy a fabric in that exact reddish-pink color and make the bag."

"A handbag with seeds? You *are* a funny one," Inger laughed while assessing Ella again with her sharp gaze. "You should come to the Lyngør summer party tomorrow night. Show us how you party in Colorado."

Mia raised her eyebrows at Inger. Ella was surprised too.

"I'll think about it," Ella said. "I'm not really into big parties though." She found large gatherings to be hard work—coming up with a good opening line, shouting over the music, all the chaos. Fitting in with the crowd was challenging enough in Colorado. It would likely be even harder to mesh with people here.

Inger nudged Mia. "Go see what Erik's problem is. Tell him to hurry, or we won't make it on time."

"Calm down," Mia replied, and then she turned to Ella. "I hope you'll join us tomorrow."

"Thanks, I'll try." On second thought, a local event might be a good way to get the information she wanted. "Mia, you mentioned the other day that Erik is around my mother's age. Is he going to the party?"

"Yes, but don't expect much; he's not exactly chatty. And he's been in a really grouchy mood," she said, chewing on her thumb.

Ella gestured toward the store. "Well, maybe now is as good a time as any, then." She reached for her mooring line. She'd never tied up a boat before, and it showed. Fumbling with the line, she fastened it to the iron cleat drilled into the dock. When she was through, her knot had bunny ears, like the laces on her boots. Mia looked confused. Inger snickered.

Mia offered, "That's not right. Let me show you how."

Inger cut in. "Erik's coming." A man with age spots freckling his face exited the front door, strode past them, and boarded his wooden cabin cruiser. He threw off the lines quickly, started the engine, and revved it.

"Hey! What's with you?" Inger shouted at him.

"Something came up. Go without me!" Erik yelled before backing away from the dock.

"Well, obviously he's not paying his bill today," Mia said. "He looks really bent out of shape. I wonder what's wrong."

"Forget it. Let's go," Inger said and blew a stream of cigarillo smoke at Ella. "Goodbye. The party is at six tomorrow. Hope to see you there." She linked her arm through Mia's, and they walked to her boat.

"Wait. Where's the party?" Ella called after them.

"Sandøya. It's an island," Inger called over her shoulder. "Look at a map."

"OK." Ella was nervous, but she had to go. The party could be an opportunity to get more information about her mom.

CHAPTER 10

Leif noticed that both Ella and the dinghy were gone, and he wondered if she was out exploring Lyngør. He had seen her just two days ago, so he was surprised at how disappointed he was at not seeing her now. It stumped him, how swiftly he'd fallen for her. He'd thought about her when he drifted off to sleep last night and he awakened thinking about her this morning. She was gorgeous and artistic, and hot—he could admit that. But whatever it was that drew him to her was much more complicated than sheer physical attraction alone. He loved that she had a creative side. And she felt oddly familiar to him, even though they barely knew each other.

It scared him a bit, when he got honest with himself. Ella might disrupt his safe and grounded routine. He knew he should forget about her and stick with Charlotte, who was at least a known entity. As he placed the can of primer next to the skiffs on the grass, he wondered why Erik had insisted that Ella return the boat. Erik loaned boats to renters every summer, and Ella needed a boat to travel around Lyngør. Besides, from what Mia said, she was only staying a couple of weeks, if that.

Rain scalloped the horizon. He could smell it coming. A

flash of red drew his attention to the dinghy coming around Lyngørsida's tip. Ella sliced the oars into the water with an air of confidence, which surprised him. She'd told him she wasn't keen on the water. He'd told himself he could never be with a woman who didn't embrace the blue waters of Lyngør, the waters that brought him so much peace.

But as the dinghy moved closer to the dock, something in his heart shifted at the sight of her. Perhaps because she wore the same yellow dress that she had the first day he saw her, warm and bright as the sun—Sunna.

• • •

Leif crouched down on the dock, grabbed the dinghy line, and knotted it to a cleat. "May I help?" He extended his hand to Ella.

Her face was sickly green. "No, thanks, I've got this. It's just that the water was rough. I'm OK though."

Right, she didn't seem OK, but he stepped back to give her space. She pressed her palms against the dock, and with a determined growl, lifted herself out of the boat. She had a glimmer of satisfaction in her eye as she rose to her feet, but her teeth chattered, the hem of her flimsy skirt was wet, and her feet were bare. She'd catch a cold.

"Learn to dress for the weather, will you?" His teasing put color back into her cheeks.

"I know how to dress, Little Boy Blue."

"Ouch," he said.

"Why are you here?" She hugged her chest.

"I delivered some tools . . ." His voice trailed off, as she was already climbing the stairs. He caught up to her, racking his brain for something witty to make her laugh, but he was fresh out of words and stood awkwardly at the door as she wrestled the key into the lock.

"Come in," she said with a half smile.

In the foyer she slid her feet into a pair of fringed moccasin boots lined with soft wool, put on a fuzzy mohair sweater, and then let out a contented sigh.

Following her into the sitting room, he regarded the damp dress hugging her hips, and desire burned through him. He averted his eyes, settling them on the trestle table where there lay a red-ink sketch of a woman, on what looked like the back of a photograph. The woman reminded him of Ella, with her corkscrew hair and wide mouth.

"Is that you?" Leif motioned at the drawing, careful not to touch it. He'd learned his lesson when he thumbed through her sketchbook.

"That's my mother." Yanking the throw from the rocking chair, she wrapped it around her shoulders.

"Beautiful. You look like her." He glanced at Ella, uncertain how she'd take the compliment, but she looked pleased. He noted the inscription on the sketch and read it aloud. "Is this why you want to go to Gåsholmen?"

"Yes. From what I can tell from this drawing, my mom went there, and I want to know more."

"Right." He rubbed the back of his neck. "Chasing the past often leads to pain."

"And you're the expert?"

"Maybe." Truth was, he knew about pain. And the past wasn't something he liked to discuss. "Scratch at wounds and they fester."

"What?" Ella said.

"You know, there's a reason I always wear blue." He scrubbed a hand over his stubbled chin. "My father, Bjorn, was a boatbuilder. He loved Norwegian folklore, Viking gods and goddesses, all of it. Same as me." Leif sat down in the oak chair and began to rock gently. "On my fifth birthday, my father gave me a book on Njord, the Norwegian god of the sea. Njord had a special fondness for the color blue, and my father always insisted we wear blue to please Njord . . . you know, so he'd be good to us on the water. But the awful thing was, my father didn't wear any blue at all one day, and that's the day he died in a boat accident."

"Oh, that must've been horrible. My heart goes out to you." She set two glasses on the serving shelf and reached for a bottle. "Join me for a drink?" she said, her voice softer. "I'm listening."

"Yes, thanks," Leif said. "It *was* horrible. It hurt so much that I sometimes wish I never knew him." Leif could see the empathy in Ella's eyes. Normally he didn't talk about his past. It made him feel vulnerable, and he'd carried the weight of it since he was old enough to understand. Now, surprisingly, he was opening up to Ella, whom he barely knew. Perhaps it was because she'd been orphaned as a child too. He stood. "No one would talk about the accident when they thought I could over-hear, but I still caught snatches of their conversations." Leif still remembered the cruelest remarks. *Drunk fool. Murderer. Killing himself and those two out-of-town fellas.*

He raised his glass, and Ella mirrored the gesture. They sipped the scotch, which went down smoothly, with nice light peat notes and a hint of ripe berries. Expensive. He studied the twenty-five-year-old bottle with its silver-encased neck and silver hammer logo and recognized it as Inger's. The Saturday before, she'd hosted an outdoor dinner party at Ringpynten to say farewell to her garden, her favorite place in the world.

"I feel a little bad about drinking it, but some renter prob-ably forgot it," Ella said, swirling the amber liquid around her glass.

Leif considered telling her that the scotch belonged to Inger, but it was too late: A third of it was gone, and Inger probably shouldn't have left it behind anyway. He also didn't know if Ella knew that Inger had planted the garden, but he didn't want to get involved, so he hid his guilty expression be-hind the rim of his glass. "Where were you rowing earlier?"

"I went out exploring and ended up at the grocery. Mia introduced me to her friend Inger. She invited me to the summer party." Ella moved to the sofa.

"Did she? Will you go?" He tried to hide his surprise.

"Yes, I'd like to meet the locals to see if any of them remember my family. I don't know if I can row the dinghy over there though." Picking up her guitar, she settled it on her lap.

"No, it's too far. Rough waters," Leif said and tipped back his drink.

"I'll figure something out." Ella strummed the guitar, humming in that smooth, honeyed tone of hers. He felt her voice in his gut—and it didn't stop there, but vibrated straight up his spine. He should take her to the party.

"Why don't I pick you up?" he asked.

"That would be wonderful," she grinned at him, strumming.

"OK. How about I swing by here at four o'clock tomorrow?" He didn't quite know what Inger was up to, but he thought he'd better keep an eye on that situation too.

CHAPTER 11

The dinghy slid into the sheltered cove at Gåsholmen. It had taken Ella thirty minutes to row there, and now small blisters bubbled on her palms. She dumped the oars into the boat and shook out her hands. The small waves had seemed like steep hills, but she had pushed through them. She was proud of herself. It felt like the first time she exhibited her work at an art festival in Colorado Springs.

She'd almost backed out of that too, with Hilda's words weighing on her: "Be realistic. There are gazillions of artists out there, and they're far more talented than you."

Ella's will to prove her grandma wrong had turned out to be stronger than her self-doubt. She sold nearly everything she displayed—dresses she'd designed and several of her photographs. It was a triumph, as was making it to Gåsholmen. She'd only been in Lyngør for a short time, and already she'd rowed from one island to another!

Clutching the mooring line, she stepped cautiously onto the algae-coated rocks, careful not to fall into the water. She could see colorful minnows just below the teal surface, and starfish clinging to the reef. She decided that in her next incarnation she wanted to be a mermaid.

After several attempts, she tied the line to the mooring pole hammered into the bank. She pushed back her sleeve and checked her watch. Two hours until Leif picked her up at Ringpynten, so she had enough time to explore the uninhabited island, a nature preserve—which according to her map was the size of two football fields—before rowing home to meet him.

She thought ahead to what she would wear to the party. Maybe if she tried to fit in, the locals would embrace her. Not that she particularly cared, since she was leaving soon anyway, but she needed them to like her enough to help her get the information she so desperately wanted.

And she really didn't care what Leif thought about her, but he did have nice shoulders. When she handed him the scotch yesterday, the air went warm and staticky between them. Chemistry, and a crazy amount of it. He'd only offered to give her a ride, so she didn't think this was a date—but was it? Maybe she should wear her favorite red dress and gold-heart hoop earrings.

She was definitely overthinking things.

The oval-shaped cove cut into the island, and she swished her fingers across the clear surface of the water. It was cold but not freezing. Maybe on warm summer days Sara had happily waded here with friends.

Gåsholmen was a romantic place for a date, with its sweet cove, pastel wildflowers, and songbirds flitting between the seagrasses. As Ella touched a cluster of cream blooms on a patch of Queen Anne's lace, she knew that Gåsholmen would somehow appear in one of her future lines of clothing. Maybe this island inspired some of Sara's designs.

Ella ducked under a thick tangle of branches and entered a clearing, then halted abruptly at the sight of a big, slanted boulder. She'd studied Sara's photograph enough to recognize the spot. Her eyes welled up, knowing that her mom had been here, spent time here with someone she cared about greatly, and perhaps even loved. Maybe they built a small campfire and toasted marshmallows skewered on sticks, or sipped champagne and fed each other chocolate-covered strawberries. Looking through her tears, Ella imagined her mom and this man snuggled up together on the blanket while holding hands and kissing.

She longed to meet the owner of the loafers in the photo, but with no clues to his identity, her chances of finding him were slim to none.

The chilly salt breeze cut through her cotton blouse. She should've brought a coat, and she needed to get back. She wouldn't have time to change her clothes or apply that lipstick unless she hurried. She made her way down the trail, but when the cove came into view, she froze. Her hand flew to her throat and her heart thudded.

The dinghy was gone.

How was that possible? As she walked to the mooring poles, the wind nipped beneath her skirt and at her legs. Her knees shook and her breath came fast in panic. *Of course,* a shoelace knot like hers wouldn't hold! Now she'd lost the dinghy, like an idiot. And worse than that, she was stranded alone on the island.

Ella looked at the sea and she shivered. It was stupid of her to travel to a foreign country where she knew absolutely no one, and not a single person would even know if she went missing. She'd probably freeze to death in the cold air tonight and later be eaten by seabirds before anyone stumbled upon her. She sank down on the rocks and began to cry.

CHAPTER 12

Leif knocked on Ella's door at 4:00 p.m. sharp, but he was met with silence, and his shoulders slumped. The dinghy wasn't at her dock. Maybe she was just running late; he'd give her a minute.

He walked around the yard and came across a cassette player and headphones on a patio chair. He held the headphones up to his ears, pushed the start button, and heard a male singer crooning about Colorado Rocky Mountain high, starlight, and raining fire in the sky. Turning off the music, he picked up one of her boots and studied the sparrows stitched on the leather. He laughed. *Oh Ella, you're charming.*

He scanned the Lyngør Sound. No sign of Ella. Why hadn't she left him a note? That stung him more than he cared to admit, but it was probably for the best if she didn't come to the party. He could relax and not feel any pressure to make sure she had a good time. Guilt poked at him for not following through with his promise to take Charlotte to the party. She was happy to do what they'd always done together, like cross-country skiing at Erik's vacation cottage in the mountains over Easter break or biking the same loop in the nearby coastal city of Arendal on sunny spring days. Charlotte never challenged him or suggested that he try something different. It was why things were so easy with her. As far as they went, anyway. On the other hand, he sensed Ella would shake up his life. He wasn't sure how, but he felt certain she would do just that if he let her into his world. *Nah, things are just fine as they are.*

Staring at the cloudy sky, he touched the leather cord that hung around his neck and inched the aquamarine pendant from his shirt. He quickly kissed the stone, saying, "Keep her safe, Njord." The pendant had belonged to his father. Now it lay near his heart, always.

• • •

Leif cut *Rán*'s engine and allowed the boat to drift into a slip at the grocery dock where Mia waited, her shoulders hunched under the weight of two bulging canvas bags.

"Hey there," she said, smiling at him. "Where's Ella? I thought you'd be bringing her."

No, she blew me off, he thought. Aloud he said, "Something came up. Let's go—I want to get there early and set up before anyone arrives." He leaned over the boat railing, grabbed the beer crate, and hauled it aboard.

As he threw off the lines, Mia eyed him from the passenger seat. "You're disappointed about Ella, aren't you?"

"Why should I care? It's good she's not coming."

Yes, she was creative and interesting—not to mention stunning—but she made his heart beat a bit too fast for comfort. He wasn't disappointed, was he?

"Everyone knows Americans are insane. Did you know Colorado has entire stores dedicated to hot sauce? And they even have fast food restaurants with drive-throughs—massive burgers and french fries—to eat in their cars. Plus, some guy named Root mixed ice cream and beer and called it . . . oh yeah, a Root Beer Float. No one in their right mind would mix ice cream and beer together. Who does that?"

"Right!" Mia laughed. "You've certainly convinced me that you're not thinking about her at all."

Backing away from the dock, Leif wondered if Ella enjoyed hot sauce and drive-through restaurants. There was nothing in Lyngør that could compete with that.

• • •

Fifteen minutes later, Leif tied up at a cleat drilled into the granite shore on Sandøya, another auto-free island just outside of Lyngør. Nautical white clapboard cottages hugged the shore, which was covered in heather. Terns soared above glazed tile roofs, and red, white, and blue Norwegian flags billowed from flagpoles. Approximately a hundred locals lived on Sandøya, and thousands of vacationers visited there over the summer. Besides a brilliant potter who sold his ceramics at galleries on the southern coast, the only businesses on this island were a mini-mart with limited hours, a small shack that sold ice cream and hot dogs, and the Propeller, a two-story red cabin that was a government-owned community center where Leif and Mia had thrown dozens of parties.

As the two of them unloaded party supplies, the sound of a familiar marine engine came into range. They waited for Erik to dock his cruiser, and then the three of them carried the food and beer from the dock to the algae-spotted rocks that fronted the Propeller.

Leif unlocked the door, and Mia piped up. "The last I counted, sixty-four people are coming tonight."

"Not everyone chipped in for the food," Erik said with a scowl. "I'm tempted to drag them to an island and leave them there. It's going to be cold and wet tonight."

Mia scoffed while Leif laughed. He flicked on the light to reveal reindeer hides spread out on the waxed floors. A whale mosaic made of cracked propellers and sea glass covered the rear wall. Leif had created it, collecting the glass and propellers from numerous beaches and boatyards, in a tribute to the club's name. The cracked propellers were a reminder that the sea demanded respect.

Near the fireplace, Mia uncorked a bottle of cabernet and poured each of them a glass. Leif set his bags on the long table beneath the mosaic and unpacked the food: smoked salmon, potato salad, fish cakes, elk meatballs, and lingonberry sauce. As he arranged the dishes, Erik sidled up next to him, reached for the dill-seasoned cod cakes, and bit into a golden patty.

"Did you happen to bring that garlic aioli sauce that I asked you to please make for the cured salmon?" Erik asked.

"Garlic aioli? Um, *no*, because everyone knows that the only proper sauce to serve with gravlax is mustard dill sauce!" Leif looked scandalized.

Mia and Erik rolled their eyes at each other. "The world won't go spinning if you break tradition," Mia teased Leif as she set a glass of wine on the table in front of him.

"Never!" Leif laughed good-naturedly and skewered a meatball with his pocketknife. He wondered if Ella ate meat. She seemed like a tree-hugger type who might not.

Erik grabbed another patty. "Delicious. You'll make someone a fine fishwife someday," he joked.

• • •

The door opened. Cigarillo smoke with a spicy clove scent announced Inger's arrival. Besides being Mia's friend, Inger was also Erik's niece. Being the same age as Leif, she was as close to a sister as he could imagine.

"What a strange day—I need a drink! But I'm OK! Everything's fine," Inger announced as she pulled a face. She gave Erik, Mia, and Leif each a peck on the cheek.

"You were supposed to come early and help," Mia lightly scolded as she handed her a glass of wine.

"I had to take care of something." Inger's gaze slid to the window that overlooked the white-capped waters, and she pursed her lips before stepping to the food table as if to put an end to the conversation.

The door banged open. Leif raised his glass to Inger's boyfriend, Axel, who loved making an entrance. Axel smiled, perfect teeth flashing against olive skin. He looked like a model in a magazine ad.

"Hey babe," Axel said. He kissed Inger on the mouth, clapped Leif on the back, and handed Erik two hundred kroner.

"To shave a little off my poker debt," he said to Erik. Axel was unlucky at cards, an all-or-nothing type of guy known for his empty pockets. Leif liked him; anyone who could live with Inger and her short fuse had his respect.

Leif placed folding chairs around the low coffee table as Mia lit the votive candles on the sills and hearth.

"Hey Leif," Erik warned in a low voice, "Charlotte, six o'clock."

Leif glanced behind him to see Charlotte enter. She was curvy with long caramel-colored hair. She narrowed her eyes at him.

"Hiya," Leif greeted her sheepishly. He'd brought her to the Lyngør summer party routinely for more than a decade. He knew she'd be disappointed that he hadn't included her in his plans this time. It crossed his mind that gossip raged with hurricane speed around the island, and she might've already heard about Ella somehow. But what did it matter—he hadn't done anything, and there was nothing to gossip about.

Charlotte greeted everyone except Leif with a kiss on both

cheeks. To him, she mouthed the word *meanie*. He deserved it, but he pretended not to notice and filled a bowl with potato chips. He wondered if Ella was back home now; maybe he should've waited a bit longer for her to return.

Inger sat down on the sofa and looked at Leif. "You best tell Charlotte about Ella." She let out a catty laugh.

"Tell her what? That I offered to give Ella a lift here? So?"

"But you were supposed to bring Charlotte tonight. Why would you ditch her for a tourist?" Erik said and shifted in his seat.

"Charlotte couldn't care less—and Inger, don't look so skeptical! How many times do I have to explain it? Charlotte and I are friends, that's it. She's not interested in taking it any further either. It works for both of us."

Charlotte approached and sat down between Inger and Erik. "Where's that summer girl? I heard Inger invited her."

"Ella stood Leif up," Inger said with a smirk.

"Cut it out—that's not even true." Leif gave Inger a hard stare and tossed back his wine.

Axel chimed in. "I dunno, Ella sounds like a strange one. Why not fish in your own pond, huh?" Leaning over the coffee table, he gave Inger a quick kiss on the lips.

"She's no friend of mine." Inger lit another cigarillo. "She drank my scotch! She admitted it when I met her on Mia's dock."

"Oh, come on. You left it in the house, so you can't blame her. What did you think she was going to do? For all she knew, a renter forgot it." Mia settled back in her seat, rested her feet on the table, and added, "Ella's one of those people you can't help but like."

"What about my garden?" Inger huffed. "I asked Ella if I could keep it, and she told me that she needed to think about it. What's her problem—why can't she just let me garden there? I need rhubarb for my wine. Now what am I going to do?"

"Maybe she doesn't see the point of some stranger using

her property, especially when the cottage is being put on the market," Leif growled.

Inger cut in sharply. "Ella told you this?"

"Yes, and I agree with her," Leif admitted. "It's not your property to do what you like with, whenever you please."

"It's not fair." Inger pressed her fingers to her temple. "What do you think, Uncle Erik?"

"I couldn't care less about some tourist." He yanked off his fisherman cap and balled it up as if he were anxious about something.

Charlotte shrugged. "Ella might be odd, and a tourist, but she owns a very expensive property. I hope she puts Ringpynten on the market and I hope I'm the one to sell it. Make sure to tell her that I'm the best real estate agent on the southern coast—I want that commission."

"I think Ella might be working with my cousin," Mia said, chewing on peach gummy candy.

"Right, we'll see," Charlotte said. She slipped several business cards from her pocket and set them on the coffee table.

"Everyone needs to lighten up," Axel said. "A shot of aquavit should do the trick."

"Oh, I'm already feeling pretty good." Inger laughed and leaned closer to Leif. With a voice barely above a whisper, she said, "I had a little fun with the tourist today." She grinned at him devilishly and sat back in her seat.

"What are you talking about?"

Instead of answering, Inger got up and set six glasses on the table. Axel filled them to the brim with aquavit and passed them around.

They stood, raised their glasses, and toasted in unison. *"Skål!"*

Axel began singing a festive drinking song: *"Å så havner vi på fyllefest igjen. Hei! Skål!"* Everyone joined in the chorus: "And then we ended up at a drunken party again. Hi! Cheers!"

They downed their aquavit—all except for Leif, who watched Inger out of the corner of his eye. What was she up to?

Charlotte challenged Axel and Erik to a game of darts, and the three of them were off. Inger hurried to the kitchen.

Mia nudged Leif with her elbow. "Hey, what's wrong?"

"I don't know. Inger just said something weird. Do you know what's going on?"

Mia shrugged. "Do you mean something with Ella? When I introduced them, they seemed to get along." She bit her nail. "Maybe Inger said something ugly to test her, you know, see if she could shove her around. I don't know. That's just Inger."

Partygoers pushed through the door and brought the cold, damp outside air with them. Leif shivered. Was Ella out in that foul weather? He needed to forget about her, right now, and enjoy the party. He flipped through the vinyl records stacked by the turntable, looking for some dance music. It seemed to him that Inger was jealous that Ella now owned Ringpynten, and the truth was, it made him nervous. She'd once had a fit on his eleventh birthday, when Erik gave him a blue parakeet. She had wanted that bird. So she mixed loads of salt in the birthday cake batter, and the next day she let the bird out of the cage. She had always been a little vengeful like that.

Leif set the turntable needle carefully on Depeche Mode's "Policy of Truth" and cranked up the volume. Inger had better come clean about whatever she was up to. He wheeled around quickly, brushed past Mia without saying a word, and headed for the kitchen.

"Slow down," Mia called after him. "Don't start a fight! It's a party, remember?"

Leif barged into the kitchen, where Inger sat on the oak counter, her long legs dangling over the edge. She was heating up the stove and had a baking sheet full of frozen rolls beside her.

Leif leaned against the refrigerator and crossed his arms. "What did you say to Ella?"

Inger picked lint off her sweater.

"Oh jeez, just tell us," said Mia, who had followed him in. She raked at her hair.

"I didn't say anything to Ella. Not a single word," Inger insisted. "I didn't even open my mouth." She wouldn't meet his eye and tapped her cigarillo ash into a tea saucer.

"Right," Leif said, "so what *did* you do?"

"It was just a joke," Inger huffed. "She doesn't belong here, and the sooner she leaves the better. I want my garden back."

Leif stepped closer to Inger, but the sound of chugging engines made him look past her through the window above the sink. He saw boats with partygoers headed to the Propeller's dock. The red dinghy that he'd loaned Ella hung off the back of a wooden skiff. Cheerful voices echoed across the water. Leif scanned the boats and their passengers, looking for Ella, but he didn't see her. All he saw was the bruised sky, and the waves shattering against the rocks.

His mouth went dry, and he touched his pendant. *Please, let Ella be safe.*

"So, my question is, Inger"—he raised his voice at her to bring her attention back from the approaching boats—"where is she?"

Inger winced. "I thought she'd notice."

"Notice what?" Leif said with a sharp edge to his voice. He fought the urge to tower over her and yell.

"She's fine. Probably a little scared is all." Inger hopped down from the counter, snatched the tray of rolls, and shoved them into the oven.

"Where is she?" Mia asked, gaping at Inger.

"OK, OK. A couple of hours ago I passed Gåsholmen. Ella had tied up the dinghy there, with one of her ridiculous shoelace knots. Bunny ears. Can you imagine?" Inger tittered. "Who does that? So, I might've loosened the knot. Just a little bit."

Silence.

Loud, happy chatter came from the next room. Axel started singing again, likely doling out more aquavit.

"Tell me you're kidding?" Mia said.

"I'm not kidding." Inger jumped back up on the counter. "I didn't think the dinghy would float away though. I was sure it would stay in the cove. You know, worst-case scenario, Ella would have to wade into the water to retrieve it."

"Are you crazy?" Leif grabbed a cookie tin from the kitchen table and sent it flying into the sink. It crashed against a glass, breaking it into pieces, and he imagined a body breaking against the surf-pounded rocks. Mia gasped. Inger blinked twice at the broken bits in the sink. They'd never seen him so angry.

Mia frowned at Inger. "You should be ashamed. That's just too much."

Inger pursed her lips at Leif. "Oh, relax! Ella will be fine. It was just a prank, and I didn't mean any harm. I'll go get her."

"Save it. You're an idiot, and I don't trust you!" Leif shouted. The back door slammed behind him.

CHAPTER 13

Leif throttled down the engine and inched *Rán* toward Gåsholmen, as the sun sank lower in the sky. He should have spotted Ella by now. Perhaps she'd found shelter amid the firs and boulders to escape the bitter wind.

He cupped his hands around his mouth. "Ella?"

But yelling her name was pointless. The wind, the engine, and the god-awful gulls drowned his voice.

Waves exploded against rocks, hissing as they withdrew. He couldn't risk being capsized by a freak wave. Or the surf could toss his boat onto the rocks, which would rip a hole in the wood and wreck the propeller. The rocks shredded people too, as they'd done to his father and those two out-of-towners. The truth of it tormented Leif. He batted away the ghastly image of his father's fate and weighed his options carefully. It would be safest to pick up Ella at the cove. Even so, it would be risky. There were no docks there, and the swells could easily shove *Rán* against the reefs and ruin the engine. Should that happen, he'd drift out to sea, away from Ella and Lyngør. He'd heard countless stories of Norwegians dying on the water: Whether they were overconfident or careless or both, their boats drifted off to no-man's-land, never to be seen again. He reminded himself that he could handle any boat, and that nothing would ever happen to Ella on his watch.

He backed the boat away from land just as Ella rushed from the trees, mid-island, and stopped near the shore. Waving her arms frantically, she shouted at him, but he couldn't hear a single word. He held up his arm in reply.

Incoming rollers almost sent *Rán* crashing against the shore. He spun the helm to port, threw the engine into reverse, and revved it. Bubbles trapped in the propeller burst forth and colored the water a milky green. As the boat backed away swiftly, he motioned to her and then pointed in the direction of the mooring poles and the cove. It was barely navigable. The cove wasn't ideal but was his best bet. Even so, getting her on board would be tricky. The southwesterly wind whipped up the sea, salt spray covered every inch of his boat, and the deck was slick as wet kelp. If she slipped when she boarded, he wouldn't be able to help her. He had to control the boat or the waves could shove the hull into Ella, smashing her against the barnacle-covered reefs. That's if the swells didn't snatch her first and fling her against the granite. Ella likely wouldn't survive that.

She ran to the cove, arms pumping. Her flimsy sandals, with their thin straps, looked about as useful as a sailboat with a busted keel on that algae-slickened shore.

"Slow down!" he yelled.

She slipped, fell forward, and landed on her knees.

"Are you hurt?" he shouted. Backing twenty yards from the island, he put the engine into neutral, spun the helm, and pointed the bow toward the cove.

"I'm OK," she called in a shaky voice as she limped toward him. She didn't look OK. Charcoal mascara streaked her cheeks, as if she'd been crying.

"Be careful!" he said. "The rocks are even slicker here."

He slid *Rán* alongside the granite shelf and throttled down the engine. The boat rocked from side to side in the rough surf, and he swayed at the helm while fighting to keep the hull from hitting the reef.

"When you can, grab the rail and hoist yourself up!" he yelled. "Do you think you can do that?"

She nodded. He noticed how much her hands shook as she yanked the preserver from her bag, put it on, and fastened it. Tucking her torn skirt into the belt cinched around her waist, she seized the railing and heaved her body up onto the bow of the boat. At the flash of red underwear, he blinked to refocus on the waves. Ella trembled as she crouched on the deck and staggered toward the helm. He reached for her arm and guided her into the seat.

"Sit and stay put."

"The dinghy floated away," she said, and inhaled a deep, shuddering breath. "It's my fault. I tied a bad knot. How stupid can I be?" Her voice caught. "I'm so glad you found me. Thank you. The dinghy is probably in Denmark by now."

Her bottom lip quivered and she wiped her eyes, but she didn't cry.

He was beyond relieved that he'd found Ella in one piece, and he hadn't wrecked his boat either. Still, he was unprepared to tell her the truth about what had happened to her boat. Inger was part of his inner circle, a sister in all but blood. Plus, Ella planned on leaving in a couple of weeks, and they'd most likely never see her again.

"Let me just move away from the rocks." Leif backed the boat away from the cove and into the channel and then he put the engine in neutral, allowing *Rán* to drift. Despite Sunna's sweater, she shivered and looked cold to the bone. He draped his sailing jacket around her shoulders.

"Don't beat yourself up, OK? Someone found the dinghy drifting not far from here. They towed it to the party, and I headed out to look for you as soon as I saw it." He was aware that he sounded annoyed, even though he was trying to swallow his fury at Inger.

"Someone found the dinghy? What a relief!" As Ella spoke, she grimaced at her knee and held it. "I think I might need a bandage."

"Let me see." He gestured at her legs. She lifted her skirt and he saw the blood trickling down her shins, blood seeping through the cotton fabric.

"You need more than a bandage," he said. Ella was in rough shape, but she didn't complain. As he throttled up the engine and headed to Ringpynten, he raised his voice over the thrumming. "I'm taking you home! We'll be there shortly, and we can patch you up."

"It's not as bad as it looks," she insisted over the wind.

Neither spoke as Leif steered past small weather-scoured islands and terns twirling in the dusky pink light. When he pulled up to Ella's dock, he cut the engine and exhaled in relief to have her home safely.

As he threw over the fenders, she hobbled across the deck and her feet slipped from beneath her. She pinwheeled her arms to steady herself. Leif jumped to reach for her and said, "Let me help."

She nodded wearily. His hands encircled her waist, and he lifted her up and set her on the dock.

"Thanks, I appreciate it." She gave him a shaky smile. "Well, goodbye."

"Those cuts look pretty bad. Why don't you let me tape you up?"

"No, I'm OK." She fidgeted with her beaded bracelets. "You should go back to the party. I can look after myself." Pushing her hair out of her eyes, she watched a hawk circle the trees on the bluff.

He could tell she was embarrassed, and he wanted to put

her at ease. He smiled at her. "Everyone falls and loses stuff. We're only human. Do you have anything at the cottage for your cuts?"

She didn't answer.

"Injuries from barnacles can cause serious infections, you know. They need to be sterilized."

She lifted her skirt again and winced at her knees. "I take back what I said about it not being so bad. It's not great, is it?"

"I can find something to bandage you up."

"All right. Thank you."

She limped across the dock, grimacing as she climbed the stairs slowly. Stubborn woman, he would grant her that. He chuckled, but only because he was sure she couldn't hear him. Grabbing vodka and a clean T-shirt from the supply locker, he followed her.

In the kitchen, Ella trembled as she patted her knee with a wet towel. Her face was drawn, and gray as plaster.

"Thanks again for helping me," she said.

"No worries." It was clear to Leif now that Ella's inexperience with boats meant that she couldn't get around safely on her own. She was a danger to herself. He set the vodka on the counter with a hard clink. "But you have to be more careful on the water."

"Please don't lecture me."

"Hop up here," he patted the counter.

She dug her fists into her hips.

"It's easier for me to bandage you if you're sitting on the counter." He twisted off the vodka cap.

"OK." She braced her palms, hoisted herself up, and planted herself on the wood surface, legs hanging over the side. "I honestly don't need a glass—just give me the bottle." She reached for the booze.

"It's to disinfect your cuts. But go ahead and take a big sip because this'll sting."

She took a swig and handed it back to him.

"Right, now take a deep breath." He held the bottle over her cuts. "I'll count to three."

Ella sucked in air before holding her breath.

"One. Two." He dumped the vodka on her knees.

She jumped, almost knocking the bottle from his hand. "Jeez, that hurts! And you didn't say *three*!" She gritted her teeth.

"It'll feel better in a second."

"You've done this before?"

"Sure. Last time was a month ago, when my friend stepped on a fishhook."

"Does she still have her foot?"

He laughed. She'd grinned, but only just. Somehow all her smiles, big or small, comforted him like a lantern in the dark, and he longed to kiss her.

"Why do you assume my friend is a woman?" He winked. "Want another sip?" He passed her the bottle, and she swallowed two mouthfuls. Using his pocketknife, he tore the T-shirt into strips and handed them to her. "This will have to do. I don't stow a first-aid kit on board, but I should."

"It'll do."

He wound the strips around her knees, and his hands brushed against her smooth skin. As he tied the strips into place, goosebumps rose on her thighs, and he averted his eyes.

"All done," he said.

She looked at her doctored knees. "Good as new. Thanks . . . really. I'm not sure what I would've done if you hadn't found me." As she hopped down from the counter, she cringed. With her injuries taken care of, he again noticed her smeared mascara. He felt awful that she'd been crying while trapped all alone on a damn island. He was getting more upset with Inger by the minute.

"You know how you can thank me? Be more careful next time," he said.

"You told me that already." She shot him a look. The ceiling light caught the amber flecks in her eyes.

He snatched the vodka from the counter. "You really should learn how to operate a boat before you go out on the water again. This isn't child's play." He heard the gruffness in his own voice, and that made him feel worse. He took a gulp from the bottle.

"I'm not stupid," she snapped at him.

"I didn't say you were." He took another swig. She was upset, but she didn't understand: The sea was moody and could turn ugly, fast. She had no idea how to read the weather or the current, and she seemed to have no clue about what was dangerous. She scowled. He tried to explain.

"Look, if you don't respect the sea, it will take your life. Why did you go to Gåsholmen, anyway? I told you I'd come by and give you a lift to the party."

"Maybe I didn't want to go to your party," she said, her temples pounding. The kitchen was silent except for the distant sound of waves clapping against the cottage dock.

"Right. I better be off," he said. "And for the record, my friend still has her foot." Vodka in hand, he headed out the door. That should show her, he thought. Although he had no clear idea what point he was trying to make.

CHAPTER 14

Beneath the cloudy morning sky, Leif split oak logs in his backyard. He hadn't returned to the party at the Propeller. He was in a foul mood and furious with Inger for tampering with the dinghy.

Inger rounded the corner of the house. He set one of the logs on the chopping block, raised the axe over his shoulder, and swung it down with such force that he split the log with a single blow. She was the last person he wanted to see.

"Morning," he mumbled. Inger had dark smudges beneath her eyes and looked green around the gills.

"Nothing good about it." She cradled her head in her hands. "I'll never drink aquavit again."

He kept splitting logs.

"For Loki's sake," she sighed. "Would you stop taking your aggression out on that wood and look at me."

He leaned the axe against the stump.

She frowned. "The party wasn't the same without you."

"Be glad I stayed away," he said.

"Whatever. How's the tourist?"

"She's fine, no thanks to you." He set another log on the stump.

"What did you tell her?"

"Don't worry, I covered for you, though I'm not even sure why. Then I listened. You should try it sometime." He scowled at Inger, split the log, and tossed the pieces onto the growing pile of firewood. "Why are you here?"

"Erik is passed out on his dock, and I need help putting him to bed. I would've asked Axel, but he's also in pretty bad shape." She lit a cigarillo and puffed on it.

"Right." In the month of June, when Erik drank enough to put King Odin of Asgard under the table, Inger often took it upon herself to clean up after him. She loved her uncle with a fierceness she reserved for family. Leif buried the axe in the stump. Wiping his hands on his jeans, he nodded.

• • •

By the time they reached Odden Island, Erik was no longer on his dock. An empty whiskey bottle lay on the ground, and Leif squinted at Erik's cottage, then into the water. He picked up the empty bottle. *Please, Njord, let Erik be asleep in bed.*

"I should have tied him up with a rope," Inger said and stepped on her cigarillo butt. "One day he's going to stumble off the dock, hit his head on the rocks, and sink."

"Stop it." Leif's gut twisted at the gruesome mental image of Erik's body washed up on the rocks, lacerated and blue.

Inside the cottage, the smell of bacon grease and cigar smoke hung in the stale air. Loud snoring came from the rear of the house, and Leif and Inger exchanged relieved looks.

In the hallway, Erik lay on a wool runner, wearing only a pair of snug gray briefs.

"Leave him, I've seen enough already." Inger covered her eyes with her hand.

"We can't leave him! Not like this." Leif gripped Erik's arm and lifted him to his feet. "Come on, old man, let's get you to bed."

"I'll get him some water," Inger said.

Leif guided Erik as he moaned and stumbled his way to the bedroom at the end of the hall. He squinted at Leif and sobbed. "It should've been me!"

"What?" Leif said, and tightened his grip on Erik, who swayed on his feet.

"I could've prevented it," Erik slurred.

"Here we go again. Oh, what a joy June is!" Leif chuckled at his own sarcasm and then gnashed his teeth, barely managing to keep a hold on his patience. Drunk or sober, Erik put up walls. The two men were like father and son, and just like many sons before him, Leif felt he'd never really known the older man at all.

"She was swept out to sea!" Erik let out another sob.

"Who?" Leif asked. He sat Erik on the bed and lifted his legs up onto the mattress.

Erik ignored the question. He curled his body into a fetal position, clutched his stomach, and let out a moan.

"Shh, it's OK. Everything's going to be fine." Leif gathered up the duvet heaped at the end of Erik's bed, shook it out, and draped it over him.

Erik grasped Leif's forearm. "Bjorn. Stay with me."

Leif flinched. Never had Erik mistaken him for his father, although the local folk insisted that Leif was the spitting image of Bjorn. As Leif pried himself away from Erik's grip, he felt a familiar twinge of despair, knowing his father was responsible for that tragedy. The last thing Leif wanted was for Erik to look at him and see Bjorn's face.

"Sleep it off," Inger said soothingly as she placed a glass of water on Erik's bedside table.

"Get out!" Erik punched at the stale, boozy air.

"Love you too, Uncle Erik." Inger blew him a kiss.

"No one loves me, it's all my fault!" Erik cried into his pillow.

Leif was too shocked to speak as he closed Erik's door behind him. Terrible enough that three men had died in the accident, but now it seemed Erik had added a woman to the death toll. Typical of Erik to get drunk and agitated and talk in riddles. A bad case of survivor's guilt. God knows, Leif wished he could help him.

"I'm worried about Erik," Inger said as she lit another cigarillo. "Axel is concerned too. He told me that Erik seems worse than ever this week. Why do you think that is? Maybe I should sit him down and ask him what's going on."

Luckily, Inger didn't hear Erik mention the woman in the accident. Even though Leif considered it the mumblings of a drunk, he knew that she'd tell everyone in the village.

"Do me a favor and leave it alone," he replied.

Even so, he wondered what made Erik say this, after all these years. He reminded himself that Erik drifted in and out of reality after a night of heavy drinking, and especially during June.

CHAPTER 15

In the guest room at Ringpynten, Ella dug through an antique sea chest that held several of Mormor's belongings. She found it odd that Mormor had left valuable family heirlooms at the cottage, like sterling silver flatware, four silver goblets, and a silver barbell-style baby rattle with the block letter *S* engraved on each end. Ella traced her fingers over the rattle that must have belonged to Sara and wondered, yet again, why Mormor wouldn't talk about her own daughter. Since arriving at Ringpynten, Ella had tried to be more generous about the choices her grandma had made. She considered that perhaps Mormor had been trying to run from the pain that these once-treasured objects may have held for her. If that were true, Ella supposed that Mormor probably continued to carry that pain with her every day, for the rest of her life. Ella couldn't help but soften toward her poor Mormor when she considered that she had buried her only child, left her house and her homeland—everything she knew and loved—and raised her granddaughter all on her own in a foreign country. Why did she want to leave, rather than lean on family and friends at that difficult time in her life?

• • •

Ella lugged the box full of silver onto the patio. She'd decided to sell it all, except for Sara's rattle, which she wanted to keep for her own child someday. Maybe Mia could recommend a store that bought sterling outright for cash. That way Ella could reimburse Mia for using the phone at her store to make calls back to Colorado. Whatever was left over, Ella planned to use it to buy her return ticket, instead of putting it on another credit card.

Ella leaned back on the lounge chair, crossed her legs, and picked up the rattle to polish it. Her knees felt better underneath the bandages. Leif's touch had been gentle yesterday, and it had calmed her so that she'd forgotten about her injuries. But when he lectured her on water safety, she wished she could click her heels like Dorothy, get the heck out of Oz, and land back home where everything made sense. And yet a part of her wanted to stick around, at least long enough to show Leif and the other locals that she could handle boats and hang with the best of them. But Leif had probably returned the dinghy already.

• • •

When someone nudged Ella's foot, she opened her eyes at the disturbance. The rattle and rag lay on her lap. She must have dozed off in the lounge chair while polishing the silver. She tipped back her head and saw Leif standing over her. She yanked off her headphones.

"You shouldn't sneak up on people," Ella said as she turned off the music—Melissa Etheridge's raspy, raw, and vulnerable album *Brave and Crazy*.

"How can you sleep through that racket?" His eyes gleamed at her.

Ella sat up. "Music helps me sleep. I live over a bar. Well, I work there too, and the walls are thin . . . it can get pretty noisy."

"You're a waitress?"

"No, a bartender."

"A bartender?" His brow flicked. "Can you even reach the bar?"

"I'm five foot five and good at my job."

"Five foot five, and bigger than all the world." He grinned at her, but his dimples flattened out as he motioned at her bandages. "How are your knees?"

"Sore, but they're healing."

"Good. I brought back the dinghy, should you like to give it another go."

"Thanks. Um, that's really generous of you. I didn't think you'd trust me with it again." Maybe she could forgive him. His broad shoulders made it tempting.

"No worries," he assured her as a smile crinkled his eyes. He slid his leather backpack from his shoulder, reached inside, and retrieved a hardback. "I have something for you—a book on nautical knots and how to tie them. You might find it helpful."

"Thanks, but you can keep it. I won't be staying long enough for all that."

"Oh, alright." He seemed hurt, and she admitted to herself that maybe she'd been a little abrupt. She didn't want to care about how he felt, but she hadn't exactly forgotten about the twinge in her chest, either.

"Well, OK, I'll just take a look."

As she reached for the book, a light breeze caught his citrus-and-mint scent, and a low thrumming moved through her. There was no reason to be rude, so she thumbed through the book.

"This does look useful," she said, and turned to another

page. "I can make a macramé dream catcher with several of them." She shut the book. "Thanks, I'll make sure to give it back before I leave for home."

"Oh, keep it. When are you going?"

"I can only stay two weeks."

"That soon?" he frowned. He seemed disappointed, and that melted her.

"Well, yeah, I need to get back to my business. I have deadlines. Plus I have to get back to my job at the bar."

"Two jobs, that's impressive. Still, there's a lot to see and do here before you leave." He hesitated. He looked like he wanted to say something, but he stared at the dock instead.

It could have been her imagination, but she thought she heard him mutter, "Do it, bonehead."

She chewed the inside of her cheek to suppress her laughter as he turned to look at her.

His eyes glimmered, and he said, "You really should experience a proper Norwegian meal before you go. Would you like to have dinner with me?"

That surprised her. His sexy, deep-set eyes traveled over her face, looking for her answer. Her gaze landed on his full lips, and she could only think of kissing him.

"Dinner?" she said. "What, like boiled fish and potatoes?" She wrinkled her nose for good measure to try to hide her singing heart. Why did she have to be so mean to him? She felt lucky that he didn't seem to notice, since he was staring at her necklace.

"It's aquamarine," he stated, as if that were somehow out of the ordinary.

"Yes. It brings good luck on the water, that's why I wear it."

"Same here. Our pendants match. Some coincidence, don't you think?" He laughed and slid his cord necklace from under his shirt so that she could see it.

"Amazing!" Was it a coincidence or a sign? Of course she'd

have to forgive him now. But he didn't need to know that her heart was beating double time.

He grinned. "We could discuss it tonight. I cook a good *lapskaus*."

"*Lap-sky-ass*? That sounds like an exotic dance."

"Nope, it's a beef and vegetable stew. So how about it? I can pick you up at four o'clock?"

How could she resist a dinner with this Viking of a man, who was also a gifted artist? As a bonus, she considered that visiting his home would be a great opportunity to see how the locals lived . . . maybe how her mom might have lived.

"OK, dinner sounds great! See you at four." She sounded as happy with her decision as she felt. And yet this wasn't a real date, she told herself. It would make for a nice memory though.

CHAPTER 16

Ella heard Leif knock on her door, and she looked at Hilda's urn. "OK, Mormor, I'm off to dinner with the cute boatbuilder. We might even make out, how about that?" She laughed as she imagined Mormor's shocked expression, knowing that her advice would have been for Ella to keep her legs crossed.

In the foyer she smoothed her ruby-red dress and fiddled with the rhinestone clips that held her hair in a braided updo. All afternoon she'd thought about Leif. She'd been so excited she changed her outfit a dozen times and painted her nails red to match her bra and underwear—not that she expected them to sleep together. Mormor had always said to wear good underwear just in case . . . even though Ella knew she was referring to getting into an accident, she decided to take what she could from this advice. And if she and Leif did make out—it wouldn't be by accident.

She opened the door and grinned at him. "Hey."

"Afternoon." He removed his sunglasses. "Wow! You look nice."

"Thank you! You look nice too." He'd shaved, and his full lips looked soft and kissable. He flashed her a wickedly sexy smile and a look that said he could somehow read her thoughts. Turning away quickly, she lifted her life vest from the coat hook, shut the door behind her, and stopped near the pink fairy roses that grew against the stone wall.

"Wait," she said. "I have a question." She touched Leif's arm and felt that same spark of heat that hovered between them always.

"Ask away."

She pointed at an outcropping of rocks wedged between the lawn and the dock. A large, thick iron ring the size of a Frisbee was drilled into the stone there. "I noticed that ring the other day, but I forgot to ask. What's it for?"

"Oh, it's from the eighteenth century. The king of Norway sanctioned several rings exactly like yours to mark mooring points in Lyngør. Sea captains and merchants had to pay to use them, but they preferred your ring over the others."

"And what was so special about mine?"

"Ships won't run aground if they tie up here." He gestured at the bank. "See how the rock disappears vertically into the water? It's very deep—no reefs. Plus, your property is sheltered from the northerly winds. Word traveled that your ring was the safest one to use. The local folk call your property Ringpynten—Ring Point—because of that ring."

"Finally, I learn some information about my property! That makes me so happy. It's the fifth-best thing I've found since coming to Lyngør."

"OK, I'll bite. What are the first four?"

"In no particular order: One, the painting of me and my mom. Two, my mom's sewing machine. Three, her sketchbook—"

"I should've asked before I thumbed through the book. That was wrong of me."

"It's OK, I forgive you." She smiled at him, and she really meant it. "Four, the photograph with the drawing of my mom, the one you saw the other day. Those are the only hints I have about her. That's why I didn't want you to touch the photo or the sketchbook." She dug into her purse for the picture. "Would you mind taking another look?"

"Sure." He reached for the photo.

"I think the woman's shoes belong to my mother. Maybe the blanket too. I wish I could track down the man who called her *sweetheart*. I sort of wonder if he could be my dad? That's not what my grandma told me, so I don't really know."

Leif scanned the photograph before flipping it over and studying the sketch of Sara, as well as the inscription. He shook his head. "Good luck. This guy could be from anywhere."

"I know the odds are against me. But it's important to me to try to learn something about her, or about my family. I've knocked on some doors in Lyngør but generally no one's at home, or they don't seem to know my family. Maybe I'm getting paranoid, but sometimes I feel like everyone I've met is hiding something." She shook her head in frustration and disappointment. "But I want to keep trying."

"I'll do what I can to help. I suppose he *could* be from Lyngør."

On an impulse, she leaned into him, slid her arms around his waist, and gave him a tight squeeze. She smiled so wide a gnat flew into her mouth, causing her to cough and splutter. Leif patted her back.

"Appetizer," she croaked, spluttering some more. She dabbed her eyes, careful not to ruin her makeup. "Your offer to help just made the list. It's the sixth-best thing that's happened to me since I came here." She wondered if maybe she and Leif were destined to cross paths. He'd rescued her at Gåsholmen. Plus he could pave the way for her to speak with Erik and other locals from that generation. With Leif in her camp, she had a real chance of learning about her family and finding out what happened to Sara.

"I'm glad to help. That way we can spend more time together, Sunna."

"Sunna?" Ella tilted her head at him in question.

"She's the Norse goddess of the sun: bright, smart, and beautiful, like you." His ears went pink as he noticed the glow on her face after he said it.

Neither of them moved as they gazed at each other. Ella felt the spark flare between them again, and she imagined kissing him passionately. His gaze flicked to her breasts, and she saw some of the same heat flash across his face. A moment passed before Leif motioned to the steps leading to the dock.

"After you," he said.

She paused to steady the weakness in her knees. They crossed the dock to Leif's boat, a wooden double-ender.

"Is this yours? It's nice, but it's not what you usually drive." She smiled at him.

"*Rán* is at home. This is *Skadi*."

"I like those names. *Rán* sounds fast; *Skadi* sounds like an exotic bird."

"In Norse mythology, *Rán* is the goddess of storms and the drowned. *Skadi* is the goddess who married Njord, the god of sailors and the sea. I built them, and I christened them."

"Well, it's smart to have a couple of goddesses on your side!" Ella gave him a wry grin, and they laughed together. "You really built them? This one has incredibly fine details. So intricate." She swept her fingers over the braided vines carved on the boat railing. Two dragons with glaring eyes, gaping jaws, and long, ribbonlike tongues were entwined in a spray of foliage.

"It's what I love to do."

"You're such a talented artist. Who taught you how to carve?"

"Thank you." He stood straighter and pushed back his shoulders. "I taught myself. But Erik whittles too, so he encouraged me. By the time I was nine years old, I was carving boats."

"Your work is so meaningful and . . . I don't know, it's speaking to me in a way I've never thought too much about . . . my Norwegian heritage feels closer to me, somehow." She touched the Viking rune, shaped like a musical note, carved into Leif's boat railing. "It's inspiring—I'm imagining this on a line of dresses."

"You'd put that on clothes?"

"Definitely. Would that be OK with you?"

"My designs on your clothing?" He laughed and shook his head like he couldn't quite believe it but was delighted all the same.

"Right now it's just an idea, but if I decided to go for it, how about I mail you my sketches and if you approve, we could talk on the phone? I would pay you for the privilege of using your art, of course. What do you think?"

"Sure, it's a deal." He grinned and shook her hand. As their skin touched, Ella reflected that her attraction to him was more than just physical; she liked him and wanted to spend time in his company.

They boarded and she cinched the straps on her life preserver. "Where do you want me to sit?"

He pointed at the rear of the boat. "At the tiller—see that wood handle at the stern? Over there. I'll join you in a second."

The boat swayed on the waves as she staggered to the tiller and plopped down on the stern bench. As she gulped the briny air, she slid a cracker from her pocket and chewed on it to try to settle her stomach.

Leif joined her and gestured at her life vest. "Water makes you that uncomfortable?"

"I don't swim. You don't ever wear one?"

"Nah, I always wear blue, and that protects me. Your ancestors were seafarers, though—no one taught you about boats?"

"Growing up, it was just my grandma and me. She hated the water and never wanted me to go near it. She passed that phobia on to me."

"That must've been tough for you. I can't imagine," Leif said, kindly. "I saw the urn. You'll leave her here when you go?"

Ella nodded. "If I knew where my mom was buried, I could put Mormor there too."

"I'm sorry you lost your mum. That must have been hard on you." He scratched at something on his pants. "I also lost my mum. She died when I was a toddler."

Before she could reply, he held up a hand and shook his head, the corners of his mouth turning up slightly. "No—no need to say anything. This is pretty heavy, but what I really want is for us to have a nice night together, some good food, and get to know each other better." He stood to throw off a line and changed the subject. "Hey, I read Colorado has rodeos and real cowboys. Is that true?"

"Yep, we have plenty of those. Cowboys are great." She couldn't help laughing at his enthusiasm. She rocked her torso, like she was riding a horse, tipped an imaginary hat, and put on her best cowboy voice: "Howdy, partner!" He let out a bark of laughter and started the engine.

• • •

Leif's two-story maritime home on Holmen Island was built in a traditional Lyngør style, with white clapboard and a glazed tile roof. It was bigger than Ella had imagined. In fact, it was one of the largest houses she'd seen here on the islands, and that surprised her. Then again, Leif was hard to figure out—a mechanic who wore button-down shirts to repair engines, and built boats that looked like miniature Viking ships. Plus he wore an aquamarine pendant on the water, just like she did.

In Leif's foyer, Ella tried not to gape at the crystal chandelier and gilded mirror. She hadn't pictured old-world antiques in his home. The rooms looked like they should have been featured in a luxury interior design magazine. Not at all what she expected from a rugged boatbuilder.

"Your house is so elegant," she said.

"Not what you imagined?"

"Oh, it's fine for you—I guess I just don't know anyone my age who owns a single antique. Let me put it this way: I bought my sofa at a garage sale, and it cost ten dollars. I can toss it on the curb when I want a fresh look, and that works for me. Change is good, right?"

"Change." He shook his head. "Mmm, not exactly my favorite word. I like to put down roots and stay attached to them."

She blinked at him and fiddled with her dress sleeves. She had no roots. He must have seen that he touched a nerve, because he blurted, "I mean, new can be good too. America is an example of that."

She set her boots next to his navy Converse. She'd learned that when you enter a house in Norway, you leave your shoes at the door as a sign of respect, to keep the floors clean, and to get comfortable.

She followed him into the kitchen. Candles and books on Scandinavian art and design were arranged on the fireplace mantel, and a painted chest butted up against blue-gray wall planks. The lid and front panel of the chest portrayed a scene from a gunboat battle; a flourished font proclaimed the date as 1812.

"That war scene is so vivid. I almost feel like I'm there," Ella said.

"The chest belonged to my great-great-grandfather, Karl Leif Arnesen. He was a gunboat commander who fought in the Battle of Lyngør against Britain—that's the battle that's painted there."

He crouched in front of the fireplace, struck a match, and lit the newsprint that he'd stuffed between fireplace logs. He

nudged the resulting flames with an iron poker as he continued. "Karl built this house, and I inherited it, along with all of
his belongings." He pointed to the kitchen table. "Karl made
that out of a century-old ship hatch. The chairs come from a
ship galley."

"Neat." She smiled at him. "The chairs would look great
painted a seafoam green, don't you think?"

"Yeah, maybe," he said, but he'd scrunched up his face, as
if that didn't appeal to him at all. "Like a beer?"

"Yes please." She followed him into a kitchen so cozy it
made her want to bake a pie—and she hated baking.

He handed her a cold pale ale before moving to the counter
and lifting the lid off a cooking pot. "This is the lapskaus. Beef,
potatoes, carrots, rutabaga, onions, bouillon, parsley. Looks a
bit mushy, but it tastes good. At least I hope you'll enjoy it." He
turned on the stove.

"It looks like a yummy beef stew." As she leaned over the
dish to sniff it, her arm brushed against his, and the air buzzed
hot between them again. She wished he'd put his arms around
her. "I can't wait to taste it."

"It'll be ready in about an hour." He grinned at her. "When
I asked you to dinner, you said you thought lapskaus sounded
like some kind of exotic dance. I have no idea what sort of
dance that is, but I'm keen to see it."

"Yes. *Lap-sky-ass* sounds like a lap dance." Ella lifted her
dress to mid-thigh and shimmied her hips. Leif laughed and
nodded in encouragement.

She laughed with him and released the hem of her dress.
"Or how about this one?" She pushed her neck forward and
bobbed it and then tucked her arms by her side and flapped
them like wings as she kicked up her feet. She might have
looked ridiculous, but she didn't care. He was beaming at her,
and that made her feel beautiful. She could be herself around
him, and that made her like him even more.

"Glad I could introduce you to the funky chicken." She bowed and smiled at him from beneath her lashes. He placed the lettuce, cucumber, and wedge of Parmesan on the kitchen table, and when she offered to help, he asked her to grab the oil and vinegar from the pantry.

She scanned its contents—sardines, pickled herring, and fish balls—and shuddered. Leif must have done all his shopping at Mia's store. Taped to the pantry wall was a newspaper clipping of Leif and Erik. Leif's arm was hooked around Erik's shoulder, and they were grinning at the camera. She pointed to it and said, "Great shot of you both. You two seem happy."

"Yup, we were at the annual wooden boat festival in Risør, about an hour west of here. Terrific festival and a great tradition." He slid a cutting board from a cabinet and set it on the table. "You met Erik?"

"No, I only saw him briefly at Mia's store. I wanted to meet him, but he took off quickly. He seemed upset."

"No surprise there. He has loads on his mind."

"Do you think you could introduce us before I leave?" She set the oil and vinegar next to the salad bowl. "He looked to be about my mom's age. Maybe he met her or knew who she was, or who her boyfriend might have been."

Leif took the scissors from a drawer. "Um, OK . . . he doesn't really get to know any of the tourists, though—he only knows their boats." He snipped at the parsley in the window box and the herb fell into his palm. "And he's very private. Let me talk to him first, and maybe I can set up a time for the two of you to meet."

"That would be great! But soon, please—if you can?"

"I'll try."

"Thanks, that would mean a lot to me."

As the stew simmered, Ella arranged the cloth napkins and dinnerware on the table and stole glances at Leif. His sleeves hugged his biceps as he tipped the cutting board over the salad bowl and pushed the diced tomato onto the lettuce with the blade of his knife. She imagined his hands tracing her skin, and the warmth of his mouth. She moved to his side.

"Table is set. Anything else I can do?"

He rested his hand on the small of her back. She felt drawn to him, a powerful pull, as if their bodies were meant to merge. He broke off a tiny chunk of Parmesan and asked, "Would you like to try a bite of this?" Ella nodded and he placed it on her tongue.

"Delicious," she said, looking into his eyes.

"You have some on your mouth," he said quietly, moving closer to her.

She lifted her chin and he brushed his thumb on her bottom lip. A lock of her hair had escaped from her updo, and he swept the strand away from her collarbone. He leaned in slowly, and his lips grazed her cheek, then traced her jawline and the hollow of her neck. She slid her arms around him and kissed him tenderly. Her head tingled, and so did her thighs. He gave her the type of kiss that could light up the night. His touch stole her breath and then handed it right back to her. She ran her fingers up the front of his shirt, and he let out a soft, low groan.

She jumped at the sound of someone banging on the front door, followed by a loud, high-pitched whistle. Ella pulled free, her breath coming fast.

"Ignore it," he said as his hands moved up her back and beneath her hair.

She tugged at her dress. "Who is that?" As she spoke, the person in question let out another ear-piercing whistle.

"It's Erik." Leif's face was red, and his tone was curt. He adjusted his pants. "I'll see what he wants. Stay here."

CHAPTER 17

Leif shut the front door behind him. The smell of baked bread and beef stew followed him outside. Erik frowned at the closed door.

"This isn't a good time," Leif said. "What's up?"

"Remember that big sale we had? The thirty-nine cuddy that we sold to that tourist. Well, the damn fool ran it aground. It's in a slip at the boatyard, but we need to pull it in."

"Can't it wait? I'm a little busy right now."

"No. The boat's taking in water. If he loses the engine, he's not gonna like it, and even though it's his fault, you know he'll try to come back to us because he just bought it. I can't deal with the hassle, and it's too much money to screw around. Just help me before it becomes a bigger problem."

"What about Axel? I've, uh, got someone here right now."

"Axel isn't home. Come on, don't gimme this. Charlotte won't care anyway."

"Fine. I'll help, but I need a minute. I'm with Ella."

"Ella?" A horrified expression swept over Erik's face as he looked past Leif's shoulder and through the large window into his kitchen. Erik yanked the cigar out of his mouth and threw it on the ground. "Why?"

"I'm making her dinner." Leif turned around to face the window. Ella gave him a stiff smile. *One moment,* he mouthed to her, holding up a finger.

"Have you gone soft? What's the matter with you?" Erik barked at him, pulling his fisherman cap low on his brow.

"What the hell is wrong with *you*?"

"Meet me, pronto." As Erik stomped off, he yelled over his shoulder, "Tell her to wait, or drop her at Ringpynten— whatever. But she's not coming."

Erik had always been a grouch, but never hostile. What could he have against Ella? But there was little point in asking; they didn't call him The Vault for nothing.

"Hey, you," Leif said lightly as he shut the door behind him. Ella sat at the kitchen table, scraping a spot of blue wax from the brass candlestick. She didn't look at him when he rested his hand on the back of her chair.

"Erik has an emergency. There's a problem at the marina, a job that needs two people. I'd much rather stay here with you, of course, but I have to go help him."

"I understand. I'd much rather stay here too. But if it's an emergency, it can't be helped. Can you take me back to Ringpynten?" Ella stood, turning to face Leif.

"Of course I will. I hate that our evening was interrupted." He clasped her hand. "How about we try again tomorrow night? I can drop by your place around five."

"OK. But how about we eat at my cottage? I doubt we'll have visitors there."

"I can bring wine and the main course?" He kissed her lips.

"Perfect. I'll make a salad and come up with a dessert."

"Good plan." As he smoothed back her hair, she leaned closer to him, and they kissed some more. She was all soft curves, soft skin and long, soft hair, and she smelled like cinnamon and sweet grapefruit. Their kiss deepened, their hips collided, and he let out a groan before pulling away.

"I want to stay, but Erik's waiting." He silently cursed Erik as he cupped Ella's face in his hands and kissed her mouth one last time. "I'll box up some stew so you can try it. Right now, that's the best I can do."

CHAPTER 18

Blue hydrangeas bloomed against the picket fence at Lyngør's only grocery store. Ella checked over the list of things to buy for her second dinner with Leif. Come to think of it, it was their *first* dinner, but second date. She counted last night as a date because they had kissed—and would have probably taken it further if Erik hadn't interrupted them. Erik, with his cold eyes and dark expression, had ignored her and didn't seem to want to talk to her at all. But maybe Leif could convince him to meet her to discuss her mom. It occurred to her that it might even be easier if Leif joined them. It would be one more chance for her to see Leif before she returned to Boulder. Her mind, in its anxiety, leaped forward to life in Boulder. If she didn't sell the cottage soon, she'd lose Little Bird.

But she definitely wanted to spend as much time with Leif as possible before leaving. Leif was stable and had a steady job and a tight-knit family of his own choosing. She'd always wanted a close family and circle of friends, and she wondered if she'd ever find that for herself in Boulder. Would she ever find a guy like Leif, who was able to express himself through his art while being so grounded?

Inside the grocery store, Bactus greeted her with a meow before strolling to a sunny spot on the floorboards where he commenced licking his paws.

"Hey, Ella! How's it going?" Mia called out, setting a large sheet cake on the checkout counter.

"Good, thanks," Ella said, smiling at her. "Any word from your cousin?"

"Yes, she said two families are extremely interested in seeing Ringpynten. She's trying to nail down a viewing date that works for both."

"I can't thank you enough for all your generosity and kindness. And along those same lines . . . I need to use your phone again," Ella said and made a face. They laughed.

"Is it nice to be on vacation, or do you miss Boulder?" Mia asked. "Is it a fun place to live?"

"Well, I wouldn't exactly call this a vacation! But once I get the house sold, maybe I can relax . . . it just feels like there's so much to do right now. But Boulder—yeah, it's fun to catch shows and indie bands. And I love seeing avant-garde films—there's a cool theater where I can do that. Let's see . . . there's good food and weekend markets and great places to go hiking and camping. The leaves are beautiful in the fall. But lately I've been too busy to enjoy any of those things . . ." She trailed off as her mind turned back to her to-do list, then she sighed. "I need to call Petal about some business issues. It's five in the morning there, but she's an early bird and probably awake. Please don't forget to give me the bill for the charges."

"No problem. You know where the phone is."

Ella called Petal from Mia's office. The answering machine clicked on. Ella rolled her eyes and then launched into a detailed message. Every day, she thought of new details that had to be addressed. She finished by saying that she'd call Petal again at 4:00 p.m., Norway time. Ella was determined to succeed, and she felt a pang of regret, wishing that Mormor were there to witness it.

Back at the register, Ella said, "Thanks. I left Petal a message; we're supposed to talk again at four. Now tell me about this dessert you're making!"

"It's *bløtkake*, a traditional Norwegian cream cake." Mia ripped open a candy bag with her teeth, pulled out a fistful of red gumdrops, and pushed them into the frosting, which looked like smooth sugar-cookie dough. "The topping is marzipan, and there are two layers of vanilla cake filled with homemade raspberry jam and whipped cream. It's a traditional birthday cake."

"It's beautiful! Whose birthday?"

"Inger's." Mia reached beneath the counter and retrieved a tray covered with pink marzipan hearts. "We're having a bonfire tomorrow night and Inger's invited everyone." She slid a marzipan heart from the tray and laid it on top of the cake.

"Do you think she'd mind if I showed up?" As soon as she said the words, Ella wanted to snatch them back. In her eagerness to learn more about her mother, as well as find the right place to leave Hilda's ashes, she'd gotten way ahead of herself. Inviting herself to Inger's bonfire was just stupid, after the way Inger had been so cold and standoffish with her.

"Um, well . . . I don't know," Mia said. "Let me check with her." She shuffled her feet in a nervous little dance and shoved red gummies in her mouth.

"Hello!" came Inger's voice from the door. She stepped behind the counter and sidled up to Mia. Sliding her tinted sunglasses to the tip of her nose, she gave Ella the once-over with her wolfy eyes. "What's up, Hippie Chick?"

"Ah, not much. I need to buy vegetables for salad," Ella said in a friendly voice.

"Mia doesn't sell lettuce." Inger plucked a red gumdrop from Mia's hand and held it over the cake but then tossed the candy on the counter instead. "There better be enough room on the cake for my name, plus the words *Happy Birthday* written in pink."

"Happy birthday!" Ella replied brightly.

Ignoring that, Inger frowned at Mia. "I told you I wanted pink gumdrops, not red ones, you nerd."

Mia said, with more than a trace of annoyance, "Jeez, how much are you paying me to make this fantastic cake?"

"Never mind," said Inger. "Thank you."

Trying to change the subject to something more advantageous for her, Ella said, "There's a cuckoo bird at Ringpynten. I sketched it and I'm thinking about embroidering it on a skirt." She slid a notebook from her satchel, tore out the sketch of the bird, and handed it to Inger. "Happy early birthday. Hope you have a great celebration."

Now invite me, Ella thought, offering her best smile.

"A cuckoo bird on a skirt? You really are something else." Inger laughed, but she gave the sketch a slight nod of appreciation before folding it into a small square and putting it into the pocket of her cardigan. "Mia, did you remember to get the candles and the lemons?"

"Shoot! I forgot." Mia chewed on her thumb.

"How could you forget? I don't have time to go to Tvedestrand! I have to work."

"Where's Tvedestrand?" Ella asked, thinking she could buy her lettuce there. Plus, maybe she could check out the real estate company and drop off her film to be developed. She wasn't totally confident she could row there—it depended how far it was—but she'd been studying the book Leif had given her and would tie a secure knot this time and eventually show them all that she could handle it just fine.

"You can take the ferry there. It's a thirty-minute ride, roughly." Mia traced her finger down the ferry schedule taped to the wall near the register. "You're in luck—it arrives in five minutes. You can catch the two thirty back here. Tvedestrand is fun. We like to drink beer on the wharf there."

Inger spoke up. "I really need those candles and lemons, but the store closes at three, and everyone I know but you"—she gestured at Ella—"has to work."

Mia and Inger started talking to each other, Mia with a frown and Inger looking smug, both speaking so quickly in Norwegian that Ella couldn't understand them, and this made her feel even more like the outsider.

"Well, see you later," Ella said. "I don't want to miss the ferry." If Inger had been nicer, or invited her to the bonfire, she would've offered to buy the candles and lemons. Inger could do her own shopping. She headed out.

"Wait! Ella!" Inger called out in English from the door. "Why don't you come to my birthday celebration? It's on Speken Island. Six p.m."

"And?" Ella blurted without thinking. She couldn't help it, but she wasn't going to offer to help for nothing. Inger had to ask her.

Inger's eyes narrowed a little, but then she smiled in a way that suggested she respected Ella's question. "Will you buy the candles and lemons and bring them to the bonfire tomorrow night?"

Inger must have been desperate. Not wanting to seem too eager, Ella slowly buttoned her coat, like she was debating the answer. But the invitation secretly thrilled her. She could meet people who might be able to help her, plus she could hang out some more with Leif.

Mia motioned toward the dock. "You better hurry, the ferry is here!"

Back on the water . . . would it ever end? Ella patted her satchel and realized with alarm that she'd left her life vest at the cottage. She hadn't planned on boating this afternoon.

"Don't worry," Mia called out, reading her mind. "The captain has life preservers on board."

"Hurry!" Inger flapped her hands at Ella, then cupped them around her mouth. "Pink candles and six lemons! Go to the Super Megamart—it closes at three!"

"Yup, I'll bring everything to the party. I'm sure Leif will give me a ride—I'll ask him at dinner tonight," Ella said over her shoulder. She resisted the urge to turn and see Inger's expression. Her startled squeak told her all she needed to know.

CHAPTER 19

Leif tied up at a downtown slip in Tvedestrand on the mainland and secured the skiff that he'd towed. The tow was for a long-time customer, and they'd arranged to meet at the Seilloftet Bistro to take care of paperwork and grab lunch together.

The Seilloftet was a local haunt known for its boiled cod and potatoes. It was tucked into a long row of century-old white clapboard storefronts bordering the cobblestone wharf. The wide windows gave diners a clear view of the ferry's comings and goings. Leif pushed open the door and scanned the two dozen tables but didn't see his customer.

That was fine with him; he was in no hurry to return to work with Erik. He was so damn grouchy lately, even for him. Never mind interrupting Leif's date with Ella last night—today, Erik had flooded Leif with invoices and paperwork that he didn't want to do himself, and his foul mood showed no signs of improving anytime soon.

As Leif sat down at the bar, a familiar spicy floral scent enveloped him. A hand rested on his arm, and a charm shaped like the letter *C* dangled from a gold bracelet. Charlotte.

"Just the man I wanted to see," Charlotte said. "I should

be angry at you for leaving the summer party to go after that tourist, but buy me a glass of champagne and I'll forgive you."

She was astute enough to position her cleavage where it would do her the most good.

"I don't have time." Leif dragged his eyes away. Drinks with Charlotte always led to sex. Exceptional sex, true, with no strings attached, but now he could only think of Ella.

She pouted her lips. "Oh, that's too bad. I just had a house sale fall through and I lost a big commission. I could use some cheering up. One drink. Pretty please." Charlotte was sexy as hell, but she couldn't hold a candle to Sunna.

"Nah, I'm just waiting for a customer then heading straight back to work. Erik's expecting me." He poked at the warm wax on the candle in front of him. It was the same ruby-red color as the dress that Ella had worn to his house last night. He was thinking ahead to picking up where they left off—with his hands running through her hair and over her soft curves. Her kisses turned him inside out with want.

He moved Charlotte's hand from where it rested on his thigh. "Stop it, I have a customer coming. And I told you, I can't."

"Oh, come on! It's been a terrible week. Two house sales fell through, and my car ran out of gas. My niece, Hannah, broke her elbow. And Bugs Bunny chewed through my purse and found my chocolate, so I had to rush him to the veterinarian. I could really use a friend right now, and just . . . you know, chill out for a second."

After inquiring sufficiently about her niece and rabbit and determining that they were both on the mend, he softened a bit. "Fine, just one drink though, nothing more." He motioned for the bartender, ordered a glass of champagne for Charlotte and his favorite Norwegian beer, Ringnes Sommerøl. Before he had time to react, she planted a wet kiss on his mouth.

As he pulled away in surprise, he looked beyond Charlotte's

shoulder, out the panoramic window overlooking the pedestrian street, and choked. Ella stood frozen outside the window, staring straight at him. He could see the hurt in her eyes, and his heart lurched. He wanted nothing more than to wrap his arms around her, rest her head against his chest, and let her know she was safe. Charlotte drew a hot-pink nail across his chest, and in a blink, Ella was gone.

"Was that Asta Nilsen? Inger told me that she stole her scotch!"

"Her name is Ella. And no, she didn't steal Inger's liquor—Inger left it at her house, dammit!" He was upset at everyone but Ella and wanted to run after her to explain, but he had no clue what to say without making it worse.

"Well, I want that property listing," Charlotte continued. "Ringpynten's worth a small fortune."

Leif caught the bartender's eye and slammed a handful of bills on the counter. "Keep the change." He'd reschedule the customer. Maybe if he hurried, he could find Ella.

"Slow down, lover boy," she protested, sipping her champagne. "Let a girl finish her drink first."

"No, I told you, I'm busy. Gotta run."

Charlotte scoffed as he rushed outside, but there was no sign of Ella.

CHAPTER 20

Ella turned from the Seilloftet and, with shopping bags in hand, hurried down the cobbled lane toward the ferry terminal. She couldn't believe what she'd seen. She dug her nails into her palms. She was disappointed and jealous of that gorgeous supermodel of a woman who'd been kissing Leif. Just last night, during her brief evening with Leif, she'd thought there might have been the possibility of romance between the two of them, not simply lust. Of course they hadn't made any promises to each other, and she was angry at herself for thinking they'd shared a deep connection. In her experience, chemistry was common but connection was rare. What was she thinking? He was a boatbuilder from Norway, and she hated the water! It was clear that she was no more than a one-night stand to him, and she felt ridiculous for misreading it. But he had seemed to enjoy their time together; she'd seen the twinkle in his eyes when he looked at her. Or had she dreamed that up too?

This was probably for the best, she told herself. In fact, it would be stupid to let her infatuation distract her from what she needed to accomplish, both in Norway and back home. She needed to be realistic. Leif was just a guy she met on vacation, a sexy almost-fling. There was no reason to feel hurt; it simply wasn't meant to be.

Ella hurried along, passing the bakery and the general store again. She'd stopped there earlier to ask questions about her family, but the employees only shrugged and explained haltingly in English that they didn't know. The real estate office was closed for lunch, unfortunately, but she worried that if she waited for them to reopen, she'd run into Leif. There was no way she'd let that happen. She knew that the ferry ran every day except Sunday; she reasoned that she could always visit the real estate office again tomorrow. Yes, she decided it could wait, and Mia had promised to help her. Ella's instincts told her she could count on Mia, who seemed kind, supportive, and honest.

She reached the ferry and hurried on board, watching over her shoulder for Leif. Tears pricked her eyes, which made her angry. She didn't need anyone. Her life was fine exactly how it was.

CHAPTER 21

Leif knocked on Ella's door and then rocked back and forth on his heels, bracing himself for whatever might happen. He'd tried to find her in Tvedestrand but bumped into his customer as he left the Seilloftet. He'd successfully begged off having lunch, but he had to pause to exchange the boat keys and paperwork. After that, Ella was nowhere to be seen.

Leif knew he shouldn't have agreed to buy Charlotte that drink. How would he ever explain the kiss to Ella? He loosened his grip on the red tulips clutched in his hand. Their stems were beaten up, like his heart would be if he lost his shot with Ella.

He knocked again. No answer. As he turned to leave, he saw her emerging from the evergreens that edged the cottage property. She had yellow flowers in her hair. His Sunna.

"Hey," Ella said as she paused near the front door, and then fixed her gaze on the bees flitting around the golden aster. She wouldn't meet his eye. He wondered if she was hurt or angry or both.

"Hey there." He grinned at her. Wiping his sweaty palms on his jeans, he held out the tulips. "For you."

"Thanks." Ella accepted the drooping flowers.

"My apologies, I was holding them too tightly." Leif held up his rucksack. "I brought dinner."

"Something came up. I can't tonight." Ella turned toward the door and slid the key in the lock.

"I have kindling on my boat."

She smiled, but barely, and she didn't invite him in. His gut rolled, like he'd eaten something rotten. He was desperate to explain himself, but he found it hard to talk about his feelings, and he feared making things worse. It tortured him not to say what was on his mind. Sweat prickled his scalp. He liked Ella—really liked her—and knew he needed to say something big, something worthy, to get her to understand how sorry he truly was.

"I feel like I have bread stuck in my throat," he rasped.

"That must feel very uncomfortable."

She wasn't going to make it easy on him either. His chest deflated and his ears burned with shame. What could he say to make Ella believe that there was nothing between him and Charlotte? The silence dragged on, until he couldn't stand it any longer.

"I'm truly sorry, Ella. I know I hurt your feelings, and I apologize. Please believe me when I say that Charlotte is just a friend of mine. Sometimes we hook up, that's all."

"That's none of my business."

"I think it is."

"Why, because we had one date?"

"I just, well"—he cleared his dry throat—"I thought you should know."

"OK, so now I know. There's really no reason to make a big deal out of it."

Leif almost breathed a sigh of relief, but her voice didn't sound as reasonable as her words. He reached for her hands, and she let him hold them.

"I didn't expect to run into her," he said. "And I didn't expect her to kiss me. I feel horrible about it."

She nodded at him.

"Really," he added, after seeing the doubt in her expression. "I've been looking forward to seeing you all day, and to spending time with you tonight. I love being with you."

"Same here" was all she offered as she let go of his hands. He reached for his pendant, the one that matched hers, and held it up.

"Fate . . . if one believes in that sort of thing," he said.

"Yeah. Fate," she said. "Like when stars collide."

They stared at each other, making room again for the chemistry that was still smoldering underneath the more difficult emotions. Leif tilted his head down and looked at her through his shaggy bangs. "I want to laugh with you tonight. That laugh of yours is my favorite sound in the world." He put on what he hoped was his cutest smile ever.

"OK." She relented with a shake of her head. "Come on in."

• • •

Ella had surprised herself by letting Leif off so easily. But she respected his honesty—in fact, she liked him more because of it. Spoiling tonight because she felt threatened by Charlotte was ridiculous she told herself. Nobody owed anybody anything. She was leaving soon, and right now she simply wanted to enjoy Leif's company.

They set the table together, with cloth napkins and Mormor's elegant Danish blue-and-white china that Ella had discovered in the antique sea chest beneath the cellar steps. They hadn't yet reestablished their earlier closeness, though they exchanged pleasantries while they worked. Mostly, Leif complimented the cottage décor that Hilda had chosen long ago.

"Oh, thanks." Ella handed him a glass of red wine. "But I've decided to get rid of almost all of it. Mia kindly offered to sell anything of value and give away the rest. If there's any money left after covering my phone bill, she'll wire it to me."

Leif looked shocked. "You're not keeping your family heirlooms?"

Ella shrugged. "It's too expensive to ship. I'll take my mom's sewing machine though. It's special to me—even though I'm not sure how I'll possibly fit it in my tiny studio apartment." She laughed.

"Yeah, I guess. That's tough. But, um . . . would you let me buy your grandma's clock? That little painting of the sea, just above the face . . . it'll remind me of you." He smiled.

"I'll give you the clock," Ella murmured. He shook his head, as if getting such an extravagant gift made him uneasy. "I won't take no for an answer," she insisted, touching his arm to help make her point. "Please. It's the least I can do, after all your help. You found me at Gåsholmen—I might've frozen to death or died from being scared out of my wits, or both."

"I was glad to help," he said, smoothing her hair lovingly. "I adore spending time with you. I hope you know that."

Leif cupped her chin gently and kissed the sensitive spot on her neck just below her ear. She felt suddenly breathless with desire and fear. What would happen if she let herself fall? But she knew that she'd already fallen for Leif . . . his intelligence and inner beauty, his shaggy hair and his good looks, his steadiness, and his passion for his designs. The artist in her appreciated that. But she also knew that they were fundamentally different. Change seemed to make him deeply uncomfortable, whereas she welcomed it with open arms. They quite literally came from two different worlds—his life revolved around boats and the small, secluded islands of Lyngør. And for her, well, it wasn't an environment in which she thrived. She wasn't sure how a relationship with Leif could possibly work, though it was difficult to think logically right at that moment, while Leif's touch was turning her brain to Jell-O. In fact, she didn't want to think about any of it at all. Ella remembered her art teacher's advice: "Trust the universe. Have faith that everything will work out as it should in the end."

He yanked his shirt over his head, and it surprised her . . . was he stripping? That would be too forward of him because of the whole Charlotte thingy, Ella told herself. She watched his abs ripple as he tossed his shirt on the sofa. He grinned in a way that suggested he could read her thoughts and that he absolutely approved of them. She wanted him and he knew it. Her face grew hotter.

"You're so captivating and beautiful—and you're hot as hell." He grinned again. She admired his extremely fit body; she was so turned on that she was starting to feel uncomfortable. He unbuckled his jeans to reveal navy swim trunks. Her eyes widened in surprise.

"I always take a quick swim in the sea before dinner." He gestured toward the window, which was lit with a yellow glow from the early-evening sun. Outside, gulls chased each other over Lyngør's waters. A sailboat made its way to one of the tiny islands.

"You swim in that cold water every night, even in winter?" Ella gasped in horror. If he wasn't so cute, she'd think he was crazy.

CHAPTER 22

At ten o'clock the next morning, Ella set off to search for stories about her family. The briny breeze ruffled the birch leaves as she rounded a curve in the path that cut through granite hills on Lyngørsida Island. She knocked on several doors, but no one appeared to be home, and the village still seemed empty. She was disappointed, but all was not lost, she told herself. Leif had suggested that she talk to the sailmakers who'd just returned from a two-week vacation and would likely be home today.

The night before, Leif had consoled her, saying, "No worries if they can't tell you anything. I'll take you around Lyngør so you can meet some more people before you leave." His kindness and support touched her. They'd talked for hours over dinner, joking and laughing as they shared stories about their lives. They'd shared long, deep kisses too. Even though she was still trying to put his kiss with Charlotte completely behind her, and even though it had put her off from sleeping with him last night, Ella had to admit she loved being with Leif. By the time he left, she was so frustrated that she ate the rest of the cake she bought for them and then did guilt yoga until she regained some perspective.

Despite her determination to not get attached, she couldn't see the harm in getting to know him better while she was in Norway. She wouldn't let herself get carried away though, she told herself. He was just a fling. A sexy, sensitive, thoughtful fling. Nothing more.

Ella walked past shuttered clapboard cottages toward the sailmakers' residence and heard music coming from some-where on their property; it was A-ha's "Take On Me" soaring from the backyard. Three flaxen-haired kids, all under the age of ten, crouched on the dock at the water's edge, scooping small crabs with minnow nets and dumping them into plas-tic pails. Next to them, two rugged men with thick, tousled hair and dark tans sipped port wine at a two-seater table. They looked like father and son.

"Hi there!" Ella called out. Everyone swiveled to greet her, and five pairs of ocean-blue eyes gave her the once-over. She flashed her friendliest smile, made sure to mention Leif's name, and explained why she'd wandered onto their property without an invitation.

The older man, Magnus, who looked about Mormor's age, shook his head. "No, I was in the navy and deployed on a ship for most of my career. I returned home four years ago to take over the family sailmaking business from my father, who's un-well. I'm afraid I can't help you."

His son, Roar, offered that he was too young to remember anything from that time. Ella politely asked if she could speak to Magnus's father, to ask what he remembered.

Both men burst out laughing. They gestured at an ancient-looking man with sunken cheeks and tufts of silver hair, doz-ing in a lounge chair on the far side of the yard.

"Dementia," Roar said sadly. He gave Ella a one-shouldered shrug and frowned. "Sometimes he remembers. But much of the time he hallucinates, or remembers wrong, or both. Last night he swore he saw forest fairies in his bedroom."

Ella persisted as politely as she knew how, and Magnus snorted and wished her luck. Roar shouted at his grandfather in Norwegian, "Wake up, Truls, you sleepy old fart!"

His grandfather's lids fluttered open, and he blinked in the harsh sunlight. His eyes widened at Ella, like he'd seen a ghost. "Where've you been hiding all these years?" he sputtered in confusion.

"What do you mean?" Ella said.

"Stop playing games, young lady!" Truls shouted at Ella. "Why did you have to disappear?"

Truls started to cry and began rambling about the forest fairies who played tricks on him in the night. He pointed at Ella. "You, be careful, or you'll disappear just like her!"

The smallest of the children skipped over to him and tipped a pail full of water and crabs onto Truls's lap. The man leaped from his chair, bellowing angrily and pumping his fists to the heavens.

"Deceit! Just like that fairy-tale witch, Huldra! She'll lead you to temptation and danger, that one will . . . before you know it, she'll have disappeared, never to return." He began to wail, loudly enough that it echoed off the water.

Roar ran to his grandfather and silenced him with several gruff words before leading him indoors. Magnus suggested that Ella ask someone else if she had any other questions. He wished her a good day, and Ella understood that she was dismissed.

• • •

Back at Ringpynten, Ella polished Hilda's urn on the window-sill and watched the light sparkle on it in swirls of electric pink.

"Mormor. That good-looking boatbuilder I told you about is taking me to a bonfire tonight. Someone there might know where you put Sara to rest. Maybe I'll put you there too."

Ella once again felt a pang of sorrow. She had always keenly felt the absence of her mother, but over the last week in Lyngør, her grief had mushroomed for both Sara and Mormor. Why did they both have to leave her alone . . . completely and truly alone?

Ella would have given anything for the chance to patch things up and tell Mormor how much she loved her. By coming here, Ella was able to realize how heart-wrenching Sara's absence must have been for Mormor. Ella felt closer to them here; was that why Mormor had fled her homeland, and why she had never been able to tell Ella the truth about Sara and all the other secrets? The sewing machine and sketchbook had shown Ella how much she'd taken after Sara. Ella realized that she probably reminded Mormor of all that she'd lost. Ella now wondered if her grandma's criticism and meanness were born out of fear of losing Ella too. Mormor ultimately wanted what she thought was best for Ella, but perhaps she couldn't show it any other way besides discouraging Ella's creativity and stoking her fears about water.

Ella sat down and moved the rocking chair closer to the table covered with fashion sketches, colored pencils, and her notebook. In contrast to these weighty thoughts, she scribbled words for a song that had been swirling around her head: *Blue Boy, blue summer dreams, desire, kiss me.* She'd incorporate it somehow with a future line that she'd already named the Leif Collection.

Then her thoughts wandered to a birthday gift for Inger— she had already given her the cuckoo bird sketch, but she should probably bring a proper gift to her party. Flipping through the nautical book Leif had given her, she stopped on a page with a diagram of a slipknot she'd tied plenty of times when she made rope jewelry, and it came to her: A boating knot bracelet was the perfect present for Inger. She could tie the knot in her sleep and wondered now why it hadn't occurred to her to use that same knot to secure the dinghy. It would be a funny gift if nothing else, especially since Inger had snickered at Ella for using a bunny knot when they'd first met. Ella gathered twine, tape, scissors, an empty cola bottle, and the beads that she'd bought in Tvedestrand.

She arranged the amethyst beads on the coffee table; the sparkly purple stones would make a stylish bracelet. Plus, some people believed that amethyst warded off negative energy, and Inger had plenty of that. Cutting a four-foot piece of twine, Ella taped one end to the bottle, winding the other in an X shape. The bracelet turned out prettier than she'd imagined, and she knew that from then on, she would tie great boating knots, as secure as any local. Perhaps she'd design a collection of jewelry using an array of colorful crystals, and give them names like Castaway or Knot Again.

· · ·

"So, this is Speken Island?" Ella smiled at Leif. Her hand rested on his thigh as he worked the tiller, squeezing *Skadi*'s hull into a spot between two wooden skiffs. "It looks peaceful, like a smaller version of Gåsholmen. There's more of that heather—I think I've fallen in love with those soft-purple blooms."

"Just like Gåsholmen, no one lives here. We can party all night and not disturb anyone." Leif jammed the anchor into a crack in the quartz-speckled bank. Ella counted seven boats at the shore. A dozen partygoers walked across the burnished rocks and around wind-twisted pines, sea grasses, and colorful wildflowers.

"Where's the bonfire?"

"It's on the other side. About a ten-minute walk. Inger will light it closer to sundown. I wouldn't risk tying up my boat near the bonfire, though—not even tonight, with decent weather. The reefs, swells, and rocks chew up boats like a woodchipper." He settled the strap of his duffel bag on his shoulder before grabbing the cooler. "We'll cook over campfires. I think the sailmaker's son, Roar, might be here tonight. Did you happen to see them today?"

"Yes, but they didn't know anything. Not really. Although the grandfather looked at me like he'd seen a ghost and mentioned that someone had disappeared. But they said he has dementia, and he was clearly confused."

"Well, hopefully you'll hear stories about Sara tonight."

"I hope so," Ella smiled. She reached for his hand, and he helped her from the boat and onto the rocks. She walked with him across the island, toward the as-yet-unlit bonfire where Inger's guests had gathered. Small tents were grouped together, and an English springer spaniel chased his tail. Ella stopped to scratch the dog's ears, allowing it to give her wet kisses on her chin. She laughed and kept scratching.

"I'm going to adopt a dog and take it to work with me when I get back home. Have you ever had a dog?" she asked Leif.

"I love dogs. But I'm always on the go, and it'd be hard to fit one into my schedule."

A loud "Hallooo!" drew their attention to a blazing campfire where a man waved a bottle over his head. "Get over here, Leif, you big dolt! Have a drink."

Leif raised his hand in greeting. "Be right there."

The man smiled, perfect teeth flashing against olive skin, and gave Leif a thumbs-up.

"That's Axel, Inger's boyfriend. He's a piece of work." He rested his hand on Ella's back. "Well, ready to meet everyone?"

"As ready as I'll ever be." She laughed and walked with him to the heart of the gathering. Wine, beer, and guitars lay on blankets spread out on the moss-matted rocks. They were a tall, fit-looking group as they gathered around small cooking fires. Two stunning big-boned women with long, blond braids skewered fish using green sapling branches. A muscular, bearded man arranged stones in a circle to build another campfire. Ella itched to take photographs of these modern-day Vikings, but thought she'd better wait. Right now, it felt like they were all staring at her and Leif.

A dozen corked champagne bottles and stacks of plastic cups sat on a rock shelf, along with Inger's birthday cake. Approaching Inger, Ella greeted her cheerfully and handed her the lemons and candles.

"You found pink candles—fantastic. Thanks!" Inger laid the candles and lemons next to the cake. "Lemons are for the seafood," she added.

"Glad I could help. Happy birthday." She gave Inger the batik jewelry bag that contained her gift. Besides making the bracelet inside, she'd made the bag too, out of the skirt that had been ripped when she was stranded at Gåsholmen.

Inger turned the bag over in her hands, examining it thoroughly.

Here we go again, Ella thought, and she forced a grin. "It's just a little something I made. Hope you like it."

"It's colorful, like you." Inger's gaze traveled over Ella's cowboy hat, flowy dress, and fuchsia tights. "Colorful," she repeated with a hint of amusement in her eyes. She placed the bag on the rock shelf.

"Open it," Leif said. "Let's see what it is."

Inger slid the present from the bag. "Jewelry?"

"A boating knot bracelet," Ella said. "The knot is used for tying lines, reef points—"

"Yeah, I know what a boating knot is." She held up the bracelet, and her mood defrosted as she studied it. "Clever."

Leif cut in. "You used the book I gave you, didn't you?" His dimples deepened.

"I've used that knot before to make jewelry back in Boulder. But I didn't realize it was also a boating knot until I studied your book. It's been very helpful," she said, and smiled up at him.

"Time to start grilling," Inger announced. She returned

the bracelet to the jewelry pouch and tossed it on the rock shelf. This wasn't lost on Ella, but if Inger couldn't see the humor behind it, that was her problem. With any luck, the amethyst beads woven into the bracelet would work their magic. Negative energy be gone.

Axel joined them, kissed Inger on the cheek, and then extended his hand to Ella. "Axel," he said.

"Ella. Nice to meet you." She shook his hand. Tall with thick lashes, he was so handsome he was pretty.

Axel tapped Leif on the arm and pointed at a boat in the water just offshore. Erik was rowing while another man was clearly bailing water. "Erik could use our help. He decided to donate his old wooden rowboat to future bonfires!" The boat was headed toward the island bank, with its razor-sharp barnacles and rushing waves.

"Oh wow," said Leif.

"What made him think he could make it to shore with cracks in the hull? Well, I guess that's what we're here for," Axel said. He and Leif laughed until Axel wiped tears from his eyes.

"Won't they get hurt?" Ella couldn't watch and sought comfort in the beauty of the low-flying seabirds.

"Nope," Axel said. "Not those two salty old codgers." He swigged from his flask. "Cognac," he said to Ella and offered it to her. She took a swallow.

"Erik should buy a fiberglass boat," Inger said. "It's more practical."

"Are you kidding? Plastic boats have no souls," Leif growled. He whispered to Ella, "We won't be long. We need to save those lunkheads from themselves."

"I'm fine," she smiled at Leif. But the thought of him hauling a boat from that rough sea and across those slick, barnacle-covered rocks had her stomach in knots. She shivered.

"I brought beer, wine, and sodas. They're in my bag. Help yourself," Leif said and kissed her cheek.

"I will." She was itching to pass around the photograph and ask if anyone knew anything about her family. Dozens of partygoers hung out around several small campfires. Near them, a man basted liquid onto a whole lamb he was roasting on a spit. He had golden-brown hair that reminded her of Charlotte's.

Ella scanned the crowd for her and realized that running into Charlotte would only be awkward if she let it be.

"Want to grab a beer?" Mia approached with a smile.

"I would love that! Hey, have you heard any more from your cousin?"

"Yup. Now it seems that four families are interested in your property, so she's going to organize an open house. She'll get back to us on the date."

"That's great news." Ella grinned, and for an instant she felt happy. "I want to stay long enough to make sure the cottage sale goes smoothly, but I do have to get back home . . . I mean, I hate to ask, but are you sure she can get it all done . . . you know, quickly?" She laughed shakily as the stress of all her commitments squeezed her lungs.

"Everything will work out," Mia patted Ella's arm gently. "My cousin is extremely motivated. She needs the commission to send her genius daughter to a private school in Switzerland, so believe me, she'll get your cottage sold ASAP. You probably won't even need to be here—she can fax you the paperwork to sign, and I could oversee the cottage until it sells. You can call me anytime to see how it's going."

"Amazing, that would be a lifesaver! Let me think about it and maybe talk to your cousin myself, just to make sure. Thank you, Mia!"

Mia plucked two beers from Leif's cooler and handed one to Ella. She picked up the jewelry bag that Ella had given to Inger and touched the little bird stitched on it. "It's so cute, and I love batik."

"Open it—it's a birthday present I made for Inger but . . . I'm not sure she liked it."

Mia pulled out the bracelet. "You made this? It's beautiful. I love it. I think I'll borrow it, maybe for keeps."

"Go for it," Ella said, and they laughed. At least someone would appreciate it.

Mia wrapped the bracelet around her wrist. "Don't let Inger bother you. She feeds on drama and loves to stir the pot. But we cut her slack."

"Why is that?"

"Well, Inger can be tough, but she's soft on the inside—and loyal as hell." Mia sipped her beer. "In school I was bullied, but Inger stood up for me and made one thing clear: If anyone messed with me, they had to deal with her. And no one wanted to deal with Inger."

Ella wasn't surprised by that last statement, but imagining Inger standing up for anyone but herself was a new thought.

Mia laughed and continued. "Inger, Leif, Erik, and I would do anything for each other. We're family. Except for Inger and Erik, none of us are related by blood, but that doesn't matter. We all know we can count on and trust each other, no matter what. And we love each other like crazy."

"I like that," Ella said. She wouldn't mind having a family of her own making. She ran through a list of whom she might choose . . . Petal? She was the closest thing Ella had to a sister, but she already had seven siblings and a full calendar. Ella had some close acquaintances among the vendors at the weekend market, like some of the potters and the beekeeper, but these people were a long way from being family.

Ella envied Mia, Leif, and the others who had deep roots in Lyngør. Even though she'd lived in Boulder since she was an infant, she still felt lonely and rootless, and was counting on the clothing shop to anchor her. She scratched at the wet label on her beer, and peeled it off the bottle. She was surprised at how much she adored her cottage that smelled of mittens warming over a fire, and the thought occurred to her: Could she possibly stay? But staying here would mean abandoning her dream store. And would she fit in any better here than she did in Boulder? Where could she sell her art? She didn't have the answers—she probably hadn't even thought of all the questions—but she had a deep sense that she didn't know where home was, or where she belonged.

These thoughts were interrupted when Inger marched past, barking orders and directing Leif, Axel, and two women as they hauled Erik's boat around a kettle of boiled crayfish. They dumped the boat on the ground near the bonfire, which was being built from wooden crates, driftwood, a banged-up dresser, and a three-legged desk. She imagined the orange-red flames and sparks against the starry sky. She would make sure to have her picture taken with Leif as the bonfire blazed behind them.

Ella surveyed the crowd, which was made up entirely of people who looked to be in their early twenties to mid-thirties. Her heart sank.

"Where's Erik?" she asked Mia.

"He's probably taking a breather after getting the boat to shore."

"And his friend?"

"Oskar. Oh, he's fine too, but why?"

"I want to show them the photograph to see if they know my mom."

"Which picture?" Mia asked.

"You've already seen it, at your shop. Remember?"

"Mind if I take another look?"

"Sure, yeah, look all you like." She slid the photograph from her notebook.

Mia's eyes skimmed over each side of the picture, and she shook her head. "Nope, nothing rings a bell."

"Are you sure?" Ella pointed at the photograph. "See the bluebells, puffins, and oyster catchers embroidered around the blanket trim? That's not something you see every day."

"Yeah, but this was taken in 1962. I wasn't born yet." Mia handed back the photo.

"I know. But I'm still hoping for answers."

Mia promised to let Ella know if she learned anything. In the meantime, she offered to introduce Ella to others who might be able to help. Mia led her toward the bonfire that was still unlit. They stopped in front of a man and a woman in their late twenties who held hands as they sat on a couch with tattered armrests. Mia introduced them as the hotel owner's son, Harald, and the baker's daughter, Frida, and they exchanged the usual pleasantries.

Leif walked up and slid his arm around Ella's shoulder. "There you are," he said, pulling her close. "Join me while I cook?"

"I'd love to, but first I'd like to show them the photograph." Ella slipped her arm around his waist as Mia excused herself.

Ella handed the picture to Harald. "I found this in my cottage. Do you happen to know anything about this picture, or the history of Ringpynten?"

As he studied the image, he scrunched his bushy blond eyebrows together. "I've only known that place as a rental. Afraid I can't help you."

"Flip over the photo," Leif suggested.

Harald looked at the sketch on the back and read aloud the accompanying words. For Sara: Gåsholmen with my sweetheart. July 1962. He shrugged. "Sorry, I have no clue. My parents and I lived in Stockholm until the eighties, when my dad bought the hotel. The staff are all our age, so I doubt you'd have luck there. Plus it's dead quiet until Fellesferie. Have you spoken to the older adults?"

"I guess a few, but none of them knew much. Or maybe

they didn't want to talk about it. Who else might know?" Ella asked.

"Beats me," the baker's daughter said, as her gaze roamed the crowd. "This group isn't from that generation; no one here is old enough to remember anything from 1962. Maybe you could talk to the elderly in town. They love to reminisce and always have a good tale or two."

Her boyfriend chimed in. "Oh yeah, they still talk about that local girl who fell though the ice about twenty years ago—and the other one, who drowned in a kiddie pool."

Inger, out of breath, asked no one in particular, "Has anyone seen Erik? He promised to bring gasoline for the bonfire."

"Erik and Oskar left," Harald said. Ella looked at Leif, who shrugged.

"Left? How could they?" Inger fumed.

"Don't worry," said Frida. "I have extra gasoline on my boat."

Inger and the couple set off to grab the gasoline. Leif asked Ella, "Are you OK? You looked disappointed."

"Yeah . . . it's just . . . well, it's a bummer that I can't ask Erik questions tonight. Wherever I look, I keep meeting dead ends. I won't let it keep me from having a good time with you tonight, though."

"Good. Because spending time with you is always a treat." He kissed the top of her head. "And don't worry about Erik. It's too noisy and crazy here to talk anyway. Better if we meet him at the boatyard. Want to keep me company while I fire up the grill?"

"OK, I guess that works." Ella had arrived eight days ago and could probably stay a little longer. She was relying on Petal for so many things already, but she was sure that she wouldn't mind meeting the electrician or finishing some of the embroidery work on the line of blouses. Ella felt that it was important to stick around long enough to put Mormor to rest and to keep searching for information about Sara.

Ella turned her attention to taking photographs. She framed Leif and his broad shoulders balancing the grill grate over the stones encircling his campfire. "What's for dinner?" she asked.

He grabbed a foil packet from the cooler. Uncrimping the foil, he held out the packet for her to see. She cringed inwardly at the fish but put on a smile.

"Looks delicious. Did you happen to bring any of your tasty beef stew?"

"I know you *think* you don't like cod, but you haven't tasted mine. I brought hot dogs and salad too."

As she tucked her camera in its case, a familiar-looking woman with long, straight caramel-colored hair sidled up to Leif. She gave him a warm hug and planted kisses on his cheek, leaving traces of peach lipstick.

The Viking supermodel ex-girlfriend had returned. Charlotte. Tight skinny jeans showed off her shapely, mile-long legs. The top buttons on her blouse were undone and flaunted her cleavage, which was cradled in a frilly push-up bra. Ella touched the scarf wrapped around her neck and the long, flowy dress that hid her curves. She and Charlotte were nothing alike. She wondered what Leif saw in her if Charlotte was his type.

Charlotte gave Leif a dazzling smile and kissed his cheek again. "Cook some for me, will you? I didn't bring any food; I've been too busy at work. What a day! But I'm here now, so all's good."

Leif rubbed his jaw in an embarrassed way. The color of his ears matched Ella's fuchsia tights.

"Ella Nilsen," Ella said firmly, and offered her hand to Charlotte.

"Charlotte." She shook Ella's hand. "I know who you are. You inherited Ringpynten." She searched her bag for a moment, then came up with her business card. "I'm a real estate agent. If you decide to sell the place, I'm the woman for the job."

Ella accepted the card while giving Charlotte a level stare. "Thank you, but I'm already working with someone."

"Well, I'm the best agent on the entire southern coast." With that dazzling smile still plastered in place, Charlotte patted Leif's arm. "Tell her."

"Ha! Keep me out of this." He snatched a stick from the ground and poked it beneath the campfire grate, his broad back to the two women.

"Come on, don't be silly," Charlotte prodded. Leif stood to face her.

"Ella is perfectly capable of making up her own mind. Let's just leave it at that," he said bluntly.

"Fair enough," Charlotte said with a nod. "Just know that I'll earn you top dollar."

"Oh? What would you put as the asking price?" Ella said.

"Well, I'd need to run the figures. But I can tell you this much: Your cottage is considered luxury real estate. I'm guessing it'll sell for megabucks."

"That would be life-changing," Ella said. It was almost too good to be true, but Mia had also suggested that Ringpynten was worth a lot of money. With that, Ella could pay off the mortgage on Little Bird and hire a couple of seamstresses and store associates. Then all she'd need was customers.

"Yep, it's a super attractive property," Charlotte said with a laugh. "In my opinion, Lyngør is Norway's French riviera. Both are stunning—and come with status. I specialize in high-end real estate. In my experience, there are plenty of people who enjoy showing the world that they've made it and can afford such luxuries."

Ella nodded as though she understood, but Mormor certainly didn't seem to fall into that category. Her grandma barely made ends meet in Boulder, and for a while she and Ella survived on food stamps. Mormor had hesitated when Ella needed braces, for heaven's sake—that didn't sound like someone who had "made it" or was accustomed to luxury. Ella wondered again why Mormor hadn't sold Ringpynten to give them a more comfortable life in Colorado.

"Listen, call me," Charlotte persisted. "We'll set up an appointment to see the property and go over the paperwork."

"Thanks, but like I said, I already have an agent."

"Well, if a contract hasn't been signed then we can fix it! I better find Inger, to wish her a happy birthday."

Turning to Leif as she prepared to walk away, she rubbed his bicep and then pulled a fifth of vodka and an orange juice carton from her designer bag. "Don't forget my dinner. I'm starving. Oh, and I brought this for us—drink up."

He cleared his throat and scratched at the back of his head. It didn't take a genius to see that he was uncomfortable. "I can't. Charlotte, I meant to tell you."

"What?" Charlotte said.

Leif looked pointedly at the two wine glasses and the uncorked bottle of merlot that he'd set on the flat rock near his cooler. The raspberry stain on one of the glasses matched Ella's lips. Charlotte's smile faded. She pinched her nose.

"Uff, I've been way out of the loop, haven't I?" She set the orange juice on the ground, cracked the vodka seal, and took a pull from the bottle. "Leif. You should have told me at the bistro the other day." She sounded confused and looked like she'd been slapped hard in the face.

"We'll talk later, OK?" he said with a dismissive edge.

"Whatever," Charlotte said before stalking off with the vodka.

"You didn't have to be rude to her," Ella chided. "And I wish you would've let me know that we'd both be here tonight." Ella valued transparency. Plus, she felt sorry for Charlotte, whose eyes were two deep pools of hurt. It was obvious that she didn't know about Ella and thought she'd be with Leif tonight. Ella wondered how she managed to feel both sympathetic to and threatened by Charlotte, at the same time.

"Yes, I should've. But why do you care about Charlotte? You're leaving soon. And it's not like you'll come back." He grabbed the tray from the cooler with such force that the foil packets fell to the ground. "Dammit. Now dinner's ruined."

"It's hardly ruined. Neither is your friendship with Charlotte. It'll be fine."

Charlotte would likely be there for Leif long after Ella returned to her life in Boulder. Even so, they could spend time together now; it'd be a shame not to enjoy it to its fullest. Picking up the foil packets, she brushed off the dirt and put them back on the tray. She did her best to sound positive. "Good as new." He looked at her with appreciation. Her belly went warm as he held her gaze.

After Leif finished grilling, they filled their plates and sat side by side on his quilt. They shared stories about their school days, marveling at how different they were. Leif drove his boat to school, played bandy, which he described as a ball sport on ice, and learned to knit in third grade because it was mandatory. Ella rode the bus to school, ditched PE whenever she could, and sketched clothes in a classroom with her art teacher, who insisted that Ella remain true to herself even if it meant staying outside the box.

"My art teacher encouraged my passion for art. She taught me that art tells a story and records history. It can help us process our emotions and even heal us to some extent. Plus it allows us to see the world differently and makes us more observant. It inspires."

"Yeah, art definitely helped me deal with the pain and grief over my father's death. It's like it kept me focused on the present, you know . . . making things gave me something to do and some sense of control. Plus, carving some of my father's favorite creatures from Viking mythology, like eagles and wolves, helps me preserve his legacy. My surname, Arnesen, comes from the old Norse word *arn*, which means 'eagle,'" Leif said quietly and kissed her on the mouth. "Maybe the bonfire will inspire designs for *you*. They'll light it soon." He motioned toward Axel, who was throwing gasoline on the tower of wood.

"It's going to be fantastic! I want to grab my camera and take some pictures. Be right back." She kissed his cheek and stood to leave. She saw Mia and invited her to join them for Leif's homemade butter cookies.

"I'd love to, but I can't right now," Mia answered. "Leif, I need your help hooking up the speakers to the stereo."

As Ella unzipped Leif's bag to grab her camera, Charlotte tapped her on the shoulder, saying coldly, "I'm surprised you're here." Ella noticed the bottle of vodka she held was one-third empty.

Ella flicked her brow. "Surprised?"

"Yes. Inger doesn't care for tourists."

Ella didn't consider herself a tourist, exactly, since her family had owned the island home for decades—although honestly, she didn't know *what* she was, and she thought it best not to provoke Charlotte, who had an angry glint in her eye.

"Well, it was nice of her to invite me. I'm having a great time," Ella said cheerfully, trying to keep things light.

"You follow Leif around like a puppy dog," Charlotte observed, and took another swig from the bottle.

What a jerk, Ella thought. Aloud, she said with a smile, "Leif's been a good friend, introducing me to locals. Everyone here is so kind." She gestured at Charlotte's fitted blazer and low-cut blouse. "I like your outfit."

Charlotte sneered. "What do you know about style, hippie cowgirl?"

Ella could have retorted that she was a designer, but she let it go. "Leif set aside some food for you."

"I suppose you know that Inger only invited you here for laughs."

Ella gritted her teeth and refused to take the bait. She closed the bag, her camera forgotten as she tried to come up with something nice and fairly neutral to say. "Well, I'm happy to be here."

"Sure, just like you're happy she nabbed your dinghy."

Ella must have heard wrong. "What do you mean?"

"When you were at Gåsholmen. She untied your dumb knot and set the dinghy free. Everyone knows, even Leif. How do you think he knew where to find you?"

Hurt avalanched through Ella; her stomach bottomed out while Charlotte smirked.

"Excuse me," Ella said, and she rushed to the evergreens to find a quiet place to calm down. Her eyes burned as she sank onto a boulder and chucked a pine cone hard against an evergreen tree. She'd thought she could trust Leif. She remembered Mia saying that Leif's loyalty lay with Inger and his chosen family. How stupid of her to think they'd ever welcome an outsider like her.

If Mormor were there, she would shake her head and say, *You're a misfit and a dreamer.* Ella put her head in her hands. She heard a cheer go through the crowd. Bonfire smoke blended with the smell of rubber and gasoline in the brisk evening air.

Ella eventually gathered herself and emerged from the trees to see dozens of people around the bonfire. Those flames should have seemed romantic, but Ella only saw furious red sparks darting toward the sky.

She walked briskly, and Axel fell in step beside her and flashed his pearly teeth. He held a jug filled with pink liquid in one hand and a stack of plastic cups in the other.

"Whoa, where you headed in such a hurry?" he said. "Try one of my drinks first!"

"No thanks." She was already buzzed, and mixing anger with more booze was a terrible idea.

"Ah, come on," he said, pouting. "You can't leave Norway without trying a Combustible Ibsen." As he poured the innocent-looking liquid into a cup, he asked, "Did you know you look like Julia Roberts?"

Ella said sardonically, "That's a first. Listen, what I really want is to hear stories about Ringpynten. Do you happen to know anything about the cottage or my family?"

"Afraid not. I moved here from Bergen ten years ago to work for Erik. I miss Bergen. It has the best nightlife in all of Norway." He pushed out his bottom lip and made another pouty face.

She sighed deeply in frustration. "No one seems to know anything—not the old sailmaker, nobody in Tvedestrand . . . I should've come to Norway over Fellesferie to meet all the summer residents who might've known my mom and Mormor, but I hadn't even heard of it until I met Mia!"

Leif and Mia joined them, and Leif kissed Ella's forehead. "There you are. Glad to see you're having a good time."

Finding out that he'd covered for Inger felt far worse than watching him kiss Charlotte, and Ella bit back the temptation to call him a jerk and traitor.

Mia pointed at the jug of Combustible Ibsen. "Beware!" she said with a snort. "That's an Axel special: aquavit, Campari, and a dash of lemon bitters."

Leif whispered to Ella, "Axel loves his aquavit, but it's potent enough to burn barnacles off a boat. Be careful with it."

Careful? She wasn't a child! She reached for the cup and took a big swallow that made her eyes water. She smiled and held back a cough.

"When I get home, I'm going to put the Combustible Ibsen on the bar menu at work. But I'm changing the name to the Axel Special."

Axel chuckled. "You do that, Hippie Chick." He held up the jug to Mia and Leif. "Like some?"

"No thanks," they said in unison.

"Meet us in ten and we'll toast Inger," Axel said. He gestured toward Mia in a way that suggested they were going to rally the crowd. Leif hooked his arm around Ella and she stiffened.

"Everything all right? You didn't come back," he said.

"I ran into Charlotte. She and I had an interesting talk."

"Oh?"

"About Inger." *And you too,* she almost said, but clenched her jaw instead.

"Are you OK?" His expression suggested he had no idea what she was trying to tell him.

No, she most definitely was not OK. In fact, she was furious at Leif for not telling her about the dinghy. But no way would she give Inger or Charlotte the satisfaction of seeing her fighting with Leif, so she'd act as though everything was OK, even if she ground her teeth to nubs. Besides, she was going back to Boulder soon and had no plans of returning to Lyngør ever again.

Axel's deep voice rang out: "Happy Birthday to lovely Inger!" He was standing with her on a granite shelf. Holding the jug of Combustible Ibsen in one hand, he hooked his other arm around her waist.

"We should join them," Ella said with a stony expression.

She found a spot between two blond women and ignored Leif, silently fuming over his betrayal. She finished off her Combustible Ibsen while listening to Axel's short speech about Inger. She was the best girlfriend in the entire world, with the biggest heart. She was his rock and made him want to be a better man. His loving words made Inger weepy, and she dabbed at her eyes with a pink paper napkin.

"Give me a break," Ella grumbled.

Axel gave Inger a long kiss while the crowd cheered. When he finished kissing her, Axel whooped. Everyone sang "Happy

Birthday" and then Mia handed out neat slices of cake on pink paper plates. From the speakers, a Norwegian synth-pop band belted out an upbeat song, and everyone began dancing around the raging bonfire.

Harald grabbed Ella's hand and twirled her around. Forget Inger and Charlotte and Leif—she'd have a wonderful night without them. So she danced until she was out of breath. Locating the jug of Combustible Ibsen, she poured another cup and chugged it. Soon enough, an alcohol fog settled over her and the ground seemed to tilt. She sat down on a flat boulder, and that's when she saw them: Charlotte was dancing around Leif, thrusting her hips at him and sticking her boobs under his nose. He stood motionless, his expression unreadable. Ella wondered if he'd lied to her about Charlotte. She marched over to them and stopped in front of Leif.

"Hey, you." He smiled warmly at Ella, with a sparkle in his eye, as if everything between them was great. Didn't he get it? A cozy love song started playing and couples began dancing slowly around the bonfire. Charlotte snuggled up to Leif and tried to kiss him on the mouth, but he turned away. She pushed out her bottom lip, muttering something under her breath before flopping on his quilt.

The romantic song dragged on as Leif pulled Ella into a hug. "Would you like to dance?"

She shrugged him off. "No thank you." Leif's gaze searched her face.

Charlotte hiccuped and said to no one in particular, "Leif sleeps with me." She blew air kisses at Leif from the blanket.

Ella stiffened. She thought back to seeing them kiss in that bistro. Jealousy erupted, and booze loosened her tongue. Ella glared at him and whispered fiercely, "You're such a liar."

His head jerked back. "Liar?"

She raised her voice. "You knew all about it and didn't tell me." Partygoers started turning to watch them.

"I'm not following you and please—lower your voice." Leif frowned at her.

Lower her voice—how dare he!

"The dinghy!" Ella yelled even louder. "Inger untied it. *You* knew."

Leif blanched. "Who told you that?"

Charlotte cackled from Leif's quilt.

Leif scowled at her and demanded, "You told her?"

"Mmm-hmm." Charlotte rose clumsily from the quilt, swaying on her feet, and then lay her head against Leif's bicep. "Kiss me—"

"What? No!" he said, his face twisting into a grimace.

"Why not?" Charlotte whined and rested her hand on Leif's chest. "Why can't you look at me the way you look at her?" She gestured toward Ella before kissing Leif's cheek. "I love you. I've always loved you." She looked longingly at Leif and began to sob.

Ella recognized all of Charlotte's troublemaking, yet she also felt sympathy for her; she looked crushed by Leif's rejection.

Mia came to her side and said quietly, "Charlotte loves being a drama queen and she hates to lose at anything. Don't worry about it."

Then Mia linked her arms with Charlotte and said, "Poor baby. Let's get you some water," consoling her while guiding her away.

Leif rubbed the back of his neck and looked at Ella with big, sorry eyes.

She wasn't ready to forgive him. Tears blurred her vision as she stumbled away, and she tripped over Harald where he sat on the ground. "Watch out, you idiot!" she yelled at him.

"Sorry, buddy," Leif said to Harald as he rubbed his shin.

"You're really spreading around those apologies tonight, aren't you?" Ella continued to cry and stumble, almost falling onto the rocks, but Leif caught her.

"I got you, Sunna," he said as he righted her and kept hold of her wrist. She vomited.

"Come on, let's get you home." He draped his arm over her shoulders. Exhausted, she hung onto his arm and let him lead her to *Skadi*.

. . .

A half hour later, Leif tied up at Ringpynten while Ella snored on the starboard bench. Scooping her up, he stepped onto the dock. She hadn't spoken a word since they'd left the bonfire. At least she hadn't attempted to swim home; apparently, he was the lesser of the two evils. He felt terrible for not telling her about Inger loosening the knot on the dinghy. He wouldn't blame her if she never spoke to him again. Misery gnawed at him; he was getting attached to Ella, and she was leaving in a couple of weeks. He didn't want his heart to break. Truth was, it was too late. He was already far too attached, and his heart *was* splintering.

In the cottage, he laid her on her warm, soft bed and drew the blanket to her chin. He was bone-tired, and her bed looked inviting. She was stunning, even if she was conked out and snoring. As he smoothed her hair, longing tremored through him, and he realized with some disgust that he was lusting after this poor drunk woman. Best to head home.

CHAPTER 23

The following morning at seven, Leif awakened to a loud rap at his door.

"Give me a moment!" he shouted from his bed and threw off the blanket. He winced at the pain in his head, a reminder of the fifth of whiskey he'd put away last night after dropping off Ella at her cottage. He wondered if he'd ruined everything. The thought of losing her was harrowing.

Erik announced himself with his shrill whistle.

"Hold on!" Leif shouted. He wondered why Erik would call around this damn early, especially after a party. Maybe it had something to do with why Erik had left before the bonfire was even lit. What Leif needed right now was to swim in the cold seawater to clear his hangover enough for him to think straight. He grabbed his bathing trunks as he headed for the front door.

Leif stepped outside and shut the door behind him. His eyes squinted in the sunlight. "Why did you leave so early last night?"

Deep lines cut into Erik's face. He still looked like crap—maybe the worst Leif could remember seeing him. He chomped on his cigar as he said, "I came down with a migraine. Oskar gave me a lift home. And son, *you* look like crap. Must've been one helluva bonfire."

"Yeah, I guess it started out that way." Leif watched a jay rush across the lawn. The bird stopped, jabbing its beak into the earth. Leif wished he could jab something. "Ella found out that Inger set her dinghy adrift, and that I've known about it all along."

"Good. Maybe she'll go back to where she came from," Erik said roughly.

"Enough." Leif glowered at Erik. He was always grouchy when it came to tourists, but Leif thought he was being particularly mean toward Ella. "What do you want?"

"Ragnar's water pump broke. I need you to fix it. You can pick up the part on the way to his place."

"You're sending me? Why?" Ragnar was Erik's best friend and lived on Jomfruland, an island four hours west of Lyngør, which meant an overnight stay. This job would delay his plans to crawl to Ella's cottage and beg for forgiveness.

"I'm swamped with service orders." Erik lit his cigar. "Ragnar is worse off than the last time we visited him. His arthritis, you know—that bum leg is debilitating. Bring some food and cook him a hot meal, will you? Make sure he has plenty of firewood. In fact, here's a list of things you can do to help while you're there." He fished a crumpled piece of paper from his pocket and handed it over.

"Yeah. OK." Leif crammed the paper into his pocket. "I better pack and head out now. Just do me a favor, will you? Ask Axel to take over the repair work on Ella's boats. I won't have time."

"No problem. He'll do it; I'll count the job as payment for his poker debt. I appreciate you helping Ragnar. You enjoyed our last trip there; why don't you stay—take a minivacation." Erik, apparently pleased with the arrangement, was overselling it.

"Right." Leif looked at the boats anchored to buoys in the narrow channel, his gaze moving to Mia's store and the clapboard cottages that clung to the shore on Lyngørsida, where Ella lived. He decided he'd ask Ella to go with him to Ragnar's cottage. It was true that Ragnar might very well have information about her mother, but he was hoping that the suggestion alone would melt her a bit. If he played his cards right, hopefully four hours together on the way to Jomfruland would complete the thaw.

Leif packed a bag and then drove straight to Ringpynten, where he tied up at Ella's dock. His mouth was dry. He owed Ella an apology and the truth, even if she might not understand his reasoning. He raised his eyes to the cloudy sky. "Please let this go well."

As he reached her lawn, Ella rounded the corner of the cottage. She carried a plastic washing bin and wore frayed denim cutoffs layered over flower-pattern tights. He longed to trace kisses over her shapely legs. When she saw him, she halted and stared daggers at him.

"Hey, you. Got a second?" he said.

After what seemed like a lifetime of hesitation, Ella nodded. She set the bin on the low rock wall and pushed her bangles up and down her arm.

Right. Here it goes. "I owe you an apology," he began.

"You should've told me what Inger did."

"I . . . I think . . . I mean, maybe you're right, and I *am* sorry, but it's not that simple. I had just met you, and I figured—what good would it have done? It could've caused big trouble with friends I've known my whole life. They're my family." Leif raked his fingers through his hair. "And you're leaving. I thought it might be best for you to leave with fond memories of Norway instead of . . . you know, nasty ones."

Her face clouded over, and he knew he hadn't convinced her.

"I thought you were my friend."

"Yes, we *are* friends. Don't think for a second that I agree with what Inger did. When I found out she loosened your bow knot, I was furious."

"Loosened it?" She glared at him. "That makes it sound like it was a harmless prank. I was trapped—alone—on an island! It was terrifying."

"Like I said, Inger was wrong. I feel terrible about what happened to you."

"Why does everyone put up with her?"

"We're used to her nonsense. It's usually harmless."

Ella threw up her hands. "So she gets a free pass to do whatever she wants?"

"No one was happy about what she did. Like I said, I was livid. I gave her a piece of my mind."

"Well, that should teach her!" Ella scoffed and lifted the bin from the wall. "What else haven't you told me?"

"A couple of things, actually . . ." His voice trailed off. Something like guilt crossed his face as he motioned at the cottage. "We had a party here just before you arrived. That scotch we drank when I came over . . . it was Inger's."

Ella's eyebrows rose to her hairline. "You turned Ringpynten into another clubhouse?"

"No! When we found out the cottage was going to be sold, we just had a farewell dinner on the patio. It was to say both thank you and goodbye to Inger's garden. Spending time here with her plants means the world to her. We only put on the dinner to let her know that we cared about her losing it. We had no idea that you would show up."

Ella looked at the flowering herbs as finches darted from the berry bushes to the roses with tangerine seedpods. The resident porcupine munched on fresh green shoots and eyed the purple rhubarb stalks hungrily. Dill with lemon-yellow flowers flourished near two fruit trees. Just looking at the garden calmed Ella. It even soothed the sting of her fight with

Leif, and she could begin to understand what this spot had meant for Inger. She smiled at him, but only slightly. "Now I understand why Inger maybe felt so emotional about it, but she had to know that . . . oh, never mind. None of this is my fault. I wish she would've talked to me about keeping the garden and told me how much she loves it. I probably would've let her continue growing things here."

"I'm telling you now."

Ella shook her head in a way that suggested she was disappointed in him. "I'll be inside while you work on the boats."

"I'm not here to repair your boats. Axel is taking over the job. I'm headed to Jomfruland for a few days."

She continued to fidget with her bracelets. "But you're supposed to take me around Lyngør to meet people. Plus, I thought you were arranging a time for me to talk to Erik."

"You've forgiven me?"

"Don't press your luck. What's in *Yum-froo-land*?" She pronounced it very carefully.

"Ragnar. Erik's cousin, a good friend. I'm helping him out with a couple of things. I thought you might like to join me on the trip. You could ask him about your roots—Ringpynten and Sara. He might have some ideas about where you could put Hilda's ashes."

"But how would he know anything if he doesn't live in Lyngør?"

"He used to live here. He's Erik's age. He's obsessed with birds, and he used to document and trap them on the islands of Lyngør. He knows everyone, including tourists, because he used to visit everyone to talk about the birds on their properties. This might be the lead you're looking for. But Ragnar is different, always has been. He dances to the tune of his own fiddle."

"You said it's an overnight trip?"

"Yes, we'll stay at Ragnar's cottage."

She dumped the bin water over the stone wall and drenched the brambles.

"Ragnar is a real talker," he persisted. "Give him a few drinks and he'll spill everyone's secrets."

"I'll need ten minutes to pack."

CHAPTER 24

The gusting wind and the thrum of the engine made it difficult to hold a conversation during most of the trip, but they exchanged smiles and nods when possible, and in more sheltered passages he pointed out the sights to her. Ella took pictures of Leif, framing his strong face against the coastline as he steered *Rán* into Risør Harbor, and others of the rocky landscape, with nautical cottages surrounded by abundant heather.

She trained her camera's lens on Leif's large artist hands as they rested on the helm. She now understood why he didn't tell her everything right away. Had she been in his place, she probably would've made the same decision. She marveled at what twelve hours, sobriety, and fresh air could do for one's perspective.

Leif cut the engine and guided *Rán* into a slip at the Risør dock on the mainland. Dozens of wooden sailboats dotted the U-shaped wharf. Ella knelt on a cushion and snapped photos of the century-old storefronts made of white clapboard and carved wood trim. Geraniums brightened their window boxes. There was an outdoor fruit and flower market, and shoppers drank beer and smoked cigarettes at sidewalk cafés. Beyond the wharf, white-painted stores edged the two-lane street; a scattering of homes and a white wooden church dotted the treed hills.

"Is there a church near Lyngør?" Ella asked. Maybe Hilda went to Sunday services when she summered there. "Also, do you think it's legal to spread her ashes in the water?"

"Yeah, Dypvåg Church. I'm not certain about the ashes, but I'll gladly take you to Dypvåg whenever you like." Leif removed his sailing jacket before gesturing at the shops. "It won't take me long to buy the part I need."

"What's the part for?" Ella put away her camera.

"Ragnar's water pump is broken, but it's an easy fix."

"Doesn't sound easy to me, Mr. Fix-It." She smiled at him.

"Well, it's freeing to be self-sufficient. It's important to me," Leif commented in a serious tone.

"You know that's how I learned to sew? When I was a kid, my mormor used to bring home the ugliest clothes, and I felt like I needed to alter them just to be able to wear them. It drove Mormor nuts that I was shortening hemlines and adding lace or patches! But I became quite good at sewing, and that was the start of my designs, and my store."

"That shows initiative. I respect it," Leif said with a smile as they went ashore.

· · ·

Ella and Leif stepped from the Risør hardware store onto the cobblestone footway. She tucked the water valve that Leif needed into her purse as she watched two men unloading bolts of fabric from a van parked at the curb. She was mesmerized by the gorgeous azure-and-apricot velvet and the burgundy corduroy. She imagined combining those fabrics to make beautiful, colorful patchwork pants.

She touched Leif's arm. "Wait. Where are they going?"

Leif followed her gaze. "Um, Nina's Sewing and Knitting. It's two doors down—the shop with the flowerpot holding the door open."

"Let's go there. Do we have time?"

"Sure. And Nina is a real character. The two of you should get along very well. She opened the store when I was small, and a while back she altered my father's old smoking jacket for me. He was slightly taller than me."

With Leif on her heels, Ella followed the delivery men into the store. She hadn't seen anything like it since coming to Norway.

The well-lit space smelled of lavender and lime. Mannequins stood on shiny walnut floors, wearing colorful, handknit sweater dresses in Nordic patterns: snowflakes, reindeer, and Viking runes. Abstract oil paintings in vibrant hues hung on pastel-orange walls. Ella could've been standing in the middle of a dream of her own shop. She loved it.

"This place is so cozy and has great energy. I hope Little Bird will feel just like this."

Leif had a sparkle in his eye as he looked at Ella. "You fit perfectly in this place. I had a feeling you'd love this store."

Leif called out, "Afternoon, Nina!"

"Be with you in a jiff!" a woman said from behind a panel of gold velvet drapes.

Ella led him to a table filled with baskets of knitting needles and yarn, and soft angora berets and scarves. She grabbed a blue scarf and reached up to tie it around his neck. He put his hand on the side of her face and moved in closer, his lips brushing hers. It was slow and sweet, and seemed to say, *I care about you, be with me.*

It made her dizzy. She couldn't imagine growing tired of being around him. No one had ever made her feel the way Leif did—like she'd swallowed a hundred sunrises, like somehow the two of them fit together perfectly, like a lock and key. She thought that maybe she was falling in love for the first time.

"Haven't seen you in years, Leif! You good?" Nina called out as she pushed through the curtain. It was amazing that she didn't topple over from the weight of her tremendous turquoise necklace and her silver-streaked beehive hairdo.

"All is well," Leif confirmed, and he gave Nina's hand a quick squeeze. "This is Ella."

"Nice to meet you." Ella grinned and shook Nina's hand.

"Likewise." Nina's lips curled up at the edges as if she were genuinely pleased. "Where are you from?"

"The United States—Colorado. I'm staying in Lyngør right now, a place called Ringpynten. Have you heard of it?" Ella was hopeful.

"Ringpynten? Nope, never heard of it." She circled Ella and reached out her hand like she might run her fingers right over her body, but she patted her own beehive hairdo instead. "The needlework on your wrap coat is extraordinary. Those finches! And the scarlet gilia flowers stitched onto these coat sleeves! Oh! Who's the designer?"

"It's my own design." Ella's face flushed with pride. She unzipped her coat, showcasing the lace hem flowing around her ankles, then took it off and held it out to Nina. "Try it on if you like."

"Your own design?" Leif arched his brow in surprise. "I'm impressed."

Ella's heart did a little flip.

"You're an extremely talented young lady," Nina said. She moved to the mirror and pushed her arms through the sleeves. Turning her body, she viewed the wrap from all sides.

"I finished the embroidery this week. It was inspired by my mom's old sketches. Maybe you've heard of her? Her name was Sara Nilsen; she was born in Oslo but summered in Lyngør."

"No, I haven't heard of her, but that's very meaningful that your mother inspires your work," Nina said with approval.

"There's something very special about your stitchwork. It's playful. I feel happy when I look at it. The details are phenomenal, and the color combo is delightful. It's been so long since I've been this excited about a design that I think I'm shaking." She grinned as she removed the wrap, but she held on to it instead of handing it back. "Is it for sale? I'll pay you fourteen thousand kroner for it."

Fourteen thousand kroner? Ella was too shocked to speak. That was around sixteen hundred US dollars—twice the amount that she'd charge for a similar coat at her shop in Boulder. Incredible, if she could get that much money for one of her wraps!

Leif let out a soft whistle. "What a great opportunity! You could break into the Norwegian market and sell your designs here. You should do it!"

"I know what I like when I see it, and I don't hesitate," Nina said firmly. "If you sell it to me, I'll display the coat on the window mannequin to show off the vivid needlework. I think it might even increase sales on my embroidery floss and silk threads." Her certainty and enthusiasm were exhilarating.

"It's a deal." Ella smiled, nearly shivering with excitement, just as Nina had said.

"Ella, this is fantastic!" Leif threw his arm around her.

Nina folded the wrap over her arm and asked, "Do you have more like this? I'd love to buy two more from you and send them to my sister. She owns two boutiques in Oslo, and when anyone is interested in buying something unique or glamorous or both, they buy from her. If the wraps sell, she'll probably order more."

"High-end designer coats at a posh Oslo boutique—wow!" Leif hugged Ella. "You could make some good money."

"Yes, thank you, Nina. This is exciting! I'm all in. I'll get to work on two other designs."

"I look forward to seeing what you come up with," Nina

replied. "This could be the start of something. I don't know what yet, but I have a good feeling."

Ella knew this was a great opportunity, and a rare one. Selling her coats in Norway might help her business in America. Maybe she could even write off at least one trip a year to Norway. That wouldn't be so bad. Not bad at all.

CHAPTER 25

The time flew by for Ella on the three-hour boat ride from Risør to Ragnar's place on Jomfruland. Leif kept *Rán* steady as he steered the boat through the waves, beyond small islands blooming in the sea, and a pod of plump seals with toffee-colored eyes. The sight of them calmed her on the choppy waters. Leif seemed to understand Ella's need for quiet to process all that happened in Nina's store. Incredible that Nina had bought the coat right off her back and ordered two more, paying double what Ella herself would have asked! Was it crazy to think that she could make a name for herself in Norway? She felt like she was on a seesaw. One moment she thought she could leverage this opportunity to grow her American business and improve her life—with a foot in both Norway and Colorado, the way some Americans were bicoastal. The next moment she decided that it was a lot to bite off. She wasn't sure that she could make room in her head and heart for anything other than Little Bird. It was everything she wanted for herself. But then Leif rested his hand on her thigh and her thoughts and emotions seesawed in the other direction, because she was unexpectedly developing a life in Norway. She had a business opportunity; she had at least two friends now. She loved having Leif around. Their relationship, whatever it was, felt natural and comfortable, and their chemistry was strong. But she couldn't abandon her life back home, could she?

Leif cut the engine and let the boat drift toward an orange buoy just offshore from Jomfruland. A great gray heron took flight from a small, ice-polished skerry near them.

"It looks different from the other islands," Ella said. Around two dozen cottages skirted the shore, each unique in color, size, and materials, but all with equal amounts of charm. The shore itself was a long stretch of pebble beach. Some of the polished stones were as large as grapefruit. Sun-dappled oaks edged a field where sheep grazed on grass carpeted with white flowers.

"Yup," Leif said. "The Vikings called this island Aur, which means 'gravel' or 'shingle.' As the glaciers retracted from the coast, they left debris—mostly ice-scoured rocks and silt that formed Jomfruland." He flung the anchor into the water and secured his boat to the buoy. He indicated a small wooden rowboat tied up next to them. "That belongs to Ragnar. I'll row us to shore."

The sun danced and seabirds sang as Ella grasped Leif's hand to board the rowboat. With a smile, he guided her to the stern bench. He placed a cushion there for her comfort, a small but thoughtful gesture that made Ella's heart race for Leif even more. The cool salt breeze ruffled his shaggy hair as he sat on the middle bench, reached for the oars, and rowed them to shore.

The bow crunched against the pebbles as Leif beached the boat. Ella shrugged off her life vest and stuffed it into her overnight bag. She thought that they'd probably sleep in the same bed tonight, and the thought gave her butterflies. Thank goodness she had shaved her legs. She combed her fingers through her wild, windblown hair, waiting for Leif, who was barefoot, to step over the bow and into the shallow water.

"May I help you ashore?" he asked.

She nodded. He reached for her waist, lifted her effortlessly, and released her only after her feet were planted securely on land. A short distance away, a small red cabin bordered the beach. Two goats grazed on the sod-and-wildflower roof; a third goat descended a plank that stretched from the stone chimney to the ground. Chewing on blue petals, it let out a bleat.

"This place looks like something straight out of a fairy tale," she said.

"You don't have goats on roofs in Boulder?"

"Nope, but I'll have you know my apartment has a lovely view of a tattoo studio and a record store, right out my living room window."

"I'd love to see it," Leif said, and winked at Ella.

She smiled. She tried to imagine him in landlocked Boulder, with vegans, weed, academics, college students, beer bongs, and football games at Folsom Field. What would he do there, with no boats to carve?

"Is that Ragnar's place?" she asked.

"Yep."

"What's he like?"

"Eccentric as hell."

"Thank goodness."

Leif laughed and pulled the rowboat farther up onto the beach. He seemed completely unfazed by its weight, dragging it six feet from shore, his muscles flexing. Crouching down, he broke off a sprig of pink blooms and then stood to face her, the delicate petals resting in his strong hands.

"This is scurvy grass. It's packed with vitamin C. Sailors collected it in bunches and ate the grass aboard ship." He motioned toward her hair and asked, "May I?"

His eyes lingered on the curve of her lips as she nodded. He moved closer and tucked the flower behind her ear, brushing her ear with his fingers. His touch was electric.

"Mm, I need to adjust this a little," he commented, and as he wiggled the stem, his hand brushed her cheek. Another surge of want sparked through her. She pushed up on her toes and brushed her lips gently over Leif's. His face lit up as if he were tickled by her touch. He kissed her back, then clasped her hand as they strolled toward the cabin.

On Ragnar's porch, wind chimes clanged and yellow canaries flew inside their standing bird cage. On the far end of the porch, Ella noticed a hammock hanging from a wooden frame and wondered if they could both fit in it.

Ragnar threw open the door and clapped Leif on the back before he'd even had a chance to knock. If Ella had thought that other people she'd met looked like Vikings, they had nothing on Ragnar. He was burly and blond, with a face cut in sharp angles. He even had a sheathed knife clipped to his belt.

"I was expecting Erik. 'Course, the two of you will do," Ragnar said warmly. The creases deepened around his eyes.

"Something came up for Erik at work. He's busy, I guess," Leif explained as he lifted one shoulder.

"For the love of Loki, where are his priorities?" Ragnar let out a deep rumble of laughter before turning to Ella. "Hiya, sweetheart, who might you be?"

"Ella Nilsen."

"She's a tourist, visiting from the States," Leif blurted before he could stop himself. Ella was startled at the label, and it stung.

"No matter, anyone with birds on their shoes is a friend of mine." Ragnar limped into the cottage and invited them in.

Ella felt right at home, and Ragnar certainly shared her love of birds. A mural of scarlet macaws spanned an entire wall of his sitting room, and avian anatomy textbooks and several feathers lay on the coffee table. She felt that the place had good energy, with giant potted plants and a burnt-honey smell.

Ragnar looked at her and tapped his leg, the one he limped

along on. "I had a fight with a rock while boating. The rock won. But that's a story for later."

Leif rolled his eyes and slid a half gallon of dark booze from his backpack. "I brought you a present."

"Vodka spiced with Turkish pepper!" Ragnar pumped one arm in the air and let out a coyote-like howl.

"What's Turkish pepper?" Ella asked.

"A spicy licorice candy," Leif said. "I added it to the vodka last week. I meant to bring it to the bonfire, but I forgot. We'll have some before dinner."

"Good plan," Ragnar said. "You can fill me in on all the Lyngør gossip. And Ella, you can tell me what brings you to Norway."

A bird let out a screech, and Ella scanned the ceiling rafters, looking for the bird.

"That's Astrid the Wonder Parrot. Ragnar's bird," said Leif. "That screech of hers could wake the dead."

Astrid shrieked again for good measure, then squawked, "Pretty parrot. Pretty parrot. No screech. Love Ragnar."

"Aw, that's so cool." Ella smiled. "It sounds like she understands our conversation." She craned her neck at the loft again and tried to locate Astrid.

"She has quite the vocabulary," Ragnar said. "African grays can collect around one thousand words, *and* they use them in context. Leif can introduce you to her if you like. I need to check on an injured barnacle goose at the bird station. Leif, give her the tour. Pick some mushrooms for dinner. Make yourself at home. I won't be long." Ragnar pushed aside a pile of *Audubon* magazines until he found his keys. He held up the vodka and added, "I'm taking this with me to give it a taste."

After Ragnar left, Ella followed Leif down the hallway and listened as he apologized for calling her a tourist. "It won't happen again," he said sincerely. "It's only . . . I didn't want him to connect you to Ringpynten just yet. With Ragnar, it's all in the timing. Wait until he's had a few drinks tonight. He gossips worse than a fishwife when he's buzzed."

She considered this. Maybe Leif had a point. "OK. I'll be patient."

At the rear of the hallway, she trailed him into a bedroom. With rose-printed curtains and lace doilies, it looked like it belonged to a genteel resident of the English countryside, not to burly Ragnar on a stone beach.

"You can sleep in here," Leif said, placing her overnight bag on the bed. "Hope you like it. Ragnar and the bird share the loft."

"And you?"

"I'll sleep in a bedroll on the floor."

"You can sleep next to me. Just don't get any ideas." She gave him a flirtatious poke in the chest with her finger.

"Oh, I have plenty of ideas," he said as he leaned toward her, cupped her face with his hands, and kissed her. His touch sent a shiver dancing up her spine.

He suggested a walk on the beach, since it was such a beautiful evening. As they strolled, she almost told him how much she liked him, how she wanted to spend every second with him, but she held back. She'd told herself that he was only supposed to be a sexy summer fling, yet she had gone and fallen for him and didn't know if she could stop herself from tumbling further. At one point he shyly removed a small block of wood from his pocket and presented it to her.

Ella moved her fingers over the outlines of a beak and wings. "It's adorable. A little bird!"

"Yes, it'll be a finch for you when I'm finished."

"It's so cute. I love it."

His ears reddened a little. He'd brought towels to sit on and spread them over the pebbles on the ground. Beneath the clear early-evening sky, Ella sat down next to Leif and scooted close enough to feel the heat of his body.

"You know, I wish I'd asked Nina more questions about

the coats. I want to show her the sketchbook and get her thoughts on some of my other designs," she said.

He tossed a pebble into the water, then wrapped his hand over hers and said, "Well, we can fit in another trip to Risør before you go back. It's another chance to be with you. How about Saturday—we can grab lunch on the wharf before we meet Nina, and make a day of it."

"I'd like that." This would mean extending her stay by a couple of days, but she told herself that she'd simply work around the clock after she returned home. For now, she slid onto his lap, kissed him, and buried her face in his neck. Their hearts beat fast for each other, saying everything without having to say anything at all.

"Do you believe in fate?" she whispered as she slid his necklace from his shirt and touched the aquamarine talisman that was identical to her own.

"I don't know . . . but I believe in us. And I like to think our pendants are a sign. I've been thinking, Ella—why don't you come back here this winter? I'll take you skiing in the mountains, and you could talk business with Nina, and probably sell your other designs here too." As he traced his thumb over her palm, tingles spread through her.

"That would be wonderful. But the truth is, I need to get Little Bird up and running and make it a success before I can take another vacation." Her internal seesaw had shifted again. Norway was growing on her, especially with Leif at her side, but thinking about a future here was a fantasy. The smartest thing she could do was live in the moment and appreciate this amazing time in Norway, with Leif.

"You're smart and talented. I have a feeling you'll do just fine with your company. OK, follow me. I've got something to show you." He grasped her hand and gestured toward the water.

"Oh, no—you're crazy. Isn't it cold?" Her high fake laugh did not mask her fear.

"It's the great North Sea that made the Vikings."

"What?"

"It's an old Norwegian proverb. Are you in?"

She had to be out of her mind to consider dipping even her toes in that cold surf. But she trusted Leif. And she recognized this moment as a chance to push past her fear of the water by actually swimming in the sea. She made up her mind.

"I didn't bring a bathing suit," she explained as she pulled her embroidered tunic over her head and threw it onto the towel. Turning her back to him, she removed her bra from underneath her tank top and set it on her tunic.

"Damn," he said appreciatively. The way his eyes moved over her body sent her heart hammering.

He yanked off his shirt, uncovering a lean body sculpted with muscle. She pictured his hands skimming her body, their hips pressed together, and it pulled her thoughts to the bed they would share tonight. A current of lust spread through her. She turned away abruptly to hide her flushed cheeks and then grabbed her trusty life vest.

"You don't need the vest. The water is shallow." He smiled reassuringly.

Still she hesitated, clamping her toes against the smooth pebbles. She looked at the water stretching out before her, where several red-throated loons floated on the surface. *They* made swimming seem effortless. She tossed the life vest back on the towel.

"I'm just curious, but why don't you like the water?" he asked, threading his fingers through hers.

"Ever since I can remember, my grandma lectured me about the dangers of water. I let that get into my head." She told him about the time she jumped off the diving board at the community center and thought she would drown. "It reinforced Mormor's warnings about the water."

Leif gave her a hug. "That must have been horrible. We don't have to do this, you know."

"No, it's OK. I want to try to swim." They walked to the shoreline. Chilly salt water sloshed over her feet and she inhaled sharply. She remembered something her art teacher often recited, a quote by Auguste Rodin, and it felt right for this moment: "The main thing is to be moved, to love, to hope, to tremble, to live."

Leif kept a firm hold on her hand and led her farther into the water until it met her knees. She glanced over her shoulder at the security of the shore and paused.

"You've got this," he said, his hand resting on the small of her back.

"Yes, I think I do." She grinned at him. But as the water rose to her thighs and the sea tugged at her, she flung her arms around his neck. "Hey, Boy Blue, didn't you say it was shallow?"

"We can stop here," he said. "But try to float for me."

Float? She was sure she looked as scared as she felt.

"Hey, it's OK—if you start to sink, I promise to grab you."

"I just need a moment." She counted to five slowly and focused on her breathing.

"Take all the time you need. I'll just be staring at your breasts until you're ready, how's that?"

She laughed.

"See? Laughter is good for your health," he said lightly. He gently scooped her up from underneath. For a moment, his touch calmed her, until the cold water lapped over her skin and carried her back to reality, and she stiffened again.

"You can do this . . . relax back slowly into the water, and let your head and shoulders recline like you're lying flat on the sofa . . . that's it. Now, if you make small movements with your hands—that's right—that will allow you to stay afloat and helps keep your mouth and nose out of the water, and to breathe naturally." He cradled her, supporting her with his arms and comforting her with his words and presence until her body gave way, trusting him.

"You're doing great. Now, relax and clear your mind. Just keep your chin up. Breathe. I'm going to release you slowly. Ready?" His advice echoed what she heard every week from her yoga teacher: Relax, clear the mind, focus on your breathing.

"Yes. Ready."

He let her go slowly.

She concentrated on the blue sky with a single cloud shaped like Cupid. She floated. The water was freezing, and she couldn't feel her toes, but it didn't matter, she was floating.

"Fantastic! You're doing it! How does it feel?" he asked, beaming at her.

"Freeing and divine . . . this must be what zero gravity feels like."

"You're funny and I'm so glad you are." He splashed her a little and laughed.

She gasped, cleared the water from her eyes, and lowered her legs until her toes grazed the smooth rocks on the seafloor. She grinned because it wasn't that deep, nothing to be afraid of, and she splashed him back.

Elated, she announced, "I'm going to dunk my whole head in!" She held her nose and took a breath, then gripped his hand. They dove under the water and kicked their feet while continuing to hold hands as they lay suspended below layers of aquamarine. Together they rose through the blue and broke the surface. As they waded to shore, she raised her eyes to the sun. She'd just floated in the North Sea—something she wouldn't have dared to do when she first arrived in Lyngør.

"Now I'm officially a Viking!" She laughed and kissed him on the lips.

• • •

Ella showered while Leif chopped vegetables for dinner. In the bedroom, she slipped her lacy camisole over her head and considered there was a good chance their clothes would come off tonight. For some reason this made her nervous in all the best ways. It was more than lust though. Being with him felt right—maybe they clicked because they were both artists and orphans. The trouble was, she didn't know how to navigate the precious brief time until she flew home to Boulder.

In the kitchen, diced onions and carrots were piled on a cutting board over the farmhouse sink, but he was nowhere to be seen. "Leif?" Ella called out.

"Look up." Leif stood near the loft railing. "I'm looking for scissors, to cut string to tie up the beef."

"Hello sweetheart!" Astrid squawked.

"Oh good! I'm ready to meet the silver-tongued bird." Ella hurried up the stairs. The spacious room featured forest-green walls and an enormous painting of a falcon. Leif leaned against Ragnar's antique desk, which was covered by science journals, a container of bird bones, and a typewriter. Astrid, with her red tail feathers and intelligent eyes, moved around her large birdcage. Ragnar really was quite an ornithologist.

"Hey there," Ella said to Leif, feeling a light tickling sensation in her stomach as she held his gaze. He was looking at her like she was his favorite shade of blue. She wanted him to hold her and never let go.

He roped his arms around her, and their lips met.

"Kissy kissy," Astrid said, clicking her beak. "Love Ragnar."

"That bird is bonkers," he said, between kisses. "Ragnar is expecting dinner. He'll be home in an hour, perhaps sooner, but I can't think of anything besides wanting you."

"Mm-hmm." Ella slid her fingers beneath Leif's untucked button-down shirt.

Leif let out a sigh. "Not helpful."

"You're right." She broke free, straightened up, and changed the subject. "I swam in the sea today—I still can't believe it!"

"Yes you did," he said with a smile. "That was brave of you. I'm really impressed."

Astrid let out a screech. "Astrid's blankie!"

Ella laughed. "That's adorable. She wants her blankie."

"Yes." Leif placed his hands on Ella's cheeks. "And I've wanted *you* since the first time I saw you in your yard at Ringpynten, strumming your guitar." The air crackled between them, and she knew this was meant to be. Their lips met again, and he gave her a long, deep kiss. Her pulse quickened as he led her to Ragnar's bed, unbuttoned her blouse, and slipped it over her head.

"Naughty boy, naughty boy!" the parrot squawked.

"Wait right here," Leif said, and he gave Ella a quick kiss before snatching the folded blanket from the foot of the bed and covering the birdcage. "Night, Astrid."

He walked back to Ella. "Now, where were we, Sunna?"

• • •

Ella and Leif were curled up on Ragnar's bed. Leif nuzzled her neck. "Being intimate with you feels so right," she said and rolled to face him.

"Mmm . . . yes, I feel content when I'm with you, like I'm right where I'm supposed to be. I'm not sure what it is . . ." He lifted his head and touched his nose against hers. "I only know I've never met anyone as authentic as you. You know what you want, and you follow your dreams. You're talented. Passionate."

"You follow your dreams too. Your boats and carvings are fabulous."

"You have no idea how I felt when you called me an artist that first time," he said.

"Same" was all she managed to say. She slid on top of him and brushed kisses across his lashes, nose, and mouth, wanting her touch to convey what her mind was struggling to process.

Astrid let out another screech. "Out! Blankie!"

Ella rolled away from Leif. She collected her clothes from the end of the bed and began to get dressed. "Maybe she'll calm down if we let her out."

"Blankie!" Astrid blurted in a shrill squawk.

Ella pulled the cover from the cage, then stopped and looked at it more closely. It was embroidered with bluebells, puffins, and oystercatchers—just like the ones on the blanket in the photograph taken at Gåsholmen. It couldn't be, could it? She flipped it over and found the initials *S. N.* stitched in large, geometric red letters on the back. *Sara Nilsen.*

She stared at the needlework in awe. The embroidery, especially the featherstitch and the stump work, could have been sewn by Ella's own hand. A new connection to the mother she never knew.

She held up the blanket. "Do you recognize this?"

"What?" Leif said.

"It belonged to Sara. My mother."

He arched his brow in question. "Are you sure?"

"Yes, look!" she said, pointing. "Just like in the picture—and look at the initials!"

"Wow! It *is* the blanket."

"He must've known my mother!"

Heavy footsteps came from the porch and Ella headed toward the door. It sounded like Ragnar was talking to someone outside, but she couldn't make out his words.

Leif gently took her arm. "Wait, hang on a minute—hear me out . . . it's just, well, Ragnar's known to borrow things. I'm not saying that he *stole* Sara's blanket. But I *do* know you shouldn't accuse him or put him on the spot, because he'll either shut down or shut you out. Last year we were all drinking at a bar, and Inger saw Ragnar slip one of the condiment caddies into his backpack. She called him out on it and he was furious at her for *months*. It's possible I'm being too cautious, but I want more than anything for you to learn about your family. I care about you." He flicked a lock of her hair behind her ear and kissed her cheek. "I'm only suggesting that you be strategic. Why don't you ask him questions about himself? Nothing too pointed or direct. We'll get information out of him in time."

"Leif, this is huge! In fact, I'm putting this blanket on the list of the best things that ever happened to me. I feel like my whole body is vibrating." She folded the blanket quickly in half, then in half again. "I don't want to wait for answers."

"I understand. Please know that you're not alone in this. I'm actually trying to help you."

Leif knew Ragnar best, Ella thought. He was probably right. "OK, you go on downstairs," she said. "I'll be right there."

She placed the folded-up blanket at the foot of the bed as Astrid began to squawk again.

"Love blankie. Love Ragnar."

"OK, pretty bird. I'm going downstairs to talk to Ragnar. Are you in or out?" she asked as she opened the cage. The bird landed on her shoulder. Ella eyed Astrid's sharp beak and was glad her hair covered her rhinestone earrings.

In the kitchen, Astrid took flight from Ella's shoulder and landed on the bird gym close to Leif, who was placing shot glasses on the table. Ella straightened her jacket and lifted a fragile down feather from her sleeve. Her mind was racing with questions. Why did Ragnar have Sara's blanket? Were they good friends way back then? What if the loafers in the photo belonged to Ragnar—could he even, possibly, be her dad? She pinched her arms as a reminder to stay calm and not fire off impatient questions. She'd take Leif's advice to tread carefully.

Opening the front door, Ragnar belted out a song about a drunken sailor. Ella gave Leif a nervous glance. He squeezed her hand reassuringly and she squeezed back.

"Don't worry," she whispered. "I'm fine. It's all good." She said this as much to convince herself as to assure Leif.

Ragnar still held the vodka in one hand, and with the other he pointed at Astrid, perched on the bird gym.

"I see you met the old gal." He limped to the kitchen island and shook the vodka in their direction. "Good stuff. Like some?" Almost half the bottle was gone. If Leif was right about Ragnar's loose lips when drunk, he wouldn't be holding back tonight.

Ragnar filled the shot glasses to the brim. Standing around the kitchen island, they raised their glasses in unison. "Cheers," said Ella. Ragnar and Leif answered with *"Skål."*

The two men downed their shots while she sipped hers. The Turkish pepper–flavored vodka tasted both sweet and spicy and went down smoothly.

"So how did you two guys meet?" Ella asked with a smile.

"When I was little, Ragnar, my dad, and Erik were close friends," Leif said. He reached for the potato chips.

"Friends since primary school," Ragnar confirmed, refilling their glasses.

"You must have lots of stories," she said, cheerfully.

"Yup, lots of stories, sweetheart. What do you want to know?" Ragnar tipped back his drink.

"I'm curious about Ringpynten, where I'm staying. It's beautiful. Did you and your friends ever go there?"

"Many times," Ragnar said with a chuckle. "Back in the day, the fellas and I knew a woman who spent her summer vacation there every year." He scooped a fistful of peanuts from the bowl, tossed one in the air, and caught it in his wide-open mouth. "Sara. She was popular with the fellas, if you know what I mean." He let out a deep growl of a laugh.

So, he knew her mom and it seemed he had stories to tell. It had been surprisingly easy to get Ragnar to talk. *Who cares if Mom kissed a few guys? So have I,* she thought.

"That Sara Nilsen," Ragnar persisted, "sure was a wild one." He tossed another peanut into his mouth.

"Likely that's just gossip," Leif said and moved closer to Ella.

"There's nothing wrong with being wild. No big deal," she said with a shrug.

Ragnar grinned at Ella. "Well, this Sara was *extremely* wild. The local fellas, like Erik and Bjorn, were crazy about her." He gestured at Leif. "Bjorn was this one's dad."

"I thought summer folk and local folk didn't mix," Ella said.

"The two of you are mixing," Ragnar said with a smirk.

"Yes, and I'm glad we are," Leif said. Ella agreed and stood on her tiptoes to kiss Leif on the mouth.

Ragnar snorted. "Now that it's settled and you two turtle-doves have made your affections clear, I'll continue my story." He snatched three oranges from a bowl, juggling the fruit as he spoke. "On many a summer night, the fellas and I helped Sara sneak out of her cottage, away from her mother, and yes sir did we party. In fact, once I saw Sara kissing Ivan—Leif, you remember Ivan?"

"No. Was I even born yet?"

"So Sara kissed him," Ella said. "What's wrong with that?"

"Oh, they did more than kiss! Ivan was so drunk he didn't even remember that night, but the next weekend he found panties under his bed with the word *Sara* embroidered on the lace. All of us just laughed at him." Ragnar tossed the oranges back in the bowl.

Mormor had called Ella's father a no-good one-night stand. Maybe Ivan owned the shoes in the photo taken at Gåsholmen. Perhaps he was her father? She rubbed her arms anxiously. Leif kissed her cheek and whispered in her ear, "It's OK."

"But that all happened decades ago. Are you sure?" Ella asked Ragnar. He might have gotten it wrong. Memories could be rewritten or exaggerated.

"Of *course* I'm sure, sweetheart. Seems like yesterday,"

Ragnar said. He grabbed an apple from the bowl and polished it on his Dale of Norway sweater. "Erik kissed her too—and he wasn't the only one, either."

"That's enough," Leif said. He shot Ragnar a stern look.

"What's gotten into you, Arnesen? She was a tourist who liked snogging the local fellas. She didn't take to *me*, though . . . probably because I called her a delicious tart."

Ella was relieved Ragnar wasn't her father. She reminded herself that he was old-school, and he'd think what he wanted but she couldn't help but feel protective toward Sara. "Excuse me, that's my mother you're talking about."

"Whoa!" Ragnar held up his hands. "You're Sara's daughter?" He shoved his bangs to the side. "Here I am going on about Sara, and you're her daughter." He yanked his knife from the sheath clipped to his belt and cut into the apple while scowling at Ella and Leif. "Someone should have told me."

"Maybe someone should have kept their mouth shut," Leif growled, his eyes sharp and angry.

Ragnar scoffed. "I've been out of the loop since I moved from Lyngør to Jomfruland. But why didn't Erik mention this when I called him yesterday?"

"He didn't know I was bringing Ella here," Leif said, defensively.

"Save it." Ragnar glared at Leif, then motioned at Ella with the knife. "When you arrived today, I asked what brought you here. You should have told me you were a relation of the Nilsens at Ringpynten. Instead you came into my house and you tricked me."

"No I didn't. I told you I was staying at Ringpynten." She almost blamed Leif, but he hadn't forced her to stay quiet. The decision had been hers alone. "I had no idea you knew my mother. I came to Norway to sell the cottage and put my grandma to rest. But then I found Sara's belongings and wanted to know more about her."

"Can't help you." Ragnar speared the apple slice with the tip of the blade.

"You must know more," Ella said, her heart thumping.

"Nope." Turning to the parrot, Ragnar said, "Can you believe these two? This one's mom and that one's dad were friends, and neither one of these kids had a clue." He looked at Leif. "Did you have a clue, boy?" Before Leif could answer, Ragnar snickered at Ella. "You, sweetheart, should be asking Leif these questions."

"Me?" Leif's eyes rounded in surprise. "Why would I know anything? If I did, I would've told her."

"Like you told me about the dinghy?" Ella frowned.

"Wait a minute—I already explained and apologized. You accepted."

"You're right. I'm sorry," she said, looking down.

"Well, look here, there's trouble in paradise," Ragnar said. He let out a bark of laughter.

"Trouble in paradise!" repeated Astrid.

Leif glowered at Ragnar suspiciously. "Did you know anything about her having a baby?"

"Arnesen, I don't care for your tone. And no, I never heard Sara was pregnant."

"But you have Sara's blanket." Ella slid the picture from her pocket.

"Blanket. What're you talking about?" Ragnar asked.

"I found this at Ringpynten. Look at the blanket."

Ragnar glanced at the photo. "Don't know." He cracked his neck and flared his nostrils in a defensive way.

"I saw my mother's blanket on your bed upstairs. If you don't believe me, look at the embroidery." With a quick jab of her finger, she gestured at the loft. "My mother's initials are on your blanket. How did you end up with it?"

Ragnar pressed his lips into a thin line. He yanked the knife from the apple and sheathed it.

"Astrid's blankie. Astrid's blankie," screeched the parrot. She flew from her bird gym and landed on Ragnar's shoulder.

"*Please* tell me what you know." Ella closed her eyes in frustration and counted to five. "What happened to my mother? Knowing would mean the world to me."

Ragnar stared at the window. Beyond it, lowering clouds veiled the sky. Ella gave Ragnar a pleading stare, tears threatening to spill.

"Sara was my mother, and I know nothing about her. Remember her mother, Hilda? That's who raised me, without ever telling me anything about Sara. I'd never even heard of Ringpynten until after my grandma died."

Ragnar's eyes softened. He covered his mouth with his hand and seemed to come to a decision. "Fine," he sighed. "The fellas were enchanted by Sara. They acted like fools whenever she was around and tried to outdo each other at every turn." He suddenly shook his head solemnly. "No, I can't do this."

"Outdo each other, how?" Ella held her breath, waiting for an answer.

"I'm done talking," Ragnar clenched his jaw.

"I assume my father and Erik were some of the fools in question?" Leif said, scratching the base of his neck.

"It's not my story to tell."

There was a moment of silence. Ella sucked in a sharp breath.

"You don't think we're siblings, do you?" she said. Ragnar and Leif laughed.

"Leif's dad was injured badly playing hockey," Ragnar grabbed at his groin and gave a mock wince of pain. "Surgery didn't help. Bjorn was sterile."

"Stop, that's too much information." Leif grimaced. "Ella. Remember I was born before you were. It happened while my mum was pregnant with me. It's impossible that we're brother and sister."

"That's terrible about your father . . . but thank goodness we're not related." To Ragnar, she said, "When was the last time you saw Sara?"

"Decades ago. But as I said, it's not my story to tell."

"Whose story is it?" She tented her fingers together in front of her, as if praying. "Please, I'm desperate to know."

"I can't." Ragnar turned his back on them both and walked to the bird gym.

She was prepared to beg for answers if she thought it would help, but he seemed to have completely shut down. Fighting off tears, she downed her shot. Maybe it would numb her disappointment over encountering yet another dead end in her hunt for facts about Sara.

"Come on, Ragnar. Whose tale is it?" Leif narrowed his eyes at Ragnar. "Give me a name."

Ragnar rubbed his bad leg and looked at Leif. "Talk to Erik."

"I'm exhausted," Ella announced. "I'm going to skip dinner and go to bed. Good night."

Alone in Ragnar's guest bedroom, Ella put on her nightgown and cocked her head at the door to try to eavesdrop on the two men down the hall, but she couldn't follow their hushed conversation in Norwegian. How well did her mom and Bjorn and Erik know each other? Did she have a serious boyfriend? Did Ragnar ever meet him? But Ragnar seemed intent on not sharing what else he might know. Snatching her hairbrush from the nightstand, Ella threw it hard at the door in frustration.

Several sleepless hours later, Leif entered the pitch-dark room and lay down next to her on the bed, rustling the sheets. She could smell his spearmint breath when he turned to face her.

"Ragnar's a fool," he said.

"Yes, he's an idiot." Ragnar's refusal to open up about Sara upset Ella—so much that she felt the urge to pick a fight with Leif. But that would just push him away further, which would make an already awful situation worse. Ragnar's silence wasn't Leif's fault. Instead, she wished Leif good night. His breathing had deepened in a way that suggested he'd already fallen asleep. She looked out the window; there wasn't a star in the sky.

CHAPTER 26

Ella awakened to find Leif's side of the bed empty. She wondered what Ragnar and Leif had whispered about after she'd left them last night. Ella didn't want to listen to gossip; she wanted facts, and she knew the facts she wanted weren't likely to come from Ragnar.

The radiator clicked. She touched the window to confirm it was cold outside and yanked a sweater over her head. From the window she could see Ragnar's backyard. Leif stood next to a pile of small boulders and was swinging a pickaxe repeatedly, tearing through the dirt like he was digging into his problems.

She wondered if he was as stunned as she was to hear that Erik had known Sara—had even kissed her but had never mentioned it. Erik must have heard by now that Ella was Hilda's granddaughter.

· · ·

On her way to the front door, Ragnar called out "Good morning!" From his seat on the sofa he waved at her casually, like one might greet a passerby on the street. A knife and a walnut lay on his thick thigh, and he tossed the nut into the air before catching it with his hairy-knuckled hand. He seemed relaxed but not overly friendly. She'd never meant to trick Ragnar. She'd only wanted him to feel comfortable enough to open up to her. Today she would act like the perfect houseguest, maybe make brunch and serve Irish coffee with plenty of the whiskey that Leif had bought yesterday in Risør. Perhaps that would loosen Ragnar up and he'd tell her more about her mom.

"Morning. I'm just going outside to say hello to Leif. Afterward, I could make breakfast?" She gave Ragnar her best smile.

"Thanks, but I need to go to the bird station." With his knife, he forced open the walnut shell. "You know, when Leif arrived yesterday, he looked happier than I've ever seen him."

Ella stopped. "He did?"

"Yup, he lights up when he looks at you." Using the point of the blade, he released the walnut meat from the shell and dumped it into a bird-patterned saucer. "Leif is usually guarded. He's been through a lot, losing both his parents when he was a little boy. And all the drama around his dad killing those poor visitors from up north. Erik stepped up for him the best he could, but, well—Leif had it rougher than most."

"Why are you telling me this?" Ella sat down on the other end of the couch.

He gave her a stern look. "The questions you're asking about your past not only affect you, but Leif too, and others I care deeply about. So you better be certain that whatever you're after is worth the price."

"I appreciate what you're saying, I really do. But wouldn't anyone want to know facts about their mother? Tell me that Leif never asked you or Erik questions about his mom when he was old enough to."

Ragnar avoided her gaze. Astrid let out a squawk from the loft.

"Could you please tell me how you got my mom's blanket?" she pleaded.

"I already told you last night; it's not my story to tell." He pushed the knife into the sheath. "I'd hate for anyone to suffer over this, especially Leif. Please consider that before you un-earth the past." He stood and limped out the door.

Ella glared after him, fed up with his cryptic answers. Who were these other people he was so concerned about, and how were they connected to Sara and Leif? Of course she didn't want anyone to pay a price; she simply wanted to learn about her family. This was becoming so frustrating, with no answers in sight. Perhaps it was time to return to Boulder. She didn't really need to stay and had done nearly everything she'd set out to do: She'd started the process of selling the cottage; she'd searched for the information she wanted about her family and arranged for Mia to oversee the actual sale. Plus she'd sold a coat and made a business connection. The one thing she hadn't done yet was to take care of Mormor's ashes. But after that, she considered, yes, maybe it was time to leave. She'd miss Leif, but it was time to get serious about her store again and prepare for the launch.

Little Bird was all she needed in her life, she told herself.

Ella walked to the table, picked up a bird skull, and turned it over in her hands. One question she still wished she could answer, though, was how did Sara die?

CHAPTER 27

Leif scooped up a small boulder and tossed it on the rock pile in Ragnar's backyard. His conversation with Ragnar the night before had gone nowhere. The stubborn old grump always gave the same answer: "That's not my story to tell. You best let sleeping dogs lie."

Raising the pickaxe blade over his shoulder, Leif braced his arm against the shock as he brought it down hard and tore through the dirt. He couldn't get a handle on what was troubling him so terribly, but whatever it was, he took it out on the ground with the pickaxe. Perhaps it was that Ella was leaving.

Or maybe it was that Erik hadn't told him that he had spent time with Sara. Even if Leif knew what questions to ask Erik, he doubted Erik would talk.

As he leaned the pickaxe against the water trough, Ella rounded the corner carrying a clear glass filled with Ragnar's homemade berry *saft*, a mixture of red currant and raspberry juice.

"I saw you working hard out here. I thought you might be thirsty."

"Thanks. I'm moving these boulders for Ragnar. He's

aiming to make a firepit. Did you sleep well?" His throat was parched, and he chugged some juice before hugging her and kissing the top of her head.

Though she'd smiled as she handed him the drink, her forehead was puckered. He couldn't read her eyes, as they were hidden behind her sunglasses.

"What?" he asked warily.

"Oh, I'm just being a grouch. It's annoying that Ragnar won't tell me anything. It put me in a bad mood," she grumbled.

"He won't talk to me either."

"I know." Ella yanked her jacket tighter around her in the brisk sea breeze. "It has to be frustrating for you too. Ragnar offered just enough gossip to raise more questions, like how your father and my mother knew each other. Which is weird, don't you think?"

"Last night was the first I heard of it, I swear," he said, and he held her gaze.

Ella rubbed her wrist as if it ached, then picked at her nail polish. "I won't let Ragnar's stories about Sara bother me, and I hope you won't let them bother you."

"No, they won't—I think no less of your mum. Ragnar tells stories because he loves to be the center of attention. It's annoying that he shut down though, just when it felt like we might be getting somewhere." He bent down, raked his fingers across the dirt, gathered up a rock, and tossed it into the wheelbarrow, wondering about Ragnar's suggestion that Erik had been keeping secrets from him. Wiping the soil from his hands, he snatched the pickaxe and scraped the blade through the dirt again.

Ella nodded. "When I was a little girl, I used to fantasize about who my parents were. Mormor told me almost nothing about my mom, and nothing about my father—I mean, I was raised as if I never had one. But he could have been anyone. What if someone around here knows who he is?"

Leif kissed her forehead and said resolutely, "I think we should pack up and head back to Lyngør. I have questions for Erik, and I imagine you do too."

CHAPTER 28

Ella unclipped her life preserver as Leif caught the dock at Ringpynten. They'd only made small talk since leaving Jomfruland. Mostly Leif had frowned at the clouds with a faraway look in his eye, and that was fine with Ella because she didn't want to talk either. She debated whether she should tell him about Ragnar's warning that her questions about the past could affect Leif too. She felt no loyalty to Ragnar, but she doubted any good could come out of telling Leif. Besides, she planned on leaving soon. Once she did, she'd probably stop chasing the past altogether.

The boat engine idled, and waves broke against the rocks. Ella was much more confident on the dock now; she was getting her sea legs.

"I'm glad we went on this trip," she said. "I met Nina. I swam in the sea. And I learned several things about my mother. Thank you for bringing me. I'm happy I met you." She wrapped her arms around Leif.

"I'm glad too." He rested his forehead against hers, and she raised her mouth to kiss him, but he only gave her a peck on the cheek. As he stepped away from her, his gaze moved to the dark waters, where it stayed.

"Is everything OK?" she asked with concern.

"Yup. I just have a lot on my mind, with Erik and all. I can't stop thinking about the things Ragnar told us last night. I'm not sure what to make of it all. Ragnar tends to exaggerate to make the story more interesting for both him and the listener. It could be that he and my father and the other local men barely knew Sara. So I need to speak with Erik, and he'd better give me answers."

There was a sadness to Leif that hadn't been there when they first met eleven days ago. She wondered if all her digging into the past had put a strain on him. She considered again that it might be time to get back to her life in Colorado. She could scatter some of Mormor's ashes around Ringpynten, then bring some back to Boulder, find a nice spot for her in Little Bird, and show her just how successful she'd become. Taking care of Mormor's ashes was the one thing she still hadn't at least attempted to do, and once that was done, she'd fly home.

But how could she leave Leif? It seemed like she had discovered her other half somehow, as if they were soulmates—if one believed in those things. Not to mention the way the air crackled continuously between them. But if she stayed, she knew she'd continue asking questions. Maybe that wasn't the right thing for Leif.

"How about I come and get you at four," he suggested. "We can find Erik."

"I'd like to see you, but I'm not sure I want to talk to him. Maybe it's best to focus on the now."

He said nothing. His brow twitched with an emotion she couldn't read.

When Ella reached the cottage, she turned to wave goodbye,

but Leif had already steered into the channel. She had a feeling that leaving would be tougher than she'd expected.

The smell of something rotten hit her as she stepped into the foyer. She dropped her bag on the shoe rack and clamped her nose between her fingers. The air tasted like ammonia and smelled of spoiled fish.

She walked into the kitchen and froze. Fish overflowed from the sink—fish with bulging eyes and gaping holes and jellied intestines. Her eyes watered at the stench, and she gagged and backed away from the horror until she bumped against the stove. Red streaks drew her gaze to the refrigerator: *Go home*—written in what she assumed was fish blood—was the message across the front panel.

Her vision grayed at the edges; she saw spots and thought she might faint but caught the stove handle for support. *Don't freak out. Think.*

From where she stood, she could see into the sitting room. The vandal had dumped a huge cod on top of her sketches, which were stacked on the table. The scotch she'd left there was gone. Had Inger done this? She couldn't rule out Charlotte either. Honestly, anyone could have done this, but why would they?

She wondered if they were still in the cottage, and sweat beaded on her back. Scared and outraged in almost equal measure, she eyed the door in case she needed to escape. A fly buzzed around a single dead cod lying on top of her sewing machine, but everything else was quiet. She grabbed rubber gloves from the cabinet and the large washing bin to use as a trash can. Breathing through her mouth, she snapped on the gloves, snatched the bloodstained fish from the sink, and flung them into the bin. It was clear that somebody desperately wanted her gone from Lyngør.

She rushed to the sitting room, where she inspected the urn that held her grandma's ashes and was relieved to see that the vandal hadn't damaged it. She retched as she began scooping up the monstrous cod lying on her sketches. Guts dangled from the fish, the metallic scent of blood filled the air, and her stomach heaved. Dropping the cod into the bin, she wished she had hazmat gear. She looked wistfully at the sketches, but they were covered in fish slime and beyond saving. She threw them away too.

Ella heard a creaking sound from somewhere upstairs, and she reflexively looked toward the ceiling. Her arm hair stood on end and a chill shot through her. Whether or not there was still an intruder, she didn't want to be there a second longer.

She ran outside, still clutching the bin, but she had no plan: There was no phone to call anyone, and she didn't even know what the heck to do with the rotting fish carcasses she was carting around. Gulls flew in and begged for the fish.

"Have at it," she said sarcastically as she dumped it all on the ground and rushed toward the hill that led to Mia's store. It was the only place she could think of going. She couldn't remember ever feeling this vulnerable and alone. She began to sob. Her doubts about leaving Norway vanished—she didn't need this headache. She had braved the water, but she saw no reason to stay for this.

CHAPTER 29

Rán was almost out of fuel, so Leif stopped at Lyngør Grocery to fill his tank. On the dock, he snatched a discarded ice cream wrapper from the ground and tossed it in the trash bin, wishing he could throw away his troubles as easily. What the hell were the secrets that Erik and Ragnar were keeping from him? He figured it must have something to do with his father, but maybe it was about Ella. Well, as far as *that* went, her life and priorities were back in Boulder. It was all he could do not to kick over the trash can in frustration.

"Leif! I need to talk to you," Mia called out from the store.

"OK, later." He wanted to head home and wind down. No, what he really needed was to disappear on a five-day fishing trip by himself to get his head straight. He unhooked the nozzle from the gas tank.

"No, now. Erik took off," she said quickly as she strode over.

"Took off?"

"Yeah, this morning, after he spoke to Ragnar on the phone." Her words tumbled out. "Axel was there, and he said when Erik hung up, he threw a mug against the wall and had a look on his face that Axel had never seen before. Axel and

Inger are worried about him, and so am I. Did something happen at Ragnar's place?"

Leif didn't respond as he topped off the tank.

"Oh, come on! What's going on?"

Leif quickly filled her in on the trip, and the partial information they'd received from Ragnar. He eyed the storm clouds on the horizon as Mia suggested they go inside for a cup of coffee.

"As long as it has lots of whiskey in it," he grumbled.

She brought him into her office in the back. Leif sat down on a stool at her long desk. She searched through the clutter, which included a cat bed and superhero comic books, until she retrieved two clean mugs. She poured the coffee and placed one mug and a fifth of whiskey in front of Leif. He smiled ruefully and pushed away the bottle.

Mia had just opened a tin of Danish butter cookies, ready to settle in and go over all of it, when the door chimed. They both started at the sound of Ella's frantic voice.

"Where are you, Mia? Something happened!"

Leif and Mia exchanged alarmed looks, then rushed out of the office and down the aisles. Ella's nose was pink and puffy from crying, and Leif could see the fear and fury in her eyes.

"My cottage was vandalized," she said in a trembly voice. "I'm scared that whoever did it might still be at the house."

"What do you mean, vandalized?" Mia wrung her hands.

"Sunna, you all right?" Leif said and hugged her tightly. She returned his hug briefly then broke free from his arms.

"No, I'm *not* all right." She grimaced. "Some jerk dumped fish all over my kitchen and on my sketches!" She clenched her hands into fists and shook them. Tears slid down her cheek and pooled on her lips. Whoever did this to her would be sorry, Leif thought. He brushed away her tears with his thumb, and she sniffled as he gave her a paper napkin from his pocket.

"Thanks," she said, offering him a small smile before

blowing her nose. "I can't believe someone did this to me. But I guess not much surprises me anymore."

"Who would be mean and crazy enough to do this?" Mia's voice rose and her eyes were wide from shock.

"Who *wouldn't* have done it?" Ella threw up her hands. "It's obvious I'm not exactly loved around here."

"They're probably long gone from your property by now. But we'll figure it out and they'll apologize and clean your cottage," Leif growled. He had visions of catching the vandals and cramming fish down their throats.

"I don't want an apology, and I don't want them on my property ever again." Ella wadded up the napkin in anger.

"I just can't believe this," Mia said. "It makes me so nervous. I need sugar." She grabbed a bag of peach gummies from beneath the register, ripped it open, and popped one in her mouth.

"My first thought was Inger," Ella said while fidgeting with her bangles. "I wondered if she might've trashed it to keep it from being sold so she could continue gardening there."

"Inger wouldn't do that," Mia said unequivocally as she chewed on the candy.

"But she messed with my dinghy already."

"Yeah, and people thought it was horrible—she wouldn't press her luck like that again, not this soon. Plus, I don't think Inger is capable of something so horrible." Mia pushed another gummy into her mouth.

Leif scowled. "We should call the police."

"No police," Ella said with a firm set of her jaw.

"Why not? Whoever did this had no right and should pay for it." Leif shook his head. "I'm furious. When we find out who did it, I'm going to shove them into a deep hole in the ground and fill it with dead fish to see how they like it."

"Sounds about right." Ella let out a shaky laugh. "But I don't want to deal with filing a police report. I've had enough. I'm done with this place. It's time for me to go home to Boulder."

"You really think so?" Leif said with a sinking heart.

"I need to get back to my life and Little Bird. I can't blow this." Ella looked like she might cry again. She turned to Mia and dabbed her eyes with the napkin. "Can I borrow your phone to call the airlines?"

Mia hugged Ella and patted her on the back. "Hey, everything is going to be OK. You don't have to book your flight now—please stay a while longer. My cousin has set up the open house at Ringpynten. The potential buyers will be here at the end of next week. I bet one of them will make an offer, and I know you'll get a great price."

"The cottage is trashed. No buyer wants that. The smell would turn your stomach. I need to clean it before anyone can set foot in there, and I'll need about a gallon of bleach."

"We can clean it together tomorrow," Mia said.

Leif clasped her hand. "Come with me to my place. I'll cook you a good dinner. I've got plenty of room and a great shower."

"Right now I need chocolate." Ella moved to the sweets rack near the register and selected an extra-large candy bar. She held it up. "How much?"

"No charge," Mia said. "And I have something else that might cheer you up." She reached beneath the counter and triumphantly held up a box of cornflakes. "I special ordered it for you."

Ella's eyes glistened. "Oh my gosh! Thank you so much!"

"You're welcome," Mia said. "Now why don't you go with Leif? Rest. You'll feel better after a good night's sleep. I'll bring cleaning supplies to Ringpynten later this afternoon. We'll need to open the doors and windows and air out the place before we start cleaning. I can help you with all of that."

"Thank you so much. I really appreciate it. It's so kind of you. I'll take the cornflakes with me now, please—to enjoy later. Thank you both." Ella moved to Leif's side. "Let's go; I'm ready."

CHAPTER 30

In Leif's foyer, Ella unlaced her mud-flecked boots and took a few comforting breaths. The house smelled like cold mountain air the moment before it rained, with the hint of a burning match. The tension in her body loosened a little, just enough to take the edge off her anger and hurt. She was glad not to be alone at Ringpynten. She hardly knew anyone in Lyngør, yet she had somehow made an enemy there. Mia had insisted Inger was innocent, but then who was responsible?

At Inger's bonfire, Charlotte had confessed her love for Leif, but she seemed too career focused to be driven by jealousy. It seemed unlikely she'd jeopardize her job and reputation with a huge temper tantrum.

Ella thought about Erik. He had given her the cold shoulder and obviously didn't approve of her and Leif's relationship. But he seemed drained and beaten down, as if living with his demons took all his energy. She supposed any of the other locals might have sent her the message to make it clear that she wasn't welcome in their close-knit community. Well, they'd made their point. She was done.

"This shouldn't have happened to you," Leif said, and

a muscle twitched in his jaw. He kicked off his blue shoes, reached for her coat, and hung it on a wall hook.

"My insides are still shaking . . . my emotions are all over the place," Ella said. "But I'm glad I listened to you and Mia and came here to calm down. Maybe it's better not to think about what happened right now." Her scalp was sweaty, her feet ice-cold. She was worn out. Leif studied her with concern in his eyes, but when he opened his mouth to speak, she held up her hand.

"You know what would be wonderful? Something to eat and drink, and a fire in the hearth."

. . .

"This is just what I needed," Ella said from a chair near the blazing fireplace. Leif turned on the stereo, old-school music: Van Morrison's instrumental "Scandinavia." She watched as he moved around the kitchen. For the first time today, he appeared calm, much like the energy of his home, and her tension eased.

Leif folded a dish towel over his forearm and mockingly inquired, "For your late lunch, Madam, you will be served leek, potato, and thyme soup with rosemary bread. Both are homemade. Does this meet with your approval? If not, I make a mean cheese toastie."

Ella laughed and felt relieved that fish wasn't on the menu. "I'd love some soup and bread. Also, I love the potted herbs in your window boxes. I can smell them from here, and it makes the kitchen feel even cozier."

"Thanks, I started growing them years ago. It might have been my birthday, but I can't remember. My great-auntie Borghild, who lives in Portugal, mailed me some seed packets—oregano, thyme, and a bunch of others. She's an herbalist and believes that herbs can cure common maladies, like . . . fennel is good for the heart. Basil prevents bad breath." He walked to the window box, snapped off a sprig of basil, and chewed on it. "Just in case!" He smiled, and his dimples deepened.

They laughed and the knot in her chest untangled further. Their meal passed in a comfortable silence. Afterward, as she set their plates in the sink, she thanked him for the food and his company, saying how much better she felt.

"I'm glad. Want to see the rest of the house?" he asked and nudged the wrought-iron fireplace screen closer to the flames.

She followed him up the stairs. At the top of the landing was a wooden ship's figurehead of a woman with thick brunette braids and large breasts spilling out of a low-cut bodice. "That belonged to my great-great-grandfather," he said. "She's a bit chipped but I love her."

He pointed out three guest rooms, each decorated with sheer curtains, century-old armoires, and queen-size beds with crocheted throws. The décor was blue and white, with no decorative accents, no quirky artwork, no bold patterns anywhere.

"Throw pillows," she blurted. He blinked at her. "I could sew you some pillows. Embroidered with birds, like the vermilion flycatcher."

"Um, vermilion?" He'd worn a similar expression on their first date when she suggested he paint his antique kitchen chairs. She had to press her mouth shut to keep from laughing.

"Yes, I'm picturing a rich red, with a bit of orange," she teased.

"Uh, well, maybe that could work," he said, but he didn't sound convinced.

At the rear of the hall, she followed him into his bedroom. The walls were painted midnight blue. A gold chandelier hung from the ceiling, and the headboard on the king-size bed had intricate carvings—crosses, more Viking runes, and an eagle. He didn't offer to share his bed, and she didn't suggest it. This holding back of words stretched between them.

Her gaze settled on the bedside table with a single candle and a copy of the book *Kon-Tiki*.

"Are you familiar with Thor Heyerdahl?" Leif said.

"Yeah, I watched a documentary on him. It's wild that he sailed on a raft from South America to Polynesia. Would you ever do something like that?"

"Me? Nah, I prefer my home, a routine . . . or at least I thought I did." He brushed a lock of hair from her shoulder. "But then you, a free-spirited, inspiring artist from Colorado, came along, and now I'm thinking maybe I could benefit from some sort of change."

"Honestly?"

"Don't sound so surprised. You're a good influence on me. You make me want to shake things up. Plus, you see me as an artist, and I love that you do." He hugged her before holding out the book. "It's one of my favorites. It's brilliant. Like to borrow it?"

"I have a better idea. How about you read it to me?" She sat down on the bed and patted a spot next to her.

They reclined against the feather pillows and he pulled the afghan over their legs. She snuggled up to him and said, "If I doze off, could you wake me in an hour?" She laid her head on his chest, the comfort of being next to his solid body and the steady beat of his heart relaxing her further.

"Good plan." He smoothed her hair, then flipped to a dog-eared page and began to read. "'May 17. Norwegian Independence Day. Heavy Sea. Fair Wind . . .'"

That was the last line Ella heard before the room with a view of Lyngør faded away.

•   •   •

Ella was awakened by a kiss on her forehead. She rubbed the sleep from her eyes and saw Leif place two bath towels on his rolltop desk. Next to the bed he'd set a tray with two mugs and two crystal cordial glasses containing a mocha-colored drink.

"I slept like a rock. Naps are the best." As she stood from the bed, evening light streamed through the window. "It's still sunny out and almost nine. I love it."

"Long summer days are glorious." He gestured at the glasses on the tray. "In case you're thirsty. Irish cream liqueur, and coffee in the mug." He touched the towels. "For when you'd like to take a shower. The facilities are down the hall."

"Thank you. I'd love to take a shower." She brushed her fingers over the towels and then his arm and gave a flirty tilt of the head. He kissed her and led her to the shower. In the bathroom, they were naked within minutes, with Leif's mouth on hers, his hands tracing her skin as she arched her back and leaned into his touch. Her fingers twined in his hair and his teeth nibbled at her throat as he pulled her against him, closing every gap they could find between them.

Beneath the steamy shower they lathered each other's bodies and shared deep, passionate kisses. When her feet slid on the soapy porcelain, he gripped her hips and didn't let her fall. In that instant, she felt free yet safe in his arms and wished she could stop time. Afterward, she cinched the belt on a blue terry-cloth robe and, leaning over the sink, sketched a giant heart in the steam on the mirror. He kissed her again.

"Make yourself at home—feel free to borrow anything. Take your time and join me downstairs when you feel like it." He put on a denim shirt and tucked his pendant inside.

"You're the best, Boy Blue." She grinned at him.

"No problem. Anything for you." He hugged her and then walked out of the bathroom.

She collected her clothes from the heated floor. Mud speckled the hem of her skirt, and she brought her blouse to her nose and sniffed rosewater, green tea deodorant, and a hint of sweat. She was relieved there was no trace of the stink of the fish dumped at Ringpynten.

She wondered again who was responsible and what had driven them to do it. Anger and hurt threatened to return, but she didn't want to invite them in again right now. She focused on the wind, which was beating at the house, but the chilly air didn't push in through the windows like it had in her drafty childhood home in Boulder.

Ella swung open the wardrobe doors, selected a plaid flannel shirt, and pushed her arms through the sleeves. In the top drawer she found a pair of handknit socks in a troll pattern. They were soft, and she tugged them up over her calves. A nautical rope belt caught her eye too, and she wrapped it around her waist, tying it off with her signature bow knot. In another drawer, her hand hovered over Leif's underwear. He did say she could borrow anything. The thought lightened her mood, and she chose a pair of sapphire boxers and slipped them on.

She found Leif in the living room, asleep in a leather wingback chair, his bare feet propped up on the coffee table. On his lap lay his whittling knife and the same small finch he'd been carving for her in Jomfruland. The gift tugged at her heartstrings.

He shifted his wide shoulders against the chair without opening his eyes. He had been like a refuge for her, a safe haven from this sometimes-cruel Norwegian island. She felt like she belonged—here, at least, in his home. Could he make it any harder to leave?

She scanned the shelves filled with art books and novels about the sea. On one shelf was a framed photograph of two men and a small boy with skis buckled to their feet. They stood side by side on a mountain of sparkling snow and grinned broadly at the camera, as if nothing could outshine that winter-wonderland moment. She recognized one of the men as a decades-younger Erik. The other man rested his hand on the boy's head. The boy mirrored the man with his prominent eyebrows, deep-set eyes, and full mouth. Her chest ached in sympathy for Leif's loss of his father.

Leif stirred in his chair and yawned. "Power naps are the best, but you should have woken me up."

She leaned over and kissed him on the forehead. "I just now came downstairs. You looked so peaceful that I didn't want to wake you. I was looking at that photograph." She pointed. "You're adorable."

"Yes, that's me, with Erik and my dad. I was four years old."

"Four years old and out skiing?"

"Well, they say Norwegians are born with skis on their feet."

"Yes, you guys look happy. You're the spitting image of your father. Bjorn, right?"

"Yup. Everyone who knew him says that I remind them of him. I'm not sure that's a good thing . . . but I don't want to think about Bjorn."

Leif always looked sad when he spoke about his father, and at that moment he seemed especially miserable.

Ella clasped her hands together. "I've been doing some thinking . . . why don't we hold off on talking to Erik. Let's stay here in the present and forget about the past for a while." She offered him a heartfelt smile to convey that she was truly OK with that.

"No, Erik is your best bet if you want to find out anything about your mum."

"But you just said that you don't want to think about your dad. Remember what Ragnar said, how Sara and Bjorn knew each other? Sadly, they're both gone, and we'll never know exactly what their relationship was. How about we let it go and imagine the best?"

"No. We can't hold off, not anymore we can't." Leif stood from the chair.

"Why is finding out about my mother so important to you?"

"Because I have questions of my own. I want the truth too."

"I understand, and I want that too. But I'm just not sure we'll find the truth we're searching for. Everyone's truth is different. Erik's. Ragnar's. Your father's. Even our own."

Leif silently gazed around the room, everywhere except directly at Ella. "Listen, I want to be frank with you. I have a theory, a suspicion. Do you want to hear it?"

"Not yet," she said. "Wait until you know for certain." He looked troubled, as though that wasn't the answer he wanted. Ragnar's warning came rushing back to Ella—that Leif and others would suffer if she kept asking questions— and she added adamantly, "Assuming, guessing, speculating, whatever—it can be costly."

He frowned as he gazed at a painting of a shipwreck on the high seas, then hunched his shoulders as if in defeat. Ella reached for one of his hands and traced her thumb over his fingers. She leaned her head against his and they stared outside at the rain-pocked channel, and the terns taking flight from the indigo waters and spreading their wings against the wet, oyster-hued sky. At last, she said, calmly but directly, "I appreciate your wanting to help me, but I'm done poking around."

"I don't understand. Up until now, you've been determined to find out whatever you can about your family. Why the change of heart?"

She hesitated. Ragnar hadn't asked her to keep his advice a secret, and Leif deserved her honesty. She waited until he met her gaze. "Ragnar warned me to quit asking questions. He wants you to stop hurting."

"Ragnar needs to mind his own business," Leif snarled.

"Well, we might both discover things we don't want to know. Why keep pushing it? I don't want you to pay a price for my curiosity."

"I don't want you to pay a price either," he said. He faced

her square-on, his blue eyes kind and earnest. He gently clasped her face and kissed her lips.

"Could you do me a favor and drop it?" she asked and wrapped her arms around him. "I want to look back on this summer in Norway and be glad for all the wonderful memories. I'm satisfied with what I've learned about Sara. I've loved spending time at Ringpynten and seeing the area. Coming here was one of the best decisions of my life. I met you."

"I'm so glad I met you too," he said and kissed her lips again. "You're wearing my shirt. It looks good on you." He untied the rope belt cinched around her waist and tossed it to the floor. He gave her ear a playful nip as he picked her up, and she squeezed her thighs around him, causing the hem of the shirt to bunch up around her hips. He laughed at her. "You're also wearing my boxers."

"Yes, and I'm not the least bit sorry."

"Good." His eyes glimmered as he carried her to the couch, and they fell back onto the cushions.

CHAPTER 31

The next morning, Leif woke up next to Ella, facing her bare back. With his finger, he traced the word *beauty* in the space between her shoulder blades. She stirred in her sleep and he nuzzled her neck, her grapefruit scent hitting him like a high. If only he could bottle that fragrance and uncork it when she was gone.

The thought of her leaving turned his mood gray. He was enchanted by her full personality and her grand ideas. She loved his work as an artist and even wanted to combine his designs with hers; he couldn't begin to explain how happy this made him. And he liked having her over; she made his house feel like a home. But he remembered her vermilion throw pillows, and that she'd probably want to change his curtains and plant hot peppers in the window boxes so she could make spicy food—without fish. She wanted goats, and canaries like Ragnar . . . or was it chickens?

He remembered something Erik always said: "Give a woman your hand and they'll take your whole arm."

He snuck out of the room and went for his morning ice bath off his dock. Afterward he put together a breakfast tray for the two of them: buttered rolls, homemade blueberry jam, and two mugs of coffee.

Tray in hand, he walked back to his bedroom and halted at the sight of Ella. She stood near his wardrobe, wearing another pair of his boxers and a lacy bra. Her aquamarine necklace was nestled near her breasts, and its long strand of beads traced a line to her belly button. With a mischievous glint in her eye and a sexy grin, she sat on the mattress and crooked her finger at him. Damn, he wanted her so badly he ached. Quickly relieving himself of the breakfast tray, he kissed her and lifted her onto his lap. She wrapped her arms around him and pinned him to the mattress. In that instant, he felt freer than ever.

• • •

He grabbed his boat keys from the dresser while Ella laced her boots. A couple of hours should be plenty of time to help her clean the fish mess from her cottage. He'd head to work afterward and stay late to make up for the time off. As he shut the front door behind them, a piece of torn cardboard fluttered on twine attached to the door knocker. The note was from Inger.

> Why won't you install a phone? Grrr!!! Come to my house immediately. Have you found Erik? We need to talk. It can't wait.
> Inger

He folded up the cardboard. *What now?* he wondered.

"Everything all right?" Ella asked.

"It's from Inger; she wants to chat straightaway."

"You're absolutely sure she didn't trash my place?" Ella asked skeptically, twisting her silver thumb ring.

Leif honestly didn't know, but Inger welcomed drama, and

he sensed Ella wouldn't put up with any more of it. He had no desire to be caught anywhere in the middle of a fight.

As if reading his mind, Ella said, "I'm going with you." She shot him a stubborn look that made it clear she'd take no argument from him.

"OK, if you say so. It's about a ten-minute walk." Leif led Ella around the corner of his house and across the backyard to the concrete path leading to Inger's place.

Ella remarked, "I'm glad I had a chance to calm down before seeing her. If I'd seen her yesterday, I probably would've accused her and said a bunch of stuff without thinking."

"I'm good at reading Inger. I'll know if she's lying." Leif kicked at a pebble, sending it skittering to the side of the path and into someone's rose garden. If she'd vandalized Ella's property, he didn't know if he could ever forgive her. His patience with Inger had run thin. "There's an adage: To make a friend, a person needs to shut one eye. To keep that friend, a person must shut both eyes. But if she's guilty, I don't think I can do that."

They walked farther yet, beyond more white clapboard homes with glazed tile roofs, roses and hydrangeas blooming against picket fences. Spotting a chocolate lab puppy chewing a squeaky toy on a stone terrace, Ella grinned.

"Do you want a dog?"

"Pets?" Leif shook his head no. "They're so much work. And they need all your time."

She clasped her hands to her chest. "But they make the best companions! I just love them."

"I do too. But with my work schedule, I can't give them the attention they need or deserve."

They passed salt-gnarled pines and boathouses decorated with colorful ceramic shells. The path took them by the Lyngør post office, located in a small nautical cottage with a stone chimney and wildflower garden. Beyond all of this was the deep blue sea.

"Every day I'm amazed at the beauty here," Ella said. "It lights me up."

"That's Inger's place straight ahead." Leif gestured at the yellow cottage sitting on a flat stretch of heather-carpeted rock.

They made their way to Inger's porch and Leif rapped on the door. A minute later Inger called out "Be right there!"

Ella was still wearing Leif's flannel shirt, and she fidgeted with the rope belt coiled around her waist. She suddenly felt slightly uncomfortable and wished she'd worn her own clothes.

The door opened and Inger announced, "You're too late. I left that note last night." Her gaze shifted to Ella and her frown lines deepened before she focused on Leif again. "I'm on my way out. I'm meeting Axel at the Propeller now. Three o'clock wine club—you forgot, didn't you?"

She closed the door behind her but continued talking. "Have you seen Erik? I don't know what he and Ragnar talked about, but it couldn't be good. Axel said Erik looked wrecked."

"Wrecked? Axel said that?" Leif rubbed the tension knot at the back of his neck.

"Yes, he said that. Did something happen when you visited Ragnar? Mia filled me in some but wouldn't say much, and I want details." Inger's wolfy eyes glittered as they bored into his. It was her way of saying that she wouldn't let this go.

"You know exactly how I feel about gossip. This is between Ragnar and Erik, so you need to ask them." Leif had been the subject of gossip ever since his father's accident, and he didn't like participating in it when it came to others either. Besides, he'd promised Ella that they'd give up chasing the past.

With a set to her jaw Inger said, "Fine, don't tell me. But tonight I'm calling Ragnar. You know how he gets at night, after he's knocked back the booze. He'll have plenty to say then." She pursed her strawberry mouth.

Ella intervened. "Someone dumped fish inside my cottage."

"Yeah? Sounds like someone pulled a prank," Inger said with an offhand shrug.

Angered by this, Ella said evenly, "I won't be bullied by you or anyone else."

"Don't bring me into this! I didn't do it. Why would I?" Inger was clearly outraged by the unspoken accusation.

"Why would you? Well, for starters, you sabotaged my din-ghy! I could've died on that island! You're right—dead fish in my house *is* a prank compared to that!"

Inger's neck turned red. For a second she scratched at the blotches on her chin, her cigarillo burning down between her fingers.

"Well?" Ella asked with impatience.

Inger tapped ashes on the ground. "I didn't trash your house—despite the long list of reasons why you annoy me. For starters, you drank my—"

Leif interrupted. "Enough! You owe Ella an apology for messing with her boat."

Inger glowered at him, and it was clear she had more to say, but he gave her a steely *Drop-it* stare, and she stopped herself. There was a first time for everything. He held Ella's hand and continued sternly, "People are going to blame *you* for trashing Ringpynten. Whoever did this will use you as their scapegoat. Do you want that?"

"I couldn't care less about what people think, and you know it!" Inger said with a sneer. But as she turned to Ella, her brow smoothed and she seemed to soften a bit. "Loosening your dinghy line was only a joke. I didn't mean for you to get stranded." She stamped out her cigarillo, effectively ending the apology. "That's why I'm going to help."

"Help with what?" Ella asked. She squinted her eyes skeptically.

"Help find out who trashed your cottage," Inger said.

"You're going to help me?" Ella let out a disbelieving laugh and shook her head. "No way."

"Let her do it," Leif said. "People know you and I are friends, so they won't open up to me. But they'll confide in her."

Inger tossed her key chain in the air and caught it confidently. "I'll ask around. Meet me at the Propeller in two hours. We'll find your culprit."

• • •

As they headed back to Leif's house, Ella threaded her fingers through his. He brought her hand to his mouth, kissed her knuckles, and asked, "Are you OK?"

"I don't know. It seems crazy to think Inger is trying to do me a favor right now, but there's no turning back."

"I'm not going to work," Leif said. "I'm staying with you today."

"I'm not sure I can face Ringpynten right now, in the state it's in. Do you think we can safely put it off a little longer? I'd really like to go to the Propeller first . . ." Ella picked several daisies growing by the side of the path and tore off a couple of petals, then observed carefully, "So, it looks like Inger is innocent, huh? But are you sure Charlotte is? She's not happy you're spending time with me. She made that clear at the bonfire."

"It wasn't Charlotte. I understand why you might suspect her, but Charlotte has a kind heart. I think this motive, whatever it may be, is more sinister."

"Sinister . . . yeah, it feels that way. Like someone would really have to hate me to do this." Ella ripped the rest of the petals from the flowers and rolled them anxiously between her fingers.

"I don't know. But we'll figure it out." Leif folded his hand over Ella's to calm her nervous movements.

"Your support means everything to me. Most things I can

handle on my own, but in Lyngør . . . well, it's very different. I'm an outsider here."

"Sunna, I'm here for you. I'm not going anywhere." He stopped, slid his arms around her, and then found her lips.

Back at Leif's house, the time that Inger had requested until their meeting stretched before them, but Leif knew just how to fill it. Ella lit the candles on the kitchen mantel. Van Morrison's "Daring Night 1" played on the stereo. She scooted her chair closer to Leif's, their knees touching as he handed her a whittling knife and a postcard-size pine block.

"Trust yourself," he said, and she loved him for saying that.

"OK." She smiled at him, then kissed his mouth and settled into her seat.

She began shaving thin strips of oak. She scraped the knife against the block, again and again, and slowly but surely she got the hang of it. Whittling was harder than she'd imagined. An image of Mia's Norwegian Forest cat, Bactus, came to mind. She could paint stripes on its tail and whiskers on its cheeks. She was glad Leif had taken the day off. Being with him and carving together took her mind off the horrors of the cottage.

As she worked, Leif whittled his own block of wood into a wolf's snout and two perfect front paws. He told her about Fenrir, a monstrous wolf in Norse mythology. According to legend, Fenrir had swallowed the sun. When he fought against the chief Norse god, Odin, Fenrir swallowed him too. Inger, with her sharp, assessing eyes, reminded Ella of a wolf. Ella prayed that she wouldn't get swallowed like the sun by the time this was all over.

The hours flew by, and she was almost disappointed when Leif announced it was time to meet Inger at the Propeller.

CHAPTER 32

When Leif and Ella made a pit stop at Ringpynten so she wouldn't have to wear Leif's clothes to the clubhouse, they discovered that Mia had already been there. She'd washed off the nasty message from the refrigerator and delivered cleaning supplies. They sang her praises as Leif steered into the channel.

Ella grew anxious as they got closer to their destination. To calm herself, she photographed the gannets that dive-bombed into the deep blue in search of food. She had always believed that everyone deserved a second chance, but she felt that this situation might be an exception.

Fifteen minutes later, she and Leif were approaching the club. Ella admired the driftwood sign that spelled out *Propeller* in shells. Leif went in first and Ella followed him.

"Wow, this place has a great vibe!" She took in the stone hearth, the reindeer pelts spread on the floor, the mahogany pool table with a mother-of-pearl inlay and claw-and-ball feet. She admired the whale mosaic and Leif proudly confessed to being its creator.

They saw Axel playing darts with a man with hooded eyes.

Axel hit the bull's-eye and pumped his fist in the air. He waved them over, saying, "Hey, Arnesen. Hey, Hippie Chick."

Ella didn't mind because his eyes twinkled affectionately when he said it.

Several people relaxed on chairs stationed around a long table, and some of them waved in greeting. She recognized them from Inger's bonfire, when she'd drunk too much and made a fool of herself. Maybe someone from that evening had trashed her place, even if she didn't think getting drunk and behaving badly seemed like a good enough reason to want to run someone out of town. She kept her chin up and put on a friendly face.

Inger and Charlotte emerged together from a dim, narrow hallway and walked toward them. Ella hadn't seen Charlotte since the bonfire and hadn't ruled her out as a suspect either. But Inger caught her eye and shook her head before stopping to chat with two blond men at the pool table.

Charlotte came over and stood next to Leif. She fidgeted with the collar on her cream blazer as her gaze shifted between him and Ella. She looked at Ella, then Leif.

"I behaved badly. And I won't blame the vodka, although I did drink almost half the bottle. I owe both of you an apology."

"I appreciate that," Leif said. Ella said nothing.

"I heard about what happened to your cottage," Charlotte said directly to Ella. "It's horrible and I wouldn't do that to my worst enemy."

"OK," Ella said and crossed her arms.

"You can think what you want, but I love my job, and I wouldn't do anything to jeopardize it—my reputation is really important to me. And since we're clearing the air"—Charlotte paused and checked her earring—"I admit that I was jealous when I saw the two of you together at the bonfire."

Ella felt Leif looking at her. Charlotte took a sip of her cola and continued. "Honestly, that surprised me. I blame it on my competitive nature. I didn't want to lose my relationship with Leif, but I'm fine now." She laughed like she was amused. "Besides, I just met the most gorgeous guy." She flicked her manicured hand at the man playing darts with Axel. Her gaze returned to Ella and Leif, and she offered a smile. "Are we good?"

Ella nodded and added Charlotte to her second-chance list. Leif looked like he might speak, until a short, stout man bounded into the room.

"Who's that?" Ella asked. He reminded her of an English bulldog, with his droopy jowls and big, sad eyes.

"That'll be Oskar, the fishmonger." Leif raised his hand in greeting, but Oskar was occupied with shaking his head at Inger, who was beckoning him over to the pool table. Mia spoke with him, then eventually led him over to Ella and Leif.

"Afternoon, Arnesen," Oskar said, and shook Leif's hand. "Did you hear that someone nicked two of my nets?" He frowned and motioned toward Ella with his pipe. "There's a good chance the crime is connected to the incident at your cottage." He tipped his chin at Mia. "This one told me what happened, and you don't deserve that terrible treatment."

"Thank you," Ella said with a small smile. "That's awful about your nets. Around two dozen fish were dumped in my cottage. Would that many fit in your nets?"

"They certainly would," Oskar said.

Axel joined them and clapped Oskar on the back. "Why the long face?" After being brought up to speed, Axel frowned and scratched at the label on his beer bottle, and then said to no one in particular, "That's odd about the fish, because I— well, never mind. It's probably nothing." He peered inside the bottle.

"What?" Ella asked. Axel looked uncomfortable, but she needed answers. "Please, say it."

"I don't know," Axel muttered.

Oskar nudged him. "The truth will come out anyway. You might as well speak up and help your friends."

"I really don't know anything." Axel frowned, then unwrapped some pink bubble gum and began chewing as if it were an effort. Leif clasped Ella's hand and brought it to his chest. Axel popped the collar on his Izod shirt, buying himself a bit more time. "OK. Earlier today I saw two nets. I thought it was strange, considering where I saw them."

"Come on, just tell us. Ella has a right to know," Leif insisted.

Axel chewed his gum.

"How would you feel if this happened to you? I can promise you, it's no fun," Ella said, cringing at the memory of fish guts on her clothing sketches. "If you know who it is, please tell me. I'm not pressing charges or anything. And I'm going back home soon anyway." She didn't care that she sounded desperate.

"I shouldn't. He's a good friend . . ." Axel wrung his hands, glanced around the room, and finally lowered his voice to a whisper. "OK. Fine. The nets are in Erik's storage chest at the boatyard."

Mia gasped.

"No. Not Erik," Oskar protested, and shook his head.

"I don't believe it! He's not a thief or a vandal." Leif put his hands on his hips, a hard expression on his face.

As for Ella, she knew Erik didn't like her. He'd made that all too clear. But she also knew that not liking someone was harmless, whereas trashing someone's home was hateful and cruel. She asked thoughtfully, "Don't all nets look the same?"

"Describe the nets," Leif demanded. Axel did, and Oskar verified the nets as the ones that had been stolen. Ella listened as they all talked over each other; she wasn't sure what to think.

"Erik's been acting weird, more so than normal," Axel said. "He took off without giving me any direction. I'm worried about him."

"Maybe we should be worried about him," Ella said. "Maybe there's something going on with Erik that we aren't aware of." She recalled that he'd been rude to her for no apparent reason and had withheld information about his past with Sara.

Leif spoke up. "Well, I need proof of Erik's guilt. If he did any of this, he needs to admit it. And I want to see those nets." He shot Ella a look. "Let's go."

• • •

On the boat ride from the Propeller, Leif told one story after another about Erik. Whether it was emptying and cleaning an elderly neighbor's cistern after she'd discovered a dead mink floating in it, rebuilding an outhouse for a one-armed man, or repairing someone's boat engine for free when they were down on their luck, it seemed Erik had done it all. Leif told these stories with conviction, as if trying to convince her, or maybe himself, that Erik couldn't be guilty. Ella tried to remain positive, but still she struggled to think positively of Erik.

She wondered why Erik seemed to hate her. Maybe he had hated Sara too.

Ella walked with Leif across the boulder-lined quay, with its clumps of seaweed and bird droppings. The briny air felt cool against her skin. Two fiberglass skiffs, resting on their trailers, greeted them from each side of the entrance of Lyngør Boatyard and Marina. Ella waited while Leif swung open the workshop's barn-style doors. The smell of engine grease and sawdust greeted them, and a couple of wooden boats sat on hoists. The evening light cut through the salt-smeared windows and cast shadows on the plank walls that were already streaked with varnish and paint. Ella was nervous about the upcoming confrontation with Erik. Finding the nets in Erik's possession would crush Leif.

Ella followed Leif into Erik's office and was intrigued by

the variety of accumulated junk that littered the wall-mounted workbench. There was a large wooden troll figurine, an oil-burning brass lantern, a glass jug full of Norwegian kroner, and a half-eaten pastry. Leif stopped in front of the storage trunk.

He bent down to work the combination lock, raised the lid, and recoiled. The orange-and-teal twine nets with red buoys matched Oskar's description of his own nets. Leif pressed his fingers to his forehead.

"This makes no sense. Erik doesn't steal!"

"Well, it kind of seems Erik *does*," she said firmly.

"But you don't know him like I do!"

"No, but he treats me like I'm contagious. He's never even spoken a word to me, Leif."

Leif kept stubbornly protesting, so Ella slipped her arm around him. "If Erik didn't do it, he hid the nets to cover for someone else. He was involved."

She reached into the trunk and pulled at a net. It stank like steamed cabbage and seafood forgotten in the heat. It weighed a ton and snagged on the trunk's rim. The twine with tiny sharp knots sliced two of her fingers, and blood rose from the small cuts, her anger bubbling up with it. Everything in her wanted to kick the trunk. What had she ever done to Erik?

The color drained from Leif's face. He dug into the trunk and pulled out an empty round bottle. *Twenty-five years old* was engraved on the silver hammer emblem.

Ella's gaze moved from the bottle, to him, and back again. "That's the scotch from my cottage. If that doesn't make it clear that he did it, I don't know what will." But her anger was softened by Leif's pain, so she rested the side of her head on his arm and said, "I know this can't be easy for you." Her voice cracked, as she was overwhelmed with concern for this man next to her, the man who was holding her heart.

CHAPTER 33

"The power should be back on by tomorrow morning," Leif said. He lit the candle on his bedside table and handed Ella a flashlight. "Just in case you need to find your way around the house."

"It's all good. I'm beat. And candlelight is soothing."

"I'm beat too." It was midnight and finally dark, as the summer sun had sunk below the horizon. They'd barely made it back to Leif's house before the storm hit Lyngør and knocked out the electricity. He lit another candle, one of a dozen illuminating his room. He was still trying to sort through all the evidence in his head. The nets were hard to argue against, and yet he had his doubts. He felt like he was walking a thin line though; he didn't want his disbelief to make it seem as though he wasn't taking her side.

"I still can't believe how fast that storm rolled in!" Ella said. "I'm glad we came here instead of trying to clean my cottage tonight. I don't even know if I have a flashlight or candles. Do you think you might still have time to help me tomorrow morning?"

"Yup, no worries. I'll always make time for you." He kissed her neck and pulled her closer. When Erik returned from his latest trip, Leif would have no choice but to confront him about the nets and scotch, but he didn't want to think about that yet.

"I'd like to borrow one of your shirts again," Ella said and kissed his lips.

"I think you're really sexy in them," he arched his brow at her flirtatiously and then slid a flannel shirt from a hanger in his wardrobe. "How about this one."

"Perfect. A beautiful blue, the color of the blue jay. Hey, I just got the best idea ever!" She grinned at him and reached for the shirt.

"What?" He laughed. He never knew what she was going to say or do.

"I'll show you," she winked. The flannel shirt hit her mid-thigh. She tugged at the hem and straightened it. Selecting one of Leif's belts, she cinched it tight around her waist, then pushed up on her toes and kissed him. "Wearing your shirts has inspired me. I'm going to design belted shirt dresses, and I'd like to create prints for them inspired by your carvings, if that's OK with you. And I'll call the line Leif. It will be one of a kind, just like you."

He felt flattered. "Come here, you." He held her cheeks in his hands and kissed her on the lips. He wondered what his life would be like if Ella stayed in Lyngør. Honestly, he'd never been so happy to be with anyone in his entire life. He'd been perfectly content with his arrangement with Charlotte—safe and steady, with excellent no-strings-attached sex—until Ella came along. But now perhaps he wanted more from a relationship, and maybe also from his life. Charlotte and everyone in Lyngør saw him only one way, but Ella saw more in him. For the first time he thought seriously about starting a side hustle carving his designs on wooden boats. He could rent a space at Erik's marina or find his own spot. What was stopping him? Nothing but his own fear. But with Ella near, everything seemed possible.

· · ·

By early morning, the power had returned. Leif pocketed his boat keys and joined Ella in his foyer.

"I'm ready," she said, and smiled at him.

Leif hugged her. "Mia's going to meet us at Ringpynten."

"I'm still touched that Mia already got rid of some of the mess. It won't take us long to finish."

As they went out the door, they nearly crashed into Inger. She looked exhausted, with bad bedhead and bloodshot eyes.

"Are you OK?" Leif asked her. "You look terrible."

"Jeez, thanks," she grumbled. "Ragnar called. Erik wants you to meet him at his mountain cabin, and to go there alone— you are not to bring Ella. Am I clear?"

Leif nodded.

"Wait, I need to see Erik too," Ella said.

Inger huffed at Ella. "Whoa, just stop. You're not in charge here. And anyway, it's your fault Erik has gone off the rails."

"What? How could that possibly be my fault?" Ella frowned.

Inger sighed. "Look. I talked to Ragnar last night. And yeah, he was drunk and didn't hold back, and from what I suspect . . . well, I think your mother and Leif's father died together. Erik was there."

"From what you suspect?" Leif's voice was loud and getting louder. "I can't believe you have the nerve to come here and say something like that! And so casually—as if you're reporting that the cost of your damn cigarillos has gone up!"

Ella's face was as pale as fish pudding. She stammered, "I don't understand . . . how could this be?"

Leif's throat tightened. He didn't want to relive the accident yet again, but it seemed there was no escaping it. Where does one thing start and the other stop? He didn't know, and he felt ill. He started to sweat. Before he could untangle his words, Inger spoke up. "It was a horrific boat accident. And if you hadn't come here, none of this would have come up again."

"A boat accident?" Ella gasped and clutched her stomach like she might retch.

"Yes," Inger said.

"A boat accident," Ella repeated, and then her eyes rounded on Leif. "Did you know how my mother died, but you didn't tell me?"

"No, I didn't know!" he shouted. "Remember a couple of days ago, I told you I had a new theory and asked if you wanted to hear it? You said no! To wait until I knew for sure!"

Ella looked at him with anguish in her eyes.

"I had no proof! And it's complicated . . ." His voice trailed off. What could he say that wouldn't sound ridiculous or weak? "You made me promise not to pursue the past. So, I buried it again." He looked out at the blue waters of Lyngør, the blue of Njord, god of the sea. The blue Bjorn wore each day, except the day of his death. Leif had recurring visions of Bjorn being crushed against the rocks as the current captured his lacerated body before tossing him around and finally dragging him out to sea. He would give anything to stop those horrid images— and to keep Ella from thinking her mother may have suffered the same fate.

"Could you please take me home?" Ella said to Inger.

"OK. My boat is at my dock." Inger gestured to Ella to follow her.

"Wait," Leif said, "please hear me out."

Ella held up her hands.

"Just give me two minutes!" he pleaded.

"Leif. Stop it," Inger said. "You aren't the only one that's been affected by this." She looked at Ella. "Time to go. Are you coming or not?"

Ella nodded, looking at Leif with the saddest eyes he'd ever seen. He was truly at a loss for words now.

He reached for the leather cord strung around his neck,

clasped his pendant, and held it toward her. "Don't tell me this doesn't mean anything!"

Ella blinked. She touched the aquamarine beads looped around her own neck. "I know . . . fate . . . maybe you and I were destined to meet."

"Why don't you hear him out," Inger said to Ella. "I'll wait in the backyard."

Leif released the breath he'd been holding. He had to weigh his words carefully and make this right. *Please let this go well.*

Aloud he said, "It crossed my mind that Sara might have been on the boat with Erik and my dad that night. But I had no proof." Grief struck him so hard, he stopped talking. But Ella had asked for the truth, so he forced out the words. "I feel horrible about all of this. I don't want it to ruin what we have— that would be terrible. In fact, I don't want you to go back to the States."

As he offered this last bit, Ella's breath caught, but she wanted to take this in order. "What makes you think she was there that night?"

Leif hesitated. His throat had seized up again, and his voice was hoarse as he continued. "When Ragnar told us that our parents were friends, that the men always got drunk and acted up to impress Sara, I wondered if she was with them the night of the accident." He scrubbed absentmindedly at his face before continuing. "A couple weeks ago, the morning after the party at the Propeller, I had to help Erik to bed. He was muttering a bunch of nonsense like he always does when he's wasted, but this time he offered something new. A woman had been on my father's boat when he crashed it. I hope that's wrong. And I pray that Inger's wrong too—that your mum wasn't there." His eyes stung, and he forced back tears. "I don't want you to suffer from knowing that. I don't want you to suffer at all."

"My poor mom." Ella's voice cracked, and a single tear slid

down her cheek. "But surely they would have found her body, right?" She shivered even asking a question like that.

Leif rubbed his wet eyes with his palms. "No. Most likely the sea would've taken her, just like it did my father and those two others. Their bodies never turned up. The rocks probably took care of them before the water did." As soon as Leif said this, he wanted to grab the words and yank them back. Ella clamped her hand over her mouth in horror and shock, her eyes darting around the yard like her bearings were scattering and she had no way of collecting them. He reached out to console her, but she twisted away and rushed toward his backyard, where Inger was waiting.

CHAPTER 34

"Did Sara really drown?"

Ella inhaled a shaky breath and held it until her lungs burned, then released it with a long sigh. She could feel Inger eyeing her as they walked together along the concrete path toward Inger's boat. Poor Mormor, the sea might've stolen her only child. That could explain why her grandma regarded the water as the enemy, even leaving Ringpynten afterward.

"Leif should've told me!" Ella fumed as she ripped a clump of fireweed from the rocks on the side of the path.

"Yep," Inger said, "if he actually knew. But it doesn't sound like he did." Cigarillo smoke curled around her finger.

The two women walked for a while in silence, squinting in the harsh morning light. As they crossed the footbridge linking the two islands, Ella tore the pink petals from the fireweed and flung them over the railing, leaning to watch them fall to the water. She wondered if they would sink or break apart in the swells and float out to sea. Her vision blurred again.

At the dock, Inger, bossy as ever, instructed Ella, "Come aboard, put on the life preserver, and for the love of Loki—don't fall overboard."

Ella untied the mooring line from the cleat, coiled up the rope, and stepped confidently onto the deck, looking as though she'd boarded boats her entire life.

"You're learning," Inger said with approval. "Soon people will think you almost know what you're doing."

"Leif showed me," Ella said, sadly.

Inger slid the key into the ignition and observed, "Leif has kind of been your rock since you came to Lyngør, hasn't he? Obviously he cares a lot about you. You shouldn't stay angry at him. I get angry easily," Inger said with a shrug, "but holding on to anger is about as useful as holding your hands to a flame."

Ella stared at her in surprise. She hadn't expected Zen-like thoughts from Inger.

"What are you looking at?"

"I'm looking at you," Ella said, smiling slightly. "It seems you're a bit of a hippie chick yourself."

"Don't push your luck." Inger smirked and backed the boat away from the dock.

· · ·

Even though Ella was getting used to boating, being out on rough waters still made her nervous. She gripped the railing on the skiff, her knuckles turning white as Inger quickly accelerated and steered through the waves. The water splashed and sprayed.

"Going fast out here is bloody fantastic!" Inger yelled over the motor.

Ella wanted to shout at her to slow down, but Inger stood proudly at the helm, a calm expression on her face. Ella longed to be calm too. She shut her eyes to the horrible new image of Sara going under the same water. More pieces of her childhood clicked, as she remembered how Mormor refused to let her attend a graduation party at Lake Estes. Things like that made sense now, if Mormor did indeed blame the water for Sara's death. Ella raised her voice over the wind and the waves.

"Do you think my grandma knew how my mom died?"

"Surely Hilda already told you how your mother died, though, didn't she?" Inger slowed the engine. "I don't want to shout over the noise," she explained and gave Ella a sympathetic look. "She would've surely told you the truth if she knew, wouldn't she?"

"I don't know. It wasn't until she died that I started learning about her *many* secrets. Maybe this was the reason she hated the water."

Ella filled Inger in, even telling her about the portrait she'd discovered in the cottage bedroom. She fiddled with the straps on her life preserver as she spoke. "If I do learn the truth about Sara's death and my grandma lied, I think I'll forgive her. I can't even begin to imagine what it must be like for someone to lose their child. She obviously never got over the pain, and that's probably why she couldn't talk to me about it even decades later. After coming here, I've realized that Sara and I were very much alike . . . I think maybe Mormor saw that too, and it made her worry more. She was only trying to keep me out of trouble so that she wouldn't lose me too."

Ella took a deep breath, realizing she'd been firing off her words like she couldn't get them out fast enough. She laughed in a way that one does when using humor as a cushion from grief. She told Inger about the old man who insisted that Sara had disappeared one day.

"That could be." Inger lit a cigarillo with one hand, keeping her other hand on the helm. "Let's just say hypothetically that Hilda knew. Maybe she didn't tell you because she was afraid that you'd ask questions, and she wanted to keep the past in the past. Certainly she had no intention of returning to Lyngør. Likely she couldn't face any of it. But she did keep the cottage, so . . . she must've wanted you to see it someday after she was gone." Inger throttled up the engine, then hollered over the thrumming, "I'm sorry you lost your mom though, and that you never got to spend time with her or with your family in Norway."

"I didn't really lose my mom. I never knew her," Ella shouted over the chugging motor. "Unfortunately, Leif and I have that in common. It's awful that he lost his father too."

"Yes!" Inger shouted back. "It's awful. I don't think Leif has ever forgiven his dad for driving drunk and killing himself and the others. It's always been a huge burden for Leif."

Inger slowed the engine again as they neared Ringpynten. "Erik was the only survivor, and guilt makes people do some very strange things."

• • •

Mia joined Ella and Inger at Ringpynten, and the three women snapped on rubber gloves and got to work. They squirted cleaner onto surfaces, poured bleach into buckets, and did what needed to be done as they chatted. Ella, who had thanked them profusely, glared at the flies circling the sink, which still contained traces of guts. She wanted to shove Erik into a vat of rotten fish.

At one point Inger commented, "This smell reminds me of something . . . once a boyfriend cheated on me, so I stuffed his curtain rod full of shrimp before I left. It took him a good week to find the source of the smell. Not that I'm suggesting you should do that to Erik!"

The three laughed grimly. Ella thanked them again for being there, and she meant it, even though she was still hesitant to trust Inger.

"Why would Erik do this?" Mia said as she wiped the refrigerator.

"Your guess is as good as mine," Inger said. Dunking her

rag in a bucket, she wrung it out with a hard twist. "Erik's sick, if he's guilty of this."

"He definitely has issues," Ella said and shooed away a fly.

Mia replied, "Yeah, but *we* can't turn our backs on him."

Ella heard that *we* and wondered if she were included. It certainly sounded like it. She wondered what it would feel like to be a part of their group. She didn't know, but she was pretty sure that it would mean playing by their established rules, and one of those was giving Erik a lot of leeway, apparently. She wasn't sure she could do that, and she doubted if she could forgive him. There was no question of forgiving Leif though, even if she was still a little pissed at him. Yes, he'd withheld his theory, but only because she'd told him she didn't want to hear it! Ella almost wished she hadn't chased the past either, because of the mental images she now had of Sara and that horrible accident. She felt awful for the agony that Leif already carried because of his father's actions. If Bjorn were responsible for Sara's death too—well, she could hardly bear to think what a burden that would be for Leif.

Mia continued, "Erik is broken and messed up, but he's not evil. He's never done anything like this. You heard what Oskar said about him—that he couldn't believe Erik was capable of stealing, let alone vandalism."

Ella noticed a fish tail poking out of the utensil drawer, so she slid it open, her eyes watering at the stench as she shoved the corpse into the trash bag. As she scrubbed a soapy sponge over the drawer's interior, it caught on the edge of the contact paper where it was covering a lump. She pulled the drawer out farther and ran her fingers over the edge of the curled paper.

"It feels like there's something stuck under here." She picked at the corner and peeled it back, revealing a ring with three keys at the rear of the drawer. They were unmarked but appeared too small for the front door. Ella held them up. "Look—I found something!"

Mia and Inger came to her side to study them. "Hmm, clock keys maybe? Mia, what do you think? Clock?"

"Yep, my mormor owned a similar set," Mia confirmed. "The large skeleton key opens the front panel, the cylinder-shaped key winds the clock, and the smallest one unlocks a drawer inside. They must go with your grandfather clock in the sitting room. I've wondered where the keys were. Hilda said they'd been lost long ago, but it didn't matter because people have wristwatches."

The women laughed and moved to the sitting room to test the keys. Dust motes floated in the soft light as Ella pulled a chair over to the grandfather clock and stood on the seat. With Inger and Mia on either side of her, she did exactly what Mia had suggested; she opened the front panel with the skeleton key and used the cylinder key to wind the clock. She nudged the pendulum, and it swung back and forth.

"Wow, it actually works! Now to find that compartment." She stopped the pendulum and ran her hand up inside the clock tower and poked around the walls, finding nothing. As she patted around the interior of the old clock, Ella wondered what family secrets it possibly held. The thought was both thrilling and scary. She might learn something deeply personal about her family, but not necessarily good news . . . there was a chance she'd uncover something dark and ugly. If that was the case, she'd rather keep it private from Inger and Mia.

Mia leaned close. "Run your hand farther up." Ella did as Mia directed, but still didn't find anything.

"Feel around for a latch," Inger suggested with impatience, craning her neck to look inside the clock cavity.

Despite Ella's mixed feelings, she pushed her arm higher into the dark chamber and paused as her knuckles brushed against what felt like a keyhole. "I think I found it."

"Open it," Inger demanded.

After three attempts, Ella fitted the small key into the hole and a drawer slid open. There were two items inside: a wooden trinket and a piece of paper folded into squares. She retrieved the trinket, leaving the paper to look at later, when she was alone. She stepped down from the chair and balanced the little object in the palm of her hand: a tiny, hand-carved brown bear.

"It's adorable," she said. "What do you think?"

"Yes, it's cute," Inger said. She reached for the bear and brushed her fingers over the rotund body. "It looks like Erik's work. Could be his carving, right, Mia?"

"It might be," Mia agreed.

Ella slipped the bear into her pocket. "How would one of Erik's carvings end up in the secret clock drawer at Ringpynten?" She hoped that the paper might shed more light on this, but she could wait until the others left. What if it was a love letter? *Did you hide both those things in the clock and the keys in the drawer, Mormor? Or was it Sara?*

"Let's see what else is up there." Inger moved to stand on the chair, but Ella placed her hand on her arm.

"No, that was it," Ella said. "I'm quite sure."

As the three of them got back to work cleaning the cottage, the minutes dragged by for Ella. It took all her restraint not to hurry Inger and Mia out the door. Finally the cottage was clean, and Inger and Mia shoved off from the dock. Ella waved a casual goodbye as she gripped the small bear in her pocket. She hurried back inside and to the clock; her fingers shook as she opened the hidden compartment and grasped the paper. Sitting down on the sofa, she wiped her hands against her skirt and unfolded the pink paper.

It was an official form, in Norwegian, with a notary stamp. Her mouth went dry as her name, *Ella Kari Nilsen*, leaped out at her in neat cursive. It was her birth certificate. Her throat ached as she traced her fingers over her mother's name, *Sara Nilsen*.

She was afraid to look at her father's given name. Mormor had different names for him: one-night stand, wandering traveler, worthless. She swore that Sara hadn't revealed his identity, but it was possible that Mormor had known and decided to keep the secret. Ella finally allowed her eyes to keep moving slowly over the document, to the father's name.

Erik Olsen.

No, it couldn't be! She wished it was anyone else—anyone at all—but there was no arguing with the name clearly printed on the official document.

She slumped onto the sofa, slid to the floor, and rested her head on the coffee table, waiting to cry tears that didn't come. She had nothing inside of her except anger and pain, for all the secrets and lies.

CHAPTER 35

Five hours after driving his Jeep away from the boatyard on the mainland near Lyngør, Leif arrived at Hemsedal, a mountainous region with snow-capped peaks and emerald valleys. He blasted alternative rock to drown out his thoughts, as the tires bumped over the stony root-ridden terrain. If he was smart, he told himself, he would let it go. But he deserved to know the truth about the accident. And besides, he thought, as he maneuvered behind Erik's cargo van on the side of the dirt road, someone owed Ella an apology for vandalizing Ringpynten, and that person appeared to be Erik.

Zipping his coat against the cold drizzle, Leif trudged along the moss-cushioned path that led to Erik's cabin. In the dense evergreen forest, a needled branch brushed against his head. He snapped the limb from the tree and tossed it to the ground. Why would Erik do it? Leif thought he had some idea, and it turned his stomach.

Above him, silver light pushed in through the pine branches. He tipped his chin at the slice of sky. *Please let there be a sensible reason why the fishmonger's nets ended up in Erik's office.*

Erik's one-story brown cabin lay ahead. A twelve-point stag trotted across the clearing and disappeared into the birch trees that bordered the snow-dusted mountain range. Leif hoped seeing the animal was a good omen.

Grass and pine shoots grew on the sod roof. Leif saw a copy of *Crime and Punishment* lying on the table on the porch and wondered if it was a sign of Erik's guilt. He wiped his feet on the bristle mat and knocked once on the door before entering the damp, dark room that seemed to promise mildew and mice. Erik sat on the upholstered sofa in front of the blazing fireplace. Flickering shadows from the flames masked his face.

"There's a twelve-point stag in your front yard," Leif said. He unlaced his hiking boots, the worn floorboards creaking as his weight shifted.

Erik leaned forward and grabbed his whittling knife and a block of wood from the reindeer rug at his feet. Leif placed his boots next to a trout rod propped against the pine wall.

"Been fishing?"

"You want to talk about fishing?" Erik grunted at Leif and pulled his cap farther down on his brow.

"No. I'm here to ask some questions and I want the truth."

"How about a drink? My first one today." Erik nodded at the bottle on the mantel. Leif found two cups and poured a finger of whiskey into each.

As always, they toasted in unison: *"Skål."* Erik tipped back his cup, his eyes still fixed on the flames. Leif shifted uncomfortably.

"What about the nets, and the vandalism to Ella's cottage?"

Erik's silence was as good as any answer. It felt like a punch to the chest.

"Why?" Leif sank down on the stool and rubbed his chin. Suspecting Erik had been terrible enough, but the truth was devastating.

"Ella was asking too many questions," Erik grumbled.

"Who cares? She wants to know about her family. There's no harm in that. What the hell is wrong with you?"

Erik ignored him. He chipped at his wood block haphazardly and pricked his hand with the point of the blade. Blood seeped from the small cut, but he continued to scrape and stab at the wood. The lines deepened in Erik's hard face.

"This is crap." He chucked the block onto the burning logs, threw the knife on the floor with a clatter, and licked the blood from his hand.

"You knew Ella's mum, Sara, didn't you? It's bad enough that you didn't tell me, but you should have told Ella."

"I can't . . ." Erik's voice tapered off. He hunched his shoulders and pressed his palms against his eyes.

Leif plowed on. "Tell me, now."

"I love you like a son. You've been through enough." Erik swallowed hard.

"It's about the accident, isn't it?"

Erik's hand trembled as he lit his cigar. The torment of that night was written all over his face.

"Yes. Ella's mother was there."

So it was true. Both grief and fury roared through Leif.

"Why keep this from Ella? She deserves to know how her mum died."

"I killed Sara."

"Bullshit!" Leif tripped over the stool as he rushed to stand before Erik. "You can be a real ass sometimes, but you're not a murderer."

Erik looked up. "I also killed your father."

"You killed them? How?" Leif pleaded, the hairs on his neck rising.

Erik reached for the fireplace poker and stabbed at the logs as he spoke to the fire. "We were on the water, just outside of Lyngør Sound. A storm came up. I thought I could handle it."

"You? What do you mean, *you*?" Leif straightened the stool and fought the urge to throw it against the wall.

"Your father was drunk. I was a little drunk too . . . but I took the helm."

"You've been lying to everyone—to *me*—all these years?" Leif felt dizzy.

"You were five when it happened. I took you into my home. If I had told you the truth, you would have hated me."

Leif said nothing. The room felt stifling, and he couldn't breathe. He raised the window with a bang. Cold valley air pushed into the room and chilled him, the sudden change making him shiver.

"Try to understand, Leif. I was driving the boat, and I was the only person to come out alive. I was racked with guilt but even more terrified of being found out. I might have gone to prison. The village would have shunned me."

"So you blamed it on my father?" Leif's throat ached in anguish. For as long as he could remember, he'd been both livid and disillusioned with his father for causing the horrific deaths, as well as their tragic ripple effects. He narrowed his eyes at Erik. "But why the fish? Why Ella?"

"When that girl showed up, something snapped in me. She looks exactly like her mother."

Leif broke into a cold sweat. He went into the kitchen, turned on the tap, and splashed water on his face. How would his own life have been different if he had known the truth? Leaning over the running water, he considered this parallel life. Perhaps he would have felt better about himself if he hadn't grown up in the shadow of his father's crime. He wouldn't have had to personally bear the pity and disgust of everyone in the village. Meanwhile, Erik—the real sinner in this scenario—was praised as a hero for taking on Little Orphan Leif.

He couldn't believe it. He swiped his sleeve across his forehead and moved back to the other room, almost in a trance.

Erik started up again as soon as Leif reentered the room, like he didn't want to waste any more time. "We were headed to Whale Island. There was a storm, but it seemed far away."

"Only an idiot would drive around Whale Island in a storm! Those waves can reach two meters high." Leif balled up his fists and shuddered.

Erik's words came faster. "We'd all been drinking. I was young and cocky, and thought I could handle the weather. By the time I realized the danger, it was too late. A rogue wave hit us." Erik's voice cracked. "The engine died, and the boat headed for the rocks."

Leif closed his eyes at the gruesome image.

"Your father and two other fellas jumped ship."

Leif quickly held up his hand. "Stop. Not another word." He never saw his father's body, but he could picture it. Sometimes when he was on the water, or when he looked at the mural at the Propeller, he thought about Bjorn slamming against the rocks. He could almost hear the crunch of bones.

"And Ella's mother, Sara?" Leif said.

"Sara fell overboard. I tried to grab her, but I was too late. She hit the rocks and disappeared under the water."

"You *must* tell Ella. You have to make this right."

Erik let out a rough sob. Leif wanted to punch something . . . someone. He loved Erik. He'd been like a father to him, but this was more than he could take.

CHAPTER 36

A loud knock awakened Ella, and she sat up groggily. It had been a night of tossing and turning. She figured it was probably Leif knocking, as he had promised to bring her news about Erik. She combed her fingers through her tangled hair as she ran down the stairs and opened the door. Her smile disappeared at the sight of Erik standing there.

She narrowed her eyes at him. "Why are you here?" He opened his mouth to speak but snapped it shut and winced at her. "Did you bring me more fish? Because I've had my fill. Thank you."

"I have no excuse," he said, as his gaze shifted to the ivy creeping over the cottage walls.

"No kidding! How dare you? Why would you even come here?"

Erik tilted his head up to the morning sky and squinted against the drizzle. "I want to explain. Can I come in?"

"I'm all out of scotch."

"I shouldn't have nicked your liquor either; I'll replace it."

"Don't bother. Just tell me why."

"Please . . . this is deeply uncomfortable for me," Erik

stammered and wrung his hands. "This might not be comfort-able for you either . . ." His voice trailed off. She was glaring at him, and she nudged her chin toward the dock as if telling him to leave.

"Look, Ella, I can explain. I'd like to do it properly and have this conversation indoors." She just stood there, so he added, "I owe you an explanation. I . . . I . . . was hoping to make you leave. To scare you off. I wanted the past to stay in the past, and you were asking too many questions. Plus it was starting to look like you were planning to stay permanently, what with you and Leif all lovey-dovey."

"You're off to a great start—I didn't hear an apology in there anywhere! And you're lying, anyway—you've been rude to me from the moment you saw me at Lyngør Grocery, well before I asked any questions!" She glared at him again and moved to shut the door.

"Please. Hear me out. It's important." He motioned beyond her shoulder, at the foyer.

She couldn't believe this man was her father. She stared at his square face, freckled with age spots, and the jut of his lantern jaw, and saw nothing familiar there. She flicked a thick lock of copper hair behind her ear. Did he know she was his daughter? Curiosity won over anger, and she stepped aside to let him pass. "OK, but make it short."

He brushed past her and stopped to unlace his hiking shoes, setting them next to her boots. He pulled up his wool socks. He was painstakingly drawing out each task. She fol-lowed him into the kitchen and watched as he ran his blunt fingers over the scratched counter.

"What?" she asked with some impatience.

"Old ghosts," he murmured with a faraway look in his eye.

"What was she to you?" Ella touched the wooden bear in her pocket and waited for him to admit to her who he was . . . unless he was trying to keep it from her . . . or maybe he didn't know.

Erik said nothing. He removed his fisherman cap and scrunched it as he walked into the sitting room and paused in front of the hutch painted with tulips and scrolls. His eyes flicked over the sewing machine.

"That belonged to Sara," he said with a solemn nod. He noticed Ella's sweater draped over the back of the rocking chair and moved to examine it, hovering his fingers over the sleeves where she'd stitched finches and flowers—and then snapped his hand back as if the sweater could burn him.

"You sew?" he asked.

"No, I glue bobbles on hats."

He let out a sad chuckle. "You sound just like her." He sank down into the rocking chair, then hunched forward and rubbed his legs.

Ella didn't care about this stranger or what he thought. He was a bully, a father only on paper. She only knew that her desire to hear about her mom was fiercer now than ever before, and it took all her self-control to play it cool.

"How did you meet my mom?" she asked.

"Sara was sixteen. She dropped off one of Hilda's skiffs for repair at the boatyard. The moment I saw her, it was as if my heart was nailed to the deck. But she was way out of my league. The next summer, I ran into her at the hotel bar . . . her voice was smooth as butter, and she told the best jokes. I'd never laughed that much, and I let my guard down. We drank too much, and . . . I don't know . . . my memory of that night is blurry. But I do remember that it felt like we'd known each other our entire lives. I'd never been able to talk to anyone like I talked to her. Over the next two years, I saw her when she came back in the summers. Each time I see you now, I think of her. I don't know what to do with those memories." His sad eyes moved to Sara's sketchbook on the table.

"When did you see her last?" Ella asked.

He was silent for a beat, then said, "The night of the accident."

"You mean the night Leif's father crashed his boat?"

Erik finally looked her straight in the eye. "It wasn't him. I was at the helm."

Ella sank down on the sofa. "But everyone says Leif's father was steering!"

"No. I was, and I killed all four of them." He was rocking in her chair, rubbing harder at his legs. Agony filled his watery eyes.

"I . . . don't understand," she said, her disbelief catching in her voice.

Erik shifted in his seat to turn away from Ella, and the rocking chair scraped against the floor. Cupping his head in his hands, he stumblingly began to tell the story of that awful night.

"Two of my navy buddies were visiting from up north. That's where they lived, and I, uh, had promised to show them around Lyngør. Your mother had asked to speak to me alone, but I showed up here, at Ringpynten, with my friends and asked her to come out with us instead." He paused to run his meaty hands over his face.

"Yeah?" Ella asked. There was a challenge in the word, an unspoken barb directed at him for not honoring Sara's wishes.

"Well, I suppose I was afraid that she might've wanted to break up with me . . . and I was excited to see her, but . . . I didn't want to be alone with her . . . you know, give her the chance to end things between us."

Ella resisted the temptation to land a well-timed insult—barely—and instead asked, "What made you think she wanted to end things?"

"Well, Sara seemed tense that night. But really . . . she hadn't answered any of my letters. We used to write to each other when she went home . . . but that year, nothing. I tried calling her at their apartment in Oslo a couple of times. But Hilda answered and told me to stop calling. She thought I was too . . . blue collar and not educated enough to marry her daughter. She wanted more for Sara."

Ella understood how Mormor's words could sting. Erik chuckled, but it wasn't a real laugh; the sound was sad and hollow. He continued to rock nervously in the chair as he spoke. "This is so hard . . . but I've already started, and I owe you this much, at least . . ." His voice trailed off again. He glanced out the window at the gray sky. "That tragic night, I pushed for us to head out in Bjorn's boat right away. Like I said, I was glad she was there, but also relieved that we were in a group. I just wanted to have a good time, and we drank way too much, way too fast. Bjorn could barely stand up to pilot his own boat, so I took the helm. It had been a cloudy day but there was no rain in the forecast, so I was surprised to see storm clouds on the horizon—but I was confident I could handle it. In less than an hour, though, the water turned rough . . . the swells beating against land—against *us*. It was bad. We didn't stand a chance."

He choked back a sob at the memory and kept his eyes fixed on Sara's sewing machine.

"How can you live with yourself? You're a coward and a liar!" Ella sputtered. She could hardly stand to look at him.

"I thought my secret was locked away for good, but believe me, I've paid a heavy price for being dishonest."

"Not heavy enough," she said firmly, with narrowed eyes.

"I love that boy as if he were my own flesh and blood— now he won't even talk to me! I can't lose him too." Erik's voice wobbled, and he gestured at Sara's sewing machine. "She'd be livid with me, for what I did to her cottage. And to you." He looked at Ella and took a shaky breath. "I'm sorry for everything. You will never know just how sorry I am."

At last, the apology. A chill cut through Ella as she looked out the window at the dark sea. As the last person to see her mother alive, he still had information she wanted, and she knew this could be her only opportunity to ask him questions. She let everything else go.

"How old was my mom, and how come no one knew she was on the boat?"

"She had just turned nineteen. It was off-season, early June. Bjorn and my friends and I were drinking in the boatyard, and she left a message on the answering machine there. If I hadn't checked my messages, I would've missed her . . . she'd still be alive."

"Wait a minute, go back—I don't understand. I thought—"

Erik shook his head gravely. "She'd come to Lyngør spontaneously that night, to see me. She said she had something to tell me. I don't know how she explained that to Hilda, but whatever story that was, I doubt it was the truth. You already know that Hilda didn't approve of me."

"Hilda could spot a rotten egg anywhere."

"Right," he allowed, and shifted in his seat. "I can see we had no business being on the water that night. I tried to grab your mum before she fell overboard but I wasn't fast enough. She hit the rocks and went under."

She didn't want to know the awful details; she already knew too much. She thought that she should probably end this conversation to protect herself from worse heartache. But she still needed facts.

"So what had Sara come to tell you?"

A brief silence, followed by, "I never found out."

Erik looked away when he answered. Ella couldn't read him well enough to know if he was telling the truth, but she saw his tortured expression.

"Where was I that night?" she asked.

"I have no idea—I didn't know she had a baby. I guess you were with Hilda, at home in Oslo." He leaned forward in his seat and clutched his stomach.

Her hands turned ice-cold as it dawned on her: He didn't know. Well, she sure wasn't going to tell him.

She had to clench her teeth to keep them from chattering.

She couldn't stop thinking about poor Sara. Her heart broke for Mormor. And for Leif, who not only lost his father, but lost something else indispensable because Erik had lied to him for so long.

"Did my grandma know the truth about how Sara really died? And if so, why would she keep it from me?"

"I spoke to your mormor after the accident." Erik winced as the miserable memory returned. "Are you sure you want to hear it?"

"Tell me," Ella said impatiently.

"OK, here it goes." He inhaled a deep breath as if drawing the courage to continue. "Two days after the accident, Hilda called the boatyard in a panic, looking for Sara. At least that's what my shop tech remembered. He told Hilda that I'd been in a boat wreck, that I was in critical condition in the hospital. I think she knew that her daughter was with me in the boat that night and was never coming home. She called the hospital, but it took some days before I was well enough to talk. When she came to see me, I thought for sure she'd accuse me of murdering her daughter and turn me in to the police. But she floored me. She wanted to strike a deal—that neither of us would ever talk about it again. Not to friends or loved ones either. Not to anyone at all. Because none of it could bring our Sara back."

He scrunched his hat in his lap and struggled to compose himself. "I was frightened that I'd spend years in prison. I badly wanted it all to go away, so I agreed with her. I said it was OK. I believe losing Sara just about killed her. Everyone handles grief differently and . . . I think your mormor's way of dealing with it was to shut herself off from anyone and everything that might remind her of Sara. I think she locked away her past in Norway and never looked back. I can certainly relate."

Ella could see the pain in his face. But there was more; he held his hand up.

"Just so you know . . . I let Hilda think that Bjorn was steering. No one knew the whole truth of it, except for Ragnar. He was the one who found me and called a medical helicopter to take me to the hospital. He stayed with me in that room for days—slept in a chair. I was on all types of painkillers, but somehow I told him the truth. He swore he'd keep my secret, and he's honored that promise all these years. It's because of him that I'm still here . . . I didn't want to survive that crash, you know. His loyalty and friendship somehow gave me the courage to live."

Ella nodded. "I met him. He seems to have a lot of love for his friends. He warned me that my digging could hurt people . . . now I understand what he meant by that. Do you happen to know why he has my mom's blanket?"

"Blanket? Oh. Well . . . the summer before the accident, me, Ragnar, and Astrid—that's his parrot, you know—visited Sara here at Ringpynten. I do seem to remember Astrid falling in love with a blanket . . . Ragnar must've borrowed it." Erik said this in a way that conveyed much more. "He was known to do things like that—plus, he'd do anything for that bird. I'm guessing he felt like that was that—or, if he ever had any thoughts of returning it . . . my guess is that he had reservations about making an impromptu visit to Hilda's house and admitting what he'd done. Your mormor thought we were a bad influence on Sara . . . and it turned out she was right." He let out another sad, hollow chuckle.

"Did my grandma ever bring me here to Lyngør?"

"Hilda? I don't think so. After Sara died, your mormor hired the grocery manager to rent out the property, and as far as I know, she never returned. She loved your mother, and I guess she couldn't bear being at the cottage without her. Lots of memories and too much grief."

"Did you love Sara too?"

Erik stood up from the rocking chair, rested his hand on

the wood frame, tucked his head to his chest, and said simply, "Yes I did."

"You did."

"Yes. Well, that's all I got," Erik pronounced, as if he'd reached his breaking point. He looked around the room with haunted eyes.

"Go on, then. Leave," Ella said through gritted teeth. She'd gotten what she wanted, and now she could be done with him. She remained in her chair as he disappeared into the foyer. The floorboards squeaked; she could hear him putting on his shoes. Finally, the door closed behind him.

She looked at Hilda's urn and said, "You were right, Mormor. He is no good." Ella knew the value of forgiveness and second chances, but Erik's lies had been calculated to save his own skin, no matter the damage to anyone else. He was that selfish and she had no patience for it.

Ella tucked her birth certificate between the pages of her mother's sketchbook to take back to Boulder. There was no need to tell anyone about Erik, especially since she didn't want him as a father. She had no attachment, no history, and no respect for him. Plus her mind was made up now: She planned on walking away from Leif, and everyone else in Lyngør, to put her energy and love into her business.

Outside the window, a colony of gulls soared over the sapphire sea. That color was beautiful. It was Leif's blue, but it was also the blue that stole her mom's final breath.

Tears blurred Ella's vision as she picked up the book on knots that Leif had given her. If it hadn't been for him, she might never have faced her fear of the water. His carvings had inspired so many designs by now; the sketches for the Leif Collection filled an entire notebook. He'd introduced her to Nina, who she hoped would be a part of Little Bird's success. Ella reflected that she owed Leif so much gratitude and hadn't thanked him properly. But she could do that now—row to his house and give back the boat. She'd say a final goodbye and wouldn't let him talk her into staying another day, because the more she was with him, the more painful it would be to leave him. It was time to book her ticket.

CHAPTER 37

Ella tied the dinghy to Leif's dock and made her way up the path to his house. Before knocking on his door, she paused for a moment on his lawn and rubbed her beads, asking for strength and luck. Luck, because she had tied a cleat hitch and hoped that it would hold. Strength, because she could really use it after that talk with Erik. She understood that his lies had hurt Leif deeply, and she wanted to offer some comfort to Leif before she left Lyngør, but she couldn't let him see how much it hurt her to say goodbye.

Before she could knock, Leif opened the door. "Hey you," he said, "I was just heading to your place, but I'm glad you're here." He seemed genuinely happy to see her, but there was pain in his eyes.

"Erik came to see me, and we talked. Are you OK?" she asked as she hugged him.

He frowned. "I've been better." Catching a lock of her hair, he brought it to his nose. "Grapefruit. Cinnamon. Sunshine. My Sunna. Just the medicine I need. Come on in."

She followed him into the kitchen, pausing near the trunk with the painted scene from the Battle of Lyngør. She was fighting a battle of her own, having decided to end her relationship with Leif—blowing it to smithereens, along with her heart. How was it that she felt closer to him after two weeks than she did to Petal, her best friend of fifteen years?

He turned down the volume on the stereo, which was playing Bill Evans's "Peace Piece," and offered her a cookie from the tin on the counter. She sat down at the table while Leif brought her a mug of coffee and placed a hand on hers.

"I should have asked—are you all right?" He pulled up a chair next to hers.

"I'm OK." She threaded her fingers through his. "I'm worried about you though. I can't believe Erik lied about your father like that."

"I've had enough of Erik's crap. I don't even know what to do . . . I mean, what do you do when your father figure has killed your actual father and then lied about it your whole life? I have no clue."

"Maybe you should talk to Inger and Mia about it." Ella knew they'd be there for Leif after she went back home to Colorado.

"Well, I'm not looking forward to *that*." He reached for a cookie and snapped it in half. "Inger, Mia, and the others might feel obligated to take sides. I don't want that."

"This has to be awful for you. I can't imagine. And I hear you—I wish I could make things better before I go." She fidgeted with the bear in her pocket. None of this would have happened if she hadn't shown up. Even though it wasn't her fault, she'd set everything in motion. Well, she knew *that* wasn't true. She was just a baby when this all started, but the unraveling of the tragedy and the lies began with her trying to solve her family mysteries, and she felt some responsibility for that.

"Do you think you guys can get past this?"

"How could he have lied to me all these years? He knew how much guilt I carried!" Leif jumped to his feet, grabbed the whittling knife from the mantel, and threw it on the hearth with a clap. Erik had probably given him that knife. Leif and Erik shared their lives and their friends, and Ella hoped that with time they might patch things up.

"Maybe you and Erik could speak with a counselor together, and try to untangle all this to get your relationship back on track?"

"Counseling? You must be joking." Leif let out a bitter laugh. "I'd have a better chance of landing a whale with a fishing rod than getting Erik to spill his guts to some stranger. Besides, it's not just what he did to *me*. How am I supposed to even look at Erik without thinking about what he's done to you? If it weren't for him, your mum would still be alive."

"I don't know. I wish I could help but I need to go home." Ella closed her eyes against the sting of her tears. No way could she stay without telling anyone that Erik was her father.

"Sunna, what's all this talk about going?" He took her hand, and she felt a spark of longing, of love. It caught her off guard.

Quickly, she asked, "Could you give me a lift home?"

"Now? But you just arrived. I thought I would cook dinner."

She swallowed hard. "I can't stay. I need to pack. I brought your dinghy back—I tied it up out there—but I don't have a way to get myself back to Ringpynten without getting a ride, so could you please take me home, now?"

"Why? I . . . I don't understand," he stammered. "Please stay—don't let Erik force you out."

"No one's forcing me out. I have my business to launch, and I'm behind schedule. And I've spent enough time here, and this feels like the right time to leave. Maybe I can come back here on vacation after I get my store up and running."

"Give me a couple more days with you," he said. "Please stay."

His voice was raw, and her heart caught at the emotion in it. "You can visit me in Boulder whenever you want." Even as she said this, she wondered how they could have any kind of real relationship from two sides of the world.

"Stay." He tented his hands like he was begging.

"I have a business, an employee, deadlines. Obligations. I have to get back to them—back to my life." Her voice wobbled and she steadied it.

Leif seemed to be grabbing at options, anything he could think of. "Just give me a few more days. Sew those jackets for Nina—I bet they'll sell fast. Have you bought your return ticket?"

"I'm booking the flight this afternoon."

There. He'd found his opening.

"Then you can stay one more day."

He moved closer and swept her hair from her shoulders. She reached out to the window box full of rosemary and rolled some in her fingers to breathe in the relaxing scent.

"Please say yes to one more day—and a date with me tonight? I'll bring you back to Ringpynten, you can pack and get ready, and I'll do everything else. You don't have to worry about it at all." He held out his hand, with the finch he'd carved for her balanced on his palm. "A little bird, named after your store."

As she took it, she swallowed the lump in her throat. "It's so sweet. It'll always remind me of you and our time together."

"It's just a small thing."

She shook her head. "No, it's not a small thing," she said in a shaky voice.

"So you'll go out with me?"

She hesitated. She slipped the finch into her pocket with the bear and secretly clutched both, out of view. She didn't want him to know that his gift had melted her, and her determination was in a puddle at her feet. She also knew that he was right; she hadn't booked anything, and she couldn't realistically leave immediately.

"Ah, come on. You'll make me the happiest man in the world if you say yes to dinner with me." His dimples deepened. She thought her heart might burst.

"OK, one final date," she said.

CHAPTER 38

Leif arrived at Ringpynten and paused to shift his bags from one hand to the other, careful not to bruise the blue delphinium poking from one of the totes. He wiped one hand on his dress pants and straightened his tie. He wanted the night with Ella to be perfect. He'd brought chocolate, champagne, and a fondue pot. He suddenly panicked, thinking he'd forgotten the cheese, but he unzipped his duffel bag and was relieved to find it tucked next to the vegetables. He shook the tension out of his shoulders. He couldn't recall ever being so anxious. This was their final night together, unless he could convince her to stay.

He halted at the sight of Ella sitting on one of the patio chairs. She was wearing a hip-hugging yellow dress and a cowboy hat, and she was strumming her guitar. This was exactly how she'd been the first time he saw her. He hadn't believed in love at first sight before that day, but he did now. When she started humming in that beautiful voice of hers, it took his breath away. He knew that he couldn't let her go and that he was going to fight for her.

"Hey there, Sunna," he said brightly, and she laid her guitar on her lap to greet him. "No, don't stop playing—it sounds so nice!"

"It's something I started writing today." Reaching for the pencil and notepad on the table, she erased a word and replaced it with another one.

"Can I hear it?"

Ella considered this as she wrote several more words on the paper. She placed the pencil back on the table and began to strum and sing.

> Lookin' back
> For someone who gives a damn.
> I'm someone, and you gotta do the things
> you can
> And I couldn't
> See when things were going wrong
> And I wouldn't change my ways and now
> he's gone

She stopped and settled the guitar into the case at her feet. "That's as far as I got with the lyrics," she explained.

"It's good."

Her voice was like velvet and sunshine. He ached to scoop her up in his arms and hold her forever . . . except soon she would be gone. Right now he felt a twinge in his chest, but he knew by tomorrow, it would be a gaping void in his heart.

Even so, he refused to ruin tonight. Ella had encouraged him to live in the moment and appreciate the now, so he smiled and offered her the champagne and flowers. This final date of theirs had to be something to remember.

CHAPTER 39

Ella woke up next to Leif in her bed at Ringpynten. She lay on her side, her cheek resting on his chest, listening to the steadiness of his heart. She was glad she decided to stay in Lyngør for one more night. They had laughed together and shared long, lingering kisses beneath the shimmering sunset. Afterward, they made love beneath the moon and stars. She wished they could stay in bed all day, but she had to finish packing before Leif drove her to TORP Sandefjord Airport in a few hours.

The thought of leaving him ripped her apart. He made her feel cherished, talented, smart, and beautiful. She lifted her chin, her eyes savoring his face—thick lashes, slanted cheekbones, strong jaw. Her heart would store what her memory might forget.

She kissed his mouth, and he opened his eyes. For a moment they looked at each other, until he reached out and gently stroked her cheek.

"I don't think I've ever felt this content," he said as he drew her in for a kiss.

• • •

Ella set her coffee mug on the dock before giving Leif a hug. "See you in a few hours. One thirty?"

"Yes," he said. "That should give us plenty of time to get to the airport. Are you still sure you want to sell it?"

Her gaze followed his to the cottage. The memories she had made while staying there had taken root in her heart. The sparkling windows. The kinship she felt for Mia and Inger when they helped her clean up the fish mess. Leif teaching her to whittle and telling her to trust herself. She loved how much they laughed together and bonded over their passion for their artwork. And then last night, the wonderful fondue dinner, and being in his arms beneath the moon. Her heart pleaded with her to keep the cottage, stay, and be with Leif, but she'd made up her mind, and her reasons were good ones: She didn't want Erik in her life, and she couldn't jeopardize Little Bird.

"Yes, I'm sure, but I still wish I didn't have to go." Her throat and chest ached at the thought of leaving him.

Leif gestured at the waters just off Ringpynten. "This is one of my favorite fishing spots, and I'll never be able to go there again without missing you. And this patio—I'll forever remember you sitting there, wearing your cowboy hat and that yellow dress, my Sunna." He kissed her slowly at first, but it quickly turned hot. She reached for his hand and considered taking him back to her bedroom one last time, but a catcall came from the channel, and she let go of him.

It was Axel, steering his wooden skiff toward her dock. He lifted his hand in the air, and his white teeth flashed even from that distance. He throttled down the engine and put it into neutral. Drifting up next to Leif's boat, *Skadi*, he leaned over and caught her railing.

"A bunch of us are meeting at the Propeller tonight. You two have to come."

"I wish I could, but I'm leaving today," she said. She was sure that the smile she offered him didn't reach her eyes.

"You're leaving? That's awful news!" Axel frowned, looking from one of them to the other.

"But she doesn't have a ticket yet," Leif said. He pulled Ella close again before kissing her cheek.

"No I don't, but I'm sure it won't be a problem booking a flight at the airport. And I don't care about the number of lay-overs; I'll take what they can give me."

"Great!" Axel said. "Then you can come tonight—we'll make it a going-away party."

"Oh, come on, you guys, don't do this to me." To avert her eyes, Ella scooped up an empty mussel shell from the dock and studied it.

Axel shook his head, tsk-tsking. "You mean you're going to deny us the opportunity to give you a proper send-off? Don't you care about us at all? Please, say you'll come." He put on an exaggeratedly sad face and blinked at her.

Leif cut in. "That face always gets him what he wants. No one can say no to those puppy-dog eyes."

Ella held up the shell. "Hey, check this out—see the dark-violet shimmer inside here? I love it! I need to find a thread to match."

The two men laughed at her weak attempt to change the subject. "You're a funny bird, and that's a good thing," Axel said. "This place won't be the same without you."

"Will Erik be there tonight?" Leif crossed his arms and got serious.

"I doubt it." Axel grimaced. "He dropped by Inger's yes-terday and told her the truth about the accident. Inger wasn't happy and I wasn't either. To think he's been lying to you all these years . . . to us, to the village?" He turned to Ella and said kindly, "I can't believe what he did to your cottage. It's terrible and seems way out of character . . . bizarre, not in his right head, but that's no excuse. Is that why you're leaving us?"

"No, it's not that at all. I need to get back to my life in

Boulder, to my store." As Ella said this, she tucked her chin so that her hair fell over her face, giving herself a moment to push away her grief over leaving.

"Right, I have to head to work myself," Axel said. He let go of the railing and gave them both a firm look as he pointed at each in turn. "I expect to see you two tonight. Don't disappoint me." He backed the boat into the channel.

"Is Axel always that persistent?" Ella said and squinted her eyes, amused.

"Yep," Leif said. "How do you think he got Inger to go out with him?" Ella laughed and he wrapped his arms around her. "One final memory together, tonight?"

Swallows flew low over the deep-blue water. "I love their little red toothpick legs," Ella said.

"They're chasing insects. That means tomorrow will be sunny. And please don't change the subject." He brought her hand to his lips and kissed it, then gave her a wry smile and asked very clearly, "Will you come with me to the gathering?"

Ella put her head down, closed her eyes, and shook her head.

"What about Hilda?" Leif asked.

"I'm going to take her back with me. Since Sara wasn't buried, I can't reunite them, and I think I'd like her with me anyhow." She picked at her nails. "Listen, I just need to go. I'm never going to believe in myself if I keep putting off going home. My business, my *dream*, is in Boulder. I can't blow this amazing opportunity—and who am I, if not a clothing designer? It's my passion, my purpose, and I can't see myself doing anything else, ever." He nodded solemnly and she reached for his hand. "Of course I want to stay. I love how I can be myself around you. I want to hold you and watch you sleep. I'd love to swim with you again and create some more happy moments whittling together in front of your fireplace. But I've only known you for two weeks. Two nearly perfect weeks, but still. I can't stay."

"I've never met anyone like you. And if I'm honest, I'm afraid I never will again." For a moment Leif looked sad, but then he pulled her close and his eyes brightened. "Now that you're staying an extra night, there's another special place I would love to show you. Let's make the most of today and tonight! What do you say?"

Her heart begged her to say yes, to be with this amazing man one more day, and so she nodded at him. "OK."

CHAPTER 40

The wicker picnic basket bumped against Leif's leg as he and Ella strolled across Kjeholmen Island. It was only the size of a hockey rink, located a short boat ride away from Lyngør. Goats roamed around the lighthouse and caretaker cottage, the only buildings on the weather-battered island. Dragonflies zipped around the heather, and Ella marveled at the elaborate geometric pattern on their translucent wings. Leif knew how much they inspired her, and that dragonfly wings would show up somehow on her designs, perhaps in the Leif Collection.

"Striking!" Ella said as she turned her camera on the light-house. Leif clasped her arm, keeping her from tripping over stones in the path. She took several shots of the white tower crowned with its red beacon.

"It was built in 1897," he said.

"Does anyone live there?" She aimed the lens at the care-taker cottage, its two stone chimneys, and its gable roof. She motioned for Leif to step closer so she could capture him in the shot too. "I'll mail you pictures of our time together."

"Thanks," he said. "Dalla, the lighthouse keeper, lives here on the island. She's quite an artist and sells her metal sculptures at the art gallery in Risør. It's near Nina's sewing shop; I don't know why I didn't take you there before." He spread a navy quilt on the ground near clusters of wild pansies. "But if you extend your stay, I'll bring you to the gallery—I bet you could sell your pictures and embroidery there."

"Wow, there are so many artists living in the area. And I'm so happy you introduced me to Nina. I'd love to sell her more of my designs and maybe even collaborate with her on some clothes in the future."

"Let's drop by her store tomorrow. Show her some of your clothes and anything else that you think she might be interested in buying. Maybe you could wear one of those beautiful dresses you made, like the one with the bluebells embroidered on the sleeves. And you could ask her to introduce you to her sister, the one with the stores in Oslo."

Ella slid her camera into her bag. "It's tempting, but you know I can't."

"Yes, I know. You need to leave," he said. "I get it." He looked crushed, so she slid onto his lap, slipped her arms around him, and nestled her face into the crook of his neck.

After they'd eaten, Leif pushed aside the cheese-and-fruit platter and held up a candy bar. "Dessert?" He broke off a small chunk and placed it on her tongue.

"I love chocolate-covered marzipan!" she said. "Mia introduced it to me."

"She's going to miss you . . . so will Inger." He began cleaning up their picnic, pressing wax paper around the cheese. His heart felt pressed too. He scooted closer so that their legs touched, and he slid his arm around her. "And I am going to miss you, very much."

"I'll miss you as well." Her voice trembled a bit and she focused on an osprey soaring above the lighthouse, until the anguish left her face.

"Stay. Give me more time."

"What will that solve?"

"Well, I don't have all the answers," Leif said as he snapped off a piece of chocolate and pushed it into his mouth. He'd almost blurted *I love you*, but he hadn't said those words in almost thirty years. He'd last said them to his father. "But I've been thinking . . . why don't you rent out Ringpynten, and move in with me? You can turn my shed into an art studio, a sewing shop, whatever you like. Decorate it however you want."

She stared at her lap, shook her head, and tore the petals from the wild pansies she had gathered. "You're not making this easy on me, you know, Leif. I've only known you two weeks and you're asking me to change my entire life!"

"The cottage already changed your life . . . but maybe not in the way you thought it would. Perhaps your grandma wanted you to come back to stay all along."

"Not likely!" She chewed on her cheek. "But it makes me wonder."

"Good—then say yes."

She looked away and rubbed her aquamarine pendant and then brushed the petals and baguette crumbs from her skirt. She leaned in closer, kissed his lips, and said, "Let's enjoy tonight, OK?"

"OK." He smiled, but he wasn't going to drop it. "Let's go to that special place I told you about."

"I thought the lighthouse was the special place."

"No," Leif said. "We have just enough time to get there before we head over to the Propeller."

"Sounds good," Ella said, giving him a skeptical look. She wondered if he'd just come up with this special place to stretch out their time together, and she thought she wouldn't mind if that were the case.

She snapped a few photos of her boots and his blue Converse lined up together on the blanket. A feminine and masculine pair of shoes snuggled together, just like in Sara's picture. As they walked to Leif's boat, a cloud passed over the island, casting a shadow over the lighthouse and them.

• • •

Silver ripples danced across the breadth of the ocean as Leif worked the tiller with Ella at his side.

"It's peaceful out here; it's like we're the only two people on earth," she said. "I'm beginning to understand why you love boating."

"We're about to enter the Skagerrak, the strait that separates Norway from Sweden and Denmark. The water may turn a bit rough, but we're seaworthy."

The bow hit a wave, and cold mist coated their faces. She inhaled sharply, looking around in alarm. "I forgot my life vest!"

"I saw you left it on the dinghy, and I grabbed it." He smiled at her reassuringly.

"You did? Thank you!"

"Yes. But it looks like you're getting comfortable enough on the water to forget about your life preserver. See? You're turning into salty, seafaring Lyngør folk, right before my eyes."

He throttled back the engine, allowing the boat to drift, then fetched her life preserver and two slickers from a bench locker. "Here you go. Soon you'll have me stowing life vests for everyone on board."

"That's actually a good idea," she said with approval. She put on the slicker over her vest, and then he rolled up her sleeves and guided the zipper to her neck. In the distance, three red poles swayed on the water. Ella pointed at them.

"What are they for?" she asked.

"They mark an underwater ridge formed by glacier activity thousands of years ago. Small boats like mine can anchor there. Deep-keeled boats avoid it. This is the special spot I wanted to show you. My father and I used to fish here, and we always brought coffee and homemade raisin rolls. God, I love this spot. Sometimes I fish here alone and talk to my father. I feel he's here in spirit."

Leif could use a good chat with his father right now, especially now that he knew the truth about the accident. Plus he was in love with Sara Nilsen's daughter. What would his dad have to say about that?

"What are you thinking about?" she asked, resting her head on his arm.

"I'm thinking there's nowhere else I would rather be," he whispered in her ear.

"Smooth talker."

He laughed and kissed her. As the boat continued to drift, he retrieved a fishing rod and a plastic bucket from mid-deck, asking, "Have you ever fished?"

"Me? No way!" Her brow shot to her hairline.

"Just think of the stories you can bring home."

"Yes, everyone should have a good fish story. I bet you have hundreds!"

He laughed. "First we troll for mackerel. We can drop them by my house on the way to the Propeller." He set the pole on the deck, grabbed the rig from the bucket, tied a sinker to the line, and handed her the rig. She studied it as if it were a fascinating puzzle.

"This looks like a kite spool. How do I use it? Should I stand up?"

"The water is a bit rough, so stay seated, but move closer to the gunwale."

She moved to the far end of the bench. "What now?"

"Face the water."

He sat down next to her, slid his hands around her waist, and nuzzled her neck. "You hold each side of the rig, like this." He folded his hands over hers to show her how. "Then let out the line like you would a kite. See all those hooks? Be careful not to snag yourself as you release them over the edge." The rig spun and the line sank into the water. "If you feel hard tugging, you've caught a fish. Reel in the line, but please—don't let go of the rig."

He moved back to the tiller and gradually brought the engine to one and a half knots. As he steered in a large loop, Ella's eyes never left the water.

"I felt a tug!" She yelled and let out a giddy laugh. "There it goes again! It's tugging like crazy—I think I caught one."

"Pull it in. You've got this!"

She reeled fast, and he gave her the thumbs-up and put the engine into neutral, the sun slipping in and out of the clouds. A skinny three-foot fish with a long needle nose skimmed the surface of the water near the stern. She'd never seen anything like it.

"What's it called?"

"That's a garfish. It has a green skeleton," he said.

Her eyes widened. "No way!"

With one deft scoop of the fishnet, Leif brought the garfish into the boat and released it onto the deck. The eel-like creature opened and closed its long jaw, which was full of tiny sharp teeth, and continued to flop around.

"Why did you bring it in here? There's no way that's edible." She took a step back.

"Are you serious? Smoked gar with black pepper. Delicious!"

She wrinkled her nose. "No thanks, I'll pass."

He snorted. After whacking the garfish on the head with a pair of pliers, he wiggled the hook from its mouth.

"Poor fish," she said.

"Don't worry, he's already forgotten it." He put the garfish in the bucket and gestured at the rig. "Like another go?"

She grinned. "Well, it was pretty exciting . . . Let's catch another good story."

. . .

A bucket of fish later, Leif moved back to the tiller and put the throttle into drive. The engine delivered a weak thump and died. He tried it again, but nothing happened except for a faint click, then silence. The only thing they could hear was the sound of the waves slapping against the hull, and the caw of a far-off bird.

"That's odd," he said. "There should be plenty of gas." He lowered the dipstick into the fuel tank and held it up. "Yeah, half full."

He slid the crank into the flywheel and spun it hard clockwise. The engine gave a short sputter before it choked out. "For Loki's sake, don't do this to me!"

"Leif?"

"We need to drop anchor."

"Is it serious?"

"I'm not sure; let me check the engine first." He threw the anchor into the sea and watched its chain disappear; in a moment, he felt the anchor tug on the ridge directly below. It had caught, but only just. They'd drifted farther from the ridge than he had realized.

"Has this happened before?" she asked.

"Not to me. It's probably a plug," he said as he bent over the engine. With the pliers, he removed the lid and loosened the spark plug to the single cylinder. He flinched in dismay: The plug was dry; it wasn't a simple fix. With alarm, he realized he had forgotten to transfer the flares and the radio from *Rán* to *Skadi*. He'd been so distracted by everything that had happened—first with Erik, and then with Ella.

"Well," she said, "I'm sure someone will come along and help the stranded, right?" She touched her pendant for luck and reassurance.

Leif didn't have the heart to tell her that the stranded died of thirst. That their boats drifted out to sea and storms blew in, hurling them against the rocks. The best course of action would be to keep her busy so she wouldn't fret. He forced his mouth into a smile.

"Do me a favor, will you? Hold the spark plug against the cylinder while I turn over the flywheel."

She moved to his side. He showed her how and where to hold the plug, and then he cranked the flywheel.

"No sparks that I can see," she reported, staring at the plug as if her life depended on it.

"Are you sure? Sparks are hard to see in the light." He cranked the flywheel again and prayed. *Please let it catch.*

"Can you fix it?" She gripped the rim of the bench as *Skadi* rose and fell on a wave.

He scratched his forehead and looked at the horizon. Earlier, the forecast had predicted clear skies, but now the clouds were flying in fast, and the wind was blowing cold and damp. He pointed at the engine and tried to sound relaxed.

"Could be a faulty coil or a busted breaker switch. I can't be certain until I take the boat to the shop."

"Now what?"

"Give me a moment to think this through. How about a beer?"

"Good idea," she agreed. She grabbed two beers from his duffel bag, twisted off the caps, and handed one to him. He took a long drink and considered the oars. On a calm day, it would take him hours to row from here to Lyngør. But thunderclouds were forming in the west, and the southerly breeze had swung eastward and picked up strength and was whipping up the Skagerrak. Rowing against it in this heavy boat would be nearly impossible, but the area saw little boat traffic, so what choice did he have? Ella sipped her beer and fidgeted anxiously with her pendant, waiting for him to say something.

"How about we row? I'm game if you are."

She gave him a determined nod.

With his knife, he sawed through the ropes that lashed the oars to either side of the gunwale, and he fitted them into the oarlocks. The boat was too heavy to row easily, and certainly not as far as they needed to row to make it to safety. But it was their only choice.

"We can take turns. I'm stronger than I look," she said, and curled her biceps.

"Good plan." He put on a smile, sat down on the middle bench, and gripped the oars. "You can take over for a bit when I tire out."

Leif rowed for an hour and battled the wind. The muscles in his arms burned, but he rowed harder. There was no time to waste, not with that dark curtain of rain rolling across the horizon and heading toward them.

Ella spoke up. "Want me to take over?" Leif was impressed with her can-do attitude, but by the way she fidgeted and bounced her knees, he could see that she was concerned. Perhaps not as concerned as he was.

"Thanks . . . soon you can." His back ached. He was exhausted, and they probably hadn't even moved forty meters.

"I really hope someone comes by soon and rescues us. I'm afraid of lightning." Ella rubbed her thighs nervously.

"Don't fret," Leif said. "Someone will grab us." But he knew that few people would be out on the water with a storm brewing.

"OK," she said with a tight smile, looking unconvinced. Even the birds had retreated to the isles. He rowed for another ten minutes. Cold drizzle fell, and the temperature dropped. Ella's teeth chattered and her fingers were pink from the chilly air.

"I want to row so I can stop thinking," she said. "I need to get out of my head."

"All right." His arms had turned to jelly. He settled the oars into the boat, and they swapped seats.

With a confident jut of her jaw, she took up the oars. Leif felt certain that he'd never loved anyone as much as he loved Ella at this moment. Ella, who refused to be defeated out in this killer storm, and bravely rowed with all her might even if it seemed impossible, even if it seemed to scare the bejesus out of her. And he had to acknowledge that she was right to be afraid; he had put her life at risk. It was inadvertent, of course, but he blamed himself. He told himself that if he and Ella survived this misadventure, he'd open his heart fully to her, and they'd somehow find a way to create a beautiful life together where they'd support each other's goals and dreams. He'd make serious changes to his life to make this happen. She was worth it.

Fifteen minutes went by before she dumped the oars onto the deck, saying, "I need to rest." Her face was flushed from exertion, eyes narrowed against the foul weather. They'd only moved a couple of meters. If that.

"You've done well," he said. "Drink?" He passed her a coffee thermos as the boat tipped from side to side in the chop. Ella sipped the lukewarm coffee, her gaze moving over the foam-streaked waves, and she began to tremble.

"Hey, everything will be OK." Leif gave her a reassuring smile, all the while punching away his own fears.

She nodded at him, but only just, and reached for the oars again.

"No, you should rest. Let me take over," he said.

"I want to help more, but it's harder than it looks." She rose from the middle bench and staggered to the stern as the boat rose and fell on the waves.

The wind howled across the waters. As Leif fought with the oars, he shot Ella a brief look and raised his voice over the fierce weather.

"We're going to get out of this. Mia and the others are expecting us. If they don't see my boat at either of our places, they'll send out a search party." This left quite a bit unsaid: If they didn't show at the party, people would most likely assume they were cozied up somewhere and wouldn't bother to check on them.

Ella found the other snag in the plan. She looked scared and shouted over the wind, "But how will they know where to find us?"

"On my way to pick you up, I saw Oskar out in his trawler near Ringpynten. I told him we were going to the lighthouse, and to my favorite spot out here in the Skagerrak." A small wave splashed into the boat. "He'll tell everyone where we are. They'll find us. In the meantime, we keep rowing."

He rowed for another twenty minutes before the thunder boomed. Ella glanced around quickly, and he could see the panic on her face.

"No worries, it's way in the distance," he said. He chastised himself for not counting the seconds between the thunder and lightning, to gauge the distance of the approaching storm. She shivered at the sight of dark-violet clouds drifting toward *Skadi*. As he continued to battle the waves, a blue flash broke open the sky. Ella let out a loud yelp and burrowed into her slicker. Leif's stomach cramped with guilt, knowing this was all his fault. Picking up the oars again, he carved them into the swells, but it was no use. The current was at least one and a half knots, and they were going against the wind, so no matter how hard he rowed, he couldn't make headway. Did Erik feel this scared and helpless when his boat went down? Leif pressed on while the sharp wind clobbered him.

A huge swell exploded against the hull and swung the boat broadside. He almost lost an oar. Ella toppled from the stern bench and landed on the deck. Leif helped her up, while the wind beat the sea into a silver-tipped frenzy.

"Are you OK?" he shouted. "That was one hell of a wave."

"That was scary." She rubbed her hip.

"Yes, it was," he said, frowning. Before he could grip the

oars again, the skies opened up, releasing a cold, hard rain. The bow slammed into a deep trough, and Ella almost fell again.

"Hold on tight and don't go anywhere!" he yelled at her and plunged the oars into the water.

"Where would I go?" she hollered. Her eyes narrowed at him in anger, and who could blame her? He shoved the blades into the swells and tried to tack and aim into the waves to avoid getting broadsided again.

"We have to do something or we're going to die out here!" she yelled, clutching the bench for dear life.

"I'll get us out of this!" he shouted. But he truly had no idea how, and that terrified him. One thing he did know: He would fight to save them until he took his last breath.

As he continued battling with the oars, he belted out the old English war song at the top of his lungs:

"It's a long way to Tipperary! It's a long way to go! It's a long way to Tipperary, to the sweetest girl I know!" He strained and pulled the oars through the frothy seas.

"Whoa! Hilda sang this song!" Ella shouted with a shaky laugh before joining in the chorus: "Goodbye, Piccadilly! Farewell, Leicester Square!"

They sang together while he rowed like mad—rowed for his life—until his muscles spasmed from exhaustion. But it was impossible to keep the bow to the weather, impossible to stop the waves from punishing the boat.

"Let me take over!" she hollered.

"No, keep singing! It helps me concentrate." He plunged the oars into the water, but the waves continued to beat back the boat.

"Goodbye, Piccadilly! Farewell, Leicester Square!" As they sang together, he pressed on, struggling, until a tremendous wave crested over the gunwale. Water rushed across the planks and swirled around their ankles. The rain stung his skin, while the salt blurred his vision. Ella let out a shriek that could wake the gods.

"Keep singing!" he shouted. He rowed with all his remaining strength, his muscles on fire. The sea struck the side of the boat forcefully. One big wave could roll them over.

In frustration, he yelled, "Arghhh!" into the sky.

"This isn't working!" Ella yelled, clinging to her seat in fear. The bow slammed into a trough and more seawater spilled in.

"I won't let anything happen to us!" he shouted. Another gigantic wave crested over the railing and dumped cold water in the boat. It rose halfway up the gunwale and swirled around their calves, and Ella let out a panicked scream.

"Grab the bucket! Bail!" Leif fought to keep a foothold on the deck and keep the bow to the waves.

Scooping up water as quickly as she could, Ella sent it flying overboard. As she bailed, freezing water pelted Leif's face and one of the oars fell into the churning current. Before he had time to react, a ferocious crest caught the hull, flooding it. Then another crest came crashing down upon them, and he tumbled sideways. He struggled to stand but lost his balance when a massive wave broke against the deck, catapulting him over the gunwale.

Skadi capsized. Leif held his breath and braced for impact.

CHAPTER 41

Ella shrieked as she was plunged into the water, then gasped and choked as the frigid sea hit her in the face. She inhaled a ragged breath, then another, and kicked her legs hard. The life vest chafed her chin, and her clothes were dead weight. She gagged at the taste of the salt water. The rain pummeled her and pockmarked the water, waves swarming around her. She knew their body temperature would drop with each tick of the clock, and she wondered how long they'd survive before freezing to death. She didn't know, but she'd have to keep moving.

Salt water blurred her vision and fear blurred her mind as her body rose and fell with the waves. Was this how her mother died—swept out to sea, alone and afraid, her skin turning blue and her heart shutting down? Or maybe it all happened so quickly that Sara felt nothing, knew nothing. Ella was terrified and wondered where Leif was. She scissor-kicked and tried to rise high enough to locate him, but a wave broke over her head, blinding her for moments that seemed like hours. She inhaled water and coughed as it streamed from her nose.

She kicked harder and dug in her arms and swam with all her strength. Riding a swell just high enough to scan the waves, she saw Leif treading water six feet away. Blood seeped from a gash on his head, and the water washed it away, but more blood trickled out behind it. At least he was alive. When she was close enough, she reached out to grip his sleeve, but the swells caught her and pushed her back.

He treaded water with one arm; the other hung at his side. As he struggled to keep his head above the surface, a wave broke against him. He gagged and coughed, then retched into the water. He fought to swim to her, clawing through the water with his one good arm. She saw that his nose was swollen, a purple lump was rising from his forehead, and the bloody gash that stretched across his hairline went down to the bone.

Her fear turned to determination, and she stretched out her arm and managed to grab his shirt. They treaded water together, and he tried to hold his chin above the waves but kept sucking in salt water and gagging. Ella tightened her grip on him.

"Go to the boat," Leif said with a raspy voice. It had settled belly-up near them. His wrist was swollen and blue, and he was clenching his jaw in pain. She wasn't going without him, and she didn't think he could swim on his own. She dragged him through the water, fighting to hold on to him and keep them afloat at the same time. She had long lost her shoes. She kicked out furiously, taking gasping breaths.

Inches from the boat, a wave carried them beyond the stern. As Ella struggled back against the current, a crest exploded over their heads. Both of them sputtered, rising and falling on the whitecaps. She kicked harder, but the tide grabbed her and smacked her against *Skadi*'s hull, hard enough to hurt her. She was too cold to feel it.

She dug her arm into the raging sea again and inched forward. Swimming another foot to the boat, she grasped the beveled planks with one hand and hooked her arm through Leif's, leaving her other hand free to seize the mooring line. She fed it through her life vest and then clenched her fist around it, doing her best to keep his head above the swells.

She felt that she was slipping in and out of consciousness, and she noticed that Leif couldn't stay alert either. But she managed to hold on to him and the rope, despite the current that threatened to rip them apart. Her teeth were chattering so hard she was afraid she'd bite off her tongue. But in this terrifying situation, shivering was a good thing; it meant she was alive. She knew this from winters in the mountains.

Blood continued to stream down Leif's face. She glanced around at the sharp, white-tipped waves. Were those shark fins slicing through the swells? Panic bit at her and her breath grew ragged. She glanced over one shoulder then the other: There were no dorsal fins, but no signs of relief either. She wondered if she was hallucinating from the cold and the trauma.

"Are there sharks here?"

"Yes."

"What?" Her gaze darted.

"Not dangerous. Just plankton feeders."

Her clothes were weighing her down, and with the rope gripped in her hand, she struggled to unbutton her jeans.

"Stop. Conserve energy," Leif said, slurring his words.

"It's harder to swim with them on."

"Insulation. And I'm wearing blue for Odin."

That made no sense, and she knew that Leif was out of it. She knew it was up to her, or maybe to someone higher. Ella prayed to the heavens and then to Njord, god of the sea. *You took our parents. Please don't take Leif.*

"Quit staring. I hit my forehead," Leif slurred again. She watched his eyes roll back in his head.

She shook him. "Talk to me! Stay awake! What about your arm?"

"Don't know," he said with great effort.

"OK, just don't sleep!" Her limbs were cold and stiff, but

she kept a firm grip on him and the rope. The rain had turned to drizzle, which should have been a relief, but the wind kept shoving the waves, which were pushing and pulling at the two of them, trying hard to carry them out to sea. A cramp jabbed her under the ribs, and it took all her willpower to maintain her grip on Leif and the boat. There was no telling how much time had passed. Was it minutes or hours? And she certainly didn't know how much longer they had left. She kissed Leif's cold, wet head.

"I'm knackered," Leif said in a faint voice. Then he dry-heaved.

"Hold on a little longer." Ella's jaw was numb. It was a challenge to speak. She felt her vocal cords locking up. Leif closed his eyes. "Everything will be OK. Someone will rescue us." She could barely see over the waves, so how could anyone possibly see them?

"My head is numb. Can't move my legs." As Leif spoke these words, he laid his head on her shoulder. She could hear that his breathing was shallow.

Why hadn't she told him she loved him, or even admitted it to herself? She didn't ever want to leave him. Ever.

"Don't you dare give up! Do you hear me?" she shouted in desperation.

"There are bees in my ears."

"Stay with me!" she pleaded.

"Make them go away." Leif's lips were blue.

"Stay with me. I love you!"

He closed his eyes.

"Wake up!" She shook him as hard as she could. "I can't lose you!"

He stopped shivering. The wind scooped up the sea around her and threw it back at her. Ella didn't know whether it was tears or salt spray that stung her eyes. She shook Leif again.

"You must hang on. We're going to get out of this! I want

to be together. I promise to learn to steer a boat." She coughed again and spit out the brine. "I'll eat fishy soup. I'll make those throw pillows for the bedrooms. Bright and cheerful. You'll love them. You'll see."

Silence. This time it wasn't the water that made her choke.

"Do you hear me? I love you. We can do this!" Her hands were so cold they burned. She knew that soon, she wouldn't be able to hold on to him or the boat.

Ella thought she heard an engine. She craned her stiff neck to search, but there wasn't a soul in sight. She thumped the side of her head to dislodge the water, and her breath sounded distorted to her. She must be hallucinating. She was probably mistaking a flock of honking geese for the sound of an engine. Maybe it was the same droning of bees that Leif had thought he heard. She kept listening over the hissing wind. Waves slapped against the boat; her limbs felt leaden. She thought she would close her eyes, just for a moment, to rest.

A deep drumming pulsed through the water. She was dreaming but knew that soon she would wake up safe in her bed, her cheek on Leif's chest.

The noise grew louder. Ella cracked open her swollen eyelids and allowed herself to believe that her hallucination might be real, that a rescue boat had come. A long, bellowing whistle drew her gaze to an approaching skiff. Erik was at the helm.

"Leif—it's Erik! Erik is here!" She shouted and shook his arm. "Wake up!"

"Erik!" She tried to shout, but her voice was feeble. Relaxing her grip on the boat hull, she attempted to hold up her arm to signal, but she could barely lift her hand out of the water.

Another sharp whistle blared from Erik's boat, and the engine churned up the water. As Ella and Leif rose and fell, her gaze never left Erik. He steered in a circle around Leif's boat. His dark eyes flickered to Leif and Ella, and then to *Skadi*, determining the best way to approach.

Erik slowed the engine, backed the boat toward them, and threw over the fenders. Moving swiftly and with purpose, Erik seized the stern line, attached it to a life jacket, and tossed it to Ella. It landed on *Skadi*'s hull.

"Put it on him in case you're separated. Hurry up. I'll pull you in."

"Bloody sea monsters," Leif slurred with his eyes half closed, clearly hallucinating.

Getting Leif into the life jacket would take every ounce of her energy, and her palms were already raw and blistered from clutching the rope. She clung to Leif in the swirling current and found that her hand was frozen stiff. She forced open her fingers, grabbed the life jacket, and jammed it over Leif's head, while assuring him, "Don't worry. I'm not letting you go."

"OK, it's on," she called to Erik.

As Erik dragged them to the boat, a big wave exploded over her. The water ripped the rope from her hand, and pain sliced through her skin. The salt water stung, but once again it was reassurance that she was still alive. They would survive, and she would live in Lyngør, and drink hot cocoa with Leif in front of his fireplace.

Leif vomited and shut his eyes.

"Hurry!" Erik hollered as he pulled on the rescue line. The waves were pushing his skiff parallel to Leif's boat. One good wave would shove Erik's boat against *Skadi*, and crush Ella and Leif between the hulls. She snatched the rope and winced, vowing that they would not die today, not while she still had breath.

Erik pulled them through the rough water. His face contorted with effort. He dragged them to the side of the boat and flipped a ladder over the railing.

"Be quick," Erik commanded.

Ella was feverish and her breathing was shallow, but she held on to Leif and gripped the ladder. Salt spray blurred her vision as she called to Erik, "Grab him!"

She released Leif from her grip, but only after Erik had folded his barrel chest over the gunwale. With his thick forearms and large hands, Erik grabbed Leif's preserver and shirt and heaved him over the railing. A wind gust rocked the boat from side to side. With Leif three-quarters into the boat, Erik's face turned purple, and he let out a roar as he gave Leif another hard tug. Leif landed on the deck and curled up on his side.

Erik leaned over the gunwale again and rammed his hands under Ella's arms. As he seized her life vest and pulled with all his might, she let go of the ladder. At that instant, another wave swung the stern around fast and slammed it against *Skadi*.

Ella heard the loud crunch. Erik jumped, and his feet staggered beneath him, but he kept a strong grip on Ella. He repositioned his legs and planted his feet securely on the deck.

Regaining his balance, he looked at Ella and assured her, "It's OK, I've got you."

As Erik hauled her into the boat, her left foot hit the gunwale loud enough for her to hear a cracking sound, but she felt no pain. Her leg was numb, leaden—a deadweight. She flopped onto the deck next to Leif. His lips were still blue, and his arm was bent at an odd angle. Ella tried to stand so she could grab him a blanket, but pain shot through her. Her head spun. Iridescent dots shimmered in her vision, and everything was distorted. A yellow wedge of sun slipped from the clouds, sparkling brightly, and burned her eyes.

"Hang on! I have blankets but right now I need to get us out of here and into calmer seas!" Erik shouted and hurried to the helm.

As the boat accelerated, Ella rolled across the hard, damp deck and landed flat on her back. The skiff continued to rise and fall on the waves, and she lay there, drained and dizzy, listening to the crackle of the marine radio.

"Axel. I found them," Erik said. "Alive. Hypothermia. Broken bones. Probably a severe concussion. Have an ambulance meet me at the boatyard. One more thing: Leif's boat is belly-up." Erik fired off *Skadi*'s coordinates.

Ella crawled to Leif, lay down next to him, and gently pressed her chest against his back, careful not to disturb his limp arm. Their legs touched, and she felt the heat of hope.

Now in smoother waters, Erik shifted the engine into neutral and snatched two blankets from the bow locker and threw them over Ella and Leif.

"Head exploding," Leif mumbled.

Erik tucked the blanket around Leif's chin. "You hit your head, son. Just don't fall asleep. We'll have you at the hospital in two shakes of an elk's tail."

Leif gave a weak grunt as Erik hurried back to the helm.

Ella nuzzled her face into the base of Leif's neck. His aquamarine pendant was still there, intact. Her own aquamarine beads lay secure beneath her sweater, solid against her skin. Her eyes closed and she gave in to the darkness.

CHAPTER 42

Ella woke to the smell of antiseptic soap. She yawned, then grimaced at the pull she felt within her ribs.

She folded back the starched sheets and stared at the plaster cast that was sticking out from beneath her hospital gown. The cast covered her leg from calf to foot. Her chipped tangerine nail polish was quite the complement to her purple-and-chartreuse toes. She flexed her sore fingers—scraped and rope burned as they were—and knew it would be a while until she could play the guitar or embroider, but it could have been worse . . . so much worse.

On the bedside table, blue hydrangeas and delphinium hugged each other in a pewter vase. Against the vase was a postcard of Lyngør and a pack of breath mints. Ella flipped the card over and read the handwritten note:

> Flowers and fun stickers from Mia. Breath mints, in case you want to kiss Leif (and not kill him) from Inger. Get well soon, Hippie Chick. Store Klemmer (big hugs).

Her eyes teared up. No, she wouldn't cry. They were alive and nothing else mattered. But she needed to see Leif, the man of her heart. She reached for the call button, but before she could press it, Erik walked into the room.

Ella studied his face. This was her father, a fact she still found too difficult to grasp. From the moment they met, he had been horrible to her. And yet now she had a different image of Erik—he was also the man who had clung to her as his own boat was threatened and had never let go. He had yanked her over the railing and onto the deck and tucked a blanket around her cold body.

She recalled the red flashing lights of the ambulance, and Erik's frantic voice, saying, "Hurry! Do something—she's hurting!" He sounded just like a father might sound. Did he know?

"You don't look so bad for a half-drowned codfish!" Erik greeted her with a shaky grin and moved to the foot of her bed.

"How's Leif? I need to see him." She eased her bruised legs and broken foot over the side of the mattress.

"You'll have to wait. He's still unconscious."

She gasped. "Oh no!"

"They gave him a CT scan. The doctor says he has a concussion, and they need to keep him quiet for a while, but he'll make a full recovery."

"I was so afraid I lost him!"

"Yeah, me too."

They smiled awkwardly at each other. She tugged at her hospital gown while Erik gnawed on his unlit cigar. They heard a deep hacking cough from somewhere in the corridor, and wheels squeaked on a steel cart. She smelled cauliflower soup and scrunched up her nose.

"Everyone's been asking about you," Erik said. He pointed at the flowers and mints on her table. "I see Mia and Inger have been here. Inger brought you a change of clothes. Yours were wrecked, but I put them in a bag for you anyway."

"Thank you," Ella said. "I don't know how to say this, but I need to . . . I know we have our differences, and I know you don't want Leif to spend time with me. Even so, thank you for saving my life. And his life."

"I have something to say too. I really, truly apologize for the way I treated you. When I heard you were in Lyngør I considered leaving town for a time . . . my guilt over what I'd done was overwhelming and . . . well, your arrival was hard for me. I told myself I was too busy at the boatyard to go away, but to be honest, I was curious to see if you took after your mum. And it *is* incredible how much you resemble her. I'm ashamed of what I did years ago, and of what I did to Ringpynten the other day. I have no excuses, I'm just sorry."

"You don't have to say anything."

"Yes I do. There's more. The nurse found this when they cut off your clothes." He pulled a small object from his pocket but kept it concealed in his big fist. He paused as his face crumbled with grief, and she softened.

"What is it?" she asked.

He extended his arm to her and uncurled his fingers. The small wooden bear stood on his flattened palm. "Where did you find it?" Erik asked, his eyes tormented.

"At the cottage. It was in a drawer inside the grandfather clock."

He nodded, as if her answer made perfect sense. As he stared at the bear, anguish folded into deep lines around his mouth. His breath caught as he spoke. "I made it for your mother. The Norse gods Thor and Odin often took the shape of a bear when they visited the human world. Sara was like a goddess to me—bears are sun animals, you know—Sara was my sun." He handed the bear to Ella. "You should keep this. I sent it to Sara as a token of a promise."

"A promise?"

He gave Ella a furtive glance. "Over that last winter, I'd

heard rumors that she was pregnant . . . that she'd met some guy from Oslo. But he didn't stick around, and . . . well, she deserved better and that shredded me, but it also meant the door was still . . . well, open for me. I sent some letters, and the bear, to her apartment in Oslo. I asked her to move to Lyngør and marry me. I told her that I loved her with all my heart, and that if the rumor was true, we could raise the baby together. That we could marry and be a family." He swiped his nose. "It was what I always wanted since the day I met her." A tear ran down Erik's cheek, and he sniffled.

"What happened?" Ella asked.

"She never answered. I loved Sara, very much."

He blew out a shaky breath and sat tentatively on the edge of the bed. "You look like Sara, with your red curls and kind almond eyes. Plus you've got a smile that lights up a room, just like she did. These memories of her that you've brought back . . . well, it's shattered me. Sara died because of me, and because of my lies I had to keep it buried all these years." He hid his face in his hands. "Sara died because of me."

Ella put her hand on his knee. "I think she loved you too."

It was clear that they'd all lost so much the night of the crash, and Ella started to cry. Erik looked at her with kind, caring eyes. He had no idea of the secret that Sara had kept from him.

Ella wiped the tears from her face. "The bear wasn't the only thing I found in the grandfather clock. There was a birth certificate too."

"Yours?" he asked. She nodded, and he gritted his teeth. "Who was the snake?"

Ella smiled at him and said, quietly but clearly, "It was you. You're my father."

"Me? I . . . I . . . that's incredible," he stammered. He pulled the rim of his cap down and lowered his head as his shoulders started to quake. They cried together. She reached for the tissue box on the table and moved it onto Erik's lap. He shoved it back at her.

"No, you need them," he said as he sniffled and ran his hand over his face. "I didn't know that her baby—you—were mine, or if there even *was* a child. I swear it. I would have driven straight to Oslo, bent down on one knee with a ring, and told Sara how much I adored her! And I would have marched right past your mormor if I had to."

"I believe you." Ella smiled through her tears.

"You're my daughter." Erik reached out as if to hug her with his big, clumsy hands, but instead he ended up patting her awkwardly. "I'm sorry for everything."

"No more apologies. You're here now." She put her arms around Erik, and he relaxed and hugged her back, gingerly. Then they grinned at each other as they dabbed their eyes.

"Wait till Leif hears this one," he said. "I wish you would stay in Lyngør. Not for me—but you must know that Leif loves you dearly."

"I love him dearly too. I realized it on the water when I thought I might lose him. And now that you and I have met properly—I don't want to lose you either. You're the only family I have."

He looked at the postcard and breath mints on the side table. "Now that I'm thinking about it . . ." His voice trailed off, but he was grinning.

"What?"

"Well, your family is a little bigger than that. Inger's my niece, you know." Ella shot him a puzzled look.

"That makes her *your cousin*," he said. She was startled.

"Oh now, you should've seen that coming," he said teasingly. "Both of you are incredibly headstrong. This should be interesting." For a moment he kept a straight face, then he let loose with a hoarse guffaw.

CHAPTER 43

Leif awakened with a fever and a fierce headache. There was no need to touch the sutures and lump on his forehead to know they existed. Plaster covered his forearm from his elbow to his knuckles, and an intravenous line stretched from his other arm to a fluid-filled bag hanging from a pole.

He drew back the sheets carefully. Sharp pains stabbed his ribs. He shrugged his shoulder, and it didn't seem torn—nothing too serious—but he couldn't remember how he ended up in the hospital. Some sort of accident?

As he searched his memory for answers, he looked out the window. The day was giving way to a murky dusk. Seeing the slice of coastline brought back the memory of *Skadi* flipping over and him hitting the water. His stomach clenched when he remembered Ella being thrown from the boat too.

A chill crept through him, and he looked at the ceiling and prayed. *Please let Ella be alive and well. Give me more time with her.*

He began looking around. The door to his room was ajar. Beyond it, a sheeted body lay flat on a wheeled stretcher. He shivered and touched his pendant. *Please, I will never ever ask for anything else in this lifetime, if only I can hold her in my arms. Hear her voice in my ear . . . her laugh.*

"Hello?" he croaked. "Is anyone there?" As he lifted his head from the pillow, the blood whooshed from his face. Heavy-headed, he focused on the door, but the room spun, and he fell back on the mattress. Everything went dark.

• • •

Hours later, Leif stirred from sleep and felt the sting of the IV in his arm. The headache kept him from opening his eyes, even when he caught a whiff of stale cigarillo smoke. It must be Inger. But where was Ella? The image of her going overboard stomped on his chest. He pretended to be unconscious because he wasn't ready to hear what Inger had come here to tell him—that Ella was gravely injured, or even gone.

He should have peeked but he was petrified. Someone cleared their throat and then hummed a soulful song, perhaps a country song . . . but it was definitely in the dulcet tones of the voice he loved.

Ella.

Thank gods. Thank Njord, and Odin, and Loki alike.

He opened his eyes and smiled. Ella sat near his bedside, close enough that he could reach out and touch her. She looked luminous, in that enchanting way of hers. She had a sparkly heart sticker on her cheek; likely Mia had been to visit.

The shadows beneath Ella's eyes matched the blue wild-flowers tucked behind her ear. The scrape along her jawline had turned into a scab and met the bruises on her chin. She was wearing Inger's old coat for some reason.

He had so many questions, but before he could utter a single word, she grinned at him and began to sing: "Beautiful Boy Blue. Get well soon. We'll kiss under the big blue moon. And barbecue fish."

"Barbecue fish?" He laughed. For a moment the pain in his head, arm, and ribs, along with the pang in his heart, were forgotten.

"I just made up the lyrics as I went, but I meant every word." She smiled at him again. Outside a big moon shone in the sky, so bright it cast shadows across Leif's bed.

"I want you," he said, his eyes roaming over her. "You look beautiful! Are you all right?"

"Yes, I'm good. In fact I've never been better. What about you?" Her smile faltered as she gazed at his banged-up forehead and broken nose, and the cast on his arm. "Does it hurt?"

"Well, I wish I felt better, but how could I not be all right? I've never been this pleased to see anyone in my life!"

He wanted to touch her, to smell her, to hear the sexy hum of her breath in his ear.

"Take that thing off, will you? It smells like smoke." He had intended to say more: *Curl up next to me, let me feel your curves, your warmth.*

"Inger's coat has kept the chills at bay," she said, tracing her fingers over the fur trim. "Mia brought me stickers and flowers, and Inger gave me breath mints."

Leif was puzzled. "Breath mints?"

"In case I want to kiss you!" she said. She slipped one of her hands from the coat, touched it to her mouth and blew him a kiss. He should have captured that longed-for kiss and put it to his mouth. Instead he stared, speechless, at her hand. Each of her fingers was taped up with gauze bandages; her hand was completely immobilized.

"You're hurt."

"I'll heal," she said as she wiggled out of the coat. "And my foot is fractured, but it's a minor break, luckily."

Leif gave her the once-over and saw that the fingers on her other hand were taped too. "I feel terrible."

"Please—don't." She leaned forward in the chair and swept

her fingers over his bicep. "As you can see, my fingers work fine. You shouldn't feel terrible about any of this. You didn't force me out there on the water. And—we're alive."

He frowned and the stitches pulled the skin on his forehead, reminding him of how close they had come to dying.

"No, but it's my fault that we almost weren't," he said.

"Your engine failed, am I right? How's that your fault?"

"I wasn't prepared."

"You brought my life vest."

He had a sudden memory of them in the water. The way she propped up his head with her body, her arm snug around him, preventing him from going under.

"You, the one who's nervous about the water, kept me afloat. You saved my life! That was brave . . . beyond brave. Just another one of the many reasons I love you."

"You love me?"

"I love you madly," he declared and smiled at her. Wet eyes be damned.

"I love you madly too," she said through happy tears of her own.

With his plaster-bound forearm, he awkwardly reached out, beckoning her closer. Using the armrests for support, she stood from her chair and winced in pain, but she didn't complain. She settled on the edge of the bed, her eyes sparkling with happiness.

He noticed. "You look lighter, excited, joyous. I guess that's what being rescued from the sea will do for you."

"There's something else that I need to tell you . . ."

Ella paused, and he prompted. "You don't want to tell me?"

"I do. I'm putting my words together." She leaned in closer, her hair brushing him as she kissed him on the mouth.

Intoxicated, he let out a moan of desire, bundled up with longing. "Please never leave," he said.

Her breath seemed to catch, and she gave him another

slow, tender kiss. But as she pulled away and met his eyes, he saw apprehension there. Perhaps she still didn't want to stay.

Before Leif could speak, she said, "If I had never come to Norway, your life wouldn't have gone through this insane upheaval. You and Erik would still be as close as ever."

"Are you kidding? I'm beyond glad that you came into my life. You brighten my world. You make me want to step outside of my comfort zone and go after my dreams, my art. I love the way you find inspiration in the little things, like the smallest petal, birch bark, the texture of seaweed. Nothing seems small to me anymore when I look at things through your eyes." He touched her cheek, taking care to avoid her injuries. "I don't want to go back to how things were before you came into my life. My house is just a house without you in it. I want a home."

"Oh, that's so lovely," she said, eyes glistening. "But first there's something I have to tell you. Something that you need to know." She put her hand gently on his chest. "This is what I was gathering my words to tell you . . . Erik is my father."

"Erik?" Leif jolted upright with such speed that he heard his broken ribs pop. "Could you repeat that?" he said as he winced with pain.

Ella told him about the birth certificate and her conversation with Erik, and Leif listened in awe. "Why didn't you tell me this as soon as you knew?" he stammered.

"I was afraid to tell you. Plus, I didn't want anything to do with him."

"Then he saved us, and you changed your mind?"

"Not even then. Not until he and I talked in my hospital room, and I saw how much Sara meant to him, how much he had wanted to be a father."

"It's good news, but . . . astonishing," Leif said.

"For the last two days Erik and I have been here, waiting for you to recover."

"Two days?"

"They sedated you in case you had brain swelling. You needed to be still."

"I think I remember the doctor telling me that."

"Do you think that you can forgive Erik, and that the two of you can work it out?"

At a loss for words, Leif was silent. He wondered if he and Erik could really mend their relationship. Even so, he was alive because of Erik—and Ella was too. He rested his hand on her lap, IV cord and all.

"Erik saved my life. In a week I'll be back at the boatyard, working with one arm, and he and I will figure it out. We always do."

CHAPTER 44

Ella cut the engine on her wooden boat, allowing it to drift into a slip at the dock near Dypvåg Church. The boat tapped against the granite bank, rocking a little, as she reached out to grab a cleat and throw a hitch knot.

A year had passed. The June sky was a clear, periwinkle blue, the perfect day for a dual memorial service when Ella would put Hilda to rest and honor Sara's memory.

As she stepped from the boat, a salt breeze blew in off the sapphire waters. She breathed the sea air and found it soothing. Her relationship with the water had changed completely since the day she arrived in Lyngør on the ferry. Everything had changed since last summer. She had found her family and her future. With Leif's help, she'd finished renovating the store in Boulder and sold it at a profit, using it to pay off her debts. She'd moved to Lyngør permanently and hadn't looked back. Instead she'd connected with Nina and other artists in Norway, like Dalla the lighthouse keeper, who welded stunning metal sculptures. They were all collaborating to sell their creations at Ella's new art center at Ringpynten.

Now Ella paused on the shale road that edged the dock and

checked her watch. It was 2:30 p.m. She'd closed the shop early to leave for the church service, with just enough time to collect wildflowers and assemble two small arrangements for Hilda and Sara's headstones.

On either side of the footpath, yellow aster, fireweed, and delphinium thrived. Ella stopped to pick some, then crossed a field of meadowsweet and collected more fragrant blooms. The headstones, which she had designed, had been erected on the west end of the sprawling, manicured property, which was dotted with gravestones and century-old pine trees. She craned her neck to spot the markers, but the church blocked her view. It was a striking building with a green copper spire crowned with a braided weathervane. The stylish black-and-white diamond pattern on the doors and shutters had inspired her new line of dresses, which she'd called Dypvåg. This place was special, particularly because her mom had been baptized there.

As Ella walked, the west end of the cemetery came into view; it was a sun-soaked spot with a hedge of orange roses. Clutching the two bouquets she'd made, she stopped for a moment on a stone bench to rearrange them. The platinum promise ring from Leif sparkled on her finger. As she tied ribbon around the stems, a dog let out several happy barks; she knew without looking that it was Freya, the mutt she and Leif had adopted.

She heard Leif calling her name, and he waved at her from the headstones. Erik, Inger, and Mia each raised an arm in greeting. Even Mia's cat, Bactus, was there, harnessed to a leash. Erik wore a wide belt with Viking symbols tooled into the leather; it was part of the Leif Collection Ella had designed. Erik had expanded his business at the marina to offer custom carving for boats, and Leif had a waiting list of clients. He was in heaven now that he was getting paid for his art. Inger clutched one of Ella's handmade purses with a fun gooseberry pattern. A cigarillo dangled from Inger's strawberry-painted mouth. Some things never changed.

As Ella drew closer to Hilda's headstone, she stopped for a moment to absorb it all. The marker was stunning. The vibrant art deco urn that housed Mormor's ashes was now encased in clear glass blocks and framed with gray granite. Hilda's life had been gray in many ways, Ella thought . . . but her gift of the cottage had made Ella's future bright and colorful. It was a future Hilda may have dreamed for herself before tragedy came into her life. Perhaps Hilda knew what she was doing when she told Ella to sell Ringpynten, as Ella often did the opposite of what her mormor wanted.

Hilda's headstone stood next to Sara's: The gorgeous rose quartz sparkled in the light, and Erik had engraved a large, fabulous bear onto the stone. The bear held the sun in its clawed paws; that sweet tribute of Erik's, and knowing how much he loved her mom, brought tears to Ella's eyes.

"Hey you! Joining us?" Leif called out. "We can't do this without you." As she walked toward him, his hand was already stretched out, waiting for hers.

BOOK CLUB QUESTIONS

1. Ella inherits a mysterious seaside cottage. If you inherited a quirky, secret-filled house in a remote location, what's the first thing you'd do—explore it, sell it, or turn it into your dream getaway?

2. Hilda kept important truths from Ella, which shaped who Ella became. How do family secrets influence the people we are? Did any revelations in the story make you rethink a character's choices—or your own family dynamics?

3. Ella faces decisions that test her instincts and courage. Have you ever had to choose between what felt right and what felt safe? How do her choices mirror real-life moments of risk or discovery?

4. Lyngør's rugged coastline, the sea, and the village feel like characters in their own right. How does the setting shape Ella's and Leif's journeys? Have you ever felt a location change your perspective or life path?

5. Ella and Hilda's relationship was complicated, full of misunderstandings and withheld truths. How did forgiveness—or the lack of it—impact their bond? Have you ever had to reconcile with someone after discovering truths you didn't expect?

6. Ella's grandmother dismissed her dreams as frivolous, yet those very dreams guide Ella's journey. Have you ever had to go against expectations to pursue something meaningful? How does this tension resonate in your own life?

7. The story suggests that hardships sometimes guide us to exactly where we're meant to be. Can you identify moments where Ella's or Leif's difficulties lead to growth or clarity? How has this idea shown up in your own experiences?

8. Lyngør is full of boats, fjords, and small-town charm. Which activity from the book (sailing, fishing, exploring the coastline) would you try first if you were visiting?

9. Imagine having a meal on the porch of Ella's cottage while enjoying the sea breeze and Lyngør scenery. What food or drink would you bring, and which character would you invite to join?

For more book club materials, visit the author's website at kimbradrake.com or scan the QR code.

ACKNOWLEDGMENTS

Many generous, wonderful people read various parts of this book, in all its messy, draft-y versions. Thank you, Michael Khandelwal, Ellen Bryson, Kelly Sokol, Lydia Netzer, Michele Young-Stone, Tim Farrington, Elaine Pollard, Lisa Grimes, Leslie Entsminger, Christian Fennell, Bev Katz Rosenbaum, Sylvia Liu, Rachel Parris, Stephen Truman Sugg, Holly McLellan Sessoms, Sarah Darrow, Chris Braig, DM Frech, Mike Krentz, David Cascio, Michelle Ross Lozano, Hannah Capin, Jessica Grace Kelley, Susan Thumm Paxton, Kelley McGee Sousa, Tamako Takamatsu, and Tiffany Wayne—and to other folks I am most certainly forgetting. I am grateful to every one of you. I am blessed by your kindness. Your notes, feedback, and encouragement helped me see the light at the end of the tunnel.

I'm immeasurably grateful for the time and talents of Caroline Leavitt, Jodi Warshaw, and Elizabeth DeNoma.

Thank you, Alicia Dekker, for all the days we wrote together and for always listening and encouraging me. You make life even better.

With appreciation to The Muse Writers Center for being such a supportive, inclusive community for creatives to learn, grow, and make new literary friends. Thank you to my friend Michael Khandelwal for creating this marvelous space for writers—including me—to thrive.

Thank you to the entire Girl Friday team for your help

launching this book, including Ingrid Emerick, Christina Henry de Tessan, Sara Spees Addicott, Georgie Hockett, Alyssa Brillinger, Reshma Kooner, and Brittany Dowdle.

To my mother, Dianne. Your love and support meant the world to me. You will always be in my heart. I love and miss you, Mom.

To my son, Dennis, thank you for helping me with "Ella's song." I love you with all my heart and soul. I believe in you! *"Go confidently in the direction of your dreams. Live a life you've always imagined." —Henry David Thoreau.*

To Kathryn Copeland, you inspired one of the themes in my novel, "chosen family," and I love you to the moon and back! Thank you for believing in me and my book and for reading an early draft—not once but twice!

With appreciation to Edel Hovland, who drew me to Norway in the first place. I cherish every ounce of our friendship. To the Hovland family—Edel, Ole, Helen, Knut, and Brede—I can't thank you enough for welcoming me into your beautiful home in Trondheim, and for making me feel like one of your own.

With love and gratitude to my "anchor," Pål Engebrigtsen, for introducing me to Lyngør—a place where we've been fortunate enough to spend our summers—and for all the meaningful memories over the years. Thank you to the entire Engebrigtsen family for all the great times at Ring Point and at your other cottages in Lyngør. Thank you, Kristine Engebrigtsen, for always letting me hit you up for information about Lyngør history and for making the best *rosinboller*—Norwegian raisin buns—ever. I'd like to give a shout-out to some of my Lyngør friends for your kindness and camaraderie and for all the cookouts: Lene Darell, Carl Christian Petersen, Claus and Heidi Petersen, Vibeke Schulz Ahlsand, Thorleif Ahlsand, Preben Bjørn-Hansen, Pål Brekke, Marianne Owesen Hoel and the Owesen family, Merete Ring, Liv Vikre, Benkt Sørensen,

Edvard and Thomas Os and the Os family, the Marcussen family, Anders Fredrick von Krogh and Karl Magnus von Krogh and their families, the Hybert family, the Glad family, Ida Melbye and the Melbye family, Øistein Grevskott Larsen, Henriette Grønn, Jonas Grønn, Anders Koppang-Grønn and the Grønn family—and Peter Grønn for the ice cream and the sunset cruises on his iconic boat, *Peter Red*.

Finally, thank you, readers, for spending your valuable time with this story and getting to know Ella, Leif, and their friends in Lyngør, Norway.

ABOUT THE AUTHOR

Kimbra Drake is a pseudonym for a published fiction writer who is also a certified book coach and developmental editor. She lives and writes in Virginia and Ireland. When not crafting stories, some of her passions include traveling, hiking in nature, photography, and watching gigs and readings at indie bookstores. *Where the Heart Meets the Sea* is inspired by her time living in Lyngør, Norway.